SM1

This book should be returned to any branch of the

SKELMERSDALE

2 0 FEB 2010

1 3 MAR 2010

1 1 JUN 2014

2 5 MAR 2015

1 2 AUG 2016

FICTION RESERVE STOCK LL60

Lancashire County Library
Bowran Street
Preston PR1 2UX

Lancashire
County Council

www.lancashire.gov.uk/libraries

D0234614

LL1(A)

Queens of Romance

*A collection of bestselling novels by
the world's leading romance writers*

**Two stories from international
bestselling author**

NICOLA CORNICK

**Nicola Cornick will whisk you back to
Regency England – where you can escape
into a world of passion and privilege…
deceit and desire!**

**Praise for international bestselling author
and RITA® finalist Nicola Cornick:**

'…vivid detail…rollicking tug-of-war…
subtle humour…'
—*Publishers Weekly* on *The Rake's Bride*

**Nicola Cornick was the runner-up in
the Romantic Novelists Association's
prestigious Elizabeth Goudge Trophy 2005,
where her work was judged to be:
'A masterclass… A vivid range of
emotions and sensations…'**

Available in the
— Queens of Romance —
collection

EMMA DARCY
Hot-Blooded Affairs

16th March 2007

CAROLE MORTIMER
Meant to Wed

20th April 2007

NICOLA CORNICK
Regency Weddings

18th May 2007

MARGARET WAY
Outback Marriages

15th June 2007

Collect all 4 superb books!

NICOLA CORNICK

Regency Weddings

Containing

**The Rake's Bride
& The Penniless Bride**

DID YOU PURCHASE THIS BOOK WITHOUT A COVER?
If you did, you should be aware it is **stolen property** as it was
reported *unsold and destroyed* by a retailer. Neither the author nor
the publisher has received any payment for this book.

*All the characters in this book have no existence outside the
imagination of the author, and have no relation whatsoever to anyone
bearing the same name or names. They are not even distantly inspired
by any individual known or unknown to the author, and all the
incidents are pure invention.*

*All Rights Reserved including the right of reproduction in whole or
in part in any form. This edition is published by arrangement with
Harlequin Enterprises II B.V./S.à.r.l. The text of this publication or
any part thereof may not be reproduced or transmitted in any form
or by any means, electronic or mechanical, including photocopying,
recording, storage in an information retrieval system, or otherwise,
without the written permission of the publisher.*

*This book is sold subject to the condition that it shall not, by way of
trade or otherwise, be lent, resold, hired out or otherwise circulated
without the prior consent of the publisher in any form of binding or
cover other than that in which it is published and without a similar
condition including this condition being imposed on the subsequent
purchaser.*

*M&B™ and M&B™ with the Rose Device
are trademarks of the publisher.
Harlequin Mills & Boon Limited, Eton House,
18-24 Paradise Road,
Richmond, Surrey TW9 1SR*

Regency Weddings © by Harlequin Books S.A. 2007
The Rake's Bride and *The Penniless Bride* were first published in
Great Britain by Harlequin Mills & Boon Limited.

The Rake's Bride © Nicola Cornick 2002
The Penniless Bride © Nicola Cornick 2003

ISBN: 978 0 263 85838 9

010-0607

*Printed and bound in Spain
by Litografia Rosés S.A., Barcelona*

The Rake's Bride

NICOLA CORNICK

LANCASHIRE COUNTY LIBRARY	
10576743 2	
HJ	04/05/2007
F	£5.99

S. LANCS. DIVISIONAL LIBRARIES

| S | S | S | S |

For Andrew

Nicola Cornick lives in the English countryside with her husband and a menagerie of cats, dogs and newts! She has been published since 1998 and these days she writes single-title Regency historicals and historical romances for Harlequin Mills & Boon Ltd.

In her spare time she teaches creative writing at her local college and she also works as a guide for the National Trust at Ashdown House. Ashdown is one of her current passions and she is researching the history of the house in order to write a book about it one day. She also studies history at Oxford, acts as organiser for the RNA New Writers' Scheme and unwinds by taking her dog for long walks in the countryside.

Nicola loves to hear from her readers and can be contacted by e-mail at ncornick@madasafish.com or via her website, www.nicolacornick.co.uk.

**Look out for Nicola Cornick's next novel,
Lord of Scandal, in early 2008.**

Chapter One

The April sunlight was as blinding as a flash of gunpowder and the rattle of the bed curtains sounded like distant artillery fire. For a moment Jack, Marquis of Merlin, wondered if he had gone to hell and ended back in the Peninsula War. He rolled onto his back and flung an arm up to shield his eyes.

"Hodges?"

"Yes, my lord?"

The Marquis opened his eyes and looked at his valet. His gaze was dark blue and very unfriendly and his voice held a dangerous undertone. "Hodges, what is the time?"

The valet remained impassive. "A little after nine, my lord."

"That would be nine in the morning?"

"Indeed, my lord."

The Marquis stretched, with a ripple of honed muscles. "As I recall, I asked you to wake me at twelve of the clock and not before. No doubt you can account for the discrepancy?"

"Yes, my lord." Hodges opened the wardrobe and took out a coat of blue superfine. Truth to tell, he had

been relieved to find that the Marquis was at home—
and alone—for neither circumstance was a foregone
conclusion. There had been plenty of occasions on
which the Marquis had spent twenty-four hours in one
sitting at White's, wandering home only to change his
clothes before another spell at the faro tables. There had
been many other mornings when Hodges had come to
wake his lordship only to discover one of his *chères
amies* sprawled naked in bed beside him. It was a sight
that would have shocked a valet of less hardened constitution and a circumstance that would have been decidedly awkward that particular morning.

"Well, Hodges? I am awaiting your explanation."

"If I could encourage your lordship to rise?" Hodges
said expressionlessly. "The Duke and Duchess of Merlin are awaiting you in the green salon—"

Jack gave an oath and sat up, clapping his hand to
his head as a wave of brandy-induced pain threatened
to lay him low again. "Damnation! My parents, you
say? Here? What in God's name could induce them to
call at such a confoundedly unsocial hour? Surely they
are not about to parade some other unfortunate candidate for my affections in front of me?"

"His Grace, your father, did not share such information with me, my lord," Hodges said, allowing himself a tight smile. "However, the Duchess mentioned
something about your cousin, Mr. Pershore, finding
himself in a difficult position—"

Jack paused, running a hand through his disheveled
black hair and making it even more disordered. "What,
again?"

"Yes, my lord. The matter involves a designing female and a hasty marriage, as I understand it. The country was mentioned, my lord."

Jack swore. It was hardly the first time that his feck-less cousin Bertie Pershore had fallen into a scrape. "Damn it, that's too much! Why could Pershore not contract his ill-conceived marriage in Town? If I have to go chasing off to Oxfordshire again just to act as nursemaid to my cousin—"

"Quite so, my lord." Hodges finished brushing down the blue coat. "His Grace the Duke did mention one thing, my lord."

"Yes?"

"He said that if you had not joined them within the half hour he would come up here himself."

Jack swung his legs over the side of the bed and reached for his shirt. He glanced across at the clock. "How long ago was that, Hodges?"

The valet gave another small smile. "A little over five and twenty minutes, my lord. I tried to wake you before but you did not stir. I was about to resort to an ewer of water—most efficacious, my lord."

"Thank God you did not," Jack said feelingly. He looked from the valet's face to the coat in his hand and gave a sigh.

"Devil take it! I suppose I must…"

"Yes, my lord," the valet said.

"Thea," Miss Clementine Shaw said, fixing her elder sister with an earnest look, "are you marrying Mr. Per-shore for his money? He is very rich—is he not?—and it seems to me most unlikely that you could be marrying for love!"

Theodosia Shaw let her needlework fall to her lap. She was trimming the bodice of her bridal gown, adding the scraps of Brussels lace that she had garnered from her mother's old dresses that were still stored in lavender in the chest upstairs. The lace was fine but a little yellow with age now and the village gossips in church tomorrow would quickly divine that the entire dress was secondhand. Thea gave a little shrug; there was no point in pretending, for everyone in the village of Oakmantle knew their parlous financial state.

"Clemmie, you really must learn not to ask questions like that," she said severely. Her sister had never understood the art of polite conversation and at nineteen possessed an outspokenness that would deter even the most persistent of suitors. "The Honorable Mr. Pershore is everything that one would wish in a husband. He is…" Here she paused, desperately trying to think of some positive attributes. "He is gentlemanly and kind and good-natured…" she floundered. "And kind…"

"You said that already," Clementine observed critically. Her perceptive blue eyes, identical to those of her older sister, scanned Thea's face. "I cannot dispute that he is kind, for has he not offered to marry you and take all of us on, as well?" She ticked them all off on her fingers. "Ned will go to Oxford and Harry to Eton, and I may have my come-out and Clara her harp lessons and Daisy—"

"Pray stop at once!" Thea said, more sharply than she had intended. To hear her sister itemize the material benefits of the match made her feel intolerably guilty, for she *was* marrying Bertie Pershore for his money and could scarcely deny it. She wished that it was not so; somehow she felt that Bertie deserved better than that she take advantage of him. Yet she was in desperate straits and he was chivalrous enough to come to her rescue. For a moment she thought back to the day when he had made his unexpected declaration and a smile, half rueful, half sad, crossed her features.

"You know I'm dashed fond of you, Thea, old girl," Bertie had said that day in the drawing room. His kindly brown gaze, so reminiscent of Theodosia's favorite spaniel, had rested on her with sympathetic concern. "Can't bear to see you struggle on in this moldering old place any longer! I'll need a suitable wife one day and you're well up to snuff—we would deal well together! So what do you say?"

Thea had not replied at once. She had got to her feet and strolled over to the drawing room window. It was early spring. The trees were still bare but beneath them the ground was starred with snowdrops and yellow aconites. It was a pretty scene but it failed to distract the eye completely from the general air of shabby neglect that hung over Oakmantle Hall.

Thea had turned back to her suitor, unsure whether to laugh or to cry. There were those who held that the Honorable Mr. Pershore, a Pink of the Ton, cared for little beyond the set of his neck cloth or the polish of his Hessians. Yet Thea had known him since they had been children together and knew him to be good-hearted and kind. She had just had the proof of it in his generous, if unromantic, proposal.

She had given him a rueful smile. "Oh, Bertie, you are most chivalrous, but I know perfectly well that you can have as little desire to marry as I! If it weren't for the rest of my family I would not even countenance it! Besides, that odious guardian of yours will surely kick up a fuss if you marry a penniless prospect such as myself, a woman older than you are, with so many dependents—"

Bertie had tried to shake his head and almost impaled

himself on his shirt points. He'd frowned as mutinously as someone of his mournful expression was able.

"Don't see what business it is of Merlin's! I'm of age and may marry whom I choose."

Thea had sighed with all the wisdom of her two and twenty years. "Bertie, only conceive of the trouble it would cause! The Duke of Merlin would never tolerate so imprudent a match, not even for a distant cousin! Can you imagine what he would do?"

"Probably send Jack down," Bertie had said, his face breaking into a sudden grin. "Jack is forever pulling me out of scrapes! Did I tell you about the time he found me at Madam Annet's when I was on *exeat* from Eton—"

"Yes!" Thea had said sharply, wincing more at the reference to their potential marriage as a "scrape" than the indelicate story of Bertie's foray into one of London's most notorious bawdy houses. From the age of five, Bertie had tired her ears with his hero-worshiping references to Jack Merlin, his cousin and idol, and as a result Thea had taken the Marquis in extreme dislike. She had never met him in person but had formed an impression of an arrogant nobleman who had been granted all of life's privileges and took them lightly, until they bored him. Bertie's assurances that Jack was a great gun and a devil with the ladies did him no favors in Thea's eyes. She knew that Jack Merlin was a rake— even in the village of Oakmantle they had heard something of his reputation.

Bertie had looked abashed. "Sorry, Thea. Dashed improper of me to mention it."

Thea had sighed. It was impossible to feel anything other than a faint exasperation for one whom she had always considered as a rather tiresome younger brother, which made the proposed marriage even more ridiculous. She already had five siblings and scarcely needed a husband who would constitute a sixth child. Yet did she have any choice? Her father had left her with a mountain of debts, a crumbling manor house and her brothers and sisters to care for. And there was scarcely a queue of eager suitors hammering on the door of Oakmantle Hall…

Thea came back to the present and cut her thread with a sharp snap. There was no point in dwelling on that now. She had made her choice and tomorrow the knot would be tied.

"Clemmie, you must understand that one cannot always marry for love." She tried to explain.

"Why not?" her sister said immediately. "Mama was most insistent that we should not compromise our principles."

Thea sighed again. Their mother had been a bluestocking in her day, one of Mrs. Montagu's circle, and had held strong views on women's education and independence. She had brought all her children up to view romantic love as the ideal, which was all very well, Thea thought crossly, but when she had no money and a family to support, high-minded principles were a luxury she could ill afford.

The true extent of their poverty had only become apparent when their father had died some six months previously. Mr. Shaw had been a scholar and a gentleman, but he had had no concept of the importance of more worldly matters such as money. They had lived in the old house at Oakmantle for more years than Thea could remember but on her father's death she had discovered that it was not their own, and now the landlord was threatening to increase the rents or repossess the house.

They had no source of income. Thea could never earn enough as a governess or schoolteacher to keep a family of six and though her brother Ned talked wildly of finding work as a clerk in the city of London, he was only seventeen and had no one to sponsor him. They had subsisted on the generosity of friends and distant relatives up to this point but now funds were running short and a more permanent answer had to be found. Bertie Pershore was that solution.

Thea shook the wedding dress out and held it at arm's length for critical inspection. Her pride had rebelled at the thought of Bertie paying for her trousseau, so as a result she would have to go to him in these faded threads.

"There, that will have to do."

Thea sighed again, repressing the urge to bundle the dress up and thrust it to the back of a cupboard, or even into the fire. "I never was much of a hand at needlework but I have done my best. It requires a hot iron."

Clementine closed her book and bent to blow out the single stand of candles. "It requires more than that! Never mind, Thea, you may have no skill with the needle but you will be able to discuss philosophy and poetry and ancient history with Mr. Pershore over the teacups…"

Thea winced but did not reprove her sister. Clementine was a sharp observer but seldom intended malice and it was not her fault that her words conjured up so ridiculous an image. For no matter how amiable Mr. Pershore was, he was no scholar. The thought of making trivial conversation with Bertie day in, day out, for the next forty years was purgatory, but Thea knew she was being ungrateful. There was a price to financial security, and if this was all she had to pay then she had escaped lightly.

The wedding service had barely begun when Thea realized that she simply could not go through with it. The omens had been bad that morning but she had tried to ignore them. A light drizzle had been falling as she made the short journey from Oakmantle Hall to the church, dampening her veil and making the embroidered roses in her circlet droop miserably. At her side, Ned glowered in silence, still smarting over the fact that she was sacrificing herself because he, the head of the family, could not support them. The church felt cold and smelled of dust, and Thea shivered convulsively in her thin silk dress. Clementine, Harry, Clara and Daisy were lined up in the front pew looking scrubbed and subdued. They were a good-looking family—all possessed the cornflower-blue eyes and fair hair of the Shaw family and all were huddling in old clothes that had been sponged down for the occasion by Mrs. Skeffington, the cook housekeeper. Thea thought that Harry looked like an undertaker's boy in his best black coat and Clara and Daisy were clutching each other's hands and looking as though they were about to cry.

Bertie Pershore was standing before the altar, looking terrified. Thea wondered if he was having second thoughts but was too honorable to say anything. Her heart sank lower than her soaking satin slippers and right down to the gravestones beneath her feet.

"Dearly beloved…" the rector intoned, fixing Thea with a severe look. He had baptized her and all her siblings and had buried her father six months before. The same villagers who had come to pay their respects to the late Mr. Shaw now bobbed and whispered in the pews behind Thea's family, noting the secondhand wedding dress and the groom's terrified demeanor. None of Bertie's family was present and Thea did not know whether she was glad or sorry.

The rector had moved on to the reasons for which marriage had been ordained and was speaking of the procreation of children. Thea, who had managed to avoid all thoughts of her wedding night, was suddenly confronted by a picture of herself and Bertie lying side by side in the ancient tester bed at Oakmantle. Under the circumstances the knowledge of Bertie's experiences at Madam Annet's hands might have been reassuring, since Thea had no experience of her own to draw on. Instead the thought was decidedly off-putting, providing as it did too much information for comfort. Bertie was kind, but Thea did not find him in the least attractive, and whilst she was not naive enough to imagine that one had to enjoy submitting to one's husband's desires, she had once hoped that she would marry a man who stirred her feelings....

"Secondly, it was ordained for a remedy against sin, and to avoid fornication..." the rector said, glaring ferociously at the congregation, who shifted uncomfortably in the pews. Bertie stared at his highly polished boots and cleared his throat nervously.

Oh, dear... Thea thought.

"I am sorry," she heard herself say politely, "but I am afraid that there has been a dreadful mistake and I have to go now."

There was a moment of absolute silence that felt to Thea as though it went on for hours. The vicar opened and closed his mouth like a landed fish, Bertie went white then red and the congregation started to flutter and whisper as they realized that something was wrong.

Then Thea found herself hurrying back down the aisle, holding her skirts up in one hand, the slap of her slippers sounding unnaturally loud on the stone floor. She looked neither left nor right, ignoring the avid faces of the villagers as they craned to see what was going on. Behind her she could hear a swell of voices like the roar of the sea, but she had already reached the door and was fumbling with the latch. Her hands were shaking so much that they slipped on the cold metal. She felt faint and light-headed but she knew that she had to escape.

The door swung open suddenly with a gust of cool spring air. Thea rushed forward, almost tripping over the threshold in her haste, blinded by her veil and the tears that were now threatening her. She stumbled a few paces down the path toward the gate, realized that she would fall if she did not steady herself, and put out a hand. She recoiled in shock as it was caught and held. Strong arms went around her, holding her close.

"What the devil—" a masculine voice ejaculated, then the veil was pushed roughly back from her face and she found herself staring up at the man who held her.

His face was heart-stoppingly close to hers. As though in a dream Thea noted the dark blue eyes with their ridiculously thick black lashes, the harsh angles and planes of his tanned face, the square chin and uncompromising line of the mouth. She could smell lemon cologne mixed with cold air and leather and it made her feel faint but in an entirely different way from before. Her knees buckled and his arms tightened about her.

A lock of black hair had fallen across his forehead and it looked soft and silky. Thea had a sudden urge to smooth it back, to let her hand linger against his cheek where the stubble already darkened his skin. Her fingers were already halfway to their destination when she shivered convulsively and snapped out of the dream that held her, stepping back and freeing herself.

The man made an instinctive gesture toward her. "Wait!"

Thea ignored him. With no thought to the rain or the slippery stones of the churchyard or the damp, clinging lace of her wedding dress, she ran from him as though her life depended on it.

Jack had seen her as soon as he came through the lych-gate and started up the path toward the church. She was hurrying toward him but he could tell that she had not seen him—there was an air of intense concentration about her that suggested she was completely wrapped up in her feelings. Then she had stumbled on the wet path and he had caught her hand, instinctively pulling her into his arms, as she seemed about to fall.

She had eyes of cornflower-blue, stricken and bright with tears now, but direct and uncompromising still. They widened as she looked up into his face and focused on him for the first time. He felt a jolt of something go through him, something like pain, deeper than desire.

Her fair hair was so soft it looked like spun gold as it escaped the confines of the wedding veil, and he had the near irresistible urge to loosen it and bury his face in the silken mass. Her mouth was tempting and voluptuous, as unconsciously sensuous as the rest of the yielding body that was pressed so intimately against his. She smelled of lavender and spring meadows and sunshine, and he found that all he wanted was to hold her closer still. Jack Merlin had never experienced so strong a reaction to a woman in his whole life. It was no surprise to find that he wanted her but it was a surprise to find himself so shaken.

''Wait!'' The word burst from him instinctively as she freed herself violently from his arms. She took no notice. He saw that her hands were trembling as she scooped up the yellowing lace skirts of the old wedding gown, then she was running from him down the path and disappearing through the lych-gate. The whole encounter had taken less than a minute.

Jack let his breath out in a long sigh and felt the tension drain slowly from his body. Behind him in the church he could hear an excited babble of voices rising to a crescendo. He cast one look in the direction the girl had gone. Unless he missed his guess, he had just met his cousin's runaway bride. But whether she was running away before or after the knot had been tied was as yet uncertain. Jack found himself hoping fervently for the former, then sighed again. When he had set off from London the last thing he had expected was to find himself envying his cousin. The whole matter of Bertie's wedding was becoming a lot more complicated than he had envisaged.

Chapter Two

"At least I was able to hold my peace!" Jack said wryly. "I'd have felt a damned fool intervening in the service at the point where the parson asks if anyone has just cause to stop the proceedings."

"Never got that far." Bertie Pershore said gloomily, passing his cousin a glass of brandy. He joined Jack by the fire. "Devil take it, Jack, if Thea didn't want to go through with it she could have told me before that! Making a cake of myself in front of the entire village… Jilting me at the altar—"

They were in the private parlor of the Lamb and Rabbit hostelry, where Jack had abandoned his carriage and his valet an hour previously. Hodges had spent the intervening time bespeaking rooms and making sure that everything was comfortable. Sampling the brandy, Jack observed that he did indeed employ a prince amongst valets.

After the debacle at the wedding, Jack had simply strolled up the aisle, ushered his shocked cousin out a side door, pressed a large financial contribution into the startled rector's hand and suggested that the jilted groom be left in peace to recover. No one had dared to gainsay him.

Jack shrugged, settling himself deeper in the armchair. "Maybe Miss Shaw suddenly realized she could do better for herself, old chap! A title *and* a fortune, perhaps…"

"Thea isn't like that!" Bertie said hotly. He saw Jack's sardonic glance and added, "Oh, I know you think I'm besotted with an adventuress, but you couldn't be further from the truth. Thea and I have been friends for years and I was only trying to help her out—"

"Keep your chivalric instincts under control in future!" his cousin advised dryly. "Not that I can blame you, Bertie. Miss Thea Shaw is devilish attractive and I can quite see why you fell for her charms, but to make her an offer—"

He broke off at his cousin's blank stare. "Attractive? Thea? I'll concede she's not a bad-looking girl, and she's game as a pebble, of course, but she's no diamond of the first water! Sure we're talking about the same girl, Jack?"

Jack raised his eyebrows. He had never felt that Bertie's taste in women was either well developed or particularly subtle and here he had the proof. His cousin had evidently been in the ridiculous position of being blind to the considerable charms of the woman he was about to marry. Jack shrugged philosophically. He was not going to point out the error of his ways to Bertie for this way he could kill two birds with one stone. He could ensure that the marriage would not be revived and he could map out a very different future for Miss Theodosia Shaw. He already had in mind exactly what it entailed.

In the hour since he had met Thea outside the church,

Jack had successfully managed to master the surprising and wholly unexpected feelings that she had aroused in him. Clearly Thea Shaw was a fortune hunter, no matter what Bertie said to defend her. That being the case, she might be receptive to an offer from him, which, whilst different from Bertie's chivalrous proposal, might still be as financially rewarding. Jack smiled, a little cynically. He was certain that he could satisfy both his own desires and those of Miss Shaw one way or another.

"I assume you have no intention of renewing your suit to Miss Shaw?" he inquired casually and was relieved when Bertie flushed angrily.

"Damned if I will! I have my pride, you know, Jack! All I ever wanted to do was help Thea out—a favor because of our long friendship, you know, and I think she could at least have been honest with me." He stared gloomily into the fire. "Think I'll eschew all women! Better off without them! No idea what makes them tick."

Jack grinned at that. "You and the rest of the male population, old chap! Well—" he stood up and stretched "—I am going to pay a call on Miss Shaw. Wouldn't want her stirring up any trouble in future."

Bertie shook his head. He looked up. "Barking up the wrong tree there, Jack! Thea won't take kindly to your interference. Why not let it lie, old fellow? Wedding's off—you can be sure that I won't be making any rash offers again. Fingers burned and all that!"

"All the same, I will be happier when I have made a few matters clear to Miss Shaw," Jack murmured. "It will not take long."

"Suppose you mean to pay her off," Bertie said, adding with gloomy relish, "Big mistake! Asking for trouble, old fellow! You'll see!"

"I have various offers to put to Miss Shaw," Jack said lazily, reaching for his coat. "We shall see which one suits her best."

"I cannot believe that I have behaved so badly!" Thea was curled up in an armchair in the blue drawing room. She had changed out of the soaking wedding dress into a plain gown of gray-spotted muslin and her hair was loose, drying in corkscrew curls about her face.

"Poor Bertie! He will never forgive me. I cannot forgive myself. Jilting him at the altar! How could I do such a thing?"

"Well, it was very bad of you," Clementine confirmed with a judicious purse of the lips, "but far better than to marry Mr. Pershore today and change your mind tomorrow. It will only be a nine days' wonder until the next scandal comes along!" She pressed a glass of Madeira into her sister's hand. "Here, drink this. I always think it the best way to ward off a chill."

"I cannot see what you can know of such strong cures at your age!" Thea said severely, forgetting her dejection for a moment. Sometimes she felt she was a poor substitute for a mother to Clementine. It was impossible to control her sister's waywardness. She took a sip of the drink and sat back in her chair.

"What happened in the church after I left, Clemmie?"

"Not a great deal," her sister said, kneeling to add a couple of applewood logs to the fire. "The rector appealed to the congregation to keep calm." She snorted. "As well try to dam the river Oak! They were chattering and gossiping when you were barely through the door." She caught Thea's eye and said hurriedly, "It will all die down before you can say 'jilt'!"

Thea glared at her. "Thank you! And in the meantime we are in as poor and parlous a situation as before. I cannot think what came over me."

"You did the correct thing." Clementine stood up and dusted her palms together to remove the wood chippings. "No matter how rich Mr. Pershore, it makes him not one whit more attractive as a husband."

Thea turned her face away. She felt restless and on edge but she knew it had nothing to do with what had happened in the church and all to do with what had happened afterward. She had not even seen the stranger in the churchyard until she had stumbled into his arms and once she was there she had wanted him to hold her forever. It was extraordinary, it was deeply unsettling, but it was true.

"Did a gentleman come into the church just after I left?" she asked casually. "I thought I saw someone on the path."

Clementine brightened. "Oh, yes! I forgot to tell you! Apparently it was Mr. Pershore's cousin, but I had no chance to meet him as he whisked Bertie away in an instant. He was most prodigiously handsome, though. That I do remember."

Thea sat upright, her heart pounding uncomfortably. "Bertie's cousin, did you say? Oh, no, I do believe that must have been the Marquis of Merlin come to stop the marriage, just as Bertie predicted..." Against her will she felt a blush rising. So it was Jack Merlin in whose arms she had taken refuge! Thea put her glass down with a snap, damning the confoundedly bad luck of the whole situation.

Clementine was sitting back on her heels and eyeing her suspiciously.

"That was the Marquis of Merlin? Is he not the one

with the terrible reputation? The rake? The one who ran off with Lady Spence, then decided he preferred her younger sister who had just wed Lord Raistrick?''

"Yes!'' Thea said quickly, wondering where on earth her younger sister had picked up such scurrilous gossip. There was no denying that Jack Merlin was rakish and dangerous—she had assimilated that in less than ten seconds in his arms. Compellingly attractive was another matter, and one she did not wish to admit to her sister.

"And divinely handsome, as well!'' Clementine sighed. "Oh, I do so wish I had had the chance to make his acquaintance.''

Thea was just reflecting that Clementine had absorbed a great deal of romance along with her mother's more stringent philosophies on life, when her eye was caught by a figure strolling around the corner of the house. There was no mistaking him, for all that she had met him so briefly. This was definitely the Marquis of Merlin come to call. Thea recoiled, stifling an urge to run away and hide upstairs. The doorbell pealed.

"I do believe that you may rectify your omission now,'' she said faintly, "for that is the Marquis at the door. Though what he can be wanting with us—'' She broke off and smoothed her dress down with nervous fingers. Oh, to be wearing her old gray muslin at such a time! This would be the second occasion on which the Marquis would see her in her frumpish clothes, just when she needed the confidence that a really modish dress would give her. But then, she possessed no such thing, so bewailing the fact was immaterial...

"Excuse me, ma'am,'' Mrs. Skeffington, the housekeeper, arrived at the drawing room door looking flustered and disapproving. Thea squashed the ridiculous suspicion that the Marquis had been flirting with her. "The Marquis of Merlin is asking if you are at home, ma'am—"

"Oh, show him in!" Clementine said, almost hopping with excitement.

Thea sent her a quelling look. "Thank you, Skeffie. I will see Lord Merlin in here. Clementine—" she turned to her sister "—it would perhaps be better if you were to leave us to talk in private."

"Oh, no!" Clementine said, adopting the severe tone her elder sister always used with her, "that would not be at all proper!"

"Lord Merlin, ma'am!" Mrs. Skeffington murmured, frowning sternly. She dropped a curtsy and moved away with a stately tread that managed to imply even greater disapproval.

The Marquis of Merlin came into the room.

Thea took a deep, steadying breath. Her heart was racing and not simply with nervousness. She had the time to study the Marquis properly now as he came forward to greet her, and she was disconcerted to discover that she had the inclination to carry on looking at him indefinitely. It was not simply that he was, as Clementine had said, prodigiously handsome, although this was not in dispute. There was something else, something more compelling than mere good looks. Here was a man who was everything that Bertie Pershore was not. In an instant Thea recognized that she had accepted Bertie because he was straightforward and safe and unthreatening. And even on so short, albeit eventful, an acquaintance, she could tell that Jack Merlin was the exact opposite—complicated, dangerous, a challenge she was unsure she wanted to accept. Such thoughts did nothing to quell the uneasy excitement that was coursing through her body.

Clementine was staring and Thea could hardly blame her. The Marquis was tall, with a strong physique and a nonchalant grace that compelled the eye. His thick, dark hair was disheveled in the kind of style that poor Bertie could not have achieved even with the ministrations of the best valet. He bowed with ineffable elegance.

"Miss Shaw?"

His voice was low and warm, sending a curious shiver down Thea's spine. She nodded starchily. "Lord Merlin."

She saw a smile touch that firm mouth. "How do you do, ma'am? It is…most agreeable to meet you again."

Thea ignored the intimate implication of his words and gestured to Clementine. "Lord Merlin, may I introduce my sister, Miss Clementine Shaw."

Jack inclined his head. "Your servant, Miss Clementine."

Thea watched with exasperation as Clementine dropped a demure curtsy and smiled enchantingly at the Marquis. She had never behaved as such a pattern card of female perfection with any of their other male acquaintance. Such contrariness was enough to tempt Thea to shake her sister—until she realized that the Marquis was skillfully disposing of Clementine's company and suddenly she was tempted to cling to her as a safeguard.

"I hope you will excuse me if I beg a private word with your sister, Miss Clementine," Jack was saying, holding the drawing room door open. "It was indeed a pleasure to meet you."

Thea sent Clementine a look that was part beseeching, part commanding, but her sister seemed blind to her appeal. She tripped out without demur and Jack closed the door gently behind her.

Thea blinked. She cleared her throat hastily, searching for a diversion.

"Would you care for some refreshment, Lord Merlin?"

Jack's gaze fell on her half-finished glass. "Thank you. I will join you in a glass of Madeira, ma'am."

Thea poured the wine herself, trying to prevent her fingers from shaking. There was something unnerving about Jack Merlin, the direct, dark blue gaze that had barely wavered from her since he had entered the room, the instinctive authority that cloaked him. This was not a man Thea wanted to tangle with. And yet a part of her, a treacherous part, wanted it very much indeed...

She handed him the glass of wine, making sure that their fingers did not touch. The memory of their encounter outside the church was still in her mind and her equilibrium, already fragile, could not withstand another onslaught. She resumed her seat with what she hoped was an assumption of ease, gesturing Jack to take the chair opposite. He did so, his eyes never leaving her face.

"I hope that you are somewhat recovered from your ordeal, Miss Shaw?" Jack raised an eyebrow. "When we met outside the church I thought that you were a little...distressed? I would have assisted you had you given me the opportunity."

There was a warmth in his tone, an intimacy, that brought the color into Thea's cheeks. His words conjured up the memory of his arms about her, the comforting strength that had somehow been simultaneously protective and inexplicably exciting. Thea smoothed her skirts with a little nervous gesture. She did not—could not—meet his eyes.

"Thank you, my lord. I am much recovered now."

"Good." Jack's tone changed subtly, the gentleness gone. "Miss Shaw, forgive my abruptness, but I wished to speak to you of the wedding. Why did you abandon Bertie at the altar? Having persuaded him to marry you, I cannot understand why you should throw away all your advantages! Unless, of course—" there was a sardonic note in his voice now "—you are contemplating a better offer?"

Thea looked up sharply. He had wasted little time on polite niceties. The gloves were off now, the contempt very clear.

"I fear that you are laboring under several misconceptions, sir," she said with cool haughtiness. "In the first place I had no need to exert undue influence in order to persuade Mr. Pershore to propose! He did so because he is a true friend and most chivalrous—"

She broke off as Jack shifted slightly. "And then you scorned his chivalry by jilting him at the altar?" he queried gently. " That was badly done, Miss Shaw."

Thea bit her lip, all too aware that he was deliberately putting her in the wrong, but equally aware that her position was indefensible. It *had* been inexcusable to treat Bertie so, but she had no intention of accepting Jack's reproofs. She looked at him defiantly.

"Would you have preferred me to marry your cousin, Lord Merlin? Forgive me, but I thought your presence in Oakmantle indicated an intention to put a stop to the nuptials rather than to dance at the wedding! Am I then mistaken and you are here to persuade me to accept Bertie, after all?"

Jack laughed. "Certainly not, Miss Shaw! My cousin
has told me a little of your situation and I cannot but
see it as a most undesirable match! No money, no connections, nothing to recommend you but…" He paused,
and his blue gaze slid over her with a mocking appraisal
that made his meaning crystal-clear.

Thea was incensed. She stood up. "You are impertinent, sir! Since you evidently set great store by wealth
and connection, I am happy to tell you that my family
is at least as old and distinguished as your own—more
so! And we are far more honorable in our conduct!"
She saw him smile and went on sharply. "So have no
fear, I do not intend to importune Bertie to give me a
second chance! Your cousin is safe from my attentions!"

"I am happy to hear it," Jack murmured. He had
also risen to his feet and was standing disturbingly close
to her. For a wild moment Thea could almost imagine
that she could feel the warmth of his body, smell the
faint scent of lemon cologne she had detected when he
had held her before. Her senses went into a spin and
she felt herself tremble. It was deeply unnerving. She
stepped back hastily and almost overturned the table
with her wineglass upon it. Jack caught her elbow to
steady her and Thea shook him off, appalled at the
tremor that slid through her at his touch.

"I cannot believe that we have anything more to say
to each other, Lord Merlin," she said coldly, moving
to pull the bell for the housekeeper. "I must bid you
good day."

Jack put out a hand to stop her. "On the contrary,"
he said, gently mocking, "there are a number of points
I still wish to make. Please be seated, Miss Shaw."

Their eyes met in a long moment of tension, then

Thea deliberately moved away to the stand by the window. She was damned if she was going to do his bidding!

"I am sure that whatever you wish to say to me may be adequately expressed with me standing here, Lord Merlin," she said. "Pray continue!"

Jack shrugged carelessly. "As you wish, Miss Shaw. My only concern was for your comfort."

"Pray make your point!" Thea snapped, allowing the tension to overset her naturally good manners.

Jack was not in the least discomposed. "Very well. In recognition of your obliging nature, Miss Shaw, I would like to make you an offer. If you undertake not to see Bertie ever again I shall be happy to contribute something to recompense you for your loss." He looked around the shabby drawing room. "It will help to tide you over until you find another suitor, perhaps..."

Thea drew herself up. She had never previously considered that she had a bad temper, but then she had never been provoked by the Marquis of Merlin before.

"Do I understand you to be offering me a bribe, Lord Merlin?" she inquired icily. "You quite misunderstand me if you think I should be amenable to such a suggestion. I have *every* intention of seeing Bertie again, if only to apologize to him! We have been friends these twenty years past."

"My dear, you are the one who is deluding herself," Jack said, sounding to Thea's infuriated ears both bored and amused. "It may salve your conscience to pretend that the arrangement between yourself and Bertie was based on chivalry, or friendship, or however you wish to dress it up, but the truth is that it was a business transaction no different in essence from the offer I am making you now."

There was another sharp silence. "I do not accept bribes!" Thea said through stiff lips. "You have my word and that should be sufficient."

Jack shrugged gracefully. "The word of a woman of principle?" There was cold cynicism in his eyes. "I wish I could believe it, Miss Shaw."

He was unfurling a roll of banknotes from his pocket and casually placing them on the mantelpiece, stacking a column of golden guineas on top to keep them in place. Thea stared, transfixed. So much money... More than she could earn in a lifetime as a schoolteacher, enough to keep a family of six in comfort for years and years....

"You see, Miss Shaw—" Jack's voice was very soft "—principles are for fools! Take it. It is yours..."

With a violent sweep of the hand, Thea scattered the guineas to the four corners of the room. They spun across the floor, clattering against the skirting board and rolling under the furniture. One of them bounced off a particularly ugly sculpture that had belonged to Thea's father and chipped its nose.

Jack picked up the banknotes, folded them and put them back in his pocket.

He grinned. "I take it that that is a refusal?"

Thea was shaking but she managed to keep her voice steady. "You are most perspicacious, sir!"

Jack was laughing at her. "A woman of principle indeed! If you wish to save my father the expense of paying you off I shall not argue with you!" He took a step closer to her. "Do not think to come begging for money in future and threatening scandal, however!"

It took all of Thea's will to respond with cool disdain when she wanted to slap him. She glared at him with the angry intensity of a cornered cat. "I have no intention of acting so! That may be *your* preferred mode of behavior, my lord—''

Jack's eyes lit suddenly with wicked amusement. Thea took an unconscious step back, warned by the predatory brightness she saw there.

''Since you ask, *this* is my preferred mode of behavior, Miss Shaw.''

His arms went around her, hard and fast, and his mouth had captured hers before she even had time to think. Thea's immediate feelings of outrage died a swift death, banished by the warm pressure of his lips on hers. Her lips parted, instinctively obeying the unspoken command; she felt his tongue touch hers and a seductive weakness swept through her, leaving her breathless with shocked desire.

There was no reprieve. Even as Thea's mind reeled under the onslaught of her feelings he deepened the kiss, his mouth skillful, demanding, making no concessions. Thea swayed a little, half astonished to find herself pressing closer to him, half wanton in her need to be closer still.

She moved slightly and her foot struck something against the softness of her kid slipper. A golden guinea. Thea's mind cleared abruptly and she pushed hard against Jack's chest, pulling away from him, utterly appalled. He released her at once.

Thea stepped back. Her voice was shaky. ''That was—''

''Exceptional.'' Thea saw a heat in Jack's eyes that mirrored the desire still shimmering through her own body. His voice was rough. She repressed a shiver. What was it about this man that turned her bones to water? She was no foolish scullery maid to have her head turned by a handsome marquis!

"My dear Miss Shaw," Jack was saying gently, taking her hand in his and reawakening all the latent feelings that Thea was trying so hard to suppress, "might I suggest an alternative future based on the... surprising...harmony we seem to have achieved? In return for your favor I should be glad to help with your financial difficulties..."

It took a second for Thea to understand, but then the shock hit her with what felt like physical force and she found it difficult to breathe. She turned away and moved a few ornaments at random on the mantelpiece.

"I collect that you mean to set me up as your mistress, Lord Merlin?" She was amazed at her own mild tone. "Or do I mistake and you intend only a short but sweet liaison? Not that it matters." She spun 'round to face him with such sudden violence that one of the ornaments, a pretty little shepherdess, clattered to the floor. "The answer to either suggestion is no—thank you! First you try to bribe me and then you offer me *carte blanche!* Your arrogance, insensitivity and conceit are truly breathtaking! Now leave this house before I throw you out myself!"

Jack raised his eyebrows, seemingly unmoved. "Your indignation is magnificent, my dear, but is it justified? Did you not respond to me just now?" His gaze, suddenly insolent, swept over her and lingered on the curve of her breast. "How many times have you used your undeniable charms to aid you in a difficult situation? When it is the only card to play?"

Thea did not answer. She brushed past him and opened the drawing room door. Then she marched out into the hall, past the startled housekeeper, and flung open the main door of Oakmantle Hall. It crashed back on its hinges, the echo reverberating through the entire house.

Jack had followed her into the hall and was now receiving his coat from Mrs. Skeffington, whose mouth had turned down so far with disapproval that it looked as though the ends would meet. Thea was grudgingly forced to admit that Jack appeared to be taking his eviction with a good grace. He even bowed to her, a twinkle of very definite admiration in those dark blue eyes.

"Your point is taken, Miss Shaw!"

Thea still did not reply. She watched in stony silence as he went down the broad stone steps, then she slammed the door so hard that the crash raised the wood pigeons from the oak trees all along the drive.

Jack strode across the gravel sweep toward the drive, his mind still focused on Miss Theodosia Shaw. *Arrogance, insensitivity and conceit...* He winced. It was a long time since anyone—except perhaps his father—had dared accuse him of any such thing. Perhaps that was half the trouble.

Jack knew that he had mishandled the situation and he also knew that in part he had done it deliberately. He had wanted to test Miss Shaw, to see if she was the woman of principle that she claimed. And yet Jack realized that as soon as they had spoken, he had known instinctively that Thea would accept neither his money nor his amorous attentions. There was an innocence about her, a straightforward honesty that made such transactions seem grubby and demeaning. Which they were, of course. It served him right to have his offers thrown back in his face.

Jack smiled a little. He had ignored his intuition and put her to the test, but Thea had triumphantly proved his instincts to be right and this pleased him more than a little. He frowned whilst he grappled with the implications of this. It would have been so much easier to have either paid her off and forgotten about her, or to have set her up as his mistress until his surprising desire for her had waned. Instead he found that he wanted her to be innocent of deceit. In fact he wanted her to be innocent, full stop. Jack whistled soundlessly to himself. Purity had never particularly appealed to him before— he had enjoyed the attentions of plenty of experienced women and had never wanted it to be any other way. This, however, was different. For a moment Jack allowed himself the luxury of imagining what it would be like to introduce Thea to physical pleasure. She had responded to his kiss with an untutored passion that was wholly arousing. Multiply that effect ten times and it gave some indication of the conflagration that would surely follow…

Arrogant, conceited… Jack acknowledged that he was being both of those things in wanting Theodosia Shaw all to himself. Further, he was certain that given the time and the opportunity he could persuade her to his point of view, convert her to his way of thinking. He did not have the time, however, and there were any number of pressing reasons why he should return to Town at once, not least because he detested country life. Miss Theodosia Shaw would simply have to remain the one lady who had escaped him…

Jack shrugged his shoulders uncomfortably, frustrated in more ways than one. He was not sure why he was hesitating when Miss Shaw had made her aversion to him crystal-clear. If he had not found himself in actual physical discomfort, he would have laughed at the irony. Jack Merlin, the ruthless rake, was aching for a woman he could not have.

To distract himself, Jack looked around at Oakmantle Hall and the neglected gardens that surrounded it. He was surprised to find that they were rather charming. The house was a low building of golden stone, with higgledy-piggledy chimneys and a pale slate roof. It was surrounded by a moat of green water, almost full after the earlier rain, and beyond that the lawn stretched to the deer park, where clumps of daffodils were showing beneath the trees. The air was mild and soft. It was a tranquil scene.

Jack paused on the edge of the moat. He could see paddocks over to the right, where a fat pony grazed undisturbed. It would make the most excellent place to keep stables. Jack told himself, jokingly of course, that if he ever lived in the country he would breed horses and set up racing stables to rival the finest.

He could hear the distant sound of children's voices and wondered whether Thea's younger siblings were close at hand. He thought that he would like to meet them, then paused, frowning. Those were two uncharacteristic thoughts that he had had in the space of a minute. Perhaps there was something in the Oakmantle air that was turning his mind. He had better get back to the inn, and from there to London. Quickly.

There was a shout much closer at hand, and he turned abruptly, but it was too late. He was struck hard on the shoulder, a blow that knocked him to the ground. He felt something sharp hit him on the head and he went out like a blown candle.

Chapter Three

"Thea, come quickly! I've shot him! I've shot the Marquis of Merlin!"

Thea was in the drawing room, tidying her ornaments, picking up the guineas and trying to put Jack Merlin from her mind. So far her mode of doing so had involved going over every part of their conversation and feeling utterly outraged, then moving on to the kiss, and feeling deeply disturbed. The fact that she had spent ten minutes thinking of nothing but Jack Merlin was something that exasperated her even more, but she did not seem at liberty to prevent it.

"Thea!"

Clementine's voice broke through Thea's preoccupation and she hurried toward the door, colliding with her sister in the hall. Clemmie was pale, her hair in disarray, her eyes wild. She grabbed Thea's sleeve and almost dragged her to the front door.

"Thea, I've shot him—"

"I heard you the first time," Thea said soothingly, noting the bow propped in a corner of the hall. She gave Clementine a quick hug, feeling the tension in her sister's body and noticing that she was close to tears.

"Calm down, Clemmie, I'm sure it cannot be so bad! Now, show me where he is!"

It was a mild afternoon outside and the threat of rain was back in the air. As they came 'round onto the carriage sweep, a horrid sight met Thea's eyes. Jack Merlin was lying on the gravel by the moat, his head resting on one of the large white stones that marked the edge of the drive. The shaft of an arrow was sticking out of his shoulder, his face was parchment-white and he was quite unconscious.

Thea took a deep breath and knelt down beside him, feeling for his pulse. The gravel felt sharp through the material of her dress. She knew it must be uncomfortable for Jack to lie on, but she also knew that she should not move him until she could ascertain his injuries.

"Clemmie, send Ned for Dr. Ryland," she said over her shoulder, "then go to the kitchens and ask Mrs. Skeffington to heat some water and find some bandages."

Clementine peered at Jack's recumbent form. "Is he dead, Thea?"

"Certainly not!" Thea gave her sister an encouraging smile. "You are not such a good shot, you know! The arrow is not in very deep but I think he hit his head when he fell."

"He wandered straight across my sights."

Thea squeezed her hand. "Never mind that now. The best way for you to help him is to fetch the doctor. Hurry!"

She watched her sister run off a little shakily toward the shrubbery where Ned and Harry could still be heard playing at cricket. The archery target was visible on the drive fifty yards away. Thea sighed. Ever since Clementine had skewered the delivery boy's hat with an arrow a few months back, she had been afraid that a worse accident would happen and now she had been proved right. That it had happened to the arrogant Marquis of Merlin was only a small consolation, for Thea found that when she looked at Jack's lifeless body it was concern that she felt rather than triumph.

She turned her attention back to him. His face was still pale, chill and clammy to the touch, but she was a little reassured that his pulse was strong and his breathing regular. She moved his head onto her lap, taking care not to jolt his shoulder. He did not stir. Thea felt a surprisingly strong impulse to brush the hair back from his forehead, and after a second she did so. It was as soft and silky as she had imagined earlier and she lingered over the feel of it before recalling herself and snatching her hand away guiltily. Then she just sat and studied the sweep of his lashes against the hard line of his cheek. It gave her a strange feeling inside, breathless, warm and protective all at the same time. She shifted uncomfortably, then hastily stilled her movements as Jack groaned a little. She held her breath, but he did not open his eyes.

It was starting to rain, the drops pattering down on the drive and dampening Thea's gray muslin dress and wetting her hair all over again. A drop fell on Jack's face and Thea wiped it away gently. She saw him wrinkle up his nose as the cool water roused him. Then he opened his eyes and looked at her. For a moment his gaze was cloudy with pain and puzzlement, then Thea saw him focus on her face, and he tried to sit up.

"What the hell—" Jack broke off with a groan as the movement jarred his shoulder and made him wince. He closed his eyes again momentarily, then opened them and frowned.

"What in God's name is going on? Miss Shaw—"

Thea laid a restraining hand on his sound shoulder. "Please lie still, Lord Merlin. You have had an accident but I have sent my brother for the doctor and we shall have you inside the house in no time."

Jack raised his right hand to his shoulder, twisting awkwardly as he tried to discover the source of his discomfort. "What is this—an arrow?" There was stark incredulity in his voice, overlying the pain. "Good God, ma'am, have you shot me to protect your virtue? I assure you there was no such need."

"Don't be so absurd." Thea said crisply. "You wandered across the target where my sister was practicing her archery. It was the veriest accident! Then you hit your head when you fell."

"A veritable chapter of accidents, in fact!" Jack gave a sigh and rubbed his hand across his forehead. "Damnation, I feel as weak as a kitten and my head aches to boot." He shifted again. "This arrow in my shoulder—"

"Dr. Ryland will remove it as soon as he gets here, I am sure!" Thea looked around a little desperately, wondering where the good doctor had got to. It seemed like hours since Clementine had run to fetch help but perhaps it was only a matter of minutes. The rain was falling harder now and she knew she had no way of getting Jack to shelter. There was sweat on his face now but he had started to shiver. Thea felt the worry clutch at her.

"If I could reach it properly I would pull it out myself!" Jack was muttering, sitting up with an effort and straining to reach the shaft of the arrow. He struggled, a groan escaping his lips. "Devil take it."

"Please keep still," Thea besought him. "You will

only make yourself worse! If you are strong enough we could attempt to walk to the house.''

Jack looked at her, squinting with the effort of concentration. ''I would gladly try but I cannot walk anywhere with an arrow stuck in my shoulder, Miss Shaw. It is damnably dangerous and could easily injure you, too, if I were to fall.'' He shook his head in an attempt to clear the pain. ''Perhaps if you were to take it out for me—''

''Oh, I do not think so!'' Thea recoiled. ''Besides, surely it is too much of a risk.''

Jack's eyes, bright with fever now, mocked her. ''What, rejecting an opportunity to cause me pain, Miss Shaw? Do you faint at the sight of blood? I assure you, there will not be much and you would be doing me the utmost favor.''

There was a silence. Thea looked at him, her face pale. He gave a slight nod, holding her gaze steadily with his. She gritted her teeth, trying to ignore the sickness inside her at the thought of hurting him. She knew she had to do it, but it was so very difficult to screw her courage up. She took a deep breath and set her hand to the arrow shaft, giving it a sharp tug. She heard the breath hiss between Jack's teeth as it came out in her hand, but he made no further sound. The blood spread from the tear across the coat of green superfine, not in a huge rush, as Thea had feared, but in a steady stream.

''One of Weston's best creations ruined,'' Jack observed dispassionately. ''He will never forgive me! Miss Shaw, might I trouble you to lend your petticoat to stem the flow? It is likely the only opportunity I shall get to encourage you to voluntarily remove a garment…''

Thea smothered a smile. For some obscure reason his

teasing made her feel much better, as though it was a sign that he was not at death's door.

"I am pleased to see you so much recovered that you can make fun of me, my lord!" she said. "I will gladly donate a strip of my petticoat, although I cannot afford to give you the whole as it is the only one I possess!"

"I will buy another one for you, if you will accept so personal a gift." Jack gave her a faint glimmer of a smile as he watched her pull up her skirts a little and hastily tear a strip from the material.

"Make it into a pad," he instructed, "then tie it in place with the loose ends…"

"You are very resourceful, my lord," Thea said, following his directions and trying to keep the surprise out of her voice. Such commonsense practicality did not seem to fit her image of the society rake at all.

Jack shrugged, then winced. "I learned to make shift as I could when I was in the Peninsula. Your petticoat is a very superior sort of bandage, Miss Shaw, compared with some of the dressings I was forced to apply then."

"You were in the Peninsula?" Thea asked, this time failing to hide her surprise. "I did not realize… That is, Bertie did not mention…"

Once again Jack's smile contained a flicker of mockery. He turned his head to watch her hands as she hesitantly wrapped the bandage about his shoulder. A lock of his hair brushed her wrist and Thea nearly jumped away, then schooled herself to carry on. She did not want him to see her vulnerability.

"A little tighter, if you please, Miss Shaw…" Fortunately Jack did not appear to have noticed her discomfort although his gaze was disturbingly observant for a sick man. It returned to her face and stayed there, thoughtful, disconcerting.

"Perhaps there is much you have to learn about me, Miss Shaw. Does Bertie speak of me often?"

"Incessantly!" Thea said briskly, tying the bandage with a little tug just to put him in his place. "He is quite boring on the subject. Now can you manage to struggle to the house by leaning on my arm, my lord? I regret that we do not have any servants who can carry you indoors…"

"No need, Miss Shaw," the Marquis murmured, "though I appreciate your offer. I believe that must be the good doctor now, and bringing Hodges, my valet, with him."

Thea looked up. Ned was hurrying across the drive, leading Dr. Ryland and a portly man who was carrying a traveling bag and wearing a long-suffering expression. Thea had the impression that the valet was accustomed to finding his master in such unusual circumstances and was wearily weighing up exactly what was required this time.

Thea accepted Ned's hand and struggled a little stiffly to her feet, then hung back as Dr. Ryland and Hodges between them managed to help the Marquis across the gravel sweep and back into Oakmantle Hall. It felt decidedly strange to see Jack Merlin escorted back into the house she had thrown him out of only twenty minutes before and Thea could not be sure if she was glad or sorry that he had not been so easy to dismiss. One thing she was certain of, however, was that she had to get rid of him again, and fast. She had no wish for Jack to realize just how much the whole experience had shaken her and how protective of him she had felt. Pulling out the arrow had taken all her courage and she had admired Jack for the stoical way in which he had accepted her fumbling ministrations. Clearly he was no mere society rake. There was indeed a lot that she did not know about him. She was not certain if it was safe to know any more.

Once inside the house, Thea was confronted by a new dilemma. Dr. Ryland was insistent that the Marquis should be put to bed and Thea saw no alternative than to donate her own room for the time being. She saw them safely upstairs then went to check that Clementine was feeling somewhat improved. Her sister was in the kitchen regaling Mrs. Skeffington with the tale of how she had shot the Marquis, but she broke off, looking guilty when Thea entered.

"A cup of tea, ma'am?" Mrs. Skeffington suggested quickly, pushing the pot toward her, and Thea sat down gratefully whilst the housekeeper poured her a cup. She let Clementine's chatter flow over her, aware that most of it was prompted by relief, and unwilling to give her sister the scolding she so clearly deserved.

Thea leaned her chin on her hands, feeling tired and out of sorts. The whole incident had left her feeling curiously vulnerable and prey to all manner of conflicting emotions. She did not want Jack Merlin in the house, but it was not because she disliked him. She knew she *ought* to dislike him intensely after what had happened between them and it was all the more disconcerting to discover that the reverse was true. Jack was too disturbingly attractive, his presence too unsettling for her peace of mind. So he had to go. She would insist that, as soon as Dr. Ryland had seen him, the Marquis be taken straight back to the Lamb and Rabbit, or to London, or to hell for all she cared. For the one thing that she did know was that even in his weakened state, if she gave Jack an inch, he would take a mile.

"Not much harm done!" Dr. Ryland said reassuringly half an hour later as he joined Thea in the library. "The Marquis has a lump on his head but his vision is unaffected and the arrow wound is slight. It may be that he has taken a fever but—" the doctor shrugged philosophically "—with your excellent care, Miss Shaw, I am certain he will be up and about within a se'nnight!"

Thea stared. She had not thought of this, had not really thought beyond the necessity to get Jack out of the rain and seen by the doctor. But for him to have to remain in bed, and for it to be her bed…

"But he cannot stay here!" she said, appalled. "My dear Dr. Ryland, that is quite improper! You know that there is no one here but my family and Mrs. Skeffington. Surely you could arrange to move him to the Lamb and Rabbit."

Dr. Ryland drained his glass of wine and put it down on the drawing room table. He was shaking his head. "Lord Merlin cannot be moved at present, my dear. Leaving aside his injury, which would be aggravated by movement, there is the blow to the head. Besides, it is raining and that may encourage the fever. There are many ways that Lord Merlin's condition could deteriorate!"

Thea pressed her hands together. "Then what is to be done?"

"We can only watch his progress over the next few days and see how soon he is recovered," the doctor said. "Besides, would you condemn Lord Merlin to Mrs. Prosper's somewhat…hit-and-miss nursing, my dear Miss Shaw? The poor fellow would certainly perish within the week!''

Thea gave a rueful smile. Mrs. Prosper's brand of brusqueness was admirable in the landlady of the local inn, but she had little time for invalids and her cooking was desperately bad. Even so, Thea felt most awkward. She did not wish to appear inhospitable but she could not explain to Dr. Ryland that what she dreaded about having Jack Merlin in the house was nothing to do with the expense or the propriety of the arrangement and everything to do with Jack himself and the way he made her feel.

"Besides," Dr. Ryland said cheerfully, picking up his bag and heading toward the door, "you have the valet, Hodges, to help with the nursing. He seems a most accomplished fellow—has been in the Marquis's service some ten years, I understand.'' His shoulders shook slightly. "By George, the things he must have seen—''

Thea waved the doctor off, having extracted a promise from him that he would call the next day, and went slowly up the stairs and along the landing to visit her unwanted guest. Her hand was raised to knock on the bedroom door when she heard voices from within and instinctively froze, listening.

"So what do you think of the place then, Hodges?'' That was Jack, sounding none the worse for his adventure. "Somewhat picturesque, eh? I feel my opinion of the country undergoing a change, you know!''

"It is most charming, my lord,'' the valet returned.

"As is Miss Shaw,'' Jack added lazily. "She is quite an original, you know, Hodges, with her quaint notions and her fancy dress!''

Thea looked down. It was just conceivable that the

ancient wedding gown could have been mistaken for
fancy dress but her old gray muslin certainly could not.
She bristled.

"She seems a most pleasant and accomplished lady,"
Hodges replied woodenly.

Thea heard Jack yawn. "Damned pretty, too, though
I understand from Bertie that the situation is not precisely as my father imagined."

"Just so, my lord." There was distinct disapproval
in the valet's tone now. "One can scarce imagine a lady
such as Miss Shaw trapping a gentleman into marriage."

Thea drew a sharp breath, the color flaming to her
face. So that was what the Duke of Merlin had thought
when he had heard of her wedding to Bertie! She
blushed all the harder to think that he had not been far
out in his assessment.

There was a noise close at hand and Thea came to
her senses and knocked loudly and hastily on the bedroom door. The voices within stopped immediately and
Hodges opened the door to her. She thought that she
detected a shade of embarrassment in his manner.

"Good afternoon, madam." He slipped past her.
"Excuse me. I shall leave you to speak with his lordship
alone."

This was not precisely what Thea had intended, but
it was too late to stop Hodges, who was already halfway
down the stairs. Thea went into the room and made sure
to leave the door open.

Jack was sitting up against the pillows, looking
faintly comical in one of her father's old nightshirts.
Evidently his traveling bag had contained nothing so
practical as night attire, and Thea wondered faintly if
he actually wore anything when he was asleep, then

hastily tried to think of something else. Unfortunately the ancient linen of the late Mr. Shaw's shirt concealed little and only served to emphasize Jack's muscled physique and superb form. Thea hastily averted her eyes, telling herself primly that she should be more concerned about whether or not Jack was running a fever rather than giving herself a temperature simply through looking at him. He gave her a faint smile that only served to make her feel warmer still and she just managed to prevent herself from turning tail and rushing from the room.

"I am sorry to be an additional burden on your household, Miss Shaw," he said politely. "I shall try to be as little trouble as possible."

Thea doubted it. "I am sorry that my sister shot you, my lord," she replied equally formally. "It is all most unfortunate."

Jack smiled. "Well, I suppose it was a little unorthodox of her, but then yours is hardly an ordinary family!" His smile faded and Thea thought that he actually looked slightly discomfited. "I meant what I said, Miss Shaw. I do not intend to be a…a financial burden to you." He met her eyes, and looked away. "Forgive me for broaching such a confoundedly delicate subject."

"I see no need for apologies, my lord," Thea said sharply. "It is but a few hours since you offered me plenty of money and your guineas are more than enough to bespeak the best medical care and hospitality for the next few days!"

Jack winced. "*Touché*, Miss Shaw! I can only beg your pardon once again for assuming in so unsubtle a manner that I knew your price."

Thea's eyes narrowed. She did not like the implication of that. "I thought that I had made it clear that I could not be bought, my lord."

There was a cynical light in Jack's eyes. He pulled a face. "Come now, Miss Shaw. Your price may be above rubies but any commodity can be bought—even innocence! It is a question of finding the right currency."

Thea's eyes turned a stormy blue. "And am I to understand that you think you will find my…currency, my lord?"

Jack laughed. "It should not be so difficult! Bertie has told me something of your circumstances and how much you would do for your family. There is your brother…Ned, is it? The one who wishes to be a soldier… A commission for him in a good regiment would be a fine thing, and such matters take influence as well as money. With my connections I could arrange such a thing as easily as breathing!" His blue eyes mocked her. "You see, Miss Shaw, it is not very hard to find a weakness to exploit…"

Thea found that she was shaking. She pressed her hands together, then put them behind her back to ensure that she did not hit an injured man.

"That is just bribery by another name, Lord Merlin! It does not impress me. Nor do I believe that you will find breathing so easy when I smother you with a pillow!"

Jack's wicked grin deepened. He leaned forward. "Very well then, Miss Shaw. How about an old-fashioned wager? No bribery or blackmail involved. Just my…expertise…against your virtue. What do you say?"

Thea gave him a scornful look. "That will be easy, my lord. You are scarce irresistible!"

Jack inclined his head. "I am willing to believe that you will prove that," he said easily. "How piquant, to pit goodness against—"

"Wickedness!" Thea finished for him. "I cannot believe you so devoid of any sense of morality, my lord! It is most disturbing!"

Jack laughed. "Perhaps you can redeem me, my sweet Theodosia."

"You need not start immediately!" Thea said sharply. "I should warn you that I am on my guard, my lord."

"That's good…" Somehow Jack had taken her hand and his warm touch was already undermining her defenses. She snatched her hand away and straightened the already straight bedclothes in an attempt to cover her confusion. She hoped that Jack would feel too weary to continue the conversation, but unfortunately he did not appear in the least bit affected by his injury.

"This is quite an unusual establishment, is it not?" he continued. "Do you have no older relatives living with you, Miss Shaw?"

Thea pursed her lips. "No, my lord. I am quite old enough to run an establishment on my own."

Jack raised his brows. "In the light of our conversation, I was thinking more of the propriety of such a situation—"

"Oh, I am well known in the neighborhood as a respectable spinster!" Thea said with spirit.

Jack gave a derisive laugh. "I do not doubt it, my dear Miss Shaw, but wearing a lace cap scarcely convinces me that you are in your dotage. Surely you are forever fending off the advances of unsuitable men."

"Not at all, my lord," Thea said, plumping his pillows with unnecessary force. "At the least, not before you arrived here. Such things seldom happen in the country and as I said, my reputation is of the most respectable. Besides, I have Mrs. Skeffington to lend me countenance."

"Oh, the hatchet-faced female who acts as your housekeeper? She doesn't approve of me, you know."

"One can scarcely blame her," Thea said hotly. "And anyway, Skeffie is the dearest creature imaginable. She has taken care of us all since our father died."

"Yes—" the laughter left Jack's eyes briefly "—I heard that Mr. Shaw died only six months ago. I am very sorry."

There was unmistakable sincerity in his tone. Thea swallowed hard, wishing that she had not raised the subject in the first place. Jack was confusing her, one moment so infuriatingly arrogant and the next so perceptive. She suspected darkly that it was all part of his planned seduction. He would lull her into thinking that he was not so bad after all, undermine her already-shaky defenses, destroy her resolution and seduce her ruthlessly. Thea shivered at the prospect, and not entirely from horror. She started to tidy the bedside table with a certain fierce energy.

"Thank you, my lord."

"A shotgun accident, I understand," Jack pursued gently. "I am sorry if my own accident raised any difficult memories."

Thea looked at him swiftly, then away. The last thing she wanted to explain to him was that pulling the arrow out of his shoulder had been so difficult because she still remembered trying to staunch the flow of blood from her father's injuries. That would make her just too vulnerable. She changed the subject rather abruptly. "Are you quite comfortable here, my lord?"

Jack accepted the change in the conversation gracefully, although Thea had the unnerving feeling that he also understood the reason for it. That blue gaze was very searching and she knew she had to defend herself better against it. Then she saw a wicked glint come into Jack's eyes, which was more unsettling still.

"Yes, I thank you, I am most comfortable. This is a very pleasant room. Yours, I imagine? If you wish to share it with me…"

Thea compressed her lips. Dealing with his flirtation was as difficult as coping with his insight.

"I shall just remove some of my possessions, my lord," she said pointedly, "and leave you to sleep."

She was very conscious of Jack's gaze resting on her as she moved about the room, collecting her bottles from the top of the dressing table and her clothes from out of the cupboard. She hesitated before going to the armada chest to take out her underwear but she had little choice. With her hands full of chemises and stockings she skirted the bed and edged toward the door.

"You need not be shy of my seeing your underwear, Miss Shaw," Jack said softly. "I am sure I have seen items far more shocking."

"I am sure you have!" Thea snapped, trying to hide them behind her skirts and only succeeding in scattering her stockings across the bedside rug.

"Your practical clothing is far more respectable than the apparel I am accustomed to seeing," Jack continued. "Though I can imagine what you would look like in something more…provocative…."

"Pray do not exercise your imagination so!" Thea glared at him. "You are outrageous, my lord."

"And you are so charming to tease! I feel such a slow convalescence coming on, by which time I am

convinced that I will have persuaded you to share more
than just the secrets of your underwear...."

"You are more likely to find yourself sharing the
moat with the swans than my bed!"

Thea vented her feelings by going out and slamming
the bedroom door behind her. It was becoming a habit
and a very damaging one, since the whole house was
so old and neglected that it might fall down around her
ears. She could still hear Jack laughing as she made her
way down the corridor. The sound was disturbing and
her heart sank to think of him occupying her bedroom
for another week. Something told her that he was going
to be a very difficult patient indeed, and then there was
the matter of the wager. Thea paused, leaning against
the paneled wall of the corridor for a moment and closing her eyes. It mattered not one whit whether or not
she had accepted Jack Merlin's challenge, for he would
try to seduce her, anyway. Just for the fun of it, just for
the thrill of the chase, just because he was a rake.
Thea's shoulders slumped. She was not at all sure that
she could resist.

Chapter Four

"You will not be able to keep Lord Merlin in bed for much longer, you know, Thea."

Thea jumped, her book sliding off her knee. Had Clementine but known it, her words summoned up all kinds of visions in her sister's overactive mind. Tending to Jack over the past three days had been absolute purgatory, not because he had been a troublesome patient but because of the sheer overwhelming effect of his presence. It had been exactly as she had feared—only worse.

Jack had developed a fever initially but after it had subsided, he had grown bored of his own company and had wanted to talk. It had been difficult, for Thea found that he asked all manner of perceptive questions and challenged her assumptions on a variety of topics in a manner that no one had done since her father had died. In a strange way it was very similar to the sparring matches she had had with Mr. Shaw, but in another way it had been far more stimulating—and exciting. She would become engrossed in their discussion, then would look up and find Jack watching her steadily. In an instant she would lose the thread of her thoughts and feel herself blushing whilst that lazy, dark blue gaze swept over her so searchingly that she was sure he could read her thoughts.

Their discussions had also been a revelation of Jack himself, for Thea knew that many of her greatest assumptions had been made about him and his lifestyle, and not one of them had survived. Well, she had dismissed all but one. She was still utterly convinced that he was a dangerous rake and that given the right circumstances, he would prove it. The wager was always at the back of her mind, an unspoken thought, troubling her, and the fact that Jack made no overt move to seduce her simply added to her concern. She could not afford to trust him.

Then there were the difficulties engendered by Jack's physical presence. Thea had been happy—relieved, even—to leave the practical nursing to Hodges, who had tended his master with exemplary skill and was fast becoming one of the household to boot.

Then, two nights previously, Thea had heard a sound on the landing and, thinking it was Daisy sleepwalking, had got up to investigate. She had found Jack, his fever returned, about to tumble down the staircase. There had been no time to call Hodges—she had had to catch Jack and support him back to bed, whereupon he had fallen in a heap on the covers and had pulled her down with him. It had taken her some time to extricate herself from his embrace, particularly since her efforts were so half-hearted because the weight of his body on hers was so peculiarly exciting. The whole experience had been deeply disturbing, and if Thea had not known that Jack was ill, she would have been convinced that he had done it on purpose. As it was, he had seemed unconscious throughout and after she had gently bathed his face, she went back to bed and lay awake for hours, tormented by the memory of his touch, the scent of his skin and the warmth of his body.

After that she had not been to visit his room for two days. She dared not.

Thea bent to retrieve her book and looked over the top of her glasses at her sister. "Whatever can you mean, Clemmie? I am not deliberately confining the Marquis of Merlin to his bed—"

"Pshaw!" Clementine snorted. Thea did not even trouble to admonish her. "You know you persuaded Hodges to keep the Marquis in his chamber today when Dr. Ryland said that he was quite well enough to get up! I do believe that you would lock him in if you could. You are afraid of what will happen once he is loose about the house."

"That is a most unfortunate turn of phrase to apply to a man of Lord Merlin's reputation," Thea said, trying not to giggle. "Besides, you make him sound like a wild animal, Clemmie, dangerous to the rest of us."

"Dangerous only to you, I believe," her sister said calmly. "You know he has you in his sights."

"I know no such thing!" Thea said hastily, wondering how Clementine could possibly have guessed. "I am only concerned that Lord Merlin should not overtax his strength, and once he is recovered he will be gone from here anyway. It is quite straightforward."

Clementine muttered something that sounded considerably ruder than "fustian," but Thea chose to ignore it and read on in a dignified silence. After a few moments she gave a sigh and cast her book down again.

"Oh, this is ridiculous! No matter how many moneymaking schemes I read about I can see a flaw in every one! At this rate Harry will have to become a climbing boy and Clara and Daisy can sell flowers in the street, whilst you and I will be teaching spoiled brats their letters and Ned will be apprenticed to some backstreet lawyer!''

Clementine put down her own book on the pedestal next to another of the sculptures that the late Mr. Shaw had delighted in. Thea was intrigued to see that the book was Mrs. Kitty Cuthbertson's *Santo Sebastiano* rather than her sister's favorite, Mary Wollstonecraft's *A Vindication of the Rights of Women.* She wondered why her sister had suddenly taken to reading romance and hoped that it was not because Clementine was developing a *tendre* for the Marquis. That would become too intolerably complicated. Thea could cope with her own foolish feelings but not Clementine's, as well.

''Well, it might not be so terrible to work for a living,'' Clementine said slowly. ''Only Harry is too big to be a sweep's boy now for he would get stuck up the chimney, and Clara suffers from sneezing fits when she is near flowers—''

''There is no need to be so literal,'' Thea snapped. ''I am sure I shall come up with something, even if it is only to sell lavender pillows or royal jelly! Oh, if only we possessed something valuable to sell.'' She took a deep breath, anxious not to add further credence to her sister's view that she was on edge about Jack's presence in the house. Her eye fell on the book again.

''What do you think of Mrs. Cuthbertson's writing, Clemmie? It is much lighter than your usual read, is it not?''

''It is all very well.'' Clementine wrinkled up her nose. ''Hodges recommended it to me, you know. He is a great reader of contemporary romances, but I find there are a little too many sentimental parts for my liking.'' She laughed. ''The hero is forever swooning at the lady's feet, you know, and how impractical is that? I fear romance is vastly overrated, Thea! Perhaps you would have done better to marry Mr. Pershore, after all!''

Jack woke suddenly, wondering where he was. For a moment he lay still, taking in the pale candlelight and the worn bed hangings, the daylight fading beyond the windows. Then he remembered. He was at Oakmantle Hall—had been there for almost seven days now—and though the fever had not yet carried him off, the starvation diet certainly would. And soon.

On the first evening after his accident, Thea had sent Hodges up with a bowl of gruel, which Jack had immediately sent back with a demand for a bottle of port and a side of beef. Ten minutes later the gruel had reappeared in Thea's own hands and she had made it abundantly clear that unless he ate it he would receive nothing else at all. Jack had submitted with an ill grace but the starvation diet had continued with a thin soup the following day and bread and cheese the day after, until Jack had wondered if it was simply that Thea's household budget could not afford anything better, the golden guineas notwithstanding. When Hodges had explained that this was Mrs. Skeffington's view of a healthy diet for a convalescent, Jack had been unimpressed, and whether it was the effect of his illness or the unaccustomed frugality of his meals, he had been unable to drag himself from the bed and had been disgusted at his weakness.

He had also been bitterly disappointed that Thea had not been in to see him for the past two days. She had accompanied the doctor upstairs on his visits—Jack had heard her voice outside the door—but she had not been into the room since the third night, the night when she had rescued him from falling down the stairs. Despite his fever, Jack could remember the details of that encounter in vivid detail, the softness of her body beneath his on the bed, the sweet scent of lavender in her clothes and hair, and the way she had extricated herself with what seemed regretful slowness from his embrace… He smiled a little. He had been too ill to take advantage, which was a shame in a way, but he would have needed to be near death not to have appreciated the experience.

Except that Thea had not been to see him since. Perhaps she was only acting out of propriety, or perhaps she was embarrassed at what had happened between them, but whatever the cause, it was deeply frustrating. He wanted to see her, to talk to her. It was a troubling realization for a rake, but he was forced to admit that he missed their discussions, which had broached topics from the London Season to the writings of Shakespeare. He had never crossed swords with a bluestocking before and he had found it a stimulating experience, almost as stimulating as holding her in his arms. But perhaps she would bring his food that night…

On the thought of food, he rolled over and sat up. And blinked.

There was a vision sitting on the end of his bed, a tiny angel. For a second Jack wondered whether he had died in his sleep and whether this was as a direct result of requesting that Hodges smuggle him in an illicit bottle of brandy. When he considered the angel more carefully, however, he realized that she was clutching a ragged toy sheep in one hand and looked about five years old. She also looked a lot like Thea, a miniature version, with tiny fair corkscrew curls and huge blue eyes. Perhaps Thea had looked like this as a child, or perhaps this was what a child of Thea's would look like. Jack felt something twist inside him at the thought. A child with fair curls and a cherubic smile… He grimaced. His illness was turning him quite ludicrously maudlin.

"Hello!" the angel said.

"Hello," Jack replied.

"Thea says that you're trouble," the angel announced, fixing him with a stern blue stare. "She says that we're not to see you."

Jack felt hurt at this apparent treachery. Did Miss Shaw really consider him a monster with whom her younger siblings were not safe? His own sisters had always praised him as a most indulgent uncle even though he had had no thoughts of setting up his own nursery—until now.

He smiled at the angel. "I think that you must be Daisy."

A nod was his only reply. Daisy was still weighing him up.

"So if your sister told you not to come here, Daisy, what are you doing?"

There was a pause. "Seeing for myself," Daisy said solemnly.

Jack grinned. It seemed that Clementine was not the only one who had absorbed Mrs. Shaw's philosophy of independence! If Thea thought that she had problems with her sisters already it seemed that her troubles were only beginning. He raised his eyebrows.

"And what do you think?"

Daisy was in no hurry to commit herself. Her cornflower-blue eyes appraised him thoroughly and Jack found himself holding his breath.

"You look very nice," Daisy said. Her rosebud

mouth curved into a smile and she crawled toward him across the bedcover. When she reached his side she simply held her arms out.

"Cuddle," she said.

After a moment of frozen incomprehension, Jack shifted obligingly so that she was curved into the circle of his good arm, her golden curls brushing his shoulder, the toy sheep clutched against his chest. Now that he could see it more closely, he realized that it was moth-eaten and more than a little chewed. No doubt toys in the Shaw household had to last from one child to the next and were never thrown away. He watched as Daisy yawned suddenly and her eyelids flickered closed.

"Story," she said.

Jack's mind was suddenly, frighteningly blank. Although he was indeed a generous uncle, his indulgence had never stretched to telling his nephews and nieces bedtime stories. After all, it was hardly his place. There were nursemaids aplenty to do such a thing. He looked down at Daisy and after a moment she opened her eyes again and frowned at him.

"Story!" she said again, slightly more querulous this time.

Jack felt panic rise in him. He glanced toward the door, but there was no sound from the landing, no rescue at hand.

"Er…does Thea tell you stories?" he asked, playing for time.

Daisy nodded. Her hair tickled his nose. "Stories 'bout the fairies in the garden."

Fairies. Jack took a deep breath, trusting to magic himself. "They live in the garden but you can't see them, can you?"

"S'right." Daisy snuggled down again. "Cos it's magic."

Jack relaxed slightly. He seemed to be on the right track. He dredged his memory for anything that he could recall about the Oakmantle gardens. It was a shame that he had not seen them properly. There were the trees, of course, and there was also the moat...

"Has Thea told you about the water sprites who live in the moat?" he asked.

Daisy shook her head a little. "No..." She sounded sleepy but willing to give him a chance. "Tell..."

Jack started cautiously on a tale about the water sprites who shared the moat with the swans and ducks. He invented a castle for them under the water and a feud with the goblins in the oak trees that had led to much magic and mayhem. He was about to launch into the story of the fairy princess who had been kidnapped and rescued by the sprites, when he felt Daisy shift and relax further into his arms, her breathing soft, deeply asleep.

Jack stopped speaking and looked down at her. Her cheeks were flushed pink, her rosebud lips parted. His arm felt warm and damp and he was tolerably sure that she was dribbling slightly as she slept.

Jack sat still, afraid to move in case he woke her. He wondered why his sisters never told their children bedtime stories when surely it was one of the best bits of having a child. That led him to wondering why the fashionable farmed their children out at every available opportunity and if they knew what they were missing. The warm weight of the child in his arms seemed to load him down with love. He almost decided that he wanted one of his own, but his mind shied away from the implications of that particular thought.

Daisy and Clara and Harry and Ned and Clementine. His heart ached suddenly for Thea, trying to do the best she could as a substitute mother for her siblings. If he could help her... Jack shook his head, as if to dispel the thought forcibly. That was the trouble with the country—he had always sworn that it addled the brain and here was the proof.

There was a step on the landing and the door was pushed wider. Thea herself stood in the doorway, a white apron over her dress, her face flushed, the hair escaping from her cap, as it always seemed wont to do.

"Oh!" She saw the sleeping child in Jack's arms and lowered her voice to a whisper, "I am so sorry! I have been looking everywhere for her! It's just that she sleepwalks sometimes—"

"She just wanted a bedtime story," Jack said softly.

Thea's eyes met his. Hers were very dark and unreadable. "Did you tell her one?"

"I did indeed. Fairies and sprites and kidnapped princesses..."

He saw her smile. "I should have liked to hear that."

Jack grinned at her. "I would gladly tell you a bedtime story anytime you wish, Miss Shaw!"

He saw the blush that came into her cheek, but she did not answer. She leant down to take Daisy from him. Her sleeve brushed his cheek. He could smell her scent, lavender and roses, faint and elusive. Jack shifted, pretending that he was simply moving his arms now that the weight of the child was removed. Perhaps it was just hunger that was making him light-headed, or perhaps it was something more.

"You have not been to see me," he observed lightly, watching as Thea scooped Daisy expertly into the crook of her arm. "I could have died in here for all that you knew…"

"No doubt Hodges would have told me if that had happened," Thea said calmly. She smiled at him suddenly and Jack felt his pulse rate increase. This fever was proving damnably stubborn to shift, or perhaps that was something else, too.

"However," she continued, "I am happy to see that you are far from death's door."

"Are you?" Jack quirked one dark brow. "Then why have you been avoiding me, Miss Shaw?"

"I must go," she said hurriedly. "Daisy will wake—"

"But you have not answered my question!" Jack protested. "Surely you are not afraid to be alone with me, Miss Shaw!"

There was a pause. "Not afraid, precisely, my lord," Thea said slowly, "but I have not forgotten your reputation. Now if you will excuse me—"

"A moment." Jack touched the back of her hand and she paused by the side of the bed. His tone was unwontedly serious. "Why did you tell the children that they were not to see me? Am I then *so* disreputable that you think I am not fit company for them?"

"Oh!" He heard Thea catch her breath. "It was not that, Lord Merlin. I simply wished you to have undisturbed rest and I thought that if the children pestered you…"

"You have permitted Bertie to visit me," Jack pointed out.

"That was different. Besides, I wished to make my peace with Bertie myself."

Jack raised an eyebrow. "So that is why he has had

the best of your attention and I have had nothing myself.''

Daisy stirred then, murmuring in her sleep. ''I must
go,'' Thea said again. Jack let his hand fall to his side
and watched as she walked slowly to the door.

''Miss Shaw?''

She paused in the doorway. ''Yes, Lord Merlin?''

Jack grinned. ''Is there gruel for dinner tonight?''

He saw the answering smile gleam in Thea's eyes
before she wiped it clean away. ''No. Mrs. Skeffington
has prepared a nourishing mutton stew for you. Oh, and
Lord Merlin...''

''Miss Shaw?''

''I have confiscated the bottle of brandy that you
asked your valet to bring up. It is not healthy. But if
you are very good I shall allow you one glass of home-
made elderberry wine.'' And she closed the door very
softly behind her.

Jack lay back on the pillows, a smile curling his
mouth. Theodosia Shaw. She might have the upper hand
at the moment whilst he was laid low in so inconvenient
a manner, but tomorrow he was determined to leave his
bed and then she would not find it so easy to avoid him.
Then he would progress his acquaintance with Miss
Shaw. He was looking forward to it immensely.

''It is plain as a pikestaff that you are still avoiding
Lord Merlin!'' Clementine said bluntly, helping Thea
to gather up the bunches of daffodils that they had just
cut for the house. ''You denied it before, but you know
that it is true and you *know* it is because you like him!''

Thea paused, her flower basket over one arm. It was
a beautiful morning and she had decided at once to go
out into the fresh air for she found that being cooped

up in the house only seemed to encourage the feelings of restlessness that she had suffered of late. And Clementine, with her usual sharp observation, had immediately identified the reason why her sister was feeling so on edge—the Marquis of Merlin.

In truth Thea could find very little to dispute in Clementine's words, for she *had* been avoiding Jack, particularly since he had become active again and was wont to pop up in all sorts of unexpected places. She knew he was deliberately seeking her out, and it was all very strange and disconcerting, all the more so since she could not ignore the speculative intensity of that dark blue gaze when it rested on her so warmly, nor the enjoyment she derived from his company. She felt as though she were being hunted—gently, patiently but relentlessly, and the feeling engendered a mixture of fascination and excitement. She knew she was being drawn into a trap, and it was one that she had to avoid, though she had little desire to do so.

"I think Lord Merlin likes you very much, too," Clementine added slyly, and Thea knew she was blushing and felt vexed.

"Lord Merlin is most amiable to everyone," she said, trying to sound indifferent. They started to walk back toward the house, their skirts swishing through the long grass. "He has been giving Harry some coaching on his cricket."

"And talking to Clara about music."

"And telling Daisy bedtime stories." Despite herself, Thea felt a smile starting.

"And chatting to Skeffie about recipes!" Clementine finished with a giggle. "She has quite altered her opinion of him, you know, and praises him to the heavens!"

Thea laughed, as well. "That, at least, is self-interest

on Lord Merlin's part! I believe he finds our diet sadly circumscribed and is longing for a side of sirloin and several bottles of port!''

They had reached the edge of the park and paused to look across the moat to the house. The golden stones of Oakmantle Hall glowed warm in the sunlight. The ducks were quacking on the water and the swans stretched their wings in the sun.

''Lord Merlin has also been speaking to Ned...'' Thea spoke hesitantly. ''About joining the army, you know.''

''Capital!'' Clementine gave a little skip. ''Ned has always wanted to be a soldier and if Lord Merlin can help.''

''Ned should be going to university!'' Thea said shortly. ''And don't say 'capital,' Clemmie—it should not form part of a lady's vocabulary!''

''Stuff!'' her sister said, clearly unimpressed. ''You know that Ned has no time for book learning and has set his heart on following the drum! If Papa had not died so untimely—''

''I will not allow Lord Merlin to buy a commission for Ned!'' Thea's words came out in a rush. ''I could not bear to be so beholden to him.'' It was impossible to explain to Clementine the conversation she had had with Jack that first day, when he had spoken of there being a price for everything and used Ned's example to make his point. It only served to prove that he could not be sincere now.

Clementine was looking at her curiously. ''Why not? He is influential and you would not think twice if there were another sponsor for Ned!''

Thea's hand tightened on the basket. ''Lord Merlin is different. He...I... He might expect...''

"Something in return for his generosity?"

"Clemmie!"

Clementine took off her bonnet and swung it by the ribbons in a casual manner that Thea considered deplorable. Not for the first time she felt hopelessly incapable of controlling her sister.

"Has Lord Merlin made such a suggestion to you, Thea?"

"Yes!" Thea said, goaded. "Several times!"

Clementine's eyes widened. "Glory! Oh, lucky you!"

"Clementine Shaw!"

Clementine did a little skip. "Well, I must leave you to fight the matter out with Lord Merlin himself, for I see him coming this way! I am sorry that I cannot stay to protect you!" She took the basket of daffodils from her sister and sped off toward the house before Thea could say a word.

Thea turned her head. Jack was indeed walking toward her, one of the spaniels panting at his heels. In Thea's father's day there had been a whole pack of dogs at Oakmantle but there were only three left now and this was the oldest and most arthritic of them all. Thea was certain that Jack had slowed his pace to allow the ancient creature to keep up and she smiled. Really he was very kind and, confusingly, that made him far more dangerous to her.

She thought that Jack was still looking a little pale, but he was immaculately elegant in gleaming black top boots, pristine white linen and a green hunting jacket that was the epitome of good taste. He was bare-headed and the morning sunshine made his dark hair gleam with tawny and gold. Feeling a certain shortness of breath that she knew was nothing to do with her exertions out walking, Thea decided that she had to be firm with him before he undermined her defenses completely.

"Good morning, my lord," she murmured as he reached her side, "did you come equipped for a long stay in the country, or do you always come accompanied by a baggage train?"

Jack smiled and Thea's heart did a little leap. He took her hand and her pulse rate increased still further. She tried to tug her hand away; he retained it, tucking it through his arm as he fell into step beside her.

"To tell the truth, it is only Hodges's ingenuity that has kept me so well turned out," he said ruefully. "I shall soon be reduced to asking Bertie for a loan of his linen. And one of his coats."

"I doubt that it would fit you—" Thea began thoughtlessly, then flushed scarlet as she realized she was expressing a view on a matter a lady should not even have considered let alone articulated. It was all very well for her to notice Jack's impressive physique— how could she avoid it?—but to give away the fact that she had been studying him... She saw him smile, felt the warmth of that midnight-blue gaze trap and hold hers, and cursed herself.

"I am flattered that you should have been observing me so closely, Miss Shaw," he drawled, proving to Thea that any opportunity she gave him would be exploited to the full. "Should you wish to continue your inspection, I am at your service."

Thea was determined to not be easy game for his teasing. "Indeed, my lord? But will I have the chance? Surely you will be leaving us now that you are so well recovered."

Jack gave her a limpid look. "Alas, Miss Shaw, traveling could be very dangerous to one of my enfeebled constitution.''

To Thea's mind, feeble was the very last thing that he looked. Rakish, perhaps. Dangerous, definitely. But feeble—the idea was ridiculous.

''I am sorry that your lordship is not in better health by now,'' she said politely. ''Perhaps you should go inside and rest? Further exercise might prove fatal to one of so weak a disposition.''

''Oh, I believe in exerting myself a little more each day, Miss Shaw,'' Jack said with a devastating smile, ''and I have not yet reached my target for this morning. Speaking of which, is your sister planning further archery practice today? If so, perhaps I might prevail on you to show me the herb garden, where we will be safe?''

Thea gave him a suspicious look, wondering what had engendered in him this newfound interest in gardening. She was certain that it was a pretense, but on the other hand it seemed churlish to refuse him, particularly as Clementine had taken the basket of flowers, and with it any excuse Thea might have had for going back inside.

They crossed the moat by a little wooden footbridge that led straight into the remains of the Oakmantle formal gardens, where Thea had only recently pruned the rosebushes for the coming season. Jack opened the gate at the end of the bridge for her, handing her through. His touch was light and warm and it filled Thea with an acute physical awareness. He was watching her, his gaze steady on her face, and she found she could not look away.

''We collect the rose petals from the bushes here in the summer,'' Thea said, a little at random, to cover her confusion. "We dry them to scent drawers and chests and...and things. And we grow herbs for eating and for perfume, as well, especially lavender..." She was rambling; she knew she was, and Jack's next words did nothing to calm her.

"So that explains why your bedclothes are scented with lavender," he said softly. His voice dropped. "And you are, too..."

Thea felt a rush of heat under her skin. The lavender scent was all around them, faint but disturbing.

"My lord, you should not say such things."

"Should I not?" Jack's voice had roughened. "I remember from the time I held you...after the wedding. And later..."

Thea moved away, along the path where the line of ragged lavender was starting to show its new spring growth. Her heart was racing, beating so loudly that she was surprised that Jack could not hear it. She could hear his steps behind her on the gravel; he was following her and she had a sudden and ridiculous urge to escape him, to run away. Unfortunately the path she was following led only to the fishpond and to flee she would have to scramble through the shrubbery on the far side. Common sense returned quickly. She was hardly in any danger and would simply walk back the way she had come. On this eminently sensible thought she turned to face Jack. And stopped.

He was a bare three steps away from her and there was something in the way he was standing—something cool, something watchful—that warned her exactly what would happen next. Jack was going to kiss her and she...

Thea felt the last vestige of sensible thought drift away from her as Jack's lips touched hers. He took im-

mediate advantage with a long, exploratory kiss that
sent a jolt of pure desire through her body from head
to toes. His arms went around her. He tasted of fresh
air and something indefinable and far more intoxicating,
and his skin smelled of sandalwood. After a moment,
Thea found herself raising her arms to encircle his neck
and hold him to her.

The kiss was softer and more persuasive than the one
in the drawing room, coaxing a response from her rather
than demanding one. Yet underneath the gentle surface
was something that made Thea shiver. It was both a
threat and a promise. He was drawing closer to his goal
all the time. And she knew exactly what that goal would
be.

It was a long time before Jack let her go, steadying
her with a hand on her arm as she stepped back—and
came down to earth. Thea frowned, trying to gather her
thoughts, which seemed to have scattered like straw in
the wind. She looked at Jack. He looked expressionlessly back at her.

"It goes against the grain with me, but do you wish
me to apologize for my behavior, Miss Shaw?"

"No…" Thea had been brought up to be truthful and
just at that moment it was a severe trial to her. "It is
not a matter of blame—"

Jack's hand tightened on her arm and for a moment
she thought he was about to pull her to him again. "A
matter of pleasure, then?"

"No!" Thea stepped back abruptly. "That is—yes,
but—"

"But no one has kissed you like that before and you
are startled at the results?" To Thea's ears Jack sounded
odiously complacent even if what he was saying was

true. She drew breath to give him a much belated set-down.

"Certainly it is true that I have not been kissed by a rake before! At least not before you kissed me the first time, sir!"

"And did you like it?"

Thea frowned stormily. "Pray stop asking difficult questions, my lord!"

"So you did. Would you like to do it again?"

"No!" Thea backed away. It was the first direct lie that she had told in a very long time and she knew at once that he did not believe her. He caught first one hand and then the other, trapping them both in one of his and bringing them up against his chest.

"Oh, Miss Shaw!" That dazzling blue gaze caught and held hers. "I had formed the opinion that you were always truthful yet now I have forced you into falsehood. It seems I am closer to corrupting innocence than I had realized..."

Thea knew that it was absolutely imperative to break free. She did not move. This time Jack bent his head with agonizing slowness to capture her mouth with his own, the touch of his lips fierce and sweet, their demand explicit. Thea's fingers uncurled to spread against his chest. She could feel the thud of his heart against her hand. The warmth of the sun mingled with her body's heated response and she felt utterly intoxicated. And totally confused. She freed herself from his embrace and felt the reluctance with which Jack let her go. He was breathing hard and his gaze, as it rested on her face, held the same concentrated desire that Thea had seen there before. She caught her breath.

"I am going inside now, my lord. I...I need to think and I cannot do so with you near me!"

"Thinking is a vastly overrated pastime in comparison to some others," Jack drawled. He followed her up the path. "My dear Miss Shaw, is there really any necessity to think at all? Can we not try something else?"

Thea warded him off with her hands. She did not want to speak since just at the moment she had lost all her *savoir faire* and knew she would only make matters worse for herself. She certainly did not want to linger here in the scented garden, where Jack's very presence was too much temptation. Besides, she knew it was all a game to him. He was simply following the dictates of the wager, proving to her just how easy it would be for him to win... The thought hardened her resolve. She would be the greatest fool in Christendom to fall into the arms of a rake who was only looking for a little entertainment.

"Pray excuse me, my lord," she said frostily, turning on her heel. "I have many household duties to attend to."

This time Jack made no move to follow her. Everything that Thea knew about him was conflicting in her head, the good, the bad and the downright wicked. She took four steps away and stopped. There was something she had been meaning to ask him for a long time.

"Lord Merlin," she said slowly, "will you answer something for me?"

Jack made a slight gesture. "If I can."

Thea's cornflower-blue eyes were troubled. "The first day we met—when you offered me the money and told me that principles were for fools—did you really mean that?"

Their gazes held for a moment and Thea had the oddest feeling that she was trembling on the edge of some precipice she did not understand. Then Jack let out his breath on a long sigh.

"Miss Shaw, you have the most damnable way of putting a fellow on the spot!" he said ruefully. "If you will have the truth, it was one of the most foolish things that I have ever said—no, I do not believe that."

Thea's expression lightened and the pretty color came into her face. "Oh, thank you!" she said.

Jack watched her until her upright figure disappeared around the side of the house, then he drove his hands into his jacket pockets and followed the way that she had gone. He whistled softly under his breath as he walked. Good God, how had that happened? He had been utterly in control, within an ace of winning his wager, yet Miss Theodosia Shaw had almost brought him to his knees with her devastating combination of honesty and innocence. He had no notion how it had happened but he could deny it no longer. He could fight it, perhaps, but the outcome was uncertain. Suddenly he was a rake who felt dangerously close to reform.

He shook his head slightly. If anyone had suggested such a thing to him a few days before he would have laughed them out of court. His parents had been nagging him to marry these five years past and he had always rejected the idea with scorn, preferring the transient enjoyment of a series of *affaires* with women who played by the same rules as he. Yet now his rules appeared to have changed when he had not been paying attention. Jack sighed. If he had learned one thing in life it was not to fight against fate. And he had a feeling that his fate was just about to catch up with him.

Chapter Five

"Sorry, Thea old thing, but it's dashed difficult!" Bertie avoided Thea's eyes and fidgeted on the rose brocade sofa. "I'd love to help you but I've a previous engagement, don't you know. In—" he closed his eyes briefly "—in Yorkshire! I'll be away above two weeks!"

Thea raised her eyebrows in patent disbelief. Bertie had always been a desperately poor liar and it was clear now that he was spinning her a tale. Now that the difficult matter of the wedding was behind them they had become friends again, but she knew there was something he was hiding from her. She decided to test him a little.

"But, Bertie, Lord Merlin is your cousin! Surely a little family feeling prompts you to offer him hospitality at Wickham…"

"Naturally I should be delighted were I to be at home," Bertie muttered, squirming, "but I've already told you I'm to go away—"

"Still trying to be rid of me, Miss Shaw?" a languid voice drawled from the doorway. Thea jumped. She had not heard Jack come in and now she blushed with vexation that he had overheard her.

She watched Jack stroll over to the carved marble chimney piece and rest one arm negligently along the top. He was standing at the precise angle where he could most easily fix her with that penetrating blue gaze. Thea shifted uncomfortably in her chair, acutely conscious of his scrutiny and aware of the blush that stained her cheeks.

Whilst Bertie and Clementine had been with them over dinner it had been relatively easy to avoid looking at Jack too much, although it was another matter to avoid thinking about him. Thea knew that she had been tiresomely absentminded for the whole meal, aware that Jack was watching her with a mixture of amusement and speculation that was deeply disturbing. When she remembered the kisses they had shared that very afternoon... But here she abruptly dragged her thoughts away. She would not remember them, for that way led inevitably to her downfall. Accustomed to ruling her heart as much as taking care of her home and family, Thea found her inexplicable attraction to Jack Merlin excessively disturbing.

"I am sorry that I cannot oblige you with my absence sooner, Miss Shaw," Jack said smoothly. "Dr. Ryland assures me that it would be foolhardy to travel before the weekend and I am anxious to take his advice. I will, however, make myself scarce just as soon as I am able."

"Forgot to mention that we are all invited to a ball at Pendle Hall on Friday," Bertie said, brightening now that Thea's attention was diverted away from him. "Lady Pendle was most insistent, even when I explained you are still an invalid, Jack! It would crown her house party to be able to boast of your attendance.''

Jack grimaced. ''Well, if we must! I suppose it would be bad manners to refuse when the good lady has been sending hothouse flowers over every day to aid my recovery.''

Thea made a business of finishing her cup of tea. In her opinion Lady Pendle was an ill-bred harridan whose motive in cultivating Jack's acquaintance was all too clear. Thea had suffered the Pendles' disdain for several years. The only occasion on which she had attended a ball at Pendle Hall had been marred for her by the patronizing way in which the Pendle sons and daughters had treated her. It had quite taken the pleasure out of her evening and since then she had refused all invitations.

''I shall not be attending,'' she said forthrightly, ''and surely neither shall you, Bertie, since you will be away?''

Bertie flushed. ''Oh, of course! I shall be in Lancashire—''

''Yorkshire!'' Thea corrected gently. She got to her feet and Bertie politely followed suit. ''Good night, Bertie, and thank you for dining with us tonight. I hope that you enjoy your trip!''

Jack moved to hold the door open for her. ''I am sorry that my cousin could not help you with your problem, Miss Shaw.''

Thea looked up at him. There was a dangerously wicked twinkle in his eye that suggested that he was not sorry at all.

''On the contrary, my lord,'' she said sweetly, ''I am the one commiserating with you. You will get your just deserts at Pendle Hall! I am sure that you will find the

Misses Pendle most attentive to you! Either of them would be overjoyed to attach a Marquis.''

Jack gave her a speaking look. ''Thank you, Miss Shaw. Might I not prevail upon you to accompany me then, for protection?''

Thea smiled. ''Do rakes need protection from respectable ladies? I am sure you are well able to take care of yourself!''

Jack caught her hand, drawing her out into the candlelit shadows of the hall. The drawing room door swung shut behind them. ''Do not be so certain of that, Miss Shaw.'' He squared his shoulders. ''All jesting aside, do you really want me to leave Oakmantle?''

Thea flushed. ''I am sorry that you heard me say that, my lord. I had not wished to sound inhospitable—'' She broke off. Here was exactly the situation that she had not wished to explain, for how did she persuade Jack to go whilst keeping a secret her growing feelings for him? She could hardly tell him the truth.

''A matter of propriety, I collect, Miss Shaw?'' Jack queried gently. ''I realize that my presence here must seem most irregular.''

''Yes!'' Thea grasped gratefully at the proffered excuse. ''For my own part I think the gossips to be idle troublemakers, but...''

''But you would not wish to give them fuel for speculation.''

Thea frowned a little. Jack seemed to be making this a little too easy for her. ''Well, no, of course...''

''Despite your respectable spinster's reputation, as confirmed by that ridiculous lace cap and the monstrous apron you have taken to wearing.''

Thea, aware that he was still holding her hand, tried to snatch it away. Jack held on to it.

"My lord, if you seek only to make fun of me—"

"On the contrary." Jack smiled at her. "I am trying to do the right thing—for once. It is not a matter that has exercised my mind very often before."

"That I can well believe!" Thea said sharply. She gave her hand another experimental tug, to no avail.

"How about a bargain, then, Miss Shaw?" Jack pursued. "I shall leave Oakmantle tomorrow and move to Wickham for a short time—if you will allow me to escort you to the ball on Friday."

Thea frowned. "But if you are leaving Oakmantle you might as well leave the county altogether, my lord! Why delay?"

She could not read Jack's expression for his face was in shadow. His voice was cool. "Perhaps I do not wish to leave, Miss Shaw. Come, your answer?"

"And if I refuse to go to the ball, you will refuse to leave Oakmantle?"

"Precisely."

"How very difficult you can be, my lord! It seems a strange, quixotic idea and I told you before that I do not take kindly to blackmail."

"Call it persuasion, Miss Shaw, and you may feel more kindly disposed toward me!"

Thea shook her head. "It seems most irregular, my lord, but I suppose it can do no harm. I accept—for the sake of my reputation..."

"Of course." Jack pressed a kiss on her palm and released her. "Thank you. I will speak to Bertie about making the necessary arrangements." He passed her a candle from the stand at the bottom of the stairs.

"Good night then, my lord."

"A moment, Miss Shaw."

"Yes?" Thea's voice was a little husky. She looked

into Jack's eyes, realized that he was really very close to her indeed, and moved reluctantly away from him. Jack smiled.

"I thought to mention that if you have not yet come up with a better moneymaking scheme, you could always sell the drawing room sculptures. There are at least two by John Edward Carew that would fetch several thousand pounds in town, although the one with the chipped nose has obviously gone down in value because of the damage." He gave her a slight mocking bow and sauntered back to the drawing room door.

"Good night, Miss Shaw."

Back in the drawing room, Bertie was finishing his port and preparing to leave.

"Have to go and pack for Yorkshire," he said gloomily as Jack reappeared, "though why the devil I had to go and choose such a far-flung place I can't imagine! Must be touched in the attic even to think of getting involved in such a scheme!"

Jack grinned at his cousin. "My thanks, Bertie! I owe you a favor!"

Bertie's shoulders slumped. "Pretending to go away just so that you could stay at Oakmantle. Devil take it, Jack, I'm no hand at deception. Thea knows there's something up, you mark my words! Sharp as a needle, that girl!"

Jack laughed. "There's no deception needed after all, Bertie. Miss Shaw and I have made a bargain. I have promised that I will remove to Wickham on the morrow in return for her agreement to accompany me to the Pendle ball."

Bertie frowned ferociously. "What, have I just pledged myself to a trip to Yorkshire all for nothing?"

"You can always cancel your fictitious invitation," his cousin said soothingly. "And it is scarcely nothing, Bertie, unless my future happiness counts as nothing to you."

"What exactly does constitute your future happiness, Jack? That's what worries me! Dash it, you had better be aboveboard with this. Don't mind helping you out, but if any harm comes to Thea—"

The laughter died out of Jack's eyes. He met his cousin's gaze soberly. "You can trust me, Bertie. I would do nothing to harm her."

Bertie shifted uncomfortably. "Better not. I'd call you out myself. You may be a damn fine shot, but principles are more important than..."

"Than self-preservation?" Jack laughed. "Acquit me, Bertie! I know my reputation tells against me but I plan to ask Miss Shaw to marry me."

Bertie swallowed convulsively. "Marry! You? Now I know you're in jest!"

"On my honor I swear it's true!" Jack passed his cousin the brandy bottle. "Here, take a glass before you go. You look as though you need a restorative."

Bertie sat down again. "Marry!" he said again. "Of all the mad starts—"

"I know," Jack said apologetically. "A vast comedown for a rake. But I fear I love her. It is inescapable!"

Bertie swallowed half the brandy in one go. "She'll never take you."

Jack went very still. An arrested look came into his eyes. "Why do you say that, Bertie?"

"Because she knows you're a rake!" Bertie pointed out. "She doesn't trust you. What's more," he added incontrovertibly, "she won't marry for money. I should know."

Jack sighed. Since he had just presented Thea with the reason why she need never marry for money, he could not argue.

"I thought women liked to reform a rake," he said ruefully. "Good God, I have spent years avoiding the lures of matrimonially minded maidens in favor of other pursuits and now you're telling me that the only woman I want will not have me? Where is the justice in that?"

Bertie grinned. "About time someone gave you a set-down, Jack," he said without malice. "I reckon you've met your match at last!"

Jack drained his brandy glass. "Now that," he said, "is where we do agree, Bertie. I have indeed."

"Oh, Miss Shaw, you look so beautiful!" Mrs. Skeffington, who had removed her cook's apron to double as ladies' maid for the evening, went quite misty-eyed at the sight of her mistress dressed for the ball. "The Marquis of Merlin is here, madam," she added. "He is waiting in the drawing room."

Thea hesitated before the mirror. It was not concern about her appearance that held her, for she had sought out her only serviceable ball gown and although it was not in the first stare of fashion, it was simple and elegant. No, she knew that what was delaying her was a sudden and cowardly desire to avoid Jack.

In the two days since he had left Oakmantle she had felt quite low in spirits. In fact, she had to admit to herself that she had missed him quite prodigiously. The children had remarked upon it and she knew that they were also feeling quite dejected. They had been difficult and noisy, withdrawn and silent by turn. Ned had got into a temper when she had spoken about him finding a job in London, and had stormed out and disappeared for several hours. Daisy had burst into tears when Thea had told her that Jack was no longer able to tell her a good-night story, and Clara had spent hours playing dirges on the old piano until Thea thought her head would burst and was fit to scream with frustration. They had all missed him, but she had missed him most of all. And now Jack was here, ready to take her to the ball, and she hardly dared to face him.

She picked up her black velvet cloak and her bag and made her way slowly down the staircase. In point of fact, Jack was not in the drawing room as Mrs. Skeffington had indicated; he might have started off there but now he was waiting for her at the bottom of the stairs. He looked up at her as she descended and Thea's heart contracted as his gaze raked her from carefully arranged curls to silk slippers, before returning slowly to her face. He smiled, the old devil-may-care, wicked smile that was so dangerously attractive and Thea feared she might melt into a puddle of longing where she stood. She steeled herself.

"Good evening, Lord Merlin."

Jack inclined his head. "Good evening, Miss Shaw. It is a great pleasure to see you again. You look quite…ravishing."

There was a look in his eye that suggested that ravishment would be high on his list of preferred entertainments for that evening. With a shiver, Thea admitted to herself that the idea held considerable appeal. But this was no good. She reminded herself sternly that she had worked hard to rid Oakmantle of Jack's troublesome presence and it was her own foolish fault if she was now languishing after him like a green girl.

She accepted Jack's proffered arm and went out with him to the carriage.

Pendle Hall was a bare ten-minute journey time away, but Thea had previously given little thought to being in a closed carriage with Jack for that time. After all, ten minutes to a rake was surely plenty of time to effect a seduction. She held her breath, but Jack behaved with impeccable and frustrating courtesy for the whole journey, handing her into and out of the carriage politely, sitting as far away from her as possible and speaking only on totally uncontroversial subjects such as his improved health and the welfare of her brothers and sisters. Thea found it perversely disappointing.

The ballroom at Pendle Hall was already crowded when they arrived, for Lady Pendle had lost no time in informing all her friends and neighbors of the remarkable coup she had achieved in tempting the Marquis of Merlin to the ball. Jack's welcome was overly warm; Thea's considerably less so. At first she thought that she was imagining the slightly barbed remarks, the exaggerated withdrawing of skirts. Soon she realized she had not. Whilst Jack was forcibly dragged from her side and marched over to dance with the Misses Pendle, Thea found herself besieged.

"It must have been *such* a pleasure to have the Marquis of Merlin as a guest for an entire week, Miss Shaw," Lady Pendle, resplendent in puce velvet, was positively purring with malice. "Such a charming man but such a shocking accident! One scarce knows whether to me more alarmed at your sister's wildness in shooting the poor man in the first place, or at the thought of you entertaining a bachelor at Oakmantle quite unchaperoned!"

Thea took a deep breath. "We were scarcely entertaining the Marquis, Lady Pendle, for he was much too ill to be seeking diversion!"

Another matron pushed forward into the group. "Lord Merlin looks much recovered now, does he not, Miss Shaw? No doubt as a result of your nursing!"

Someone tittered, hiding behind their fan. Thea looked 'round the sea of faces. Some were avid, some openly disdainful. None was friendly. There was nowhere for her to seek refuge.

"My family and I were happy to be of assistance to the Marquis," she said colorlessly. "We all did what we could to help his recovery."

"And does Lord Merlin intend to stay long in Oxfordshire?" Lady Pendle pursued.

"I am not party to Lord Merlin's plans, ma'am," Thea said. She spoke coldly although she was feeling increasingly heated. "However, I believe he is soon for London."

"No doubt having exhausted the pleasures Oakmantle has to offer," another dowager said meaningfully. "I believe he tires easily—"

"One often does after an illness, ma'am," Thea said. Her temper had quite frayed away. She gathered her skirts up in one hand, about to flee the gossips but with no clear destination in mind. "If you will excuse me—"

"Care to dance, Miss Shaw?" The drawling tones of the Honorable Simon Pendle stopped her in her tracks. He was a well set-up young man who had often looked down his nose at her, but just now Thea grasped him as a lifeline.

"Thank you, Mr. Pendle!"

They moved onto the dance floor and away from the circling harpies. Thea breathed a sigh of relief. It was short-lived, however, as Simon Pendle drew closer to her than the dance steps dictated.

"So how have you got on with Merlin, Miss Shaw? Is he not a splendid fellow? Generous, too, I hear!"

Thea's eyes narrowed. Her nerves already on edge, she was still willing to believe that she had misread the freedom of his words and his tone—but only just.

"Lord Merlin has certainly been generous to my family, sir," she said coolly.

Pendle guffawed. "No need for false modesty, ma'am! I was hoping you and I might have a little chat later—sort out a few things…" He squeezed her shoulder in a disgustingly familiar manner.

"I do not believe that we have anything to discuss, Mr. Pendle," Thea said frigidly, moving away.

"Oh, come now…" As the dance drew them together again, Simon Pendle deliberately let his hand brush intimately against the side of her breast and Thea recoiled, the color flaming to her face. "I hear Merlin is to return to Town on the morrow. Then you may be more inclined to talk to me—"

Thea itched to slap him rather than speak to him. She kept her voice low but her tone was arctic.

"You mistake, sir. I have nothing to say to you!"

Pendle leered at her. "Hoity-toity miss! You won't be so quick to refuse when Merlin's money runs out—"

"Servant, Pendle. Miss Shaw, may I beg this dance?" Jack's voice cut smoothly through Simon Pendle's insults and through the angry words clamoring for release in Thea's head. She had not even noticed that the music had ceased, nor that Jack had approached them.

Simon Pendle bowed slightly. For the first time Thea realized that he was more than a little drunk.

"Evening, Merlin. I was just telling your charming *inamorata* here that—"

He broke off, gulping, as Jack stepped intimidatingly close. "I think you mistake, Pendle, as no doubt Miss Shaw has told you already." Jack's voice was dangerous, suggestive of an inclination to take Simon Pendle by the throat and choke the life out of him. "If we were anywhere other than in your parents' ballroom I would show you the error of your ways. As it is—" Jack stepped back "—if I hear you speaking at all for the rest of the evening, I shall call you out!"

He offered his arm to Thea and they moved away.

"That should ensure a little peace for the rest of us," he said dryly. He glanced down at Thea. "Are you quite well, Miss Shaw?"

Thea knew that her hand was shaking and was sure that Jack could feel it, too, for after a moment he pressed her fingers comfortingly with his. She could see the Pendles' guests whispering and gossiping behind their hands. The words burst from her.

"I wish to go home now. At once!"

"You cannot run away." Jack seized her arm in a hard grip. "Do you wish the scandalmongers to say that they drove you out? I did not think you so poor-spirited, Miss Shaw."

Thea's eyes flashed. "It is all very well for you, Lord Merlin! I am just another of your conquests—"

Jack's face was tight with anger, but Thea sensed it was not directed at her. "Thea, you know that is not true—"

"I know that it is not true, but these people—" Thea gestured wildly "—they will only believe the worst!"

The music struck up again. Before Thea could move away, Jack had pulled her into the dance.

It was a shrewd move. Thea realized at once that it was almost impossible to quarrel whilst performing a minuet, for the stately music and the movement of the dance demanded a show of perfect decorum. It was the slowest and most mannered dance and it was the exact opposite of the wild, ungovernable feelings that were pent up inside her. Yet every time she opened her mouth to launch a blistering attack on Jack the dance steps forced them to part.

"It is all very well for you," she began as they came together, "coming to Oakmantle and causing all this trouble—"

They stepped apart. And together again.

"That is a little unfair," Jack murmured. "You were the one who started it all by planning to marry Bertie. And a more hen-witted scheme could not be imagined."

They moved away, joined hands and circled the other couples.

"Pray do not blame me!" Thea whispered crossly. "You came to Oakmantle to prevent the marriage!"

"Indeed. And a good thing, too. And it was your sister who obliged me to stay here by shooting me..."

Thea ignored this undeniable truth and swept on. "And now you are trying to distract attention when it is *your* behavior that has been disgraceful—"

They moved apart. And together. Jack grinned down at her.

"I protest! I was an exemplary invalid!"

"Do you deny that you offered me *carte blanche?*" Thea hissed. "*And* tried to seduce me?"

They executed a complicated twirl.

"I do not deny your first accusation, but the second?" Jack raised his brows. "That is scarcely fair. I most certainly did *not* attempt to seduce you!"

"Yes you did! You even wagered that you would be successful, but I won *that* bet!"

They stepped apart, turned and linked hands again.

"I admit that I issued a challenge to that effect," Jack conceded, "but I abandoned the idea of the wager after I kissed you in the garden—"

"Hush!" Thea threw a scandalized glance over her shoulder at the other dancers. "Someone will hear you."

Jack shrugged. Thea hurried in to seize the moment.

"Am I then supposed to believe that I only won because you let me, Lord Merlin? And am I also supposed to accept that if you *had* tried to seduce me, I should have noticed the difference in your behavior?"

"Most definitely you would! And—"

"And?"

Jack raised his eyebrows. There was a twinkle in his eyes that made Thea even crosser. "My dear Miss Shaw, you would have succumbed! I would bet any money!"

"Oh!" Thea stamped her foot, and then tried to pretend it was one of the dance steps as others in the set looked at her curiously. It was infuriating, particularly as he was right. She sighed angrily, caught Jack's eye and the gleam of speculative amusement in it, and almost squeaked with annoyance. "Lord Merlin, you are the most provoking man! I am trying to quarrel with you but you persist in funning me! Yet it is *not* amusing. You are here being feted by these obsequious people whilst I am suffering their censure!"

Jack bowed. "I acknowledge that. It was foolish of me not to anticipate it."

"You have ruined my reputation!" Thea said wildly, feeling her self-control slipping perilously yet seeming powerless to stop it. "Worse, you have wormed your way into the affections of my family, making them unhappy! Now Ned wants to join the army and Harry wants to be a Corinthian just like you when he grows up and...and Daisy wants a new father! You have turned our heads when you should have left well alone!''

She broke off, realizing that her words had struck a sudden chill. She saw the amusement leave Jack's eyes. He still spoke softly, but there was an undertone of something in his voice that froze her and made all her anger shrivel away.

''If you truly believe that I have deliberately upset your family then you are right to reproach me, Miss Shaw. And if you have a concern for your reputation, I suggest you think hard, for you are contributing to your own downfall even now with your intemperate behavior!''

It was only then that Thea became aware of every eye upon them, every ear flapping for the next snippet of scandal. She could not believe that she had handed it to them on a plate. She wanted the earth to open up and swallow her whole, but worse than her humiliation was the coldness she now saw in Jack's demeanor, the formality with which he offered her his arm to move off the dance floor. Thea knew that he would not abandon her to the gossips but she also knew that he was performing his duty with no sense of pleasure anymore. She could not be certain how those undeniably bitter words had spilled out. Yes, she had been worried about her siblings—oh, yes, Jack had turned their heads, it was true, but more importantly he had turned hers. *That* was what had made her so miserable. She had fallen in love with him and she had no one to blame but herself.

Thea closed her eyes briefly and reopened them, hoping that the sea of curious faces might somehow have disappeared, that the clock would be put back, that she could have another chance. The unyielding hardness of Jack's face, the rigidity with which he kept his distance, told another tale. Around her the sea of tittle-tattle rose and fell and she felt like a cork tossed on its surface. Thea was just wondering in despair whether matters could possibly get any worse when the ballroom door swung open.

There was a silence. Then there was a commotion. Thea saw Lord and Lady Pendle detach themselves from the couple they were speaking with and rush forward with undignified haste. She saw Jack turn, and heard him swear under his breath, but before she could even wonder who had arrived so late in the proceedings, and why they were causing such a fuss, the butler cleared his throat to announce portentously, "The Duke and Duchess of Merlin!"

Chapter Six

Thea drew in a sharp breath.

The Duchess was a tall, patrician *grande dame* in pale gold, with an ice-cool countenance. The Duke, who looked startlingly like an older version of Jack, was equally tall and austere.

Beside them, looking shifty and ill at ease, stood Bertie Pershore.

Thea experienced an almost overwhelming urge to turn and run away, but it was too late. The Duke and Duchess were already disentangling themselves from the Pendles' eager overtures and were coming toward them. Thea made an instinctive movement and Jack's hand closed around her arm like a vise, holding her by his side.

"Jack, darling!" To Thea's amazement the Duchess's face broke into a smile of startling sweetness. She came up and kissed her son on the cheek, then turned the full warmth of her smile on Thea, taking both her hands.

"Miss Shaw. Bertie has told us all about you. We are so pleased that you are going to marry Jack!"

"I…" Thea shot Bertie a look of confusion and dire

retribution. Her former friend seemed to shrivel beneath her glare. "I am very pleased to make your acquaintance, Your Grace, but I fear—"

She broke off as Jack's hand tightened on her arm almost murderously. He moved smoothly into the gap.

"Pray do not put Miss Shaw to the blush, Mama! We had not announced our betrothal yet."

Thea shot him a glance of mingled horror and confusion. Jack smiled back at her blandly.

"No doubt you were wishing for us to meet your fiancée, Jack, before making a formal announcement!" The Duke of Merlin now stepped forward to shake his son by the hand. Thea felt his gaze on her face, as direct and searching as Jack's own. He smiled at her. "I fear the Duchess is precipitate, my dear Miss Shaw, but it is only because she is so pleased to welcome you into the family!"

"Of course!" The Duchess enveloped Thea in a scented hug. Thea submitted, wilting with shock. "Miss Shaw—Thea—may I call you Thea as you are to be my daughter? I could scarce believe it when Bertie told me. But I am so pleased!" The Duchess turned to Jack with shining eyes. "It is high time you settled down, dear boy, as we have been telling you this age past—"

"Yes, Mama!" Jack said hastily. "Perhaps we could continue this conversation later?"

"By all means," the Duke murmured. He turned to Thea, his eyes twinkling. "Will you grant me a dance, my dear, to grace the Pendles' Ball? They will be *aux anges* to be first with the news and to be able to boast that the Duke led out his future daughter-in-law!"

Thea realized that this was not so much an invitation as a direct order. Jack clearly did, too. He gave her a rueful smile, kissed her fingers in a way that sent Thea's

feelings into even more of a spin, and offered his arm
to his mother.

"May I offer you some refreshments, Mama? You
may then tell me how you come to be here, for I am
all agog—"

Thea was desperate to know, as well, but the Duke
was waiting. She took his arm gingerly, almost as
though she were afraid he would explode on touch. She
was convinced that this extraordinary masquerade must
come to an end very soon. The Duke covered her fingers
very briefly with his own in a gesture that Thea was
surprised to find gave her immense reassurance.

"No need to look so terrified, my dear!" the Duke
murmured. "I am the gentlest of fellows, despite my
reputation!"

Thea laughed a little shakily. "I do not doubt it, Your
Grace, but if you were to find that your good nature
had been abused by a misunderstanding—"

Merlin's dark blue gaze, so like his son's, fixed upon
her. He spoke with emphasis. "But I shall not do so,
shall I, my dear Miss Shaw? I am persuaded that you
are the ideal wife for my son, and further, I am delighted to see that it is a love match!"

Thea was silent. Indeed, she was not certain what she
could say. The Duke of Merlin was clearly too intelli-
gent a man not to have read the situation correctly, but
she realized that for reasons of his own he had chosen
to interpret it differently. Indeed, the warning in his tone
as he led her into the dance told her not to pursue the
subject, least of all in public. She would be a fool to do
so—the arrival of the Duke and Duchess had transformed her situation from one of scandalous misfortune
to blazing triumph. All around her Thea could hear the
buzz of censure transformed into pure envy.

"Betrothed to the Marquis of Merlin!... Why did she not say so before... Dear Thea has so much natural delicacy... Indeed, the Duke seems much taken with his future daughter..."

It was true that the Duke did seem most attentive to her, Thea thought, feeling more than a little dazed. His conversation was light but he complimented her sincerely on her dancing and at the end said, just loud enough for the gossips to hear, "Thank you, my dear. I suppose I must hand you back to my son now before he starts looking daggers at me! He is to be envied such a charming bride..."

Jack was indeed watching them and his expression was quite different from the coldness he had shown Thea a brief half hour before. His gaze fixed on her face with an intensity that made her feel strangely self-conscious. She knew that he was only playing up to the situation, but it added to her confusion. As the Duke escorted her from the floor, Jack took her arm proprietorially in his.

"If you are not too fatigued, my love, will you grant me one waltz before we retire? Now that our secret is out, there can be no need to dissemble..."

Thea narrowed her eyes. Jack seemed to have moved from the formality of addressing her as "Miss Shaw" to the intimacy of "my love" rather too swiftly. There was a spark of amusement in his eyes that suggested he was about to play the situation to the full, and she itched to give him the set-down he so richly deserved. But the Duke and Duchess were smiling indulgently and as she hesitated, Jack slid an arm about her waist and steered her back onto the dance floor.

"My lord," she began, as soon as they were out of earshot.

"Jack," the Marquis murmured, his lips twitching. "You really must address me by my given name now that we are betrothed...Thea!"

"We are *not* betrothed." Thea hissed. "I have no notion how this occurred but I have no wish to be married to you—"

"Hush!" Jack touched her lips fleetingly with one finger and the contact silenced her more effectively than any words could. "Is it your wish to reverse your good fortune? Half an hour ago you were berating me for ruining your reputation. Now you are triumphantly restored and about to throw it all away."

The music struck up and they started to circle the floor. Thea pinned a bright smile on her face, one that she hoped successfully portrayed the happy sentiments of a young lady in love.

"Yes, my lord."

"Jack."

"I perfectly understand that, but the price of such a situation—"

"Is too high?"

Jack's hands moved against her back, drawing her closer to him, and Thea was suddenly and devastatingly aware of him. All coherent thoughts flew straight out of her head. She looked up into Jack's face and felt herself tremble at the look of unabashed sensuality in his eyes.

"Are you sure, Thea?" Jack's breath brushed her cheek, sending the shivers down her spine. His lips just grazed the corner of her mouth. Thea tried to think straight, tried to cut through the web of desire that threatened to envelop her. It was no easy matter.

"Surely this is all a pretense, my lord," she said breathlessly. "You cannot wish for a wife! You are temperamentally unsuited to such an enterprise as marriage.''

''I assure you I am becoming more inclined to it by the moment.''

Jack's hands slid into the small of her back, holding her hard against his body so that their legs almost tangled. The sensation of the hard length of him pressed against her softness was almost her undoing. Thea gasped.

''Jack!''

''Well, that's an improvement!'' There was a note in Jack's voice that threatened to undermine her completely. He was making no secret of the fact that he wanted her. It was in his voice, in his touch.

''You must accept what has happened, Thea,'' he continued softly. ''My parents have trapped us both— so neatly I have to applaud their strategy! They have wanted me to marry for a long time. Finally I have presented them with the opportunity to enforce that wish and I cannot find it in my heart to regret it.''

''But surely we are to call off this fictitious betrothal?'' Thea searched his face unhappily. It seemed extraordinary to her that Jack might be prepared to go through with it. ''Surely you cannot wish to marry me!''

Jack looked down at her and she saw his gaze soften. ''Why not? You are delightful and entirely suitable.''

''But...'' Thea made a despairing gesture, ''I know you are putting a good face on this, my lord, but I do not expect that you even like me very much, let alone wish to marry me! After what I said to you earlier—''

Jack's smile faded. ''Did you mean it, Thea?''

Thea looked away. His gaze was too penetrating. It made her feel vulnerable. But even so she was aware that she had treated him badly and owed him an apology.

"No. I am sorry. It is true that you have turned our heads, my lord, but I acquit you any deliberate intent."

"Thank you!" Jack flashed her a grin. "Then we are reconciled…and betrothed—my love."

Thea blushed at the warmth of his tone. She was aware that he had skated very adroitly over her objections, but she could be as stubborn as Clementine when she chose. She frowned. "But—"

Jack's arms tightened about her again. "Thea, If you make one more objection I shall kiss you here and now."

Thea felt a shaky smile start. "Oh, Jack—"

"Well, perhaps I shall kiss you anyway…"

"Pray be serious!" Thea tried to focus her mind. "You have been trapped into this—"

"Yes, and I do not object at all!" Jack's tone became more serious. "Do you?"

Thea looked away from that searching blue gaze. "I do not know." What she did know was that she loved Jack but she was afraid. Afraid that whilst there was an undeniable attraction between them, that was not sufficient to sustain a marriage. Afraid because his society lifestyle was so different from her own that she was not sure she could adapt. Afraid because suddenly she felt that she did not know him well at all. She knew that she loved him, but she did not dare to tell him so.

"I do not know," she repeated softly.

She missed the fleeting expression that crossed Jack's face as he looked down on her bent head, the combination of disappointment and hurt, chased away by determination. His arms loosened about her. The dance was finishing, anyway.

"Come," he said, "I'll take you home now."

When Thea glanced at him his expression was quite blank, but she could tell from his voice that he had withdrawn from her. The excitement, the sensual pleasure, had drained away, leaving her feeling uncertain and cold, and suddenly she was not at all sure what she was going to do.

The Duchess talked for most of the journey back to Oakmantle, directing her conversation to Thea with an excitement that was both touching and disconcerting. Jack, who knew his mother of old, realized that now she had the bit between her teeth she would be as irresistible as a tidal wave. Yet when the Duchess started to speak about wedding dates and trousseau and Thea turned her away with slight answers, Jack felt his heart sink. Here was the confirmation of what Thea had said earlier—she was not at all sure that she wished to marry him.

Jack shifted a little on the carriage seat and maintained his silence, cursing himself for failing to declare his feelings before the Duke and Duchess had arrived. Now that they had been trapped into an engagement, Thea would never believe that he genuinely wished to marry her anyway. The only thing that had prevented his declaration before had been Bertie's assertion that Thea did not trust him. A rake's reputation, Jack thought bitterly, was a damned encumbrance when one wished to make the first honorable proposal of one's life.

She would not marry him for his money. Jack acknowledged that he had known that even before he had told her of the value of her father's sculptures. A smile curved his lips in the darkness. So he would have to persuade her of the genuineness of his feelings. He would have to court her with irreproachable decorum. The problem was that that would take time and he did not feel inclined to patience. And he might even fail to convince her. In which case he would have to seduce her.

Desire shot through him at the very thought. He shifted again, concentrating fiercely on the intellectual side of his predicament rather than the physical. Just how persuadable would Thea prove to be? Surely a bluestocking should be susceptible to an approach through the intellect? Yet she was convinced that he had been obliged to offer for her against his inclinations and once she had an idea she could be very tenacious.

How persuadable did he want her to be, in truth? Jack watched the carriage lights flicker over Thea's bent head and smiled again. If the thought of wooing her was sweet, the thought of seducing her was even sweeter.

"Very sorry, Thea, old thing, but what could I do?" Bertie spread his hands apologetically. He looked like a whipped spaniel. "There was Merlin demanding to know what was going on, and there was I—"

"You were supposed to be in Yorkshire, not London!" Thea abandoned her seat beside him on the garden bench and leaped to her feet. "Really, Bertie, this is absurd! Whatever can you have said to the Duke and Duchess to send them down here with the harebrained notion that Jack wanted to marry me?"

Bertie looked acutely uncomfortable. "Anyone could see the way that matters were tending between you and Jack! Once I had told Merlin a little about you and explained that you had captured Jack's affections he became positively indulgent to me! Never seen the old man like that before!''

Thea glared. "Yes, because you handed him what he wanted on a plate! Oh, Bertie, you know that the Duke has been angling to marry Jack off for these five years past and now you have played right into his hands!''

"Nothing wrong in that," Bertie said virtuously. He ran a finger around his collar where his neck cloth was feeling particularly tight. "Don't see the problem myself. Thought you'd be glad to be rescued from that nest of vipers at Pendle Hall, Thea. Ripping your character to shreds—''

"That is beside the point!" Thea threw her hands up in the air. "Jack will not release me from this so-called engagement and my future mother-in-law is setting a wedding date—''

"Good thing, too!" Bertie got to his feet. "Just the thing for you to marry Jack. All your brothers and sisters are delighted—Ned was telling me only yesterday how pleased he was—''

"Well of course he is! Now he has someone to sponsor him through the army!''

Bertie looked at her mildly. "Tell you what, Thea, I'm glad you didn't marry me. You used to be such a sweet-natured girl and now you've turned into a shrew! Perhaps Jack should change his mind before it's too late.''

Thea stopped pacing and stared at him. Bertie's words had somehow hit home. He was right. She could remember a time when few matters had ruffled the smooth calm of her temperament. Certainly she had never been as cross-grained and shrewish as she was now. That had been...three weeks ago. It felt like a lifetime, and it was Jack Merlin who had effected the change by stirring up her life until it could never be the same again. She sat down a little heavily.

"Oh, dear. I have become so very cross about everything, have I not!"

Bertie patted her hand. "Never mind. Perhaps you can make up for it, old girl. Especially to Jack, for he does care about you, you know. He told me so."

To hear that was the final straw. Thea burst into tears. Bertie backed away hastily, a look of horror on his lugubrious features.

"I say, there's no need for that, Thea!"

"Sorry, Bertie!" Thea sniffed, groping for her handkerchief, grasping after her self-control. She gave a hiccuping sob. "I shall be better directly."

She blew her nose hard, trying not to give in to the abject misery that threatened her. She felt wretched. She had quarreled with Jack from the night of the ball until that very morning, six days later. During that time he had called every day, taken her driving, courted her in exactly the conventional way that her parents would have approved. He had been the epitome of good behavior, he had gently rebuffed all her attempts to break the engagement and his baffling good humor and steadfast persistence had made Thea want to cry.

Only that morning he had pressed her gently about a wedding date and she had snapped at him that she would not marry him, would never marry him. She had seen an expression cross his face so quickly she had wondered if she had imagined seeing the hurt there, and then he had turned on his heel and gone out. Thea had gone up to her room and cried, without really understanding why, and then she had kept herself very busy until Bertie had arrived. Now, despite herself, another small sob escaped her.

Bertie gave a hunted look around. "Shall I call your sister?" he asked hopefully. "Needs a woman's touch, and all that!"

Thea shook her head. "Everyone is out today. Ned and Harry are playing for the village side at cricket, Skeffie has taken Daisy and Clara to watch, and Clementine is visiting with the Duchess." She brightened a little, scrubbing her eyes. "Do you know, Bertie, the Duchess believes that she might even make Clemmie presentable! Can you believe that? She was talking about giving her a Season next year." She slumped again. "But, of course, if I do not marry Jack…"

Bertie snorted. "Marry or not, you're going a step too far there, Thea! Clementine presentable? I'll wager a monkey against it!"

Thea gave a watery giggle. "Maybe you are right and it is too much to hope for! Oh, Bertie—" she gave him an impulsive hug "—you are the very best of good friends and I am sorry that I have been so horrible to you!"

After Bertie had left, Thea donned an apron over her old blue muslin and walked listlessly to the herb garden. It was a beautiful spring day and the clumps of mint, parsley and thyme were flourishing in the warmth by the old brick garden wall. Thea walked on, past the hyssop and rosemary, until she reached the lavender bed. She took a small knife from the pocket in her apron and cut some new sprigs before going back inside the house.

Oakmantle Hall was very quiet. Thea went softly up the stairs and into her own bedchamber, where she busied herself folding the clean bed linen and storing it away in the armada chest. She folded the sheets, put the sprigs of lavender between them and closed the lid.

The scent of lavender was on her fingers, reminding her of that day in the garden, the way that Jack had held her. Perhaps he would not come back now that she had been so horrible to him. Thea blinked the tears back. She seemed to be turning into a watering pot these days and it was most infuriating.

She did not hear the front door open or the tread on the stairs, did not even realize anyone was there until she heard a step in the bedroom doorway and turned to see Jack lounging against the doorpost. He did not speak, simply stood there watching her. There was a look in his eyes that made Thea catch her breath. The words dried on the tip of her tongue.

"Jack."

"Thea?" Jack straightened up and came toward her, moving with what seemed to Thea's unnerved eyes to be the predatory concentration of a cat. Two thoughts occurred to her simultaneously. One was that they had never been completely alone together in the house. The second was that Jack was a rake. And even as she thought it she realized his intention and her heart started to race. She took a step back, crushing one of the sprigs of lavender that had fallen to the floor. The lavender smell entwined itself around them. Jack stepped closer, his eyes darkening as he inhaled the scent.

Thea's words came out in a rush. "Jack, I must speak to you."

Jack barely paused. "We'll talk later."

"But—"

A second more and Thea realized that he was not going to waste his breath arguing with her. Not when he could kiss her. He leaned forward, closing the distance between them slowly, sliding one arm about her gently. His lips barely brushed hers, the merest touch, yet Thea felt the echo of that contact all the way through her body. Her hand came up to rest on his chest and she made one last effort, leaning back a little.

"Jack..." She found she had to clear her throat. "What are you doing?"

The danger and gentleness in his eyes made her feel weaker still.

"I am going to seduce you, Thea." His voice was as husky as hers. "I have courted you with decorum, I have tried to reason with you, but if this is what I have to do to persuade you of my genuine desire to marry you...."

Thea's eyes were huge. "Oh! I am persuaded!"

Jack shook his head. "Too late. If I let you go now you will think of another reason to refuse me. This is the only thing that I can do to claim you for my own..."

To claim you for my own... Thea gave a little gasp that was lost as his mouth took hers again, this time holding nothing back. The kiss was hot and hungry, spiraling down into desire. Thea felt the passion flood through her like a riptide, huge, powerful, too urgent to resist. She did not even try—at last her mind was telling her that there was no need to hold back, for Jack wanted her for herself alone, not to rescue her reputation nor to help her family but because he wanted to claim her as his, body and soul.

She was trembling as Jack drew her down onto the yielding softness of the bed, and she lay back gratefully for she was not certain that she could stand any longer. The kiss had softened into sweetness now, long and lingering but no less breathless. Finally Jack propped himself up on one elbow, pulled the lace mobcap off her curls and tossed it across the room.

"I have wanted to do that for a long time," he murmured. "And as for this monstrosity of an apron—" His fingers had found the ties and were tugging hard.

Thea murmured a faint protest and Jack bent his head and kissed her again. And again, until she could scarcely speak.

"Thea…" When Jack let her go this time, Thea simply looked at him in mute silence. "I wanted to tell you that when you ran into my arms that day at the church I felt something far stronger for you than I had ever felt for any woman before."

His fingers were undoing the buttons of her gown with deft skill. Thea smiled a little as she watched him. "Was that not desire, Jack?" she whispered.

"Perhaps," Jack conceded. "Yes, definitely. But it was not just that…"

He opened her gown and slid his hand inside, baring her small, gently rounded breasts. Thea gasped and arched against him. She was filled with the most sublime ache and when Jack bent his head to her breast and captured one rosy peak in his mouth, she felt a simultaneous rush of exquisite relief and an even deeper need, awoken by the roughness of his cheek against her skin, the teasing of his tongue.

"It was much more than that," Jack continued, his lips against her skin. "My feelings did not take long to deepen into admiration and…love. So you must be gentle with me, sweetheart, for it hasn't happened to me before…"

Thea's heart seemed to do a somersault. "Do you really love me?"

"Yes…" Jack's hands were drifting over her skin in distracting circles, stroking, soothing, making her melt again with love and desire. He leaned over to kiss her long and hard. She could feel her body softening again, aching for him, opening as Jack moved across her, one leg sliding between hers.

"I think you have done this before, though," she murmured.

"It's different..." Jack's words were a breath against her bare skin. He bent his head to her breasts again, teasing her until she dug her fingers into his back in exquisite agony. Her whole body was slipping and sliding down into delicious pleasure. She never wanted it to stop.

Jack sat up reluctantly and tugged off his boots, tossed them aside, and dealt summarily with the rest of his clothes. Neither of them spoke as he rejoined her on the bed and removed the rest of her garments with equal ruthlessness. The touch of his skin against hers made Thea gasp in shock and pleasure. She shivered as he started to kiss her again, long, slow kisses that drugged the senses until she was desperate for him.

Urgency caught them both then, sweet and strong, and Jack shifted again, drawing her to him, parting her thighs, sliding into her gently.

Thea gave a soft gasp and Jack lowered his head, brushing his lips across hers.

"Thea?"

She opened her eyes, dazzling blue, bright with desire. She did not speak, simply raised a hand to tangle in his hair and bring his head down to hers so that she could kiss him again. All the love and triumphant possessiveness fused within him then, and slowly, with infinite gentleness, he made her his.

When Jack awoke the sun had moved across the room and was lying in a bright bar across the tangled bed linens. Thea was kneeling at the end of the bed, craning her neck to see the clock on the mantelpiece, the sunlight turning her hair into a web of bright gold, light and insubstantial like a fairy net. It was a net that had trapped him firmly and would never let him go. Jack examined the thought, the strange but satisfying rightness of it, and felt a smile start to curl his lips. He stretched luxuriously.

At his slight movement, Thea turned her head toward him. She was in shadow, every curve outlined in black like a silhouette. Jack felt his body stir. He told himself that he had a lifetime in which to watch Thea, to memorize her face, to explore all those tantalizing lines and curves. However, when she almost lost her balance on the tangled bedclothes and leaned over the foot of the bed to steady herself, the need suddenly seemed urgent.

Jack moved swiftly, catching Thea around the waist and tumbling her back down beside him. She lay still looking up at him, her eyes widening as his desire communicated itself to her. Jack brushed the hair away from her face, bending to kiss her.

"I am thinking that whilst I have made a most humbling declaration of love to you, sweetheart, you have not actually told me that you love me..."

Thea looked at him. Her face was flushed pink, her lips parted. "Oh... I thought that you knew. Yes, of course I do..."

Jack kissed her softly again, his lips clinging to hers. She felt sweet and warm and wonderfully yielding.

"In that case I must go and get a special license. At once. There is not a moment to lose."

He felt Thea shift beneath him. Her hands caressed him tentatively and he drew in a sharp breath.

"Jack—" it was a whisper "—can it not wait a little?"

"Well…" He moved inside her again, gently, tantalizingly. Thea gasped. He bent his head to her breast. "Perhaps it can wait just a little longer…"

Whereas he knew that he could not. As he reached for her and she responded in full measure, all Jack's good resolutions fled. He had meant to be tender, to introduce her to the pleasures of making love gradually and with consideration, but her natural sensuality swept all of that aside. This was a wild lovemaking with none of the gentleness of their previous encounter and at the end they were both dazzled, sated with pleasure. Jack wrapped his arms about Thea as they slowly drifted down to earth.

"The children will be back soon," she murmured against his shoulder.

Jack made a sound of sleepy contentment.

"We must get up." Thea wriggled out of his embrace and groped around for her clothes, which seemed to be scattered to the four corners of the room. "Daisy will want her story, and Clara will want to play for you and the boys will want some more cricket coaching if the village team lost—"

Jack rolled over and looked at her. His midnight-blue gaze raked her lazily from head to foot. "And what do you want from me, my love?"

"Oh, just to marry you," Thea said airily. "That will suffice!" She looked at him and smiled. "I know those sculptures are worth a fortune but I could not bear to sell them for sentimental reasons! My father was prodigious fond of them! So I am sorry, Jack…" She bent over to kiss him, "I have to marry you for your money! It is the only solution!"

* * * * *

The Penniless Bride

NICOLA CORNICK

Chapter One

The offices of Churchward and Churchward in High Holborn had seen many secrets. The lawyers' premises exuded a reassuring discretion that was highly valued by their noble clientele. On this August day in 1808, Mr Churchward the younger was dealing with a matter of inheritance that should have been straightforward. War, and the vagaries of his eccentric clients had, however, made it a matter of some delicacy.

The new Earl of Selborne had arrived some twenty minutes earlier and after the conventional greetings had taken place, Mr Churchward had offered his condolences and had taken out the last wills and testaments of both the Earl's late father and his grandmother. At the moment they were still studying the terms of the late Lord Selborne's will and had not even touched on the Dowager's dispositions. Mr Churchward, who knew what was still in store, had the depressing feeling that matters were moving downhill rather more swiftly than a runaway carriage. He settled his glasses more firmly on his nose, a manoeuvre designed specifically to give him time to study the gentleman sitting in the comfortable leather armchair before the desk.

Robert, Earl of Selborne was looking a little grim. He had the thin face and chiselled features of the Selbornes, with dark hair and eyes that hinted at his distant Cornish ancestry. Though tanned from several years of campaigning in the Peninsula on General Sir John Moore's staff, Robert Selborne was pale and somewhat tight-lipped. And no wonder. He was confronted by a dilemma that no one would envy. Mr Churchward was grimly aware that he had not had the opportunity to raise the details of the second will yet. That was, if anything, even worse.

As Mr Churchward studied him, Lord Selborne looked up and said, 'I should be grateful if you would run through the terms of my father's will again, Mr Churchward, to be sure that I fully understand.'

His tone was clipped.

'Certainly, my lord,' Mr Churchward murmured. He suspected that the Earl had understood the will perfectly from the first, for he was no fool. At six-and-twenty years old, Robert Selborne had been away fighting since he had achieved his majority, first in India and then in Spain. He had been mentioned twice in despatches, commended for his courage under fire and his heroic rescue of a fellow officer. Unfortunately it was young Lord Selborne's preference for the army over the merits of settling down young that had led him into the situation in which he now found himself.

Mr Churchward scanned the will again, although he was entirely conversant with its contents. In many ways it was a simple document. And in others… He cleared his throat.

'You have inherited the Earldom of Selborne and all entailed property absolutely as the only son of your predecessor, the fourteenth Earl Selborne of Delaval.' Mr

Churchward looked grave. 'All unentailed property and monies accruing to the title…'

'Yes?' Robert Selborne's dark eyes held a mixture of exasperation and resignation. Mr Churchward allowed himself a very small, sympathetic smile. He had seen young gentlemen squirm on such a hook before, although he had never come across such specific terms in a will as these.

'Will come to you the day that you marry.' Mr Churchward's tone was dry as he read the next paragraph of the will word for word.

My son is to choose a bride from amongst the young ladies present at the marriage of his cousin, Miss Anne Selborne, and is to marry one of them within four weeks of the wedding. He is then to reside at Delaval for the following six months. Otherwise all unentailed properties and monies relating to the estate of Delaval will pass to my nephew, Ferdinand Selborne, Esquire…

'Thank you, Churchward.' Rob Selborne's tone was as dry as that of the lawyer. 'Alas, I did not mishear the first time.'

'No, my lord.'

Rob Selborne got to his feet and strolled over to the window as though the office felt a little too small for him.

'So my father managed to clip my wings in the end,' he said. He spoke conversationally, almost to himself. 'He swore that he would find a way to do so.'

Mr Churchward cleared his throat again. 'It would seem so, my lord.'

'He always wished for me to marry and settle down to produce an heir.'

'Most understandable, my lord, as you are the only son.'

Rob Selborne flicked him a glance. 'Of course. Do not think that I did not appreciate my father's feelings, Churchward. In his situation I would very likely have behaved in the same manner.'

'Indeed, my lord.'

'Who knows—I might even have invoked such a draconian condition myself.'

'Very possibly, my lord.'

Rob swung around. 'Even so, I am tempted to tell my father's memory to go hang, disrespectful as that might be.'

'Very natural under the circumstances, my lord,' Mr Churchward said soothingly. 'No gentleman likes to feel himself coerced.'

Rob clenched his fists. 'Ferdie may have the money. I will not marry simply to inherit a fortune.'

There was a pause.

'You are aware, my lord,' the lawyer said carefully, 'that the extent of the fortune, even when assessed conservatively, is around thirty thousand pounds? It is not a huge sum, but it is not to be dismissed lightly.'

The grim line of Robert Selborne's jaw tightened a notch. 'I am aware.'

'And that the estate of Delaval, whilst bringing in a reasonable income under normal circumstances, has fallen into disrepair after the epidemic that carried your parents off?'

Rob sighed. 'I have not yet seen Delaval, Churchward. Is it in so bad a condition?'

'Yes, my lord,' the lawyer said simply.

Rob turned abruptly towards the window again. 'I did not go away because I cared nothing for my family or for Delaval, Churchward. I wish you to know that.'

The lawyer was silent. He knew it perfectly well.

From his earliest youth, Robert Selborne's love of Delaval had gone very deep. He might have been away for the best part of five years, he might have wanted to prove himself by serving in the army, but his attachment to the place of his birth—and to his family, for that matter—was unquestioned.

'I wish now,' the Earl said, 'that I had not been away from home for so long.'

There was a wealth of feeling in his voice.

'Your father,' Mr Churchward said carefully, answering the sentiment rather than the words, 'was away for three years on the Grand Tour in his youth.'

Their eyes met. Robert Selborne's grave expression lightened slightly. 'Thank you, Churchward. I suppose that we must all strike out for our independence in our own way.'

'Indeed so, my lord.'

There was another pause. Robert Selborne drove his hands into the pockets of his beautifully cut jacket of green superfine, thereby spoiling its elegant line.

'My cousin Anne's wedding is when, exactly?'

'Tomorrow morning, my lord.' Churchward sighed. The timing of the whole matter was most unfortunate. He had been summoned to Delaval urgently at the start of the year, when the old Earl of Selborne had realised he was dying. The late Earl, though ravaged by fever, had consigned to Churchward's care his new will, with its eccentric codicil. In vain had Churchward argued that such a condition was unnecessary. The Earl had been adamant that he did not wish his son to take up his title and march straight back to the Peninsula.

Churchward had returned to London and had sent urgently to Robert Selborne in Spain, telling him of the scarlet fever that had decimated the entire village of

Delaval. His first letter had never reached its destination. He had written again a month later, by which time the Earl had died and his wife and mother had also been taken with the fever. That letter had eventually caught up with Robert Selborne at Corunna and he had returned home immediately, arriving in London seven weeks later. By then both his parents and his aged grandmother had been dead for over six months, a dreadful piece of news to greet his homecoming. It was no wonder, Churchward thought, that the young Earl looked somewhat bleak, for in addition to his bereavement, the estate of Delaval had suffered shocking depredations and would need time and money to put to rights. And the money would only be forthcoming if Robert Selborne married within four weeks…

'So I must find a bride on the morrow,' Rob said, with a parody of a smile. 'I had best find something to wear to a wedding, and try to remember how to make myself agreeable to the ladies. A vain hope, I fear, when one has been on campaign as long as I have, but I will have to try if I want to restore Delaval.' He laughed. 'It will be a remarkable bride indeed who will be ready for her wedding within a month. My father clearly had no idea of how long a lady requires to prepare for her nuptials!'

Churchward took a careful breath. 'You have decided to fall in with your father's plans, then, my lord?'

Rob gave him a mocking smile. 'It seems to me that I have little choice if I wish to set Delaval to rights. I might wish that my father had been a little less proscriptive in his arrangements, however. Do you know why he chose my cousin's wedding as the place for me to find a wife?'

Churchward shuffled the papers on his desk. He had

asked the old Earl the same question, arguing that it would have been fairer to his son to give him a wider field of choice. The Earl had retorted that he did not wish to be fair. His son was already acquainted with many of the ladies who would be present at the wedding, and that way he knew Robert would be obliged to marry the right sort of girl. By which, of course, he meant a lady of quality.

'I believe your late father may have thought it best for you to contract a match with a connection of the family, or at least an acquaintance,' the lawyer said.

Rob laughed. 'Then I do not know why he did not go the whole way and simply arrange the match himself,' he said wryly. 'You had best wish me luck on my bride hunt, Churchward.'

'I am sure that no luck will be needed, my lord,' Churchward said. 'Your lordship is a most eligible *parti.*'

'You flatter me, Churchward,' Rob Selborne said. 'The field is narrow. The young ladies present at my cousin Anne's nuptials, eh? Let us hope they have a long guest list!'

'Yes, my lord,' the lawyer said unhappily. He fidgeted with his quill pen. Now that the moment had come to reveal the contents of the second will, that of the Earl's grandmother, he was feeling even more ill at ease. But there was no doubt that the Dowager Countess had been of sound mind. She had turned all the more eccentric since the death of her husband in a shooting accident ten years previously, but she could never be described as mad.

'My lord, there is the matter of your grandmother's will as well,' he said, uneasily. 'I am afraid...that is…the Dowager Countess of Selborne was somewhat unconventional…'

Rob looked up, an arrested expression in his dark eyes. 'I do not think that any of us doubt that, Churchward, but what is it that you are trying to tell me? Surely my grandmother's will is quite straightforward?'

Mr Churchward placed the late Earl's depositions in a drawer and drew the second will towards him. It was much shorter.

'You were aware that the Dowager Countess intended to leave you her fortune, my lord?'

'My grandmother did mention it to me when we last met,' Rob Selborne said. 'Naturally I assumed that it was a nominal sum. She had no property of her own and the jewellery was all family items…'

Mr Churchward gave a thin smile. Old Lady Selborne had so enjoyed her little jokes. Pretending to penury was one of them.

'Her ladyship had investments that totalled forty thousand pounds, my lord.'

Rob Selborne looked winded. He came across to sit down again. 'How is that possible, Churchward?'

'Mining, my lord,' the lawyer said succinctly. 'Iron ore. Most lucrative.'

'I see,' Rob said. 'She certainly kept that quiet.'

'Yes, my lord. I believe that the Dowager Countess thought her mining interests were profitable but not to be mentioned in polite society.'

Rob shrugged. 'Grandmama was high in the instep. I do not particularly care where the money comes from as long as it enables me to do my duty by Delaval.'

'This sum should enable that, my lord,' Churchward said drily. 'Together with the amount your father left it will do the job very nicely.' He cleared his throat again. There was no way around this. He took a deep breath.

'There is a certain condition attached to the Dowager Countess's will, my lord…'

Rob leaned back in the chair. 'Of course there is,' he said ironically. 'Why did I imagine it would be straight-forward?'

Churchward took his glasses off, polished them violently, then put them on again. He paused. Rob Selborne was looking at him somewhat quizzically.

'You seem to be in some agitation, Churchward,' he said. 'Would it be easier for me to read the will for myself?'

The lawyer breathed a sigh of relief and passed the paper over. 'Thank you, my lord. I do believe that that would be preferable.'

There was a silence, but for the tick of the long case clock in the corner of the office and the snap as Mr Churchward broke the nib of his pen between his anx-ious fingers. Rob perused the will quickly, then read it a second time, a sudden frown between his brows. Churchward held his breath and waited for the explo-sion. It did not come. Instead, the Earl burst out laugh-ing.

'Good God!' He looked up, unholy amusement light-ing his brown eyes. 'It is a shocking pity that my father and his lady mother did not compare notes!'

'It is indeed, my lord,' Mr Churchward said fervently.

Rob read the will for a third time. 'Pray, Mr Church-ward, correct me if I am wrong but…I inherit thirty thousand pounds from my father if I marry to his or-der—'

'Indeed you do, my lord—'

'And I inherit forty thousand pounds from my grandmother if I remain celibate for one hundred days from the reading of this will…'

Churchward almost blushed.

'Ah…um…that is correct, my lord.'

'So I am to marry within a month and remain celibate for three months!'

Rob read aloud, his tone dry: *'In order to prove himself worthy of his inheritance, I require that my grandson, Robert Selborne, demonstrate the same temperance in his private life as I shall expect him to do with his fortune. I should add that I do not believe this condition should prove too difficult for my grandson, who has always shown the greatest restraint in his behaviour—'* Rob looked up. 'Thank you, Grandmama!' *'—but it will do him no harm to exercise some self-control. The youth of today can be quite without discipline. So I am setting a condition of celibacy for one hundred days from the reading of this will…'*

Rob put the paper down, the smile still lingering about his lips. 'The devil! I cannot believe it. Is it legal, Churchward?'

The lawyer shifted in his chair. 'I believe so, my lord. The Dowager Countess was in sound mind when she made the will and it is witnessed and signed entirely properly. You could contest it, of course, but I would not advise it. You would have to go through the courts and it would cause much speculation.'

'I would be a laughing-stock,' Rob said. His gaze flicked over the rest of the will. 'I see that my cousin Ferdie inherits from my grandmother as well if I fail to fulfil the conditions. That seems a little harsh. Ferdie would not be able to be celibate for ten days, never mind one hundred.' The amusement lit Rob's eyes.

'How is the requirement to be enforced, Churchward? Surely I am not to report to you every day?'

This time the lawyer did blush. 'Please, my lord, do not jest on this matter! I am sure that Lady Selborne never intended anything so indelicate. I do believe that the matter is left to your conscience.'

Rob stood up. 'I apologise for offending your sensibilities, Churchward.' There was still a twinkle deep in his eyes. 'There does not seem a great deal more to say, does there? In order to inherit sufficient fortune to restore Delaval I must conform to the requirements of both wills. A hasty marriage followed by one hundred days of abstinence.' He held out a hand. 'Thank you, Churchward. You have been most helpful, as ever. I apologise if my response to the stipulations of my relatives' wills has been less than courteous...'

Mr Churchward shook his hand vigorously. 'Not at all, my lord. I understand your feelings. I assure you that I did advise both my clients to abandon the eccentric terms of their wills, but both were adamant.'

Rob grinned and his face lightened again from the rather grave look that it held in repose. 'Thank you, Churchward, but you had no need to tell me that. I am aware of the difficulty of your position and I appreciate your support.' He raised a hand in farewell. 'I will contact you again when I have met the conditions of the wills—or when I have not.'

He went out and Churchward heard his confident tread on the boards outside, his voice bidding the clerks a pleasant good day. The lawyer sat down heavily in his chair. His hand strayed towards the bottom drawer of his desk where he had a secret bottle of sherry hidden away for emergencies. The meeting with the Earl of Selborne surely fell under that description. He had never experienced the like of it and it was only Robert Selborne's equable nature that had made it tolerable.

He poured out a small measure of sherry and sipped it gratefully. He dearly hoped that Robert Selborne could find himself a bride at his cousin's wedding. He was fond of that young man and wished him well of his marriage. Such a match made hastily and under duress ran the risk of starting badly. Or of ending that way. Mr Churchward shook his head sadly. It would take an exceptional woman to bear with the Earl of Selborne whilst he sorted out the competing demands of his relatives' wills.

Mr Churchward drained his glass and pushed the Selborne papers back into their drawer. Then he poured himself a second measure of sherry. He felt that he had earned it.

Miss Jemima Jewell bent down and pulled out the Armada chest that was pushed into a corner of her bedroom. When she opened the lid the faint smell of lavender floated up and tickled her nose. At the bottom, under the pile of crisp sheets, pillowcases and other items set aside for her trousseau, was what she termed her wedding outfit. She took it out and held it up to the light.

'Here it is. It needs a press but it will do…'

Her brother Jack was lounging against the foot of the bed. He put his head on one side critically.

'You haven't grown again, have you, Jem?'

'Of course not.' Jemima flashed him a glance. 'I am one-and-twenty years old, Jack, not a schoolgirl.'

Her brother grinned. 'Nevertheless, it's short. It will show your ankles.'

Jemima sighed. She detested her wedding outfit. It

was the chimney sweep's Sunday best outfit, trotted out for weddings and special occasions. It had a stiff black cambric skirt, slightly flared, a white chemise and a tight black jacket with glossy buttons like pieces of coal. There were black silk stockings and shiny black boots in the cupboard. And for her hair, a beaded net embroidered with jet.

Jemima's parents had dressed her up to earn money for as long as she could remember. Even as babies she and Jack had been paraded at weddings, where the ladies had cooed over their good looks and kissed them for luck. A chimney sweep at a wedding was supposed to bring good fortune and they had always been popular. These days the ladies still loved Jack, who at three and twenty had black curls and wicked dark eyes that made them quiver with excitement. Jemima dryly thought that there was nothing so appealing to a lady of quality as a bit of dalliance with a man from the wrong side of town.

As for the gentlemen, there were plenty of occasions on which she had been obliged to turn away their propositions with a smile and soft word when what she really wanted to do was kick them where it hurt. Hard. The assumption that a tradesman's daughter was fair game for a so-called gentleman was so commonplace that it barely surprised her any more.

'Is Father taking the cat with him?' She asked. Along with his children, Alfred Jewell always arrived at weddings with his black cat, Sooty, perched on his shoulder.

'Of course,' Jack said, grinning.

Jemima pulled a face. 'It is all so false, Jack. I loathe the pretence! Sweeps' children dressed up in their Sunday best like a sideshow for the nobility!'

'It is lucrative,' Jack said drily. 'Papa may have made

his fortune these days but he will still not turn down the offer of good money.' He sat down on the top of the Armada chest. 'You will be attending your own wedding soon, I suppose, Jem,' he added, looking at her out of the corner of his eye. 'Father is talking about having the banns called.'

Jemima shrugged, refusing to meet his gaze. She tried to appear cool but her heart skipped a beat and the fear rose in her throat. She had been betrothed for two years and had almost started to imagine that the wedding would never happen. Her fiancé, Jim Veale, was the son of another High Master of the Sweeps' Guild, who, with Alfred Jewell, held the lion's share of the chimney-sweeping business in the fashionable West End of London. Their client list read like *Burke's Peerage*. Marrying into the Veale family was a good dynastic match for the Jewells, particularly as Jack was also betrothed to the Veales' daughter Mattie. There was only one difficulty. Jemima did not wish to marry. Not Jim Veale. Not anybody.

'It will never happen.' Her voice sounded calm, disinterested.

'Yes it will, Jem. Best accept it.'

Jemima turned to see pity in Jack's eyes. She dropped the black skirt and the white blouse abruptly on to the bed and went over to the window, looking out over the jumble of rooftops. The moon was half-full with a scatter of ragged cloud scudding across in front of it. The smoke from a thousand London chimneys hung like a haze above the roofs. A single star winked, then disappeared. Jemima stared at it and wished fiercely and silently for her world to change. She clenched her fists.

'Will you be happy with Mattie Veale, Jack?'

She could see Jack's face reflected in the panes of

the window. He was wearing his slightly simple expression, the one he always adopted when asked a question that was deep, or to do with his feelings. Once, years ago, Jack had been in love. But that had all ended miserably and now he did not even pretend to care for Mattie. Jemima knew that whatever he would have with her could only be a pale reflection of what had gone before.

'Of course I will be happy,' Jack said, after a moment. 'Mattie's a good girl. Just as Jim Veale is a good man, Jemima.'

Jemima wrapped her arms about herself. 'I know he's a good man. That makes it worse somehow.' She swung round sharply. 'Jim is kindly and gentle and utterly dull. I shall feel stifled within a week…'

'He's a good man,' Jack repeated. 'He will never beat you like Father beat us—'

'Like he beat you,' Jemima corrected, smiling a little. 'I almost always escaped because you were in the way.'

Jack shrugged uncomfortably. 'My shoulders were broader than yours. I could take it.'

They smiled at each other for a moment and then Jemima sighed. 'All the same, I do not believe you can get in the way this time, Jack. And perhaps you do not want to? Perhaps you think I should take Jim and give over complaining?'

Jack kicked moodily at a splinter of wood coming away from the polished floorboards.

'I think they should never have sent you to that fancy school,' he said gruffly.

'Because it has given me ideas above my station?' Jemima asked.

'Because it has made you unhappy,' Jack said.

Jemima sighed. Her brother was right. These days she

felt as though she was a very square peg being forced into a very round hole.

Matters had been so much simpler when they were small and their father had used them both to climb chimneys. Jemima had been a climbing girl until the age of eleven, but by then Alfred Jewell had started to make good money and he had employed an apprentice, and sent his daughter to the school established for the children of sweeps by Mrs Elizabeth Montagu, the noted bluestocking. Jack, who detested book learning, had always skipped off from lessons at the Sunday school and as a result could barely read or write. But Elizabeth Montagu had discovered in Jemima a quick intelligence and rare interest in learning, and had taken her under her wing. Jemima was sent away to study at another of Mrs Montagu's foundations, an academy for young ladies in Strawberry Hill. As a result, she was a very accomplished young lady indeed, but not in the arts that would make her happy as the wife of a tradesman.

Jack came across and gave her a hug. 'Do not look so sad,' he said roughly. 'It won't be so bad...'

Jemima knew it would.

'I have been educated beyond my place,' she said, into his shoulder. 'I did not fit into their world and now I do not fit into my own.'

'I know.' Jack loosened his grip a little. 'But I still like you.'

Jemima felt a tiny bit more cheerful. One of the things that she loved about her brother was that he was resolutely unimpressed by her book learning. Her father was full of bluster around her, as though he had created something that he did not understand. Her mother looked at her with a wonder that made Jemima feel very uncomfortable. Her old friends shunned her because they thought she had grown too grand. Only Jack was exactly the same to her as he had always been.

'What would you do if you did not marry?' Jack asked now, curious.

Jemima smiled. She knew that they were speaking of dreams now rather than reality. 'Oh, I would read, and go to lectures and exhibitions, and play music—'

'And become bored.' Jack's black gaze was mocking. 'You know you cannot bear not to be doing something.'

Jemima paused, wrinkling up her face. It was true. She had always worked, first climbing chimneys, then at her books and now on the clerking side of her father's business. At school, she had met many young ladies who did not understand the concept of working for a living and their naïveté had amused her. Not everyone had that choice.

'Then I would become a musician, and sing in the theatre.'

Jack sighed. 'That is no respectable trade for a woman.'

'Oh, and chimney sweeping is?'

'No. You know what I mean. A woman's only respectable recourse is to marry.'

'Nonsense!' Jemima scowled at him. 'A woman may become a teacher or a governess—'

'You are the only person I ever heard of,' Jack said, 'who actually *aspired* to become a governess.'

'It would suit my position in life,' Jemima said. 'Neither one thing nor the other. Betwixt and between. Not gentry nor servant...'

'And instead you must marry Jim and become a stalwart tradesman's wife.' Jack moved restlessly across to the walnut bookcase and picked up some of Jemima's novels, peering at the spines. 'Old man Veale will have to build some bookshelves in his house. I hear he is mighty proud to be getting so talented a daughter-in-law.'

Jemima grimaced. She was not vain and she did not like to be thought of as a trophy. She also knew how quickly that pleasure in her accomplishments could turn to bafflement. She had seen it happen with her own father. It was not that she thought herself too good for her family and friends, but somehow she could not fit in any more and they sensed it.

Jack pulled a face too when he saw her expression. 'Father is only trying to do his best for you, Jem, arranging such a match.' A shadow crossed his face. 'And he's doing the best for himself as well, I suppose. Marriage into the Veale family will be to everyone's advantage.'

Jemima nodded. 'I know.' She spoke briskly, without self-pity. 'It is the way of the world. Even were I born with a silver spoon rather than a short-handled brush, I would still be married off for profit.'

Jemima had learned that early on. She was cynical about marriage. Servant girl or Duchess, she observed that it made little difference. Marriage was business and love was irrelevance and that was the end of that.

'You won't refuse to marry Jim, will you?' Jack said. He looked suddenly anxious. 'You know how angry Father would be…'

Jemima felt a pang of mingled fear and misery. Alfred Jewell had always prevailed with his fists. She turned back to the bed, picking up the black cambric skirt and shaking out the creases.

'No,' she said slowly. 'I won't refuse.'

Chapter Two

It had been a fine morning and Rob had taken his accustomed walk early on, strolling through Hyde Park whilst the rest of the world was barely astir. When he had been in the Peninsula it was the only time that he had had to himself, in the cool of the dawn, before the sun had risen and the day had heated like a furnace. He had taken to going out alone then, enjoying the fresh quiet of each day as he listened to the call of the birds, the hum of the insects waking and the muted sounds of human life stirring. His fellow officers had laughed and called him 'Solitary Selborne'—until his early morning meanderings had helped him stumble across and foil a plot on the General's life, after which they had shown him considerably more respect.

This morning there were no such dramas to face, only his cousin's wedding, which was beginning to take on the unattractive appearance of a cattle market. Which of his cousin Anne's unfortunate friends or relatives was to be the recipient of his hasty proposal of marriage? Rob, who had never suffered from the failing of vanity, shuddered at the thought. Such calculated wooing was not his style.

The previous afternoon, after his meeting with Churchward, Rob had called on his Aunt Selborne to acquaint her of the fact that he was returned from the wars and would be delighted to attend Anne's nuptials the following day. His family had all fallen on him with cries of pleasure, especially Ferdie, who had always been a good friend to him. Rob had been less pleased to see Ferdie's younger sister, Augusta, who had changed from a shrewish schoolroom miss into a fully fledged termagant in the time that Rob had been away. He reflected ruefully that were he obliged to marry Augusta his time on campaign would take on a whole new charm.

It was that afternoon that Rob first received the hint that the wedding would not provide him with a great deal of choice in his hunt for a bride. It was to be a small affair. Mrs Selborne was not specific about just how small, and Rob did not wish to pry for fear of making her curious, but the situation did not seem promising.

So it proved. Rob had seldom been to such a subdued wedding. It was clear that the late Earl of Selborne's death had cast a pall over the whole proceedings, which seemed a little unfair to his cousin Anne. The pews were barely half full, the organ played extremely quietly and even the flowers looked disappointed.

'Here's the thing, old fellow,' Ferdie said, sliding into the pew beside his cousin and lowering his voice to a hushed whisper. 'With your father dying less than a year ago, Mama wanted to postpone the ceremony until next season.' He cleared his throat. 'You know what a stickler for propriety she is! Only Anne wouldn't hear of a delay, so they compromised on a small wedding instead.' Ferdie made a noise of disgust. 'Pretty poor show, if you ask me.'

Rob risked a quick glance around the half-empty church. A feeling of doom was starting to spread through him.

'Just how small is small, Ferdie?' he enquired.

'In this case, tiny,' Ferdie confirmed gloomily. 'Immediate family only.'

Rob swallowed hard. 'Fifty guests?'

Ferdie gave him a look. 'More like forty. You know we only have a small family, Rob.'

Rob did some quick mental arithmetic. Forty people, of whom half would be female… Except that the Selbornes almost always had sons, not daughters. His Aunt Clarissa Harley, for instance, had five sons…

He glanced around again. By his estimation there was a grand total of fifteen female wedding guests present and most of them looked to be married already, or to be too young or too old.

Augusta Selborne, the only adult bridesmaid, looked self-important in an orange organdie dress with too many embroidered roses on it. Lady Caroline Spencer, a distant family connection with a sullied reputation, sat across the aisle from him looking decadent in a plunging gown of blue silk. She winked at Rob, patting the seat beside her. Rob pretended to be afflicted by sudden short-sightedness. It seemed that Caro and Augusta were the only eligible women there. His doom moved a step closer.

The organ music swelled slightly as the bride started her progress up the aisle and Rob looked straight ahead, determined that he was not going to spend the service ogling the congregation. There was plenty of time later for his worst fears to be confirmed.

* * *

Afterwards the small but fashionable crowd thronged the steps outside. Rob paused and scanned the gathering for Ferdie, eventually locating him in the press about the bride and groom. Anne was receiving the traditional kiss for luck from the chimney sweep and was emerging pink and ruffled from a hearty embrace. Rob thought that her bridegroom looked distinctly put out, as well he might, for the sweep was a well set-up lad of about three and twenty, with twinkling black eyes and a wicked grin. He looked quite capable of eloping with the bride from under her new husband's nose.

Rob smiled wryly. He could do with some luck himself but he did not fancy embracing a handsome chimney sweep, not even for his father's fortune.

The crowd parted a little and Rob saw that the sweep had evidently brought his wife with him, for a young girl was standing a little way apart. She was dressed in the traditional costume of black fitted jacket and stiff flared skirt. The skirt was a little short, showing a pair of very neat ankles in black boots, and the jacket was tight and framed a very shapely figure. She had jet-black hair, piled up on her head and confined within a black net, on which jet beads glinted in the sunlight. Her skin was translucently pale and she had wide-set eyes in an oval face. She was very pretty.

She turned her head slightly, as though aware that someone was watching her, and her eyes met Rob's. He felt slightly winded, as though someone had hit him hard in the stomach. He saw that her eyes were very a deep violet blue. She did not look away from him, but held his gaze with just a hint of haughty composure.

Rob found himself moving forward without conscious thought. He brushed past the crowd as though they were not there, completely ignoring the greeting that someone called out to him.

He reached the sweep's girl in four strides. She was small. The top of her head was level with his shoulder and she had to tilt her face up to look at him. She was looking at him now, and he could see that her composure was ever so slightly shaken. She was looking at him as though she was not at all certain what he might do next.

Rob fumbled in his pocket and produced a guinea. The summer sun struck sparks off the gold.

'I need some good fortune,' he said. 'I will trade you this guinea for one kiss. What do you say?'

Jemima had been watching Jack with the bride, cynically reflecting that the little henwit looked more in love with her brother than she did with her bridegroom. She loathed these occasions, with the snobbish, twittering, aristocratic crowds and her father exuding bonhomie and playing the part of fulsome master sweep to perfection. It was all so false. The reality of a sweep's life was choking soot and roasting heat; calloused feet, bleeding elbows, lungs full of dust, cold hard floors and bone-aching tiredness. It was a world away from this perfumed throng. But they would never want to know about it. They paid for the fiction and her father would do anything for money.

Suddenly she felt a prickle along her skin, a shiver of awareness. Someone was watching her. She turned her head very slowly.

A man was standing on the edge of the crowd. He was quite tall, though not as broad as Jack, and he had thick chestnut-coloured hair, ruffled by the breeze. He had a hard, handsome face, tanned and a little grave in repose.

Jemima's stomach did a little flip. She realised that she was staring and that the man had evidently taken this as some kind of encouragement, for he was now cutting a path towards her through the wedding crowd. She saw him brush past an acquaintance, who accosted him and then fell back, looking startled to be ignored. As the man drew close Jemima felt hot and then cold, unable to move away. He reached her side in five strides.

Instinctively she tilted up her face to look into his. He was handsome in the same devil-may-care way as so many young noblemen—arrogant, accustomed to command. It was an attitude she disliked intensely.

His eyes were a very dark brown and they contained a warmth deep inside. His mouth was firm and turned up at the corners slightly, as though he smiled often. When he did smile, as now, it drove a very attractive crease down his cheek.

He was holding a guinea in his hand.

'I need some good fortune,' he said, quite as though he were ordering a punnet of strawberries. 'I will trade you this guinea for one kiss. What do you say?'

Jemima almost gave him a set-down. Then she saw that her father was watching, a calculating look in his eye as his gaze rested on the coin. She took the guinea and bit on it, conjuring up the saucy look that was all part of the act.

'The real yellowboy,' she said, adopting the chimney-sweep patois of her childhood. 'An' I reckon you must be a real gennelman, sir.'

She tossed the guinea in the air, before slipping it into her pocket.

The gentleman looked amused. The laughter deepened in his eyes and Jemima felt a tingle down to her toes.

'I assure you that both of us are genuine,' he said. 'I would not cheat you.'

His voice was smooth and warm as the sun on the stones beneath her feet. Jemima felt as though they were rocking very slightly. She was not entirely sure what was wrong with her.

'A' right then.' Her own voice came out slightly husky. 'One kiss for good luck.'

She offered her cheek to him, expecting the customary peck. Instead he bent his head and his lips took hers lightly, then with an insistence that made the blood sing through her veins.

He stepped back and Jemima opened her eyes again, blinking as his own laughing gaze came into focus.

'That will have to do, I suppose,' he said. 'I have no wish to offend your husband.'

Jemima followed his gaze. She felt shaken, a little off balance. 'That's not my husband,' she said. 'That's my brother, Jack.'

She realised her mistake a second later, when she saw the wicked light leap into the gentleman's eyes.

'In that case I'll have my money's worth…'

This second kiss was so thorough it made her head spin. Sensuous, slow and deep, it swept her away. Sensation burned through her body. Her hands came up to clutch at his jacket, then slid around his neck to keep him close to her. She had forgotten where she was. The wedding, the crowd, the noise and colour of the street faded away to nothing. There was no reality except the stunning power of his kiss, the hardness of his body and the racing of her heart.

Jemima was no sheltered innocent. She had grown up on the streets and had no illusions about love or romance. As a child she had seen plenty of relationships between men and women contracted for every reason from lust through to money. Some had had the benefit of clergy, some had not. When she had gone to Mrs Montagu's school the romantic sighs of her fellow pupils had made her laugh. They had swooned over the fashionable gentlemen and dreamed about the brothers of their friends. Jemima had held her own counsel but she had known that those selfsame girls would make good marriages because their families demanded it. A few might marry for love, and of those few some would fall out of love just as quickly as they had fallen into it.

Jemima did not wish to marry Jim Veale, but it was not because she did not love him. That seemed almost an irrelevance to her. In her world, love played no part in marriage. Love made you vulnerable. She had seen that when she had seen Jack fall in love with Beth Rosser. After Beth had died and their child was taken away from him, Jack had gone very silent for months, and after that he had turned into the careless seducer who entranced the ladies now.

Jemima had always thought that love was not for her. Yet despite these hard lessons she could suddenly see how one could be blinded by it. Suddenly she understood how it might be, in another world, another existence.

The kiss eased a little; their lips clung and parted and Jemima pushed away from him, one hand against his chest. She could feel the hammering of his heart against her palm. Just for a moment his gaze reflected all the heat and excitement that she felt spinning inside of her.

Then reality intruded. She was a chimney sweep's daughter who was betrothed to another man and she was not prone to lose her head over a handsome gentleman.

'You ask for a deal too much good luck, sir.' Jemima had recovered herself. She spoke unthinkingly in the cut-glass tones that her seven years at Mrs Montagu's school had taught her.

She saw the gentleman's eyes narrow. 'And you are suddenly become a lady, mistress. How can that be?'

Jemima hesitated, aware that she had given herself away comprehensively. Then a feminine voice said, 'Robert, dearest! I am so glad that you were able to come today! But kissing a little chimney sweep's girl?' The lady offered a powdered cheek to Rob for a rather more chaste salutation. 'Really! You never know what you might catch!'

Jemima looked at her. The lady was about Jemima's own age, with a thin, haughty face and a sneering expression. She was dressed in an over-decorated bridesmaid's gown and had a head-dress of rampant roses. Jemima privately thought that she looked as though she had fallen into a flower cart.

'Good morning, Cousin Augusta.' There was a note in the gentleman's voice that made Jemima glance at him quickly. His face had tightened with something that looked like anger but Jemima did not wait to hear his response. She took several steps backwards until she felt Jack's reassuring presence at her elbow.

'Are you quite well, Jem?'

'Yes,' Jemima pulled herself together. 'Yes, thank you, Jack.'

'I saw you with the flash cove,' Jack said, an edge to his voice. 'Want me to sort him out for you?'

'No!' Jemima grabbed his sleeve. 'No harm done.'

She glanced back at the gentleman. He was still talking to his cousin, but he was looking over Augusta's head at her. There was a faint hint of concern in his eyes. It made Jemima feel strange.

She turned away. 'Let's be going, Jack. I've had enough, and Father has his money…'

It was true. Alfred Jewell's pockets bulged and he was cheerfully jangling the coins. The black cat, Sooty, was perched on his shoulder, surveying the wedding guests with a disdainful air as he washed his paws.

Jemima slipped her hand through Jack's arm and resisted a last glance over her shoulder at the gentleman. She could feel the outline of the guinea against the lining of her jacket and after a moment she slid her other hand into the pocket, rubbing her fingers over the hard edge of the coin.

A guinea for a kiss from a little sweep's girl… It would be foolish to think of their encounter as anything more than that. Love was a foolish extravagance after all.

'Come on,' Jack said, pressing her arm comfortingly. 'I'll stand you some spiced gingerbread from Sal Stanton's stall.'

'You're on,' Jemima said.

Alfred Jewell had other ideas, however. As they turned to leave, he came bustling up, Sooty clinging on to his shoulder by virtue of digging his claws into the thick material of his black coat.

'Where do you think you're going?'

'To the gingerbread stall,' Jack said. There was a hint of insolence in his tone, as so often when his father challenged him. The older Jack got, the more they clashed. One day, Jemima thought, there would be an almighty disagreement…

'Oh, no, you don't,' Jewell said, his face reddening angrily. 'We're booked for the whole day. Wedding breakfast and dancing to follow. You're to dance with the bride, Jack.'

Jack sighed heavily. 'Won't be eating with the nobs, will we?'

'Of course not!' his father snapped. 'We eat with the servants in the kitchen.'

'Just so long as we know our place,' Jack muttered, under his breath. He took Jemima's arm again. 'Come along, sis. Time to put on the act again.'

Augusta Selborne had wandered off to talk to some of the other guests, leaving Rob feeling irritable and on edge. If anything had confirmed him in his reluctance to marry her it was that short encounter. Augusta had been trying to charm him, but she had marked her own card from the moment that she had insulted the sweep's girl. Rob had felt a protective anger stronger than anything he had ever experienced before. Augusta's slights were often poisonous, but over the years he had grown to ignore them. This time, though, they had got straight through to him. He told himself that it was because he had been away and had forgotten just how sharp Augusta could be.

He looked around for the chimney-sweep girl, but she had gone. It had been particularly unkind of Augusta to make a target of a tradesman's daughter who could not defend herself. The girl had been very sweet as well. She had smelled of apricots and tasted of honey... Rob shifted slightly, telling himself not to be a fool. He was in the market for a wife, not a mistress, and it was not his style to go around buying kisses from anyone. He was not entirely sure what had come over him.

He thought that the girl must be a clever mimic to be able to ape a lady's accent so accurately. That had thrown him. That and the potent sweetness of the kiss. His mind had been so addled that he had not even asked her name.

He bent down and picked up one of the trade cards that had fallen into the gutter with the confetti thrown over the bride. The card was the size of a handbill, embossed on expensive paper, and bore a fine Royal coat of arms.

'Alfred Jewell, Chimney Sweeper and Night man, No. 3 Great Portland Street' was inscribed with many flourishes. Rob smiled slightly. Clearly Mr Jewell was a High Master of the trade and knew the value of advertising. He folded the bill and tucked it absentmindedly in his pocket. Should he ever need a chimney sweep he would know where to find one. And should he want to find the girl... He shook his head slightly. That was about the last thing he should be thinking of at the moment. He needed a wife. And he was no closer to finding one.

Ferdie and Bertie came up to him. Ferdie clapped him on the shoulder. 'Looking glum, Rob. Not surprised, if Augusta's been trying to charm you. Mama has placed you next to her for the wedding breakfast, I'm afraid.'

Rob grimaced. The attractions of his club suddenly seemed very strong. Then he remembered the chimney-sweep's daughter. Perhaps she would be dancing at the wedding. Perhaps he should not seek her out. And perhaps he would do so anyway.

It was late when Jemima managed to escape the dancing and slip outside into the cool of the evening. The feasting had gone on long into the afternoon, but she and Jack had sat around twiddling their thumbs as they waited to be summoned to join in the dancing. Jemima reflected that her father must have been well paid indeed to put his business aside for a full day at the whim of some lord. At some point the beleaguered servants had managed to feed them on baked potatoes and stew between dashing out to the marquee to keep the wedding guests well supplied with food and drink. Eventually the dancing had started and Jemima had found herself passed from gentleman to gentleman, rather like a well-used bottle of port. She hated it. There had been nothing overtly suggestive in their behaviour, just the odd innuendo and some hands that strayed with rather too much familiarity. But she was supposed to accept it all with a saucy smile for the sake of the guineas and notes that were stuffed down the bodice of her gown. Her father was watching her, his black eyes hard and calculating. Jack had practically disappeared, besieged by a group of eager ladies vying for his hand in the dance, chief amongst them a ravaged-looking widow in plunging blue silk.

Outside it was cold, with the promise of autumn in the mist that was creeping up from the river. Jemima walked slowly down the path that led away from the house. The music tinkled in the background. Jemima hummed a strain of music under her breath: 'A north country maid up to London had strayed although with her nature it did not agree...'

There were flambeaux lighting the way, but the gardens were empty. She paused by a stand of tall oaks. The ground beneath her feet was thick with fallen leaves that crackled as she walked.

'Taking the air, mistress?'

Jemima gasped. She had not been aware that she was

sharing the gardens with any of the guests. She recognised the voice at once. It was the lazy, amused tones of the man who had kissed her outside the church. Robert Selborne. The Earl of Selborne, the bride's cousin. During the wedding breakfast, Jemima had heard all the gossip about the Earl—how he was but recently come in to his title and it was rumoured he was looking to settle down; how he had been estranged from his father because of his insistence on joining the army; how he had covered himself in glory and that General Wellesley himself spoke highly of him. The ladies thought him dashing but a little distant. He did not flirt and it was said that his only love was Delaval, the family estate in Oxfordshire.

Jemima had seen him earlier at the wedding feast, but he had not been dancing. A small part of her had been disappointed. Nor had he been looking at her—at least not when Jemima had cast a covert glance or two in his direction.

She saw his shadow now, dark against the paling sky. He had turned towards her and he was smiling. Common sense prompted her to leave, but instinct made her want to stay. She was drawn to this man's company in a way she did not understand, but she knew she had to fight the impulse. She turned to go.

'Excuse me, my lord. I had no notion there was anyone else here—'

'Do not leave on my account,' Rob Selborne said. Jemima saw him tilt a bottle to his lips. 'I am merely standing here and admiring the view. I have been away and had forgot how beautiful it was.'

The view was indeed very fine. The Selborne house stood on a slight rise above the river and the streets tumbled away down to the water's edge. The sun was setting in a blaze of gold, wreathed in the city's habitual curtain of grey smoke.

'Would you care for a drink?' Rob asked. He held the bottle out to her.

Jemima lifted the bottle and took a cautious sip. It was sweet and warming. 'Port. Just right for a summer evening.'

Rob laughed, turning back to contemplate the scene across the river. 'I have seldom seen so fine a sight as London on a clear evening.'

Jemima smiled. 'It does indeed look very pretty.'

'"When a man is tired of London he is tired of life,"' Rob said softly.

'"For there is in London everything that life can afford,"' Jemima finished the quotation for him. She passed the port bottle back to him. 'Are you tired of London, my lord?'

She saw Robert Selborne's shadow turn towards her. She could tell that he was surprised at the question and surprised at her for asking it. The servant classes seldom asked impertinent questions. Nor did they generally quote Dr Johnson. After a moment, however, he gave her a straight answer.

'No, I am not. I could never tire of London, Miss Jewell, although I do prefer the country. And yourself? You must see a different side to the city, I imagine.'

Jemima was surprised that he knew her surname. He must have picked up one of the handbills her father had had printed. It was even more surprising that he had remembered what that name was. In her experience the nobility had difficulty realising that the working classes were called anything at all other than 'you'.

'I have certainly seen up enough London chimneys

to last me a lifetime,' she said. 'I suppose that you could call that a different perspective.'

Robert Selborne laughed. 'And have you also had enough of dancing at aristocratic weddings?'

Jemima looked at him. 'Did I look as though I was not enjoying myself?'

She could not see Rob Selborne's expression, but she could hear the amusement still in his voice. 'You looked as though you would rather have had a tooth pulled. Your mouth was smiling, but your eyes were not.'

Jemima hesitated. 'You see a great deal, my lord.'

Rob Selborne shifted slightly. 'I was watching you.'

A shiver ran along Jemima's skin, giving her goose pimples. 'I hope that no one else was doing likewise,' she said.

Rob laughed again. 'Oh, a great many people were watching you, Miss Jewell, the majority of them men. But do not worry—I do not believe that they saw what I saw. To all intents and purposes you looked to be having a fine time.'

Jemima smiled. 'As did you, my lord, with that charming bridesmaid to entertain you.'

'So you were watching me as well,' Rob Selborne said. 'That is interesting. Alas for my cousin Augusta that I prefer your company to hers, Miss Jewell. As you will perceive.' He made a gesture. 'I am out here talking to you rather than in there dancing with her.'

There was a rustic bench between two of the oak trees. Jemima sat down and settled her poplin skirts about her.

'I do not believe Miss Selborne need repine, my lord.'

'How so?'

'Because I overheard two ladies discussing that you

might be looking for a bride and that your choice could fall on your cousin.'

Rob turned towards her. He was but five steps away. Jemima could see the crisp white of his shirt and neck-cloth in the first, pale moonlight.

'I fear that that is true, at least in part,' he said, 'though I am not certain how anyone knows. My father's will decrees that I am to choose a wife from the ladies assembled here tonight, Miss Jewell, if I am to inherit the fortune I need to restore my home.'

Jemima raised her brows. 'How piquant, my lord. And it is your cousin whose candidature you favour?'

'No, it is not. Perhaps I am too nice in my requirements, but none of the ladies appeal to me. What would you do in my situation, Miss Jewell?'

Jemima raised her brows. 'What would *I* do? Choose the one who bored me the least and get on with it, I suppose.'

'The one who bored you the least?'

'Yes. You might be married for fifty years. How intolerably tedious would that be if you were stuck with a lady who did not hold your interest?'

Rob inclined his head. 'Sound advice. But you do not mention love, Miss Jewell.'

Jemima smiled a little. 'Oh, I do not have much time for that.'

'I see. Plenty of literature is against you. Poets and novelists are often extolling the pleasures of love.'

'And the pain of it.'

Rob came to sit beside her. Jemima imagined that she could feel the warmth of his body even though he was not touching her. She told herself not to be fanciful.

'Do you speak from experience, Miss Jewell?' he asked.

'Not I!' Jemima said. 'I speak from observation, my lord, and nothing else.'

Rob took her hand. 'Yet you kiss like an angel.'

Jemima drew her fingers away, but not before they had trembled slightly within his. She rather thought that he had felt it too. The mention of the kiss had sent a flutter of sensation down her neck like the brush of a moth's wing.

She spoke severely to counteract the trembling inside. 'That has nothing to do with love.'

'I see. What does it have to do with?'

Rob's tone was very low and just the sound of his voice seemed enough to have the most peculiar effect on her. Jemima looked accusingly at the port bottle. Perhaps she had taken more than she thought.

'Kissing is…oh, you know what I mean! Kissing is about desire and physical attraction and all those dangerous things—'

'Dangerous?' Rob leaned forward. His sleeve brushed her arm. Jemima's throat dried. He was very close to her now and she wanted him closer still. She made a grab for the shreds of her common sense.

'They are dangerous because they are misleading,' she said. She made to get to her feet. 'Excuse me, my lord. I am paid to dance at this wedding and that is what I should be doing.'

Rob's hand closed about her wrist, not hard, but in a gesture that stayed her when she would have moved away.

'A moment. I could pay you more to stay with me.'

There was a silence but for the whisper of the breeze stirring the leaves at their feet.

'I think not,' Jemima said. 'Only some of my services are up for sale, my lord, and those right reluctantly.'

She saw the flash of his teeth in the darkness as he smiled. 'Do you include your kisses in that, dangerous or not?'

'I do not,' Jemima said.

'You granted me one earlier.'

Jemima's heart skipped a beat. She was sure that he could feel her pulse racing beneath his fingers. 'You took more than you paid for.'

'That's true,' Rob said. 'Did you object?'

There was a silence. His fingers still encircled her wrist but lightly now.

'No,' Jemima said with reluctant honesty. 'I did not object. But I will not grant you another.'

'Why not?'

Jemima gave him an old-fashioned look. 'Need you ask, sir? If a tradesman's daughter is free with her kisses, then she gains a reputation of being free with other things too…' She shrugged.

She heard him laugh but he did not press her. 'I understand. That is when matters may become misleading and dangerous.'

'Just so.'

Rob let go of her and moved away a little, leaning back against the bars of the wooden seat. Jemima started to breathe again.

'Then talk to me instead.'

'About what?' Jemima's voice was cool. She had to keep her defences in place.

'About where you learned to quote Johnson. And to speak like—' He broke off.

'You were going to say "like a lady" were you not, my lord?' Jemima enquired.

'I beg your pardon.' Rob sounded uncomfortable and Jemima liked him for it. 'I did not intend to be rude.

No doubt ladylike qualities, like nobility, are not a birth-right.'

Jemima smiled. 'They certainly were not *my* birth-right. I am the daughter of a chimney sweep and the granddaughter of a rat catcher. It is only because I was educated by that most strict moral arbiter, Mrs Elizabeth Montagu, that I could impersonate a Duchess if I wished.'

Rob gave a low whistle. 'A protégée of Mrs Montagu! That is no mean thing.'

'Thank you. I was immensely grateful for her interest in me.'

'And yet despite your education you consider yourself a counterfeit lady?'

The crescent moon was rising, entangled in the branches of the tree above their head. By its light, Jemima could see that Rob was sitting back and studying her thoughtfully.

'You may give the sweep's girl an education,' she said, smiling a little, 'but at the end I am still here dancing at the wedding.' She turned a little towards him. 'You said that you had been away, my lord. Maybe you know how difficult it is to go away and then have to come back again.'

Rob gave her a crooked smile. 'Very perceptive, Miss Jewell. I went to the Peninsula and when I returned, everything that I had been fighting for had changed.' There was a note of passion in his voice that struck Jemima forcibly. 'My family died in an epidemic. I never expected not to see them again.'

Jemima put out an impulsive hand.

'I am sorry. That must be very hard for you. Not to be able to say all the things you might have wanted to say to them, I mean.'

Rob caught her outstretched hand and once again his fingers entangled with hers. He did not speak, but his touch conveyed gratitude. Gratitude and something more. His fingers stroked hers very gently and Jemima felt her pulse leap. This seemed like madness, this attraction to a total stranger. And yet the night was warm and scented with the smells of late summer and there was a romantic little crescent moon overhead...

This time when he leaned forward she did not draw back. His stance was relaxed, but there something watchful in his eyes. It was a warning. Jemima's stomach turned over.

'If I wanted to kiss you again now...' Rob's voice was low '...would you refuse?'

He was so close that Jemima could smell the sharp lime scent of his cologne, mixed with the warmer smell of his skin. Her head swam. She tried to speak, failed, and cleared her throat.

'It's...probable. Are you in need of more good luck?'

'I need a great deal of it. But that is not why I want to kiss you.'

Danger beckoned, supremely tempting. Jemima closed her eyes for a second. One kiss... Surely there was no harm in it—and a great deal of pleasure? Except that this man was looking for a wife, and that was certainly not the role that he envisaged for her...

Jemima stood up abruptly. 'My father will be wondering where I have got to,' she said. 'I really must go.'

Rob stood up too. 'Miss Jewell—'

Jemima stepped back, deliberately putting distance between them.

'Lord Selborne?'

Her use of his title and the coolness of her tone were

intended to keep him at arm's length. Nevertheless, Rob Selborne just smiled and took a casual step closer.

'Farewell then, Miss Jewell. And good luck.'

Jemima felt tense, though she did not know in all honesty whether it was from apprehension that he would kiss her—or fear that he would not.

'I wish you good luck too, my lord,' she said lightly. 'In restoring your home—and in marrying your cousin.'

Rob nodded slowly. She saw the shadow of his smile. 'Do you really wish me luck in my marriage?'

'No, not really,' Jemima said. 'In restoring your home, of course I do, but not in marrying your cousin. I think that she will probably drive you to bedlam within a twelvemonth.'

And before she could betray herself further, she turned from him and hurried up the path and away into the night.

Chapter Three

Rob was dreaming, tossed on a restless sea of memory and horror. There were scenes of carnage everywhere, bodies tossed in the street, women and children running for their lives. The excitement of bloodlust was in the air, tangible, thick as treacle. He could hear the screams, feel the sweat and blood and heat as though he were still in the Peninsula. Worse, he felt that desperate helplessness, that impotence that told him that no matter how he tried, no matter how many he helped, there were those beyond his saving. Men tortured, women raped, children murdered like stuck pigs. The knowledge burned through his mind, bringing with it the now-familiar nightmare. He was on horseback, riding through the town, and from the gutter a child reached out to him; a child dark-haired and dark-eyed, holding up her arms to him in a mute plea. He was leaning down, within an inch of touching her fingertips with his own, when she was quite literally cut down in front of his eyes. The scene dissolved, his head was full of noise and blood and unimaginable misery, and he woke up gasping, to find himself entangled in the sheets and drenched in sweat.

He lay still for several minutes, allowing his breathing to calm, not attempting to shut the images from his mind, for he had found that that simply made the experience worse. Gradually the hideous scenes receded and he could see beyond his nightmare; see that the dawn was breaking and the light was creeping around the bed curtains.

He got up, stripped off his nightshirt and splashed some water from the ewer on to his face. Then he walked slowly across to the window and edged the curtain back a little. London, early on an August morning, looked drab and grey, but it also looked immensely reassuring. Street vendors were already setting up their stalls and there was the rumble of wheels on the cobbles, the cry of the seabirds in the air.

With a sigh Rob let the curtain fall back into place. His heart ached for the country, for the lush fields and wooded chases of Oxfordshire. He thought of Delaval, half-ruined now from neglect and decay, and a fierce determination took him. He would not let it fall down and his heritage tumble like the stones into the long grass and be lost forever. If he could not fulfil the conditions of the two wills then Ferdie would inherit all the money and he would simply have to find some other way to achieve his ambitions.

The faint light fell on a crumpled handbill lying beside the hearth. Rob picked it up and recognised it as Alfred Jewell's trade card.

He smiled to himself. Miss Jewell had suggested that he should marry the lady who bored him the least. Ironically, all the ladies at Anne Selborne's wedding had struck him as infinitely tedious, cardboard cut-outs of society ladies. All except Miss Jewell herself…

Rob tapped the paper thoughtfully. An idea was start-

ing to come into his head, an idea so preposterous yet
so appealing that he scarce knew whether to embrace it
or to dismiss it out of hand. Yet what did he have to
lose? She could always tell him to go hang…

He tucked the handbill into the pocket of his jacket
and pulled the bell to call his valet. Now that he had
resolved on a plan, he did not wish to waste any more
time. He would call on Miss Jewell that very evening
and make her a proposal.

'I cannot do it!' At the last minute Jemima had
changed her mind, broken her word to Jack, and told
her father that she could not marry Jim Veale. They
were in the sitting room of her parents' comfortable
home in Great Portland Street, cluttered with the furniture and china ornaments and polished brasses that her
mother so lovingly collected. It was as though Mrs Jewell, having spent so many of her years in poverty, had
tried to reassure herself by stuffing her later life with
the material symbols of prosperity.

Sometimes Jemima thought that her mother did not
know how to stop collecting. China dolls jostled for
space on the mantelpiece with an ugly marble clock and
several branches of candles. The walls were papered
with paintings of the sweet, sentimental type. One sofa
and no less than five fat armchairs were squashed into
the space, between three polished walnut tables. There
was not a speck of dust and the chimney did not dare
to smoke. Jemima remembered Mrs Montagu's words:
'Less is more, Jemima. In furnishings and in personal
attire, the most elegant style is always the simplest.' Yet
Jemima had a great deal of affection for her mother's
magpie acquisitiveness.

Alfred Jewell looked out of place amidst this muddled gentility. It was not a room that he frequented very often for he was more at home out and about on his business, or supervising the work of his clerks. A stocky man, he had a ruddy countenance and a magnificent moustache and side-whiskers. Now, as he contemplated his daughter's disobedience, his ruddy face grew redder still.

'You cannot marry him? There is no *can* about it, miss. You *will* marry Jim Veale, aye, and the banns will be read next week!'

Jemima locked her fingers together. She was sitting on the sofa, the wooden arm pressing uncomfortably into her back as she cowered away from her father. Mrs Jewell sat opposite, her pale eyes moving from one to the other in trepidation. She was murmuring under her breath:

'Oh dear...oh dear... You must do as your father says, Jemima dear, indeed you must...'

Jemima knew that her mother would never intervene to support her. Once, Mrs Jewell had confided that it was a shame her daughter could not marry a gentleman now that she was such a pretty-behaved girl, but when the match with Jim Veale had been mooted she had never uttered another word on the subject. Nor was Jack there to help her. He had gone to the alehouse and it was anyone's guess when he would be home.

Jemima stared up into her father's angry black eyes. She tried to speak calmly. 'I cannot marry Jim Veale, Father. I would be stifled.'

The frown gathered between Alfred Jewell's brows. 'Stifled? What sort of talk is this? Jim Veale is a good man—'

'I know he is,' Jemima said desperately. 'It is just

that he…that I…we are not suited to each other. Not any more…'

She could feel her words beating pointlessly against her father's bafflement and indifference. What did Alfred Jewell care that she would be suffocated by the stolid worth of a tradesman's home? It did not matter to him that she and Jim Veale had nothing to say to each other, that without books and conversation and wider interests her life felt intolerably constricted. When she had left school her father had reluctantly permitted her to continue visiting some of her former teachers, but that would be at an end on her marriage. Mrs Jim Veale could not go gallivanting about London mixing with bluestockings and visiting the art galleries and theatres. It would make her husband a laughing-stock in the community.

Her father took her by the shoulders and shook her slightly. His fingers bit into her skin.

'See here, girl, you'd best learn what's good for you and that right quickly! The only reason I sent you to school was so that you could read and write, and help Jim balance the books. Should've known you'd take on these airy-fairy notions! Well, you can let them go again—as quick as maybe!'

He shook her again, a bit harder. Jemima shrank back, squashed into a corner of the sofa, trying to avoid his angry bloodshot eyes and the spittle that had started to fly, as it always did when he became enraged.

'Father, please! If you could give me a little time—'
Alfred Jewell made a sound like an outraged bull.

'Time! How much time does a girl need?'

Turning, he swung out one arm and knocked Jemima's books off the small side table on to the floor. They fell with a clatter on to the polished wood. He picked them up and tossed them one by one into the fire, where they flared briefly, the paper charring, the printed word fading to ash.

'Take that for your book-learning and your lady's airs and graces! Too good for us now, aren't you, my girl! Well, I don't give a fig for your fancy education.'

Jemima took a deep breath and forced herself to stay calm. Her precious copy of *Castle Rackrent* was disappearing up the chimney, but at least she had left *Frederick and Caroline* upstairs in her bedroom. She felt the tears prick her eyes. How foolish to have provoked her father thus, but her refusal had been instinctive, borne of fear and a desperate feeling that she would die a slow death in Jim's father's house, deprived of all the things that she had come to hold dear...

Her mother's twitterings had increased in speed and reached a higher pitch as she twisted her hands together in an agony of misery.

'Jemima, dear, young Jim is such a good boy and so gentle and kind! You could not ask for a better husband. You will have a lovely home close by, and children of your own, and when Jack marries Mattie we shall all be one happy family—'

'Ingrate!' Alfred Jewell bellowed, making his wife and his daughter jump. 'Useless little bitch!'

Jemima drew in a sharp breath. When she had been a child such language and worse had been the cant on the streets and it had neither shocked nor disturbed her because she had grown up hearing it. Now, after years of education and refinement, she could feel herself go hot with surprise—and disgust. It was part familiar and part revolting. She tried to keep her feelings out of her face but it was too late. Her expression changed and

Alfred Jewell, watching her, narrowed his hot black gaze in anger.

'Oh, so my language offends your dainty ears, does it, miss? Time to cut Miss High and Mighty down to size!'

The first blow caught Jemima's ear and set her head buzzing. She raised one of the fat cushions to protect herself, and the vision of herself as a small child flashed through her head. She had been small then, dodging the blows, running rings around her father's legs. Not so now. Now it was Mrs Jewell who was hanging on her husband's arm and trying to pull him back, and stuttering the words that must surely only fan the flames: 'Alfie, stop. You cannot hit Jemima. She's a lady now. You wanted her to be a lady!'

'Aye, and see what's become of her,' her father growled. 'Too much reading! Too much thinking!'

The hysterical laughter bubbled up in Jemima's throat even as the second blow slapped her hard across the cheek and knocked her backwards, her head connecting sharply with the arm of the sofa. A dull pain burst inside her skull. Dimly she could see her mother sent flying across the room to crash into the fire irons with a whimper. There was a commotion in the corridor outside. Jack's voice was raised in anger; his fists were pounding at the door. Jemima felt a rush of relief followed by a plunging despair. The door was locked and now her father was coming for her.

Mrs Jewell stayed where she had fallen, her grey hair tumbling about her face, her eyes tired and defeated. Jemima tried to struggle to her feet the better to defend herself, but she became entangled in her skirts and lost her balance. She felt her father's belt snake about her shoulders, felt the vicious, remembered pain of the buckle bruising her collarbone, and grabbed the end of it, wrenching it from her father's hands. The impetus swung her backwards so that her head bounced sickeningly against the floor. She saw her father's face as he loomed over her, then there was a crash as the door splintered open and Jemima closed her eyes in relief and lay still.

It had not occurred to Rob that gaining an audience with Miss Jewell might be in any way difficult. He had found the house in Great Portland Street without a problem, for there was a golden pole and a sweep's brush marking the door. It was only when he was standing on the doorstep that he realised that the entire family might well be at home and that explaining himself to them all, before he had had time to speak to Miss Jewell alone, might prove somewhat awkward. He was hesitating on the doorstep, his hand raised to knock, when he noticed that the front door was ajar. A second later there was a crash from inside and the sound of voices raised in altercation. This time Rob did not hesitate. He pushed open the door and walked in.

The scene in the hallway was confusing. A little maid was standing with her apron over her head, wailing loudly, whilst a man Rob recognised as Jack Jewell was setting his broad shoulder to one of the doors, cursing when the heavy wood did not budge. He turned when he heard Rob's footsteps behind him and there was such violence in his eyes that Rob felt himself stiffen instinctively, all his training coming to the fore and overriding all other considerations. Then there was a crash from inside the room, the sound china breaking and a female scream that cut off abruptly. Jack Jewell said:

'Help me. She's in there.'

And Rob understood without the need for further words, and set his shoulder to the door beside Jack so that the lock burst on the first attempt and they both fell into the room to face the horror within.

She was lying on the sofa with her head on a cushion. Someone was holding one of her hands very gently and she could feel the cool dampness of a cloth against her face. Jemima's mind was supplying disjointed bits of information one at a time. She could hear a voice, very calm but with the unmistakable ring of authority. She opened her eyes.

Rob Selborne was sitting beside her on the sofa and it was he who had applied the cool water to her temples, for the cloth was still in his hand. As Jemima's eyes focussed on his face she saw him smile at her with astonishing tenderness and it made her blink in shock. His hand was warm on hers and he smelled familiar. The scent of him tugged at her senses, confusing her. She felt weak and suddenly close to tears. One slipped from beneath her lashes before she could help herself and she closed her eyes again, despising her weakness.

'Lie still.' Rob spoke softly. 'You are quite safe. Your brother has taken your mother upstairs and I believe—' Jemima heard his voice harden '—that he is helping your father to come to his senses under the pump in the yard.'

A faint splashing of water from outside confirmed his words. Jemima tried to sit up. 'I must go to my mother—'

'Presently. The maid is with her. But you—are you hurt?'

Jemima moved a little. And winced. She saw the grim line of Rob's jaw tighten a notch and realised with a sudden pang of the heart just how much self-control he was exercising. There was concentrated fury in his eyes, held on the tightest rein. She knew without him saying a word that he wanted to go outside and hit Alfred Jewell across the yard and that his respect for her was the only thing preventing him from doing so. She felt profoundly shaken by the knowledge. She also felt ashamed that he knew so much about her family—things that she did not want anyone to know.

'I am sorry—' she started to say, but Rob interrupted her.

'You have nothing to be sorry for.' His voice was still hard. 'Are you injured at all or can you move?'

Jemima succeeded in sitting up. She put a hand to her forehead. 'My head aches a little but that is all. I shall be better directly.'

'You have a bruise coming up on your collarbone.' Rob's tone was dispassionate. Jemima blushed and flicked her dress back into place to conceal the mark.

'The buckle of the strap just caught me. It is nothing.'

They looked at one another for a long moment.

'You cannot stay here,' Rob said. 'I need to know that you will be all right—'

'She'll be fine. I'll look after her.'

Jemima jumped as Jack strode back into the room. Suddenly the air crackled with renewed tension. There was a belligerent jut to Jack's jaw and he looked Rob Selborne over with the cold assessment of a prizefighter. Rob looked amused and slightly disdainful and did not back away.

Jemima put out a hand. A further demonstration of male aggression was the last thing that she needed. Whatever solidarity had drawn Rob and Jack into temporary alliance, it was over now. And she was the reason why.

'I think,' she said clearly, 'that we should thank Lord Selborne for his intervention, Jack.'

Both men looked at her. Neither moved. Then Rob sighed, and held his hand out.

'I am reassured to think that your sister will be safe under your protection, Jewell.'

Jack stared at Rob's face, then at his outstretched hand. Jemima glared at him. Jack sighed and shook Rob's hand grudgingly.

'Thank you for your help, Selborne.'

Both of them looked as though they were having teeth pulled. The sight made Jemima want to laugh. She felt a tiny bit more cheerful.

Rob turned to her. 'Good night, Miss Jewell. I shall call tomorrow to see how you are.' He bowed and went out, passing Jack in the doorway without a second glance.

'What the hell did he want?' Jack asked, as the front door closed.

Jemima frowned. Her head felt fuzzy and there was an ache behind her eyes. She wanted nothing more than to go to bed and sleep forever.

'I do not know,' she said, in surprise. 'I did not even think to ask him why he was here.'

Jack looked at her. 'I don't suppose it was to arrange for his chimney to be swept,' he said, at length.

Jemima looked away. 'No,' she said. 'I don't suppose it was.'

Later, when the maid had brought a cold compress for her head and some salve for her bruises, Jemima lay on her back on the bed and stared out of the window

at the tumble of roofs and the stars above them. Jack
had gone out again—back to the flash house—to get
well and truly drunk. It happened every time he quarrelled with their father. It was the only way he knew to
deal with the situation. Jack had not mentioned Rob
Selborne's visit again and nor, surprisingly, had their
father when he had staggered in from the yard, dripping
and swearing quietly. Jemima assumed that he was the
only one who had thought that Rob *had* been there to
arrange for his chimneys to be cleaned. No one spoke
about what had happened. It was as though the whole
previous hour was to be wiped from their minds, as
though it had never happened.

Except that Rob Selborne had said that he would be
back. And Jemima believed him.

She knew why he had come. He was going to ask
her to become his mistress. And for the very first time
in her life, she was tempted. For a second she thought
of Rob; of his kiss and his touch and the look in his
eyes. He was an honourable man and there was something so seductive about that strength and integrity
when you lived in a world that lacked it. But it would
be madness to give in to Rob, for what would happen
when it ended? The only examples of love that she had
ever seen had all ended in unhappiness. That was no
way to gain security or the independence she craved.
Nevertheless...

Jemima stared hard at the patch of sky above her
window. It was inky black, the stars hard and bright.
The bruises on her shoulders were aching now and the
cuts where the strap had broken the skin were sore.
Jemima was used to physical pain. As a child she had
climbed chimneys until her feet were rough and raw,
and had worked from before dawn until after dark, when

she had fallen asleep almost where she stood. What was more painful was the emotional ache, the feeling that she had got lost somewhere along the way. Too much thinking… Her father had been quite right. Elizabeth Montagu had taught her to question, to think for herself, and now she could not stop.

She thought about running away and taking a post as a governess or schoolteacher. It was one way in which young ladies could support themselves, and it was not as though she was a delicate flower unused to fending for herself. The difficulty was that society was against her. She had testimonials from Mrs Montagu and Miss Hannah More, but the type of families that were looking for a governess would not wish to employ a chimney sweep's daughter in the role. She could always ask her former school for a job, of course, and she was sure that the headmistress, Mrs Gilbert, would be only too happy agree, but then it would be all too easy for her father to trace her and force her to go back with him. Jemima winced as her bruises chafed her. Independence of mind was one thing. Achieving freedom was quite another.

A shooting star flashed across the small, black square of sky, a golden flash so quick Jemima thought she had imagined it. She stared out into the dark.

'I shall call tomorrow to see how you are.'

She knew that he would come. And she would have to decide what her answer was going to be.

Chapter Four

Rob gave his card to the little maidservant and asked if Mistress Jewell was at home. Despite the fact that she had seen him the previous night, the girl stared at him like an owl. It was clear that she could not read the card either. She repeated as if by rote that the Master and young master Jack were out on business and that if he wanted to speak to them he should call later. Rob explained again that it was Mistress Jewell whom he wished to see. The maid stared at him with her mouth open, then offered the information that the mistress was out marketing. It took another five minutes to explain to her that it was Miss not Mrs Jewell that he wanted, and even then the maidservant looked dubious. She left him in the sitting room and disappeared, leaving Rob with the conviction that he might never see her again.

He was fascinated by the contents of the room in which he had been left. He had never been inside a wealthy merchant house before last night and then he had had no time to notice anything. Now he looked about him with curiosity. It was a very modern house, with expensive furniture in a rather bland design. A long case clock ticked sonorously by the window. There was a hotchpotch of ornaments filling every available space. A dozen china ladies danced across the mantelpiece, entangling themselves in the branches of several candlesticks. There were at least seven squishy cushions on the sofa and three filling each chair. The tables were laden with various trinkets: empty glass scent bottles, tiny pottery houses, gnomes and fairies. There was what looked like a bead-embroidered wedding veil lying over the back of one chair. There were no books, except for in the fire grate, where he could see the charred remains of what looked like several pages of print. He knelt down on the hearthrug for a closer look.

'Lord Selborne?'

Rob stood up so quickly that he almost bumped his head on the wooden mantelshelf. Miss Jewell was standing just inside the door, dressed in bright jonquil muslin. Her black hair was tied up with matching yellow ribbons. She looked just like a débutante, fresh, young and very pretty. She was holding his card in her hand. He noticed a small ink stain on her fingers, and wondered suddenly if she had been working. Her voice, smooth and well spoken as a lady of quality, was calm this morning. All her defences were back in place, as though the events of the previous night had never occurred. Yet when he looked closely he saw the telltale beat of a pulse in her throat that suggested she was not quite as unruffled as her outward demeanour suggested.

'It is kind of you to call,' she continued. 'It gives me the opportunity to thank you formally for your help last night.'

Rob smiled slightly. There was a frosty reserve in her manner and he could tell that she was not going to invite him to sit down and was certainly not going to offer him any refreshment. It might be because she was embarrassed about the situation in which he had found her the previous night and had no wish to discuss it further with him. Or it might be that she had had time to wonder why he had sought her out—and had come to the obvious conclusion. Whatever the case, he could not give her the chance to dictate their interview. He had to breach those defences, and quickly.

He bowed and took her hand in his. 'Good morning, Miss Jewell. I hope that I find you recovered this morning?'

Her pulse fluttered beneath his fingers and she tried to withdraw her hand from his. The pink colour came into her cheeks and Rob felt a rush of masculine pleasure that she was not indifferent to him.

'Thank you,' she said, evading his gaze. 'I am very well.'

There was a pause. 'When I called last night, I was hoping to speak with you,' Rob said.

That brought her gaze up to his. She raised her brows, a faintly cynical expression in her eyes. 'Were you indeed, Lord Selborne? I cannot imagine what you have to discuss with me.'

Rob gestured to the chairs. 'May we sit down and talk about it?'

She gave the question full consideration rather than treating it as a formality. After a moment she nodded, and took the chair on which the wedding veil rested. She folded it quickly, neatly, and placed it to one side. A sudden thought occurred to Rob.

'Yours?' he asked, nodding to the veil.

'Yes.' Her voice was flat and lifeless suddenly and so was the expression in her violet eyes. 'I am to be married in three weeks.'

Rob felt a sharp disappointment. 'That rather makes my proposition redundant.'

Her gaze was fixed on him. 'What proposition is that, my lord?'

Rob shrugged a little awkwardly. He was hardly going to importune her to marry him when she was already betrothed and on the point of marrying another.

'It does not matter. There was something I wanted to ask you, but it is not appropriate.'

'You may ask me all the same.'

Rob looked at her. Her voice was quite expressionless but there was something in her eyes now, a glimmer of flame. There was also a certain weary knowledge. He could see that she knew all about propositions from gentlemen. He wondered how many she had received. And how many she had accepted...

'You may remember from our conversation a few days ago that I am in need of a wife,' he said. 'I was going to ask you to marry me.'

He saw her eyes widen with shock and realised that she had genuinely expected him to ask her to become his mistress. This different suggestion had thrown her utterly and convinced her, not unreasonably, that he was mad. She got to her feet and moved towards the fireplace to ring the bell for the maid. He got up quickly and caught her hand before she could press the button.

'Wait! It is not as you think. Let me explain.'

She stared at him for a moment, her eyes very wide and dark. Then she smiled. It was a mischievous smile and it lit sparks in her eyes and made him smile in return. She shook her head slightly, as though she could not quite believe what she was hearing.

'How you do surprise me,' she said. 'Very well, Robert Selborne, you have five minutes. And it had better be good.'

Half an hour and a pot of tea later, Jemima could see that Rob's plan could not possibly work. First, and most obviously, there were the terms of his father's will. Terms that she quite definitely did not fulfil.

'Your father's will specified that you should marry a lady present at your cousin Anne Selborne's wedding,' she said, wrinkling her brows.

Rob sat forward. 'That is correct.'

'But when it came to the point you could not bring yourself to apply to your cousin or to any of the other ladies present?'

Rob grinned boyishly. 'I confess that I could not stomach Augusta as a wife. As for the other ladies, there were only about four who were eligible in principle but none were suitable in practice.'

'And I am ineligible since I am no lady,' Jemima said. She saw the flicker of amusement in Rob's eyes and amended hastily, 'That is, I mean, of course, that I was not born a lady.'

'Maybe not, but you are indisputably a lady by education and behaviour,' Rob said.

Jemima looked at him. A small smile played around his mouth. He was watching her closely and his scrutiny made her feel hot and a little bit bothered. His brown gaze was very warm on her. It felt like a physical touch. And it was impossible to ignore the fact that he was quite handsome. She had noticed it outside the church and she noticed it again now. He had straight, dark brows the same colour as his hair, and his face was triangular, tapering to the firm line of his jaw and to a very determined chin. Jemima remembered his quiet strength and authority the previous night. She cleared her throat, made self-conscious by his regard.

'I am indubitably a chimney sweep's daughter, my lord.'

'You were educated as a lady, you speak like a lady and I am sure that you act like one as well.'

Jemima could not help a small smile. 'Sometimes I do. And sometimes I do not.'

Rob laughed. 'I hope to be on hand when you decide not to behave as a lady, Miss Jewell,' he murmured.

Jemima gave him a very direct look. 'I only mean that there are occasions on which I prefer a pint of ale to a thimbleful of Madeira.'

'Well, if it comes to that, so do I,' Rob said easily. He shifted. 'What we are discussing here is the fulfilment of the terms of the will, Miss Jewell, and whilst marrying you might not have been precisely what my father intended me to do, I do not think that anyone will dispute that you meet the conditions.'

Jemima frowned again. 'Your lawyer—'

'Will accept that you are the appropriate wife for me in every way.'

He seemed very certain. Jemima shook her head. She was sure that it could not be so easy.

Rob took her hand. 'Shall we move on to your next set of objections?'

The warm touch of his hand distracted Jemima, who had indeed been rehearsing her next point in her head. She looked at him suspiciously.

'How did you know that I had further reservations?'

Rob laughed. 'You have a very expressive face, Miss Jewell. I can see your doubts lining up in an orderly row.' His thumb brushed the back of her hand lightly. 'Come, tell me what the problem is.'

Jemima sighed. 'Even were I to agree that I fulfilled the criteria to become your wife, my lord, I am not entirely sure I understand what you are asking of me. You mentioned a marriage in name only.'

Rob released her hand and sat back. Jemima had the distinct impression that he was uncomfortable about something.

'That is correct,' he said. 'The marriage is to be a formality only. After the wedding I shall go directly to my home at Delaval in Oxfordshire. It is perfectly in order for you to stay in Town. I shall rent you an establishment and pay you an allowance to enable you to remove from your father's house—'

'—and when you come into your inheritance you will give me a lump sum from the capital,' Jemima finished. 'Once the fortune is secured, the marriage will be annulled. And all you demand in return is my discretion and my name on the marriage lines.' She frowned. 'I understand all of that, my lord. What I do not understand is why you are doing it.'

Rob shifted in his seat, and once again she had the impression that he was uneasy about something. 'It seems a convenient arrangement,' he said. 'I achieve my inheritance and you are free from the tyranny of your father.'

'Whilst neither of us is obliged to make a marriage that we dislike.' Jemima jumped to her feet. The plan sounded straightforward and yet she still had a strong conviction that it would not work. She turned to look at him.

Rob looked at her enquiringly. 'What is it?'

Jemima made a slight gesture. 'Why, merely that there is so much potential for something to go wrong!'

She bit her lip. 'You are intending to keep this a secret and I distrust that.'

'How so?'

'Simply because of your family! There is always a curious relative lurking in everyone's background. Mark my words—someone will discover what is going on and then we shall be in trouble!'

Rob laughed. 'I do not have many close relatives and I rarely see the ones that I do have.'

Jemima shook her head, unconvinced. 'What about Mr and Mrs Selborne and your cousins? You seemed quite close to them.'

Rob shrugged. 'I rarely see them. Ferdie Selborne is a friend of mine, but when I return to Delaval I doubt I shall even see Ferdie. He detests the country.'

'Hmm.' Jemima narrowed her gaze. 'What about your other friends?'

'I suppose that I should claim to have some or you would think me odd.' Rob smiled. 'I do have a couple of close friends and any number of acquaintances. Is that acceptable?'

Jemima tried not to smile. 'Pray take this seriously, sir! I have the conviction that something will go awry with your plan.'

Rob shrugged lightly. 'I do not see why it should. We shall tell no one of the marriage, we shall go our separate ways...' He stood up and came across to her. 'It is a simple plan and those are always the best. So do we have an agreement, Miss Jewell?'

Jemima hesitated. There was no denying that this unexpected offer had come at precisely the right moment to rescue her from a different, unwanted marriage. With some money behind her she might fulfil some of her dreams—to open a discreet establishment of her own where she might teach music and languages and various accomplishments in much the same way that Mrs Montagu had taught her. To follow in her mentor's footsteps would be a fine thing. At last she would have a measure of independence, far more than if she had had to sell her body to achieve it...

'How much allowance will you pay me?' she asked.

She saw Rob relax a little, as though he realised that her decision was made. He named a sum that made her head whirl. With an immediate payment of fifteen hundred pounds she could easily achieve her aim of establishing a school. And then to have a lump sum at the end of it as well... But she needed an establishment, of course.

She looked at Rob from under her lashes. 'You mentioned that you would rent me a house?' She took a deep breath. 'I shall require somewhere of decent size. A villa in Twickenham would be perfect.'

Rob did not look offended. On the contrary, he looked amused. 'I feel as though I am bargaining for a mistress rather than a wife, madam.'

The wayward images crowded Jemima's mind without warning. Rob visiting her at the villa...a boudoir full of tumbled sheets...his touch on her skin... A wave of heat suffused her whole body and made her tremble. But this was no time to be thinking such thoughts. Their agreement was purely business.

'I apologise,' she said, glad that her voice was steadier than her pulse. 'I grew up on a hard street and had to struggle for everything I gained, Lord Selborne. Forgive me if I sound determined to extract a good bargain.'

'Of course.' Rob inclined his head. He was watching her closely and Jemima knew that her heightened colour had not escaped him. She hoped that he was putting it down to embarrassment rather than arousal.

'Since I am demanding your discretion in this matter, I appreciate that I must arrange something suitable for you,' he said. 'You may leave it with me.'

Jemima let out a little breath of relief. This was simpler than she had expected. Rob Selborne seemed very easygoing. And of course he wanted this arrangement as much as she. Yet she knew that he was no soft touch. She had already seen a hard core underneath that easy exterior. She hesitated, then took a gamble.

'And I would like a small carriage, if you please.'

'Only a small one?' Rob was still smiling, but his dark gaze had an acute edge to it. 'Not a coach and four?'

'I believe that you are teasing me,' Jemima said. 'A small carriage will suffice. I am not greedy.'

Rob nodded. 'My man of business will attend to everything.' He smiled at her. 'Do we have a bargain, then, Miss Jewell?'

Jemima smiled back. 'I believe we do, sir.'

Rob relaxed. 'I will procure a special licence.' He paused as a thought struck him. 'I suppose that you are old enough to marry without your parents' consent?'

Jemima laughed. 'I am one and twenty, sir. How old are you?'

Rob raised his brows at the bluntness of her question. 'I am six and twenty, mistress.'

Jemima put her head on one side and studied him. He looked a little self-conscious under her scrutiny. 'Sometimes you look older,' she said, thinking aloud. 'As though you have seen too much.'

A shuttered look came into his eyes. 'I fear that that can be one of the effects of an army career,' he said, and though he spoke lightly Jemima heard the hardness in his voice. He took her hand. 'I will send word when all is arranged.'

Jemima nodded. 'And the house—and the money?'

'Will all be ready for you as soon as we are married.' Rob smiled. 'I will have my lawyer draw up a contact, Miss Jewell. I swear I would not cheat you.'

'I know,' Jemima said. 'You said that before—when you gave me the guinea.'

'I remember.' Suddenly there was an intent look in Rob's eyes and Jemima wondered if it had been a good idea to remind him about the guinea—and the kiss. But this was a business arrangement, a marriage of convenience. No kissing was required. All the same, she wondered if he would give her a peck on the cheek to seal the bargain.

After a second Rob held out his hand in a formal gesture. 'Thank you, Miss Jewell.'

Jemima put her hand into his. His own was cool and his touch made Jemima feel very hot. She tried to snatch her hand away, but Rob kept hold of it.

'What is your name?' he said abruptly.

Jemima felt slightly surprised to realise that he did not know. So much had happened between them already, but not the intimacy of a name.

She looked up into his eyes. They were very dark brown and flecked with green, the colour of moss. He had thick, dark lashes. She felt ever so slightly dizzy. No one had ever had this effect on her before and she was not entirely sure that she cared for it.

'My name is Jemima Mary Jewell. I suppose you need to know for the marriage licence?'

'I do,' Rob said, 'but that was not why I asked.' He

smiled slightly. 'Jemima Mary. That is pretty. You already know that my name is Robert.'

'Just Robert?' Jemima asked.

Rob looked slightly embarrassed. 'No. Robert Guy Lucius Cavendish Selborne.'

Jemima bit her lip to stop a smile. 'No wonder you settle for Rob.'

She did not imagine that she would have much opportunity to use his given name. It seemed a pity.

'Why did you ask me to marry you?' she said impulsively. 'Why me, particularly? I know you said that the other ladies at the wedding were not appropriate, but why ask me?'

There was a pause. Almost immediately, Jemima wished that she had not asked. She knew that he had chosen her because he had thought he might buy her. She was a tradesman's daughter and as such understood the value of every commodity. She was no sheltered lady. And she had agreed to be bought.

'I asked you because I thought you might agree,' Rob said. He smiled. 'And I am glad that you did.'

Jemima smiled too, reluctantly. She did not believe him, but she appreciated his gallantry. Rob gestured to the wedding veil, folded on the table beside her.

'You are sure that you will not change your mind?'

Jemima shook her head. She wondered if he would think her mercenary, prepared to throw over a suitor of her own kind for a more lucrative offer. He could not be more wrong, of course—this marriage was her only hope of escape from her father and at least he understood that much.

She smiled at him. 'I promise I shall not change my mind.'

She made to open the door for him, but he touched

her arm to detain her. 'You are sure that you are recovered from last night?'

The sudden intimacy of the subject caught Jemima off her guard. Her hand went to twitch the neckline of her dress in a telltale gesture that made sure the material covered the offending bruise. She saw Rob's gaze narrow.

'Is it very bad?'

'Not really.'

Jemima moved away from him and went over to the window. He had not even touched her, but she found that she was shaking and she was not sure why. It was something to do with the gentleness of his voice and the pity in his eyes. No man had ever treated her this way before. Jack was kind, but he was gruff with it and Rob's tenderness twisted her heart.

She looked up and saw that he was still watching her. 'Why did your father become so angry last night?' he asked.

Jemima touched the wedding veil lightly. 'I refused to marry the man of his choice.'

Rob's expression was grim. 'Was that why you agreed to marry me? To escape both of them?'

Jemima shrugged. 'In part. The options are limited for a female, my lord, particularly one in my situation.'

Rob took her chin in his hand and turned her face up to his. 'You should not take the responsibility for his behaviour on yourself, Jemima.'

'I don't.' Jemima slid out of his grip. 'You forget that I am not a lady, my lord. I have grown up with such things. Violence is commonplace on the street.'

Rob looked stubborn. 'I do not doubt it. But make no mistake, Jemima—violence is no respecter of persons. It can happen to anyone, gently born and bred or not. And the ugliness of it is the same, be the victim man, woman or child, Duchess or—'

'Chimney sweep's apprentice?'

'Precisely so.' Rob smiled slightly. 'Are you sure that you will not come with me now?'

Jemima smiled. 'I will not. But I thank you for the offer.'

Rob let out his breath on a sigh of resignation. He took her father's handbill from his pocket. 'Do you have a pen and ink?'

He waited as Jemima fetched some from the bureau, then scribbled quickly on the back of the handbill.

'This is my address. If you need to, you may come to me at any time.'

Jemima nodded. Her throat felt strangely tight. 'Thank you, my lord.'

Rob kissed her cheek. His lips felt soft against her skin—a butterfly touch.

'Goodbye then, Jemima. I will send word to you in secret when the marriage is to take place. I will arrange it as quickly as I can.'

At the door he paused, removing his signet ring from his right hand. 'Here, take this. It will be too big for you and you could not wear it without arousing suspicion, but I want you to have it.'

Jemima stared, turning the ring over between her fingers. It was made of solid gold and it was heavy and worn. It felt warm from contact with his body. She could see the patch of paler skin on his hand where the ring had been.

'But you cannot give this to me—'

'We are betrothed. You are mine now and I want you to have the ring.'

Rob sounded adamant. Jemima felt a tiny shiver. She slid the ring into her bodice.

'Thank you. I will keep it safe.'

She gave him her hand and he kissed it, old-fashioned style. Jemima reflected that, for all his youth, there was much that was old-fashioned about Robert Selborne. She wondered if it was his army experience that had made him grow up so quickly. He was not at all like the gilded youth who roistered in the streets, turning over the street-sellers' carts for a jest, destroying a man's livelihood and moving on without a thought.

She saw him to the door, then went back into the sitting room and collapsed on the sofa, clutching one of the fat cushions to her breast. She felt breathless with disbelief and release. Her head was buzzing.

She could not believe that Rob had so carelessly bestowed on her the means to achieve all that she had ever wanted. It mattered nothing to him—all he needed was her name on a marriage certificate so that he could meet the terms of his father's will. But for her it was the whole world. At last she could achieve her dream.

She would have bookshelves from floor to ceiling and visit Hatchard's to stock them. She would buy a piano—a grand piano, since the rooms of the villa in Twickenham would surely be large enough to contain one with ease. And she would buy a harp and a spinet. She would need to practise the harp though, since she had never been as good at playing that as she had with keyboard instruments. Then there was the sheet music. She would buy piles of it, enough to fill the air like confetti…

Jemima laughed, throwing the cushion up in the air in relief and light-headed pleasure. To have money and yet to have no husband or father commanding her behaviour... It was almost too good to be true.

She thought of Rob Selborne, with his aristocratic looks and his courteous manners. He was what the sweeps would call a swell, a real gentleman. He was so *nice* that he was asking to be robbed blind.

Jemima shook her head. It was lucky that Rob had made his bargain with her, for she would never cheat him where others might. He was a real gentleman and, though she was only a counterfeit lady, they had made a deal. A marriage convenient to both.

She remembered the current of attraction that had run between the two of them and put the thought aside with another shake of her head. Physical desire was a snare that brought unhappiness. The hard-headed cynicism she had learned as a child on the streets told her that. It would be foolish in the extreme to build too much on the feelings that she already had for Robert Selborne, to build on the respect—and the attraction. Their arrangement meant that they would be spending very little time in each other's company, married or not. Rob would go directly to his estate in Oxfordshire after the wedding and she would go to Twickenham, and very likely they would only communicate via Rob's man of business. And after a year or so, the marriage would be over.

Jemima felt a pang of disappointment that she could not deny. She knew that she wished to spend time with Robert Selborne. She wished to know him better. He was to be her husband and, ironically, she would know nothing of him at all.

She got to her feet and moved over to the window. The early morning mist had lifted and the sun was coming through, pale and golden. It looked like being a lovely day.

Jemima picked up the wedding veil and draped it over her head. She was just twirling in front of the mirror, smiling as she watched her reflection, when her mother came in. Mrs Jewell smiled too when she saw what her daughter was doing. For a moment mother and daughter stood before the mirror, united in their happiness but dreaming very different dreams. And against Jemima's skin Rob Selborne's signet ring felt very warm.

Chapter Five

'You've gone mad,' Jack Jewell said flatly. 'Stark staring mad. You should be locked up in Bedlam.'

Jemima and her brother were standing on Blackfriars Bridge, side by side, leaning their elbows on the parapet as they ate their dinner. Below them the river flowed, brown and ponderous at low tide. The mudlarks skipped across the exposed flats looking for pieces of coal and the seagulls screamed overhead.

Jemima scooped a piece of hot eel out of the packet in her hand and swallowed it whole. It was salty and smooth. She licked her fingers. Mrs Montagu had always said that food tasted better served on a plate and eaten with a knife and fork, but then Mrs Montagu had probably never eaten fresh, hot eels in spiced gravy direct from the stall, nor oysters at four for a penny. There were some experiences that gentility could not buy.

The breeze off the river was chilly and the food was cooling quickly. Jemima gulped down another slippery piece of eel.

'I know you think I am unwise—'

'No, I don't. I think you're idiotic. I've just told you.' Jack scowled. 'You are going to marry a man you do not know, and all because you cannot bear to wed Jim Veale.'

'It isn't that simple.' Jemima crumpled up the empty packet and wiped her fingers clean. 'You don't understand—'

'Oh, yes, I do. People always say that when they know you understand perfectly.' Jack's scowl deepened. 'You haven't thought any of this through, Jem. Who is this gentleman? Is he straight or will he swindle you?' He turned round to face her abruptly. 'Will he tell you this is a business arrangement—and then demand his married rights and privileges?' Jack drove his hands into his pockets. 'Because if he does, Jem, there's not a hope in hell that you can avoid it.'

Jemima sighed. She understood her brother's concern—appreciated it, even—but she was not going to let his scruples stand in her way.

'You are making this a deal too complicated, Jack. Lord Selborne and I have made an agreement. My name on a marriage certificate in return for his money.'

'Suppose he doesn't come through with the money?' Jack said. 'I thought he was supposed to be poor? When he has what he wants he'll leave you high and dry. And how would you explain that to Father when you run crying home?' He smashed his fist down on the stone parapet. 'He's using you, Jem! And you are so blind to everything but your desire for an independent life that you are prepared to accept it!'

Jemima turned away, staring out across the water. The cold breeze stung her cheeks. Jack could always be relied upon to speak his mind and there was a lot of truth in his words.

'We are both using each other, Jack. It is a means to get what we both want. I want my independence and the chance to set up a school. Rob—Lord Selborne—wishes to gain his father's fortune—'

'A fortune hunter!' Jack looked disgusted. 'Why can he not marry an heiress, one of his own kind?'

Jemima sighed. 'I have explained all this to you. He had to marry one of the ladies at the wedding and none of them was suitable.'

'They probably all turned him down, more like. There must be something wrong with him.'

'No, there isn't,' Jemima said. She smiled a little. 'Indeed, Jack, he is…a very personable man.'

More than just personable, in fact, but she was not going to tell Jack that.

Jack snorted. 'Even so, there must be something wrong with him. It's just that you don't know it yet. But you'll find out quick enough.'

'Maybe I will.' Jemima folded her arms against the cold wind, huddling a little deeper into her coat. Now that the warming effect of the eels had worn off she was feeling chilled. Inside and out. Jack had planted the doubts in her mind and they were growing. It was three days since Rob had called and she had been carried along by excitement and anticipation—until she had decided to confide in her brother and he had made her see the truth of her plans. At best it suddenly looked like a tawdry bargain and at worst she could be making a huge mistake.

And yet she had trusted Rob Selborne. She had no notion why, but she was convinced that he would not cheat her. He had given her his word, and shown her great kindness. Perhaps I am easily bought, Jemima thought. Speak kindly to me and offer me something that I truly want…

'You seemed glad enough of his help the other night,'

she said crossly. 'You know that you could not have broken that door down on your own.'

'I would've fetched an axe,' Jack said, scowling. 'I didn't trust the man then and I don't trust him now.'

'You thought he wanted me to be his mistress then,' Jemima pointed out. 'You should be glad that it's marriage he's offering me.'

Jack made a noise of disgust. He turned so that he was leaning back against the stone parapet. 'Of course, there is another explanation for your behaviour,' he said casually.

Jemima raised her brows, suspicious of his bland tone. 'Oh yes?'

'Yes. You have fallen in love with this Selborne fellow, or think you have, and are therefore prepared to do anything he asks. You've read too much about love in those books of yours, and now you want to experience it yourself.'

Jemima glared. 'That is not funny, Jack. What has love got to do with it? You know I have no time for that nonsense. Rob Selborne and I have met less than a handful of times.'

'And the first time you met, he was kissing you as though he meant it.' Jack gave her an old-fashioned look. 'And then he wants to marry you. Funny that.'

'I…he…' Jemima floundered. 'He was kissing me for good luck at the wedding. Just as you were kissing the bride, if you recall.'

'I wasn't kissing her as though there was no tomorrow,' Jack said bluntly.

'No,' Jemima said, feeling defensive, 'you save that for Lady Alford, do you not?'

Beatrice Alford was the widow of a City Alderman and had had Jack's undivided attention for almost a year. Jack always said that chimney sweeps had unrivalled opportunities for seduction. They had access to the entire house—including the bedrooms.

Jack shifted, blushing as much as one of his swarthy complexion was able. 'That's at an end.'

'Is it? Why is that?'

'For the same reason that you cannot be happy with your flash gent. I was sick of being a backstairs lover.' Jack scowled down at the cobbles. 'Oh, I was welcome in milady's bed, but not to grace her table.'

'I did not think that was what you wanted from her.'

Jack flashed her a black look. 'Don't be stupid, sis. I didn't want to sit down to eat with her. But I needed to feel that I could if I *had* wanted. Do you understand? It's all about respect—and knowing one's place.'

Jemima wrinkled up her brow. She knew what Jack meant. It was demeaning to be treated as though you were not good enough. 'Yes, I do understand.'

'Then don't go getting any silly ideas about being Countess of Selborne. You'd never be accepted. You'd be nothing better than a backstairs wife. Everyone would turn away when you walked by. They'd put their parasols up in your face like they did to Lady Denbigh.'

'She was a circus rider.'

'Circus rider, chimney sweep's daughter—where's the difference?'

'It is different when the daughter of a rich cit wishes to marry into the nobility.'

Jack drove his hands into his pockets and started walking. 'Of course that's different. Usually they are several generations away from the smell of the shop. Or if not, they are so rich it can be overlooked. But we don't even smell of the shop, Jemima. We smell of *soot*.

We're way down the pile, and not even Mrs Montagu's scented parlour can change that for you.'

They were walking towards Westminster now and Jack set a brisk pace. Jemima trotted along beside, trying to keep up.

'I would agree with you if I was secretly desiring the sort of match you describe. But I have no thoughts in that direction.' She paused, feeling the tiniest pang of guilt. Perhaps that was not quite true. She *had* allowed herself a very small dream about being the Countess of Selborne in reality and not merely in name only. It had been delightful when Rob had kissed her and it had started to undermine all her cynical beliefs about love. But to think like that was foolish. Love was a luxury that was not for the likes of her.

'Neither Lord Selborne nor I look at the marriage in that way, Jack,' she said. 'I keep telling you that there is no sentiment involved, only business.'

'And does your self-respect not revolt at that, Jem?' Jack glared at her. 'You would take the money of a man who would not wish you to grace his table—or his name, for that matter, since the truth of this marriage is to be kept a secret?'

Jemima flushed. She raised her chin. 'Evidently my self-respect is not such a delicate thing as yours is, Jack. I will take Lord Selborne's money and be grateful for the chance it gives me!'

Jack swore under his breath.

'And,' Jemima added crossly, ignoring him, 'it seems I cannot do right for doing wrong in your eyes! Firstly I am a fool for apparently falling in love, and then I have no self-respect for accepting an arranged match! Make your mind up, Jack!'

There was a silence between them until they reached the corner of East Chepe, then Jack spoke again.

'And you are quite happy to cut yourself off from your family in this way?'

Jemima sighed. This was the aspect of the case that made her the unhappiest, for clearly she would have to keep her whereabouts a secret from her father, at least until his anger had had time to abate. She had no real regrets about that, but she was sorry to hurt her mother.

'I shall not be utterly cut off. I shall have you.'

Jack gave her an exasperated look. 'And our mother? She does not deserve this of you, Jem.'

'I know,' Jemima said, unhappily. 'But in a little while, when Father is resigned to it, I may come back and see you all.'

Jack was shaking his head. 'You are living in a fool's paradise. He will cut you off, Jem. He will forbid Mother to see you. There is no generosity in him. This is a man who still sends small children up the chimneys even though there are machines that will do the work instead. He is not quick to change—or forgive.'

'Nor am I.'

Jack sighed. 'No. You have a great deal in common, you two. Perhaps that is why you can no longer live together.'

They had argued themselves to a standstill. Jemima could see the stubborn lines settle about Jack's mouth, then he relaxed on a sigh.

'Very well. Since you will not listen to sense, do you still wish me to be your bridesmaid?'

Jemima gave a little squeak and threw herself into his arms. 'Oh, Jack! Thank you! You will be the most handsome bridesmaid in the whole of London!'

Jack grinned. 'I still think you are making a monumentally stupid mistake, Jem,' he said, as he hugged her back. 'It will all end in tears. Just you see.'

'No, it won't,' Jemima said. She stepped back. There was something that she wanted to say, but it was a great risk.

'Jack, I thought that, once I was established in Twickenham I might arrange to visit Tilly.'

Jack's expression was suddenly as remote as stone. 'So that's what you intend to spend your new-found fortune on? Don't be stupid, sis. Tilly is content and settled. She doesn't need an interfering aunt—nor a father neither.'

Jemima wrinkled up her face. She knew she was treading on dangerous ground here, opening old wounds. Jack never spoke of his daughter, but that did not mean that he never thought of her.

'I wanted to know for myself that she was well and happy,' Jemima said hesitantly. 'For Beth's sake.'

Jack's eyes were black with fury now. 'Well? Of course she's well! She is the ward of a nobleman and far better placed in the world than we have ever been. There is nothing we can give her. Leave her be...'

There was a silence. 'I thought that you would want to know,' Jemima said.

'Well, I don't want to know,' Jack said. 'Let it go, Jemima. If you must marry your fancy lord, do it for any reason you like, but don't do it for this.'

'You are taking a very great risk, my lord,' Jemima observed. Some fifteen minutes previously the maid had brought a note from Rob Selborne into the office at the back of the premises in Great Portland Street and five minutes after that, Jemima was in a hackney carriage with him driving through the streets of London.

Rob raised a lazy brow. 'Why is that?'

'Because someone might see you,' Jemima said. 'I thought that we were not to meet until the wedding?'

Rob shrugged. 'I wanted to talk to you. I did not wish simply to summon you to the church like some sort of servant.' He frowned. 'That's too shabby, Jemima.'

Jemima felt a warm glow of pleasure at his words and quelled it at once. He had wanted to see her, to talk to her. That was precisely the sort of behaviour she should be discouraging. The two of them were destined to go their separate ways and they might as well start now. Even so, she did not demand to be taken straight back home.

'Where are we going?' she asked. 'Do we drive around London until we have finished talking, just to make sure that no one notices us together?'

Rob shot her a look. 'I had not quite decided where we could go.'

'What about the Tower of London? Only tourists go there.'

Rob shook his head. 'It is not the most pleasant of days for walking outside. Besides, I wished to sit down and talk to you properly.'

'Then I have the very place,' Jemima said. 'The Hoop and Grapes in Drury Lane.'

Rob looked a little startled. 'Is that not a flash house?'

'It is.' Jemima gave him a challenging look. 'I thought that you wished to be unrecognised? I assume no one would know you there?'

Rob sat back with a grin. 'I imagine not. We shall go there if you wish.'

The taproom at the Hoop and Grapes was almost full, but Jemima found a small table in a corner and slid along the bench, leaving Rob the seat on the old settle that faced outward into the room. The air was thick with the fug of smoke and the smell of ale, and although the conversation did not stop when they walked in, Jemima knew that everyone was watching them. She could see that Rob knew it too. There was a faint smile on his lips but it was belied by the watchful look in his dark eyes. Jemima was not surprised. There were half a dozen men there who would slide a blade between your ribs first and ask questions later.

'Do you come here often?' Rob asked, raising a hand to summon a serving girl.

Jemima watched in mixed surprise and chagrin as two girls converged on their table and started to squabble over who should serve them. It was rare enough to get any service in the Hoop, let alone the undivided attention of two of the servants.

'A jug of ale, please,' Rob said, giving a coin to the nearest girl. She held on to his hand for a moment and giggled. Jemima felt extremely irritated.

'Yes, sir.' The girl dropped a curtsy, her expert gaze assessing him. 'Yes, my lord,' she amended. 'And if you're wanting anything else, my lord...'

Rob gave her a smile that made Jemima's irritation levels soar. 'I'll be sure to let you know,' he said.

Jemima set her lips into a straight, disapproving line. It was her own fault for bringing Rob here. It had been a childish impulse, to show off and also to see if he would object. So far he was passing the test with rather more aplomb than she had imagined.

'Regretting it yet?' Rob asked affably.

Jemima looked at him sharply. 'Regretting what?'

'Bringing me here.' Rob gestured around the tap-room. 'Did you want to scare me?'

Their gazes locked. 'Could I?' Jemima asked.

Rob leaned back against the plaster wall and stretched out his legs. He looked extremely elegant in the squalor of the Hoop and Grapes, but also, to Jemima's surprise, rather tough. In such surroundings he could hold his own.

'I doubt it,' he said. 'I have drunk in far worse places than this when I was on campaign.'

Jemima nodded. 'I imagine so. I did not think that you scared easily, Lord Selborne, not even if I told you that the fellow in the corner is a scamp—that is, a highwayman.'

'Is he?'

'Oh, yes. Ned Macaine. He works the Great North Road.'

Rob's lips twitched. 'He seems to like the look of you, Miss Jewell.'

It was true. The highwayman, a strikingly handsome young man, raised his glass to her. Jemima, sensing the opportunity for revenge, smiled back sweetly.

Rob laughed. 'So. We are all square, I believe. But you did not answer me. Do you come here often?'

Jemima shook her head. 'Not any more. This is Jack's favourite tavern, which was why I knew we would be safe here.'

'Your father does not drink here?'

'No.' Jemima laughed. 'Father is far too proud to frequent the Hoop these days. He thinks himself too good for places like this.' She looked around. 'Those gentlemen over there—the ones with the clay pipes, playing the game of cribbage—they are master sweeps. Do not worry. They will not give us away.'

'I'm not worried,' Rob said. He poured some of the ale into her tankard. 'I am sure that you will protect me from all comers, Miss Jewell.'

'I am sure that you can look after yourself,' Jemima said truthfully. She took a mouthful of ale. 'So, what is there for us to discuss?'

'The wedding, for one thing,' Rob said. 'It is fixed for ten o'clock in three days' time, at the church of St Saviour.'

'At Borough?'

'I am afraid so.' Rob scowled into his glass. 'In the interests of discretion…'

'I understand. And do not worry—I have walked around worse neighbourhoods than the Borough.'

'I dare say.' Rob flashed another glance around the tavern. He looked moody. 'It is not that I do not think you can stomach it, Miss Jewell, it is that I feel it is not good enough for you.'

Jemima felt an errant tug of emotion. 'You are very kind, but I assure you it will do very well. It is only a means to an end, after all.'

It seemed the wrong thing to say, ungracious, somehow. Rob's scowl deepened. 'I suppose that your brother will be accompanying you?'

'Yes, he will.'

'No doubt I should be glad.'

Jemima sighed. 'You do not like each other, do you?'

Rob's expression eased slightly. 'It is more that I believe your brother does not trust me and I understand why.'

'So do I.' It was Jemima's turn to frown. 'I still think the pair of you are very annoying.'

Rob laughed. 'I beg your pardon. By the way, I shall also be bringing a wedding guest. My cousin Ferdie is to be my groomsman.'

Jemima drained her tankard of ale. 'Have you told him everything?'

'I have. And sworn him to secrecy.'

There was a silence between them.

'Do we go back now?' Jemima asked. 'Now that that is all decided?'

'Not yet,' Rob said. 'I am enjoying myself far too much.'

Jemima looked him over thoughtfully. He did indeed look entirely at ease as he lounged on the settle, one shoulder propped against the wall, the folds of his coat falling open to reveal the buff pantaloons and plain navy jacket beneath. Every inch of him spoke of quality, from the linen of his shirt to the high polish on his boots. No wonder the serving girls were positively panting after him.

'I hope that your brother will be able to keep an eye on you when you go to live in Twickenham,' Rob said. 'Although Churchward, my man of business, will attend to anything that you wish, it will be comforting to know that you have other people to call on.'

'Oh, I shall still see Jack,' Jemima agreed. She felt slightly guilty. She had resolved not to tell Rob of any of her plans for a school, thinking that he might cut up rough at the thought of her working for a living. She might be the Countess of Selborne in name only, soon to be Countess no more, but in the interim he would probably expect her to live quietly.

'So, what do you intend to do with your time when you are there?' Rob asked.

Jemima jumped. It seemed that he could add an ability to read her mind to his other attributes.

'Do?' She knew she sounded evasive. 'I understood that ladies did not ''do'' anything. I have been looking forward to doing nothing at all.'

Rob grinned. His hand covered hers, vital and warm. Jemima jumped again, for a different reason.

'Try telling me the truth, Jemima,' he said. 'You don't strike me as the sort of lady who would be content to sit about doing nothing. So what are you planning?'

Blue eyes met brown. There was a distinctly quizzical twinkle in Rob's own. Jemima capitulated.

'Oh, very well! If you must know, I intend to open a school.' She saw his expression and hurried on. 'Do not worry—I was not going to use my own name! No one will know! But I should run mad if I had nothing to do with myself all day. Besides, the good wives of Twickenham would have smoked me out within days. Genteel females have a way of weighing up newcomers amongst them.'

Rob looked slightly startled. 'Whatever do you mean?'

Jemima laughed. 'Why, merely that a mysterious lady who appears from nowhere and has no visible means of support is quickly designated as being of shady virtue. It would cause a monstrous amount of gossip. Whereas a teacher of music is pegged as an indigent gentlewoman and everyone allows her to get on with her business, whilst pitying her a little, of course.'

Rob shook his head ruefully. 'Jemima, you are a dreadful cynic!'

Jemima shrugged. 'Doubtless I have seen more of the world than other ladies of your acquaintance. I know for a fact that the ladies of Twickenham would consider me either a dangerous widow out to snatch their husbands, or a retired courtesan pretending to respectability. This way they will know that I am nothing more than a schoolteacher and we may all be comfortable.' She looked at him. 'You do not object, I hope?'

'Would it matter if I did?'

'Well, of course! You hold the purse strings!'

Rob laughed again, but there was bitterness in it. 'Damn it all, Jemima, is that all that it means to you?'

Jemima blushed. She did not wish Rob to think her mercenary, but on the other hand she had sworn to herself that sentiment had no place in this match. She was not about to make matters more difficult that they needed to be.

'I thought that we had a business arrangement, my lord?' she queried lightly. 'How else would you like it to be?'

She realised her mistake when Rob's hand came up to brush a strand of hair back from her cheek. His touch was gentle. His gaze held hers. 'Did you never wish to marry for love?'

Jemima shifted uncomfortably on the bench, looking away. 'Not particularly. Marriage and love do not generally go together, do they, my lord? For your class as well as mine, marriages are made in the bank and not in heaven.'

'You did not love the man to whom you were betrothed?'

Jemima had almost forgotten Jim Veale. 'Jim? No! He was pleasant, but that is all. The marriage was intended to be a dynastic one.'

'So—no love.'

'Love is lust dressed up in pretty clothes,' Jemima said. 'No more, no less. It always ends in tears.'

Rob was frowning a little now. 'Has somebody hurt you, Jemima? Is that what this is about?'

Jemima rested her chin on her hand. 'Not in the way that you mean.' Her gaze sought Rob's, begging for understanding. 'There were girls who climbed chimneys with me as children and now they are in the Haymarket, selling themselves.' She shrugged. 'Talk of love seems dishonest to me. Sex is a counter people play to gain what they want—power, money, privileges, or simply to survive. And love is just the name they give it to make it seem more acceptable.'

Rob grimaced. 'It is usually the male of the species who is cynical about love.'

'Then what about you?' Jemima challenged. 'Have you ever been in love, my lord?'

Rob gave her a long, slow smile. It did strange things to Jemima's equilibrium. 'No,' he said. 'I have never been in love. But I would never rule it out.'

The sounds of the alehouse faded then as he captured and held her gaze with his. The heat flooded Jemima's body at the expression in his eyes. His leg brushed against hers under the rickety table and suddenly she felt acutely aware of him. She shifted on the seat, wanting to escape yet somehow pinned to the spot. Then from above them a voice spoke.

'Want to throw the swell over and come with me instead, darling?'

Jemima tore her gaze from Rob and looked up into the admiring face of the highwayman Ned Macaine. She smiled sweetly.

'No, thank you, Mr Macaine, but I am flattered by your offer.'

The highwayman shrugged. 'Can't blame a man for trying.'

Rob straightened. 'No, indeed,' he said, 'but the lady is already spoken for.'

Macaine gave him a comprehensive look that lasted fully five seconds, then he nodded and slapped him on the back. 'Lucky man,' he said. He bowed to Jemima. 'If you change your mind, darling…'

Jemima laughed and got to her feet. 'We had better be going, my lord, before one or other of us is carried off!'

Rob took her hand and tucked it through his arm as they walked out of the taproom. 'You will find Twickenham so dull after this,' he observed. 'I do not know how you shall bear it.'

Twickenham. Jemima felt a chill touch her. She had completely forgotten that she was to go her own way and Rob his. That was the agreement. There was nothing that she could do about it.

Chapter Six

'Fetching little thing, ain't she?' Ferdie Selborne said in Rob's ear as together they watched Miss Jemima Jewell making her way up the aisle of St Saviour's Church off Borough High Street. 'Don't follow your logic in doing this, Rob, but I can't fault your taste.'

Rob gritted his teeth. He would far rather have asked one of his other friends to be his groomsman, but most of them were hopelessly indiscreet and this was a situation that demanded the utmost secrecy. At least Ferdie could be relied on to hold his tongue about the wedding, even if he would probably try to seduce the bride from under Rob's nose.

The Church of St Saviour was tucked away down an alley in the unsavoury part of town that had once housed the notorious prisons of the Clink and the Marshalsea. It was an insalubrious and downright dangerous area, and Rob was ashamed to have chosen it. He had done so because it was a place where nobody asked any questions. The priest had glanced at the special licence with absolutely no interest whatsoever but had brightened considerably when Rob had pressed a fat purse of money into his hand. Rob had been happy with the arrangements until he had met with Jemima a few days before, and then he had felt ashamed. This simply was not good enough for her.

Rob felt this keenly as he watched Jemima walk towards him on her brother's arm. Jack Jewell was looking grim. In fact, he looked as though he wanted to knock Rob to the ground.

Jemima, in comparison, looked quite serene. Loosening his neckcloth, which suddenly felt intolerably tight, Rob wished that he could match her apparent composure. He felt tense and unsure.

Jemima was wearing a simple dress of mauve figured silk, and a straw hat with matching ribbons that framed her piquant little face. The sun, striking through the dusty glass windows, touched her face with a luminous light. Rob caught his breath.

She reached his side and glanced up at him. Her gaze seemed a little shy. For a second Rob saw an echo of his own nervousness in her eyes. He took her hand in his own and felt her fingers cling briefly to his.

The marriage service passed in a blur. He heard himself making the responses and Jemima's voice, quiet but sure. In a strange way her presence steadied him. She spoke with dignity, as though she had every intention of honouring her wedding vows. Rob felt wretched when he thought of the planned annulment. He was making promises which he had no intention of keeping. His parents had not always been in accord, but they had stayed with their marriage through thick and thin. What he was doing did not feel right, but now it was too late. He must simply concentrate on Delaval and remind himself that he now had the means to restore it.

'You may now kiss the bride.'

Jemima tilted her face up to his and for a brief second their lips met. Then she stepped back.

There was an awkward silence for a moment after the service had finished, then Rob offered the bride his arm and they moved towards their guests. As in Great Portland Street, Rob offered his hand to Jack Jewell and after a long pause Jack shook it. Both of them understood without words that Jack was only doing it for Jemima's sake. Rob suppressed a smile. Jack Jewell did not like him and he could hardly blame the man.

'How do you do, Jewell?' he said politely.

'How do you do, Selborne?' Jack responded, blank faced.

Rob turned to Ferdie. 'May I introduce my cousin, Ferdinand Selborne?'

Ferdie bowed. 'Lady Selborne. Mr Jewell.'

Rob saw Jemima's eyes widen to be addressed by her married name, as though the reality of the situation was only just becoming plain to her. She coloured prettily and Rob felt a rush of unexpected pleasure, tempered by a certain exasperation with himself. On reflection it had probably been a big mistake to propose a marriage of convenience with a lady to whom he was so strongly attracted.

When he had first had the idea of marrying Jemima it had seemed perfect, a marriage in name only that would enable him to fulfil the terms of both wills in one fell swoop. Their marriage would meet his father's requirement, but because Jemima would not be living with him, he need never disclose the terms of his grandmother's will to her. He could achieve his bride and his celibacy in one simple move. Best of all, he could devote himself to restoring Delaval and go some small way to assuaging the guilt he felt at neglecting his home and family.

Yet the reality seemed to be less simple. Already he was starting to care rather too much for Jemima. When he had left her ten days ago at her father's house, it had been one of the most difficult things that he had ever had to do. The compulsion to take her with him, to tell her that she must accompany him, had been incredibly strong. And when he had seen her again, his feelings had simply strengthened each time. He was aware that he barely knew her, that she was no sheltered débutante in need of his protection, and yet the urge to defend her was overwhelming. He had never experienced a feeling like it. It seemed he could not help himself.

Ferdie had struck up an easy conversation with Jemima now and was at his most urbane. 'If you require anything whilst Rob is out of town, you must not hesitate to approach me, Lady Selborne,' he was saying, in a manner that set Rob's teeth on edge. 'I should be delighted to visit you at Twickenham.'

Rob felt Jack Jewell stiffen beside him. For another brief moment they were united in the same cause. Jack gave Rob a meaningful look. Rob intervened.

'There will be no need for that, Ferdie,' he said sharply. 'Churchward may attend to any matters of business for Lady Selborne, and I am sure that Mr Jewell will be on hand if my wife requires any help whilst I am out of town.'

He felt Jack Jewell's dark gaze rest on him mockingly and met his eyes very directly. 'Will you not, Jewell?'

After a moment Jack bowed slightly. 'Of course, Selborne.'

Rob took Jemima's arm. 'If you gentleman would excuse us for a moment...'

Both Ferdie and Jack looked surprised, as though Rob could not possibly have anything he wished to say to his bride. After a moment they moved aside a little, awkwardly avoiding each other's eyes and conspicuously not speaking. Rob drew Jemima into the shelter of a pillar and took a letter out of his pocket.

'I did not think that we would have much opportunity to talk on the journey to Churchward's chambers as I assumed you would wish your brother to accompany us. I have written everything down for you. If you need anything in future, send for Churchward. He will come to you at once. He is a good man and is to be relied upon. I have written his direction here, along with all the other information you need, but you will see where to find his chambers shortly.'

Jemima nodded. She was biting her bottom lip and for a moment looked a little apprehensive. Rob tapped the letter for a moment, then handed it over to her with a sigh. Although he had done his best to think of everything that she might need, his letter, like everything else on this curious wedding day, seemed inadequate.

'Churchward will escort you to the house at Twickenham on the morrow. Only attend him in his chambers whenever you wish to go.'

Jemima nodded again. Her eyes were very wide and dark. Rob wished he could read her expression and know what she was thinking.

'And for God's sake do not ask Ferdie for any help, nor tolerate his company if he should seek you out.'

A spark of humour lit Jemima's eyes. 'Have no fear, my lord. I am not such a fool as that. I know exactly the sort of gentleman your cousin is.'

Once again Rob was reminded that he was not dealing with a naïve young girl. 'Yes, of course. I do not wish him to importune you, that is all.'

He saw her brows lift very slightly. 'He is your cousin, my lord. I must still be civil.'

Rob smiled. 'Ferdie is indeed my cousin, which is how I know him so well. I would not trust him with my sister, let alone my wife. If you need to be uncivil, do not let it trouble you for a moment.'

Jemima gave him a glimmer of a smile in return. 'I shall remember that. Do you then have a sister, my lord?'

'I do. Camilla. She is married to a naval captain and is living in the Indies at present. I told you that my close relatives would not trouble us. I will tell you all about Camilla one day—' He broke off, thinking that if all went as they had planned it then he would not have the opportunity to speak to Jemima very much, let alone chat about his family. He would secure his inheritance, pay her off, meet the condition of the hundred days celibacy and have his marriage annulled... And that would be that. The Countess of Selborne would disappear as though she had never been.

'I will come and see you when I return from Oxfordshire,' he said abruptly, making a spur of the moment plan to return to London. 'I shall be up in Town in a month or two.'

Jemima looked startled. 'I do not believe that that would be a good idea, my lord. If you were seen calling on me it would give rise to speculation, which is precisely what we wish to avoid. I shall not be using my married name and of course our association remains secret. It will be better if we conduct all our business through Mr Churchward.'

Rob nodded. He could not fault her logic even if the arrangement seemed a little cold. It was precisely the sort of agreement he should be seeking himself. A marriage in name only, severed as quickly as it had been contracted. The fact that this was no longer exactly what he wanted was a problem that he would have to deal with. He felt irritable and frustrated, and was not sure why. If only he did not feel this damnable responsibility for her! And an even more inconvenient urge to seek her company…

He suddenly remembered that he had one other thing to give to her. He groped in his pocket and retrieved a small parcel wrapped in brown paper.

'Here. I have a wedding gift for you. It is only a small thing…'

Jemima took it and unwrapped the paper. She was silent for so long that Rob hurried into speech again, afraid that she did not like it.

'It is nothing special. I merely saw the book in the grate and thought you might have lost your copy to the fire.'

'I did.' There was a strange, wondering tone in Jemima's voice. '*Castle Rackrent.* How kind of you.'

Rob felt a rush of relief. 'You like it?'

'Of course. Thank you, my lord.' Jemima looked up at him. Her brilliant smile made Rob feel slightly dizzy. He blinked as she touched his arm lightly. 'It is no small thing at all, and I am extremely grateful.'

They stood looking at one another until Jemima seemed to wake up of a sudden.

'Should we not be going? If we are to see Mr Churchward this afternoon—'

'Of course,' Rob said. He offered her his arm. 'My carriage is round the back.'

'Then let us hope it still has its wheels,' Jemima murmured. 'Excuse me, my lord. I must speak with my brother. I should be glad for him to accompany us to Mr Churchward's office.'

Rob watched as she went over to Jack Jewell. Jack straightened up from where he had been propping up one of the pews, and came across to join her, wrapping the black cloak about her and steering her towards the door. She looked very small. Rob felt a mingled pang of envy and possessiveness. It was he who should be escorting Jemima from the church, not her brother. He saw that she was tugging the wedding ring off her finger as she walked and stuffing it in her reticule. The sight made him feel angry, although he understood her reasons. This was not a neighbourhood in which one walked around displaying jewellery made of gold.

Rob turned to find Ferdie at his elbow. His cousin was also watching Jemima's small figure and he was smiling wolfishly.

'Damned fine filly, Rob, you lucky so-and-so. Wouldn't mind consoling her on your behalf—'

Rob swung round on him so violently that Ferdie flinched back, a look compounded of amazement and fear on his face. 'I say, old fellow, wouldn't hit a man in a house of God, would you?'

'That depends on the provocation,' Rob said icily. 'You're speaking of my *wife*, Ferdie.'

'But she's a sweep's girl,' Ferdie pointed out. 'Fair game. Suppose I should have got in before the wedding, though.'

Rob took his cousin's neckcloth in his hand and pulled tight. To hear Ferdie speak slightingly of Jemima and make assumptions about her virtue was intolerable.

Ferdie wheezed, 'Steady on, Robert!'

'Never speak about Jemima in that way again,' Rob said, through his teeth. He let Ferdie go and stood back.

'I'll take that as a no to consoling Lady Selborne, then,' Ferdie said, unoffended. He adjusted the set of his coat. 'No idea you were so possessive, Rob.'

'Well, you know now.' Rob's mouth set in a hard line. He had not known either. He remembered that when he had started his bride hunt he had nonchalantly assumed that he and his wife would go their own way. At the time he had thought that he would not expect fidelity from a woman who was bound to him in name only. Yet the thought of Jemima indulging in amorous dalliance with Ferdie or, indeed, anyone made him feel a white-hot anger and a flaring jealousy.

He hurried to catch up with Jemima and Jack. They were chatting together and he envied them their easy intimacy together. It was he who was the uncomfortable third in this trio. He seemed to be learning a great deal about himself on his wedding day, and none of it was easy to stomach.

Ferdie plucked at his arm. 'I say, Rob, could you give me a lift back to the West End? Can't be wandering around this neighbourhood on my own. I'll be robbed before I take ten steps…'

Rob sighed. He supposed that it might make the journey into town slightly less uncomfortable for Ferdie to be with them. He had no wish to sit opposite Jemima and Jack, glowering in silence at the sight of their comfortable friendship.

Rob was not sure how it had happened, but already his ambitions for his wife had changed. He wanted her to come to Delaval with him. He wanted to get to know her better. But he also knew that they had made an agreement and he could not break the terms now. He knew it was impossible.

Jemima liked Mr Churchward on sight. The lawyer toasted them discreetly with a glass of warm champagne, pulled out the deeds to the house in Twickenham and ran over all the arrangements, and made no observations on the rather unusual circumstance of a gentleman renting a separate residence for his brand-new wife. It seemed that Mr Churchward was entirely conversant with the unusual situation in which Rob found himself under the terms of his father's will. Indeed, Jemima suspected that there was something the lawyer knew that Rob had not told her, for on one occasion reference was made to the will of the Dowager Countess of Selborne, Rob's grandmother, which was something that Rob had not mentioned to Jemima at all.

Nevertheless, matters were proceeding smoothly until the very end of the meeting, when there were voices upraised in the office outside and a considerable commotion. Mr Churchward's clerk stuck his head around the door.

'I beg your pardon for interrupting, sir, but Lady Marguerite Exton and Miss Exton are outside. Hearing that you were occupied with the Earl and Countess of Selborne, they requested that they might be permitted to join you—'

Glancing at Rob, Jemima saw that he had turned quite pale. She grabbed his arm.

'Who—?' she began, but before she had time to get any further the door burst open. A tall, patrician-looking lady swept in, followed by a small blonde girl of about Jemima's age with the sweetest face that Jemima had ever seen. The girl gave Jemima a look of lively curiosity, then uttered a squeak and hurled herself into Rob's arms.

'Robert! What a splendid surprise to see you here! When the clerk told us that the Earl and Countess of Selborne were within we could scarce believe it! We thought there must be some mistake!' She turned to Jemima and beamed all the more. 'Hello! I am Rob's cousin, Letty Exton. And you must be Rob's new Countess! How wonderful to meet you!'

Chapter Seven

'Cousin?' Jemima's lips formed the words as she looked at Rob accusingly. She raised her voice a little. 'I thought that you said that you had no relatives, Robert?'

Rob was still trying to disentangle himself from Miss Exton, who was hugging him hard and telling him how wonderful it was that he was home again. He looked part pleased and part harassed, and Jemima almost laughed to see his expression. He freed himself and turned to the older lady, whose somewhat haughty demeanour had slipped now into a smile of genuine affection as she viewed the reunion.

'Robert, my dear,' she said. 'Not only home, but married as well! When you wrote to me last week you made no mention of a wife. A poor show when your own grandmother has to find out by accident!'

Jemima winced. This patrician lady was Rob's *grandmother*? She began to see that her new husband's definition of close relatives and her own might be considerably divergent. She also began to see that they were in a very tight corner indeed.

Miss Exton gave a little shriek. 'Yes, Rob, you beast!

I wanted to dance at your wedding. Are we not good enough for you to acknowledge us now that you are the Earl of Selborne?'

'Letty!' Lady Marguerite said in gentle reproof. She leaned forward and coolly extended a cheek for Rob to kiss, before turning to Churchward. 'Good afternoon, Mr Churchward. Pray excuse this interruption. When I heard that Lord Selborne was with you—'

'And Lady Selborne!' Letty said, bouncing with excitement.

'And Lady Selborne,' Lady Marguerite said, with a glacial smile in Jemima's direction, 'I thought that we should pay our respects.'

Jemima suddenly felt very small and vulnerable. She would have liked to have had longer to prepare to meet Rob's family and she was suddenly conscious that Lady Marguerite might view her as an adventuress at worst and as a jumped-up nobody at best. She glanced instinctively at Rob for support. They had no story prepared of how they had met—or married. They had not thought that it would not be necessary. And now Rob's grandmother and his cousin were standing in front of them; they clearly expected an explanation.

Rob came forward to stand next to her. His presence at her elbow was comforting and he took her hand in his.

'Grandmama,' he said, suddenly very formal, 'may I present my wife, Jemima? Jemima, this is my maternal grandmother, Lady Marguerite Exton.'

Jemima dropped Lady Marguerite a curtsy. 'How do you do, ma'am? I am delighted to meet you.' She cast Rob a fleeting glance. 'Robert quite assured me that he had no family, but I could not believe him.'

'How horrid of you, Rob!' Letty Exton looked reproving. 'And to keep your new wife hidden from us as well! If we had not been passing today we should never have known.' She turned to Jemima. 'Grandmama and I reside in Oxfordshire, you know, and seldom come up to Town. We are only here now to see dear Mr Churchward because I am one and twenty next month and we needed to consult him about my inheritance.'

'I sent a note around to your lodgings as soon as we arrived, Robert,' Lady Marguerite said. 'I assume that you did not receive it?'

'No, Grandmama,' Rob said, and Jemima could hear the amused resignation in his voice. 'I was not aware that you were in Town.'

There was a rather awkward silence.

'Never mind!' Miss Exton said, smiling gamely. 'We are very happy to meet you now!'

Jemima smiled back gratefully. She rather liked Miss Exton, who seemed the polar opposite of her grandmother, warm where Lady Marguerite was chilly, friendly where her ladyship was decidedly aloof. But then, Jemima thought fairly, Rob's grandmother would necessarily think the marriage a strange, havey-cavey affair and so could hardly be blamed for not welcoming Jemima with open arms. They had definitely got off on the wrong foot.

Jemima suddenly caught sight of Jack, who was also eyeing Miss Exton with interest.

'Excuse me,' she said. 'I have been most remiss. Lady Marguerite, Miss Exton, may I introduce my brother, Mr Jack Jewell?'

Jack bowed to the ladies with immaculate politeness, then spoiled the effect by giving Letty a comprehensively admiring look that was not in the least gentlemanly. Jemima could feel Lady Marguerite positively radiating grand-maternal disapproval. Letty blushed and laughed.

'How do you do, Mr Jewell?'

'How do you do, Miss Exton?' Jack said, smiling warmly into her eyes. Letty blushed harder and lowered her gaze.

Jemima could feel Rob's eyes on her and looked at him a little quizzically. He was trying to convey some message. He looked pointedly at her hand, then at her reticule. With a little jump of her heart, Jemima remembered that she had removed her wedding ring immediately after the marriage service and hidden it away in her bag. It was precisely the sort of detail that Lady Marguerite would notice at fifty paces. She furtively undid the clasp of her reticule and burrowed about inside.

Letty, who was leaning over Mr Churchward's desk, gave a little squeak. 'Oh! Are you purchasing a house in Twickenham, Rob? Whatever do you need that for when you have Delaval and a house in Town?'

Jemima's heart missed a beat. With superb aplomb, Mr Churchward swept the deeds to the Twickenham house and all of Jemima's other paperwork underneath a large sheet of blotting paper. 'Those papers appertain to another client, Miss Exton,' he said. 'Very reprehensible of me to leave them lying about. Very reprehensible indeed.' He took off his glasses and polished them furiously on his pocket handkerchief, as though taking the blame for something that was not actually his fault was almost too much for him.

There was another pause.

'Would you care for some champagne, Grandmama?' Rob asked.

'I would love some!' Letty piped up. 'Are we celebrating?'

She gave Jack a luscious smile as he poured a glass for her.

'Yes, we are celebrating indeed.' Rob smiled. 'Jemima and I were married this morning. A quiet affair—' He turned to spike Lady Marguerite's guns in a preemptive strike that Jemima could not but admire '—as I am still in mourning.'

'A shame you could not control your ardour until you were *out* of mourning.' Lady Marguerite sniffed. 'Or at least long enough to introduce Jemima to the rest of your family. Most improper! This whole marriage seems a very hasty business. Have you known each other long?'

'No,' Rob said. It was clear that he was intent on offering as little information as possible and equally obvious that Lady Marguerite was intent on extracting as much as she could. He smiled at Jemima and she felt a strange, warm prickle of sensation. 'That is immaterial, however. I knew as soon as I saw Jemima that I wished to marry her.'

Letty sighed soulfully. 'Oh, Rob, how sweet and romantic.'

Lady Marguerite made a snort like a disapproving camel. 'How impulsive.'

Rob drew Jemima closer still to his side. His touch was warm and reassuring and the look he bent on her seemed full of affection. Despite the difficulties of their situation, Jemima found herself relaxing a little.

'I do not believe that I know your family, Lady Selborne,' Lady Marguerite continued, fixing Jemima with a gimlet eye.

Jemima felt Rob's hand tighten on hers. 'No, ma'am,'

she said politely. 'It is unlikely that you would know them.'

'In what sense is it unlikely?' Lady Marguerite's tone was arctic. It was clear that she thought Jemima the veriest fortune hunter.

'Grandmama!' Letty said, embarrassed.

Jemima smiled. She knew it was important to tell the truth as far as she was able. On the other hand, she had no intention of revealing her antecedents to this aristocratic lady. Lady Marguerite would probably require the smelling salts if she knew her grandson had married a sweep.

'You would not have met my family because we do not go in to society, ma'am,' she said sweetly. 'My mother is much occupied in the home and my father…' she hesitated '…is involved in property.'

She heard Jack smother a laugh.

'I suppose you did not invite the rest of the family to attend the wedding?' Lady Marguerite continued.

Rob shifted. 'Ferdie acted as my groomsman,' he said unwillingly.

'Ferdie Selborne!' Lady Marguerite's perfectly plucked brows rose an inch. 'Ramshackle! Very ramshackle indeed.' Her gaze swung back to Jemima, itemising the mauve silk dress, the bonnet and the reticule, noting the lack of jewellery and dwelling thoughtfully on the wedding ring. Jemima suspected that she had been found seriously wanting.

'And where did the two of you meet?' Lady Marguerite pursued.

'Outside a church,' Rob said. He released Jemima's hand, but only so that he could slide an arm about her waist. His lips brushed her hair tenderly. Jemima found the effect disconcerting rather than helpful. His proximity disturbed her. She tried to move a little away and found herself held very firmly.

'I see,' Lady Marguerite murmured. Jemima could tell that she was still very suspicious. 'Engaging in conversation in a public place is a very dangerous occupation for a lady. One never knows whom one might accidentally acknowledge that way.'

'But it was in front of a church, Grandmama,' Letty pointed out, eyes dancing. 'One can be sure of meeting a good quality of person in such a location.'

'Rather like a lawyer's office,' Jack put in.

Letty looked at him under her lashes. Jack smiled at her. Lady Marguerite gave him a glare that could have iced the Thames over, but Jack appeared impervious.

'Are you up in Town for long, Lady Marguerite?' Jemima enquired hastily.

'No.' Lady Marguerite took a tiny sip from her champagne flute. 'Merely to settle Letty's inheritance and to visit our acquaintance. We hope to travel back to Oxfordshire in a few weeks.' Her cool gaze slid back to Rob. 'Are you travelling to Delaval shortly, Robert, or do you remain in Town? If so, we must all have dinner together soon.'

Jemima shot Rob a quick, agonised look. He could hardly tell his grandmother that he was intending to travel to Oxfordshire immediately, but that she would be staying in London. That would look most odd. On the other hand, if he said that Jemima was accompanying him to Delaval, sooner or later Lady Marguerite would return home to find the new Countess missing and that would appear odder still.

Rob looked down at her. A faint smile touched his mouth. Jemima had a sudden and strange feeling that matters were about to get very complicated indeed.

'We do indeed go to Oxfordshire, Grandmama,' Rob said. 'In fact, we plan to travel to Delaval as soon as possible to begin the restoration work. We are hoping to set off tomorrow.'

Jemima felt cold with shock. She drew an indignant breath to refute the statement, then froze as Rob put his lips very close to her ear. His breath tickled her and sent a little shiver down her spine. He said, softly but very firmly, 'Don't say a word.'

Their gazes locked for a long, tense moment, then Jemima let her breath out again silently. She supposed that she could understand his dilemma. If Rob had said that they were to be in London for any space of time, then his grandmother would surely have insisted on seeing them for dinner that very night. Jemima repressed an exasperated sigh. They were well and truly trapped, but she wished that Rob had left them slightly more room for manoeuvre.

She felt Rob relax as he realised she was not going to argue. He gave her a slight smile that conveyed his gratitude and Jemima gave him a look in return that promised retribution.

Fortunately Letty and Lady Marguerite had largely missed this byplay.

'It is good that you have a project to occupy you once you return home,' Lady Marguerite said. 'A husband and wife should always be busy or in other company. It spares them the boredom of spending the whole time together. We shall let you know as soon as we return to Swan Park, Robert, and we shall expect a visit.'

'Thank you, Grandmama,' Rob said. 'We shall be delighted to call.'

'Perhaps we may go shopping together in Cheltenham, Lady Selborne,' Letty said enthusiastically. 'For although London has the finest shops of them all, Cheltenham is most elegant and exclusive. I should be delighted to take you there.'

'Thank you,' Jemima said, feeling that matters were spiralling a little out of control, 'you are most kind, Miss Exton.'

'Oh, call me Letty as we are to be friends!' Letty said warmly. 'I shall call you Jemima, if I may.' She turned to Jack and smiled at him most charmingly.

'Will you be visiting your sister at Delaval, Mr Jewell?'

'You may depend upon it, Miss Exton,' Jack said, ignoring Jemima's discouraging stare.

Lady Marguerite looked down her nose at him. 'Are you in property as well, Mr Jewell?'

'Frequently, ma'am,' Jack said. He bowed. 'If you will excuse me, I have an appointment.' He turned to Jemima. 'I assume that I will see you before you… ah…leave for Oxfordshire, Jem?'

'Of course,' Jemima said, trying not to feel cross with her brother for adding colour to the deception. 'Good day, Jack.'

Jack went out and Letty gave a little sigh. 'Oh, Lady Selborne, your brother is quite the most charming and handsome man that I have met in a long time! Is he spoken for?'

'Letty!' Lady Marguerite said with a fearsome frown. 'Such forwardness in a gel is most unbecoming.'

'I fear he is,' Jemima said, trying not to feel sorry for Letty as the girl looked quite crestfallen at both the reproof and the unwelcome news of Jack's engagement. 'Jack's betrothal is of long standing and is to a family friend.'

Lady Marguerite at least seemed pleased to hear this

news. She held her hand out to Jemima in a much more
cordial fashion.

'We will see you again soon, I hope, Jemima, and
then we shall have time to get to know one another.'

'I shall look forward to it, ma'am,' Jemima said politely and untruthfully. She turned to Rob. 'Robert, I do
believe that we have certain urgent matters to discuss…'

Rob tucked her hand through his arm. 'Of course, my
love. I am at your disposal. Grandmama, Letty—' he
kissed them both '—we shall see you shortly. Enjoy
your stay in Town.'

He ushered Jemima out.

'Oh, Grandmama,' she heard Letty say, as the door
to Mr Churchward's office closed behind them, 'isn't it
famous to have Robert home! And of all the wonderful
things—he is in love at last!'

'I do believe, Lord Selborne,' Jemima said coldly,
'that you have taken leave of your senses. Whatever
induced you to say that we were returning to Oxfordshire together tomorrow? Not to mention the *tempting*
offer to visit your grandmother once she returns home!
You have left us no space for compromise. Have you
utterly forgotten the terms of our agreement?'

They had left behind the bustle of High Holborn and
were sitting on a bench in the quiet of Gray's Inn Gardens. The sun was high and the trees cast a cool
shadow. Jemima was glad of their shade. The champagne she had taken in Mr Churchward's office had
gone straight to her head and, when taken alongside the
agitation engendered by their situation, it was making
her feel very hot and bothered.

Rob, on the other hand, looked cool and undisturbed.
He sat half-facing her on the bench, long legs stretched

out in front of him, the slight breeze ruffling his dark hair.

'I apologise if you feel that I have overstepped the mark,' he said. 'I had to make a quick decision in response to my grandmother's arrival, and that was the decision I made. If you do not like it—'

'Of course I do not like it!' Jemima narrowed her eyes at him like an angry cat. 'How could I possibly like it? Our agreement was that we should go our separate ways, you to Oxfordshire and me to Twickenham. Now I find that I am promised to accompany you to Delaval without so much as a by your leave! And to visit that starch pants of a grandmother of yours as well! And that is another matter. You promised me that you had no relations, my lord, yet here they are, scuttling out of the woodwork faster than mice!'

'I am sorry.' Jemima did not think that Rob looked particularly apologetic. 'My grandmother so seldom leaves Oxfordshire that I thought the risk was negligible. How was I to know that she would choose to come up to London just as I was returning from abroad?'

'You should have guessed!' Jemima snapped, thoroughly out of sorts. 'That makes one grandmother and a cousin on the Exton side, and one aunt, one uncle and three cousins on the Selborne side of the family… Oh, and a sister who will probably reappear from the Indies at any moment! Do you have any other relatives you forgot to mention, my lord?'

Rob frowned slightly. 'I do not believe so. I have godparents, but they do not count.' He took her hand. 'Jemima, please stay calm—'

'I do not feel calm!' Jemima said sharply. She took off her straw bonnet, which was making her head itch in the sun, and ran her fingers through her hair impatiently.

'You might have anticipated that your whole family would use the same lawyer, my lord. Such an omission shows a great lack of foresight!'

'I knew that everyone in the family uses Churchward, of course.' Rob bent an amused look on her. He seemed untroubled by her display of temper. 'I simply did not think that it would signify.'

'You have this collection of relatives and yet you thought that you could get away with not telling any of them that you were married?'

'Precisely.' Rob shifted a little on the seat. 'I thought that you would go to Twickenham and I to Delaval and that once the inheritance was secured, the marriage would be annulled and no one would be the wiser.'

Jemima bit her lip. 'But now your family know that we are wed. Your grandmother will interrogate all your other relatives about your marriage, and they will all be curious and want to know what is going on. She will ask Mr Selborne—'

'Very probably. I know that Ferdie will be discreet, but this is why I need you to be with me at Delaval. I have no wish to make my entire family aware of the terms of my father's will, so we must make this look like a genuine love match.' Rob moved a little towards her. 'Would that be so difficult for you, Jemima? I am sorry for the way that this had happened, but you carried off the meeting in Churchward's office with aplomb. There is no reason why you could not do carry off the role of Countess of Selborne in the same manner.'

Jemima fought against several conflicting emotions. She liked Rob Selborne, even if he had been foolish enough to get them into this situation. She liked him very much, and a part of her strongly wanted to fall in with his plan and agree to accompany him to Delaval. But the consequences of that were too great. Instead of being his wife in secret she would be the Countess of Selborne in reality and everyone would know it.

She knew she could carry off the part. That did not worry her. It was all the other difficulties that provided the rub—the need to conceal her background, the risk of someone who had attended Anne Selborne's wedding recognising her and, most importantly, the abandonment of her own plans of independence. She had wanted her school very badly and now it had all been snatched away from her.

And yet her very freedom had in fact been dependent on Rob's generosity all along. It had been an illusion to think that she was independent. If Rob chose to break their agreement, if he rescinded the offer of the house in Twickenham and the money, if he insisted that she accompany him to Delaval, then she had no choice. She was his wife. She was trapped.

She made a small noise of despair and fury. 'Oh! You swore that you would not cheat me.'

Rob's gaze was very steady. 'I am not seeking to cheat you, Jemima. I wish to persuade you to my way of thinking.'

Jemima made an angry gesture. 'Semantics! Fancy sentiments! I am obliged to change my plans because you wish me to do so.'

Rob sighed. She could tell that he was holding on hard to his own temper and a part of her wished that he might lose it so that they could have a big quarrel and relieve the frustration. Except that that would never do in the Inns of Court Gardens, and especially not if one was the Countess of Selborne. She took a deep breath.

'I am sorry, my lord. I simply cannot do this. We must stick to our original agreement.'

Rob nodded slowly. 'Very well.' He raised his brows. 'May we discuss this?'

Jemima scuffed at the grass beneath her feet. She did not wish to talk about it because she knew just how persuasive Rob could be. When he had first asked her to marry him she had been determined to refuse him, yet he had convinced her. She would not be in this predicament now if she had stuck to her guns.

'There is nothing to discuss,' she said. 'Can you not simply explain matters to Lady Marguerite?'

Rob shook his head. 'Jemima, you have met my grandmother. She is a noticing sort of person. For a wife to appear suddenly is suspicious enough, but for her to disappear again is most irregular, and I doubt that any explanations of mine would persuade her otherwise.'

'Then tell her the truth!'

Rob shook his head. 'That would cause an unnecessary scandal and it would damage your reputation as much as mine. More so, in fact, since a lady's reputation is so fragile a thing. I would not want anything to hurt you, Jemima.'

Jemima shot him an exasperated look. 'Do you imagine that I care about that? Such a consideration has never been in the least relevant to me!'

'That may be so, of course.' Rob shrugged. 'But it matters to me. This touches my honour and I cannot allow your reputation to be damaged.'

Jemima sighed. 'Then I shall think of an excuse to stay in London. I could have a sick mother…'

'Permanently sick and permanently requiring your

presence? It is a possibility, but not a very convincing one!'

'Then tell Lady Marguerite that I have left you—' Jemima broke off. For a moment Rob looked quite angry; angry and as stubborn as she, and it shook her. He spoke very quietly.

'I cannot do that, Jemima. Not unless that is truly what you wish to do.'

Their gazes met and held. Jemima was the first to look away. She knew that her words had hurt him even though he had not said so. When they had made their agreement they had had no intention of keeping their wedding vows but somehow—already—something had changed. There was a link that bound her to this man now. She had made promises to him, promises that she had not imagined she would be obliged to keep. Yet now everything was different. She even felt different...

'I am sorry, Rob,' she said, at last. 'I should not have said that.'

Rob relaxed a little. The shadows of the trees played across his face. He was watching her very closely and Jemima felt a little breathless under his scrutiny. She dropped her gaze.

'It is not that I do not feel I could fulfil the part of Countess of Selborne,' she said after a moment, 'but I believe there are those who would think it most inappropriate. I am persuaded that Lady Marguerite would not wish you to marry into trade, even were I bringing a fat dowry.'

Rob looked rueful. 'My grandmother's bark is much worse than her bite. Once she decides to like you, you will find her the kindest of creatures.'

Jemima gave him a frankly disbelieving look. 'And

when will she start to like me? Before or after we tell her I am a chimney sweep's daughter?'

Rob's jaw was set in a stubborn line. 'I am not ashamed of marrying you, Jemima, chimney sweep's daughter or not. If people discover your antecedents, then so be it. If they choose to cut you, then they are not people I would wish to have as my acquaintance.' He laced his fingers through hers. 'You are my *wife*, Jemima, and that is all that counts.'

Jemima smiled and let it go. She knew that matters were not so simple. Rob's family could hardly be expected to applaud his marriage to a penniless girl of poor family and country society would probably be even less forgiving. She remembered Jack's fierce words about snobbery and self-respect. *'They will never accept you…'* If she tried to keep her background a secret, it would be bound to come out sooner or later. Secrets always did. Yet if she was open about it, then people would shun her. It was another impasse.

She was distracted by the realisation that Rob had moved closer to her along the bench. She was not sure whether it was deliberate or not, but it certainly flustered her. His thigh was pressed lightly against hers through the lilac silk; his arm brushed hers. Jemima tried to wriggle surreptitiously away and found she was already backed into a corner. She closed her eyes for a moment. She was not at all sure that she could concentrate with Rob in such close proximity.

'Jemima?' Rob sounded concerned.

Jemima opened her eyes and squinted at him. She put her straw bonnet back on to shade her eyes. Her head still felt muzzy from the champagne and suddenly she had a strange desire to rest it on Rob's shoulder. She could even feel herself starting to lean towards him. She sat up straighter.

'Jemima, are you quite well?'

There was a gleam in Rob's eyes that made Jemima feel very hot. 'Oh, yes, thank you! I am merely a little sleepy from the sunshine…'

'Well,' Rob said, his gaze warming from speculation to outright interest, 'if you wish to take a nap, then please feel free to do so. You could rest your head against my chest and I could put my arm about you.'

Jemima jumped and blushed at the images he had conjured. 'I would not dream of doing anything so improper, my lord! Besides, we were talking.'

'Talking,' Rob murmured. 'So we were. Anything else will have to wait, I suppose…'

Jemima frowned. 'There will not be anything else, my lord. If I fall in with your plans, then this will be a *pretence* of a love match, not the actual thing itself.'

'Of course,' Rob said. He raised his brows. 'So are you going to fall in with my plans, Jemima?'

Chapter Eight

'I do not know.' Jemima frowned. 'I had such high hopes for my school. It is very difficult to relinquish something that I was looking forward to so much.'

Rob nodded. 'I understand that, but if you come with me to Delaval you may open as many schools as you may choose.'

Jemima laughed. 'Almost you persuade me, my lord!'

Rob leaned closer. 'I understand that I have defrauded you in a way, Jemima. We made an agreement and now I am asking you to accept a change of terms, but—' he made a slight gesture '—I would be honoured if you were to help me restore my home at Delaval, and the village there *will* need a school, if you still wish to set one up. There is no reason why you cannot follow Mrs Montagu's example.'

For a moment Jemima felt her heart soar at the prospect, then she forced herself to be sensible. 'I doubt that it would be appropriate for the Countess of Selborne to teach in a school, would it?'

Rob looked slightly uncomfortable. 'Not to teach, no. But you could establish it, show a benevolent interest…

That is what your mentor did, after all—' Rob broke off. 'What is wrong?'

Jemima gave him a wry smile. 'My lord, I have worked for all of my life and am not accustomed to sitting around being benevolent. You yourself commented as much when you asked me what I would do in Twickenham. I need to be active.'

Rob laughed. 'Believe me, Jemima, there would be plenty for you to do at Delaval. The place is falling apart!'

Jemima rubbed her fingers over the rough wood of the bench. 'And the annulment, my lord?' she asked, looking at him from under her lashes. 'I take it that there would not be an annulment now?'

'No,' Rob said. 'There would be no annulment.'

Jemima felt her heart twist just as it had when Rob had been so tender to her that day in her parents' house. For all his kindness, he had never intended her to take her place as Lady Selborne of Delaval. Their marriage was supposed to be an expedient match, quickly ended. But if they took this course, there would be no annulment and no quick end to the marriage. The Earl of Selborne would be stuck with a chimney sweep's daughter as his countess when he had never intended for that to happen. Jemima felt a lump come into her throat at the sudden irrevocable nature of it all.

'Pray remember,' she said, with difficulty 'that it was not a part of your original plan to be encumbered with a wife.'

Rob's expression softened. 'That's true. Originally I had no such intention. But now I believe I would like it very much.'

Jemima's blood was beating quickly and hard. The tone of his voice stirred something in her that she had not experienced before. She could not deny that she was drawn to him. It complicated matters; confused her. She could not look at him.

'When I proposed our original arrangement I did not know you very well, Jemima,' Rob went on. His voice was very gentle. 'I thought that all I wanted was to gain my inheritance so that I might restore Delaval. The marriage was to be a means to an end.' He put a hand on hers. 'Please look at me, Jemima. I do not wish there to be any misunderstandings when I tell you this.'

Jemima looked up. The intensity of his gaze almost burned her and she fought the urge to look away again.

'There is no one whom I would prefer to be Countess of Selborne,' Rob said, very slowly. 'You are my wife, Jemima, and I am proud of that.'

Jemima freed herself and got to her feet. She took a few steps away from the bench, seeking the shade of a nearby oak tree. She felt terribly torn. She put her hands up to her head in a gesture of despair.

'This was not supposed to happen,' she said.

Rob had followed her. He turned her gently to face him now, and touched her cheek, a featherlight touch. 'If you truly feel that you cannot go through with it I shall explain the situation to all my family. It is my fault that we are in this position and there is no reason why you should suffer, my dear. I shall honour our agreement.'

Jemima's shoulders slumped. It was the only logical outcome, it was the conclusion that she had argued for and yet now it did not feel right at all. She looked at Rob. His face was set and expressionless but somehow she could tell that he was disappointed. The knowledge made her feel unhappy. She felt as though she had let him down. And a small corner of her heart felt excited and pleased that he should want her with him. It was dreadfully confusing.

'I would not be a *conformable* wife,' she began, and saw Rob's face break into a grin as he realised that she had capitulated.

'I would rather have the sort of wife who can help me restore Delaval than a fine lady who cannot bear to get her hands dirty.'

Jemima felt an answering smile starting. They looked at one another. Rob drew her deeper into the shade of the spreading oak. His expression was suddenly serious.

'So you *will* come to Delaval with me?'

Jemima felt a tug of something inside her, something that felt like apprehension and excitement. 'Yes, I will.'

'I am very glad,' Rob said quietly.

Jemima felt the colour wash into her face. She seldom blushed but Rob Selborne seemed to have the power to make her do so simply by looking at her. And there was one thought that made her feel more nervous still. She cleared her throat.

'About the pretend love match…'

'Yes?' Rob was smiling slightly.

'I…' Jemima floundered a little, uncharacteristically shy. 'I…am anxious that we are clear that it *is* a pretence. I mean—this is still a marriage in name only…'

Rob's smile deepened. Jemima's blood fizzed with champagne and something else, something hot. 'Of course,' he said.

Jemima looked at him. In her experience, gentlemen were rather more persistent in gaining what they wanted and Rob's casual attitude made her deeply suspicious. He had already kissed her, so she knew that he was attracted to her. It was in every gesture, every look he gave her, which made his apparent lack of interest in consummating their marriage even harder to understand.

'I am concerned that we are clear on this,' she said again. She took a deep breath. 'I would like a celibate marriage.'

Now Rob was positively laughing. 'So would I. At least for the time being.'

Jemima frowned. 'You would? But—why?'

Rob raised his brows. 'Are you trying to persuade me to change my mind?'

'No, of course not! I barely know you and I am not in the habit of propositioning gentlemen.' Jemima could feel herself growing flustered and fought for composure. 'It is simply that the gentlemen themselves... In my experience...'

'Yes? Are you very experienced when it comes to gentlemen?'

Rob had taken her hand again and was rubbing his fingers over the pulse point at her wrist. It was distracting. Her skin prickled beneath his touch and her pulse jumped.

'No, I am not. I have told you my opinion of love before, and despite my background I have no knowledge of...of amorous affairs. I am used to gentlemen pursuing me, but—'

Jemima cast a despairing look at him. She felt very embarrassed.

'But you have not succumbed?' Rob suggested. She saw him smile. 'I dare say that I should not be so predictable, but I find that rather pleasing.'

Jemima fiddled with the rim of her straw hat. It felt very personal to be discussing such matters with Rob. She had always been a rather private person and now it felt like giving a bit of herself away.

'My experience or lack of it is not the point,' she said, trying to get the conversation back on course. 'We were speaking of our supposed love match. It must be understood that whatever the impression we give the outside world, our marriage is in name only.' Jemima pressed her hands together nervously. 'I do not know you well, Rob, and I should not feel comfortable with an intimate relationship.'

Rob put up a gentle hand and brushed the stray strands of hair from her face. 'I understand, Jemima. I understand your scruples from the things that you have said to me before. It would be remarkable indeed if you were to feel comfortable with me when we have known each other so short a time. But despite your reservations I would like to think that there might be a chance for some stronger feeling to grow between us.'

Jemima was feeling exceedingly hot and bothered. She had always thought of physical attraction as a dangerous trap, and of love as something that made one as vulnerable to heartbreak as Jack had been when he had fallen in love with Beth Rosser. She had avoided both on principle. Yet now this man—her husband—could undermine her certainties with a single touch and it frightened her. She sought reassurance.

'You have said yourself that you were content to have a marriage in name only,' she reminded him. 'If that is not what you truly wish, then I think you should say so now. It is important to be honest.'

Rob sighed and drove his hands into his pockets. 'I said that I was content to have a celibate marriage *for the time being*. That is the operative phrase here, Jemima.' He gave her a crooked smile. 'My instinct and necessity are in conflict, I am afraid.'

Jemima's interest was well and truly piqued. Instinct

she could understand. Necessity was another thing entirely. 'Necessity? Whatever do you mean, my lord?'

To her surprise, Rob took her hand and drew her as far into the deep shadow as they could go. He sat down on the dry grass and pulled her down beside him.

'There is something that I have to tell you.' His expression was serious. 'Except that I find that I do not *want* to tell you at all.'

Jemima raised her brows and waited. Rob gave a sigh and leaned back against the tree trunk. There was a little silence. Rob frowned.

'Perhaps I could guess,' Jemima said, after a moment, 'since you seem to be finding this unconscionably difficult, my lord.'

'You could guess all day but not come up with the correct answer.' Rob turned his head against the tree trunk and looked at her. He took a deep breath.

'You will recall the terms of my father's will,' he said.

Jemima nodded. 'Of course. Why else would we be here?'

'Indeed. Well, my grandmother was carried off by the same epidemic that killed my parents.' Rob hesitated, looking awkward. 'She was somewhat eccentric. She left me her fortune of forty thousand pounds, but on one condition.'

Jemima frowned. 'It seems to be a habit in your family.'

'It is. And it is one that I could do well without,' Rob said feelingly.

'So what was the condition?'

Rob traced circles in the parched grass. He did not look at her.

'She required that I should remain celibate for one

hundred days in order to be worthy of inheriting her fortune.' He looked up suddenly. 'Are you laughing?'

Jemima was indeed feeling the irrepressible laughter well up inside her. She put her hand over her mouth. 'Of course not, Rob.'

'You are!' Rob seized her shoulders. 'Jemima—'

'I am sorry,' Jemima said, bursting into giggles, 'but it *is* funny, Rob! Did your father and your grandmother not know what the other was doing?'

'I hope not,' Rob said feelingly, 'or I would consider them unwarrantably cruel.'

Jemima looked at him, her eyes still brimming with laughter. 'No wonder you wished to marry a stranger and to part again on your wedding day. To have married someone you already knew and then be obliged to disclose these conditions would be most embarrassing!'

Rob gave her a speaking look. 'Thank you for pointing that out. I am aware. It is quite embarrassing enough as it is.'

Jemima smothered another giggle. 'And no doubt if you had married a lady of your acquaintance you would have found the abstinence a most shocking strain!'

Rob gave her a look that quelled her laughter. 'That, my dear Jemima, is already a problem. As I said, instinct and necessity are at war here.'

Their gazes locked. Jemima looked away and twisted a blade of grass between her fingers.

'Perhaps we should reconsider the circumstances,' she said slowly. 'You must own that living with each other will be very difficult. Being in close proximity with a person does tend to lead to intimacy.'

'Does it?' Rob said. 'Then we shall find out, shall we not?'

Jemima met his eyes and looked quickly away. 'So

where does that leave us?' she asked hastily. 'With a marriage in name only?'

'Temporarily,' Rob said. He moved a little closer. 'Jemima, I have to be honest about this. I cannot envisage myself wanting a celibate marriage for any longer than the one hundred days. And even that will be torture.'

Jemima blushed. She liked Rob Selborne a great deal and was obliged to admit that she had enjoyed his kisses, but she did not want to tumble into unguarded love with him. Life, as Jemima knew, could be hard and cruel without making oneself even more vulnerable. She tried to match his honesty.

'Thank you for telling me this, Rob,' she said. She cleared her throat. 'I cannot pretend that I am indifferent to you and I shall not try, for you could disprove my claims with a single kiss. But—' she put out a hand as she saw his instinctive move towards her '—I still have my reservations…'

'Of course.' The look in Rob's eyes made her feel quite dizzy. 'I am aware that I shall have to earn your trust, Jemima.' His fingers brushed the back of her hand. 'I have eighty-five days in which to woo my own wife…'

A shiver went through Jemima. 'Eighty-five days?'

Rob's eyes were dark and amused. 'Actually eighty-four days, ten hours and something in the region of thirty-five minutes. You might conclude that I am counting.'

Jemima caught her breath. 'You mean…you are intending…'

Rob smiled at her. 'I intend to seduce you, Jemima. By the end of my period of enforced abstinence I intend that both of us will want to seek the pleasures of our marriage bed. You have been warned.'

It was past midday as they left the Inns of Court Gardens and made their way down a sloping alleyway that led towards the river. Jemima had been very quiet since the discussion under the oak tree and Rob had no idea what she was thinking. She had not commented on his final statement and had merely told him composedly that she was hungry and that the champagne had gone to her head. Then she had taken his arm and steered him towards the waterfront. Rob hoped that they would not end up in another flash house. The thought of some ardent highwayman attempting to spirit his bride away on their wedding day was enough to arouse all the emotions that he was keeping under such careful control.

He had had no wish to frighten Jemima, but he thought it imperative that she should not take away the mistaken belief that this marriage, starting as it was in name only, would continue that way forever. When he had stated his intentions so clearly in the gardens she had not replied, but he had read a great deal in her face. Her eyes had widened with a mixture of apprehension and a shy interest she could not quite hide. Her lips had parted on a small gasp and Rob had found himself wanting to kiss her very much indeed. He had watched her struggle with the concept of his courtship, had seen the colour fluctuate in her face as she thought about it and had watched the final struggle in which Jemima's common sense eventually triumphed over her wilder imaginings. It had been a close run thing and next time he spoke to her of love, Rob thought, there would be a different outcome. He was planning a slow campaign, but he had every intention of making a little progress each time.

But for now they had to eat.

'Where are we going?' he asked.

Jemima pointed. 'To the oyster stall. They are fresh from the river. You can try some eels as well if you wish, my lord.'

Rob shuddered. 'No, thank you. I detest eels.' He flashed her a look. 'As for the oysters—are they not rumoured to be an aphrodisiac?'

Their eyes met. He saw Jemima blush slightly. She looked away. 'No oysters, then,' she said brightly. 'Perhaps we should go to the potato stand and you may wash it down with some of Mrs Miggin's coffee. Jack assures me that it is the strongest in London, and death to passion! He says that they should give it to prisoners to calm their frustrated ardour!'

'Just what I require,' Rob said wryly.

In the end they partook of a cup of hot pea soup and a baked potato from the stall, eaten in a corner of King Street tucked away from the chill wind off the river. Rob, who would never normally have ventured down any of the narrow alleys by the river without first checking he had a pistol on him, was intrigued by the whole experience. The soup was good and hot, and as they sat there a score of urchins came slipping out of the dark alleys and gathered around them, rather as though they were a peep show. They all seemed to know Jemima, who chatted to them easily while she ate her food. Some she introduced as sweeps' apprentices. Others were potboys from the inns, stable lads or children from the docks. All were barefoot and ragged, and the apprentice sweeps were black with soot from head to toe. All accepted Rob without comment. One even went so far as to lift his watch when he was not paying attention and was ordered sternly by Jemima to give it back. Rob ate, and watched his wife talking to the children, watched the breeze stirring her hair and the sunlight on her face, and felt proud and possessive.

When they got up to leave, the little crowd parted to let them through.

'Who's the swell?' one of the urchins piped up.

Jemima smiled. 'This is my husband,' she said, taking Rob's hand, and Rob felt ridiculously happy.

'Cor,' the urchin said, looking Rob up and down.

After lunch they wandered along by the river, hand in hand.

'I am glad that you didn't give the children any money,' Jemima said, as they stood at the end of Blackfriars Bridge and watched the barges ease up the river. 'Most gentlemen would have done, and would have thought that they were being kind in doing so.'

Rob turned to look at her. 'I did think about it,' he admitted, 'but it seemed the wrong thing to do. Almost like giving money to a friend when they hadn't asked for it.'

Jemima smiled. He watched the light reflect in her eyes. They were astonishingly blue, almost purple. The deep blue of cottage-garden lavender.

'That is it exactly,' she said softly. She folded her arms. 'I must go home now. I told my mother that I was visiting a friend today, so I cannot be too late.' She hesitated. 'I thought to tell her tonight where I was going. Father is away on business, cleaning the Duke of Bedford's chimneys and will not be back before the morrow. If you wish, you may collect me as soon as you are ready in the morning…'

Rob tossed a pebble moodily into the river. It was

only now, when the time was approaching for them to part, that he realised how little he wished to be apart from her. Even a few hours was too long.

'It is our wedding night,' he said.

'So it is. And you will spend it at your lodgings and I will spend it at my home.' Jemima smiled. 'And you may go to sleep thinking about your grandmother's forty thousand pounds, my lord. That should keep you warm.'

Chapter Nine

It was not the thought of forty thousand pounds that occupied Rob when he and his new Countess set off on their journey to Oxfordshire the following day, but more the thought of the eighty-three days to go before he had fulfilled the terms of his grandmother's will. The more he tried not to think about the days of abstinence, the more he seemed unable to concentrate on anything else. The more he tried to distract himself from the thought of bedding his wife, the more he ached to do precisely that. He had been awake for almost the whole night and he had spent almost all of that time thinking about Jemima.

He could remember in perfect detail the way in which her lips had trembled beneath his when he had kissed her briefly at their wedding and, having kissed her before, he was burning to do it again. It was not the sort of experience one could forget or undo. Having taken such a step forward, it was impossible to retreat and Rob did not want to try. What he wanted was his wife.

He closed his eyes as the coach lurched through the countryside. Eighty-three days. The rest of August, all of September and October and the first part of November… A groan almost escaped him. He was going to have to take stern steps to avoid going mad with sexual frustration.

From the moment they had driven off from Great Portland Street that morning, it had seemed to Rob that he had been unable to focus on anything but his wife. Jemima had been looking delectable in a travelling dress of deep green that fitted every rounded contour of her body. He had appreciated her elegance and style, but he had wanted to take that dress off her as soon as he saw it.

Then there was her scent. Jemima smelled of flowers, of the sweet, pale scent of jasmine that had grown in sun-warmed profusion against the south wall of Delaval when last Rob was there. He had wanted to drink in that perfume from her skin, a desire that led his wayward thoughts in all sorts of interesting but ultimately unfulfilling directions.

Jemima had insisted on driving with the window open, for the day was hot, and gradually the scent of jasmine had mingled with the fresh smell of cut hay and made Rob feel uncomfortably lustful. He was not sure what it was about hot summer days and the verdant sight of the countryside that put such thoughts into his head, but after a couple of hours he was fidgeting uncomfortably and Jemima, who had been engrossed in the scenery for the best part of the journey, commented on his restlessness. Rob wished that he had thought to ride beside the carriage rather than sit with Jemima in the enforced intimacy of the interior. After five hours with her he was so tense that it was with great relief that he realised they had arrived in Barrington and rolled into the yard of the Fox Inn.

Jemima, in contrast, had looked cool and restrained

for the entire day. She had shown the greatest interest in the countryside and all the villages that they had driven through, and now, as they contemplated their lodging for the night, she looked as unruffled as Rob felt disturbed. He reflected ruefully that there was no reason why she should feel as on edge as he. She had responded to his kisses with a tentative passion that had hinted at the depths beneath, but she had also held something back from him; quite a lot back, in fact. She was an intriguing mix—the little sweep's girl who had learned hard lessons on the streets, overlaid with the lady of quality that Mrs Montagu had fashioned. Rob suspected that it might be quite a while before he got to know her properly and even longer before she fully trusted him. But he had months... Months in which to court his own wife. If only his unruly impulses did not get the better of him first.

His good intentions suffered a blow almost immediately when the landlord ushered them into the parlour with much obsequious bowing and many apologies for the fact that the inn was so crowded. They would have to share the parlour and, more to the point, share a small bedchamber. Rob was almost tempted to travel on to Delaval. It was only another twenty miles, but one of the carriage wheels had started to splinter, and as evening was approaching he had decided that there would be no harm in stopping overnight. Now he was not so sure. The thought of sharing a chamber and, moreover, a bed with his wife, a prospect that would fill most newly-wed husbands with cheer, made him feel gloomy and frustrated. There were times when eighty-three days of abstinence could feel like a lifetime and Rob had the lowering conviction that by the end of it he was going to feel much, much worse.

* * *

'This is very pleasant,' Jemima said, as the innkeeper steered them towards a secluded corner and sent a boy scurrying for refreshments. She liked the crooked low ceilings of the Fox and the golden flagstoned floor. 'I shall have a pint of ale, Mr Hinton, and some of the mutton stew, if you please.'

The landlord looked briefly scandalised. 'A pint of ale, my lady? Harrumph! Yes, certainly… And for you, my lord?'

'I will have the same, Mr Hinton,' Rob said. He looked as though he was trying not to laugh at the landlord's outraged expression. He turned to Jemima. 'I do believe you may set a new fashion in local society, my love, for ladies to partake of ale!'

Jemima slid into her seat on the long wooden bench.

'I will only have a little, my lord,' she said with composure. 'It would be rather foolhardy to drink too much in our situation, would it not? I have often thought that there is nothing like getting foxed for affecting one's judgement.'

Rob drew on his glass of ale and looked at her thoughtfully. 'A sound observation, my love. I can see that with your practical common sense we need not concern ourselves with the possibility of breaking the terms of my grandmother's will.'

Jemima looked at him. 'It would help if you were to exercise some self-control as well, my lord,' she pointed out. 'I cannot be expected to do this on my own.'

Rob grinned. 'I shall do my best,' he said. 'Alas that my self-control may not prove infallible.'

Jemima sighed. She had a feeling that the next few months were going to be very difficult in more ways than one. Young ladies might swoon at the prospect of becoming Countess of Selborne, but she was of a rather more practical bent and knew it would not be easy. There would be a huge adjustment to make in terms of taking on the running of a big house and she had no background that might have prepared her for such an undertaking. If it came to that, she had no knowledge whatsoever of the countryside, where life was incomprehensibly different from her own experience of living in a city.

Then there were family, friends and neighbours to meet. And then there was Rob himself...

Jemima studied her husband as he drank his ale. He had a kind of careless authority that made his presence felt without being overpowering. Rob was no dandy, but he had a casual elegance that Jemima found all too attractive. She had never spent five hours in close contact with a man before and she had found the enforced intimacy of the carriage to be strange, though not in an unpleasant manner. She and Rob had conversed easily on all manner of topics prompted by the journey, from the time it took to travel from Delaval to London to the different crops that were being harvested in the fields around them. It was only when she had caught Rob's gaze upon her, bright and hard with a desire that she could read all too easily, that she had felt her colour rising and a strange warmth seep through her veins.

When she had gone to bed the previous night she had told herself that it was essential that she kept her head when in company with her husband. Her heart had already shown an erratic and unhelpful inclination to override all common sense, but Jemima felt that her position was still tenuous in the extreme and if she allowed herself to fall into Rob's arms then she would have surrendered completely. She had to remind herself that they did not know each other well despite the strange and persistent conviction she had that she already knew and understood him. Such flights of fancy were alien to her nature and they worried her, at the same time as exciting her. Now, seeing that Rob was watching her in that particular way again, she squashed down the excitement and sought a safe topic of conversation.

'So you say that we are now some twenty miles from Delaval, my lord? Whereabouts are we exactly?'

'We are close to the town of Burford at present,' Rob said. He glanced away from her as the two steaming plates of mutton stew were delivered. 'In point of fact, we are near the estate of the Duke of Merlin at Merlinschase. We turn south from here to reach Delaval…'

Jemima was no longer listening. When she had heard the name of the Duke of Merlin she had felt frozen and a little sick, with a buzzing sound in her ears that made her wonder if she might faint. The Duke of Merlin. Merlinschase. Tilly's home. She had had absolutely no notion that her niece would be so close to Delaval. Since the angry exchange with Jack that day she had thought no more about seeking Tilly out and now, ironically, it seemed that she would have to do the opposite and do everything in her power to avoid her.

'I thought…' Her voice sounded croaky and she cleared her throat. 'I thought that the Duke of Merlin resided somewhere in Gloucestershire…'

'He does.' Rob looked up, a faint frown creasing his brow as he took in her face. 'Are you quite well, Jemima? You have gone a little pale.'

'I? Oh, yes…' Jemima pulled herself together and picked up her fork. She toyed with her stew, then put the fork down again and picked up her ale. The drink felt cool against her lips, but she could not seem to taste it.

'I do not suppose… That is…I imagine that the Merlins are far too high in the instep to have anything to do with the rest of us?'

'Not at all,' Rob said easily. 'We shall see them once we are established at Delaval. The Duke's nephew, Bertie Pershore, is one of my oldest friends. Merlin is, in fact, my godfather.'

Jemima's glass of ale trembled in her fingers and some of the liquid jumped and spilled on the oaken table. Aware that Rob was looking at her quizzically, she put the glass down. She hunted for an excuse to explain her sudden nervousness.

'A Duke for a godfather? Good gracious!'

Rob smiled. 'There is no need to be concerned. Merlin is a very pleasant chap. You will like him.'

Jemima had no intention of ever meeting the Duke, but she could not tell Rob that. She imagined ruefully that she would need a whole host of imaginative excuses to avoid his godfather. She drew a deep breath and tried to think calmly. There was no immediate danger. Delaval was twenty miles from here, in Oxfordshire. She need not meet the Duke of Merlin and there was no reason to suppose that she would ever meet Tilly. Unless the child resembled her closely, there would be nothing to connect them at all. Jemima felt tired and dispirited. She thought about trying to explain to Rob about Tilly, but shied away from it. It was bad enough that Rob was saddled with a chimney sweep's daughter as a Countess. To spring upon him the fact that her illegitimate niece was his godfather's ward… Well, that would have to wait until she knew him a little better. Just for now, for the sake of both Tilly and herself and the secrets they hid, she would have to avoid any possibility of seeing her niece.

She looked at Rob. He was still applying himself to his stew and did not seem to suspect that her sudden pallor had stemmed from anything other than surprise and a natural apprehension at meeting more of his acquaintance. She started to eat her stew. It was hot and reviving and after a few mouthfuls she felt a little better. She had another sip of her ale. One day soon, she promised herself, she would tell Rob the truth about Tilly. There should not be any secrets between them.

'Do you think that the landlord might light the fire?' she asked, deliberately seeking a change of subject. 'Although it has been a warm day, these old stone buildings have quite a chill.'

The landlord, when applied to, was apologetic.

'I am sorry, my lord, my lady, but the chimney smokes like the very devil. Plenty of business it's lost me in the winter, spewing smoke all over my guests, and me spending a fortune on a chimney doctor all the way from Oxford to no avail! Charged three guineas and made not a ha'porth's worth of difference!'

'Have you tried putting the goose up the chimney?' Jemima enquired. 'They say that the flapping will brush all the soot down.'

The landlord looked embarrassed. 'Thought of that, my lady, but yon goose is the wife's pet and she'd no more put it up the chimney than she would one of our children! Besides, the soot is nasty sticky stuff. Take more than a goose's wing to dislodge that.'

Jemima finished her ale. 'I know the very thing. Do you have a shotgun, Mr Hinton?'

The landlord looked a little perplexed. 'Course I do, ma'am. Most country people do, like.'

'Then pray bring it in. And bring some big sheets with you as well.'

The landlord looked even more puzzled. 'Ma'am?' He turned to Rob. 'Milord—'

'If my wife wishes to inspect your shotgun, Hinton,' Rob said smiling, 'then I should comply.'

'Well, yes, my lord...' Now the landlord evidently thought that they were both mad. He hurried out, to return a moment later with an ancient-looking shotgun, his wife, four curious children, a pile of sheets and a mongrel dog.

'Spread the sheeting around the fireplace,' Jemima instructed, 'so that you may catch the soot. That's it— hang that one across the beams so that it acts as a curtain. Robert, would you move that table back, please? Thank you. Now, Mr Hinton—' she turned to the landlord '—take your shotgun and stand in the inglenook and fire it directly up the chimney.'

'Madam!' The innkeeper looked aghast.

'Would you like me to do it for you?' Jemima asked, in kindly fashion.

The other guests had gathered around by now and watched in amazement as the landlord stepped into the grate, pointed his gun up the chimney and released a deafening report. The building shook. Outside, the chickens and geese set up a huge honking and squawking, and all the birds rose from the surrounding trees giving calls of alarm. The ladies screamed and pressed their hands over their ears. All except Jemima, who stood, hands on hips, smiling broadly. Then there was a rumbling and a shaking, like a cart going along the road outside, and with a huge whoosh the soot fell down the chimney to engulf the landlord and pile up on sheets in the fireplace.

'I do apologise,' Jemima said, looking at the landlord and trying not to laugh. 'I forgot to tell you to step away from the fire.'

The landlord shook himself like a dog coming out of the water and the soot flew in all directions. He was smiling, a big white grin that split his face.

'Well, I'll be damned! You're worth more than any fancy chimney doctor, Lady Selborne, and that's a fact!'

'Thank you,' Jemima said modestly. The other guests, realising that the inn would not be tumbling down, gave a big round of applause and went back to their seats and resumed their meals. The landlord and landlady scooped up the sooty sheets and went out and Jemima sat down again and tucked into her stew quite as though nothing had happened. She gave Rob an innocent look.

'What is it, my lord? Do you wish me to give the chimneys at Delaval the same treatment before the winter comes?'

Rob was looking slightly stunned. 'Good God, Jemima, that was remarkably effective. And not a spot of soot in my stew either.'

'I thought you knew what I intended to do,' Jemima said, her mouth full. 'When I sent for the shotgun—'

'Oh, I guessed what you had in mind.' Rob frowned. 'I suppose I should have stopped you, but I fear I am not that sort of husband.'

'No harm done,' Jemima said. 'The landlord is very grateful. But first the ale and then the chimneys…' She looked at him, head on one side. 'I do believe that you are very tolerant, Robert Selborne. How far *would* you let me go before you stopped me?'

Lavender-blue eyes met brown. Rob smiled slightly.

'Do not put it to the test, Jemima,' he said. 'You might be surprised.'

And Jemima, remembering how much steely determination lay beneath Rob's deceptively cool exterior, shivered a little. She thought that he might be right.

'We may put a bolster down the middle of the bed,' Jemima said, as they stood in the chamber later that evening. 'I am sure that that would help.'

Rob was not at all sure that it would help at all. He had been temporarily distracted earlier by Jemima's chimney-cleaning exploits, but as the evening had worn on, his lustful thoughts had returned to plague him with increasing intensity. He had watched entranced as Jemima drained her second beaker of ale and her elbow slid along the table top, causing the neckline of her dress to dip a little and reveal the enticing, shadowy cleft between her breasts. He had watched her animated little face in the candlelight as she chatted to him and had found it difficult to concentrate on the answers to her questions. Now they were alone in their bedchamber he was so tightly wound up that he thought he might explode.

'I will get ready for bed first,' Jemima said, still briskly practical, 'if you would be so good as to leave the room, and then, when I am ready, you may come back…'

Rob repressed a groan. All he seemed capable of seeing was the image of Jemima in her nightgown, lying in the big four-poster bed. And that was only in his imagination. Once he saw her in reality… He shifted, feeling the hardening in his body that presaged an extremely uncomfortable night.

'Perhaps I could sleep in the chair,' he said, nodding

towards the overstuffed and distinctly uncomfortable-looking armchair that stood before the fire. The chair, the bed or the taproom—it made little difference, since he knew he would not sleep a wink.

For a moment Jemima looked amused.

'If you wish it, my lord.'

'Of course I do not wish it,' Rob ground out. 'It must be obvious to the meanest intelligence that I would like to share the bed with you—in every sense—' He broke off, trying to get a grip on himself. He saw Jemima's gaze drop to his pantaloons and a blush suffuse her cheek as she saw what was outlined there. She stood clutching her nightrail to her chest and she suddenly looked very young and innocent. Rob cursed himself and tried to speak more gently.

'Forgive me, Jemima. I did not mean to be rude. It is simply...' He gestured hopelessly. 'This marriage seems to be a great mistake...'

He was aware of having made things much worse. Now Jemima looked positively miserable. He tried again.

'I mean that it was a mistake to marry someone—you—whom I find so very attractive. It would have been better to wed cousin Augusta and then I could have endured her company beside me in bed with the utmost indifference.'

Jemima gave a little giggle. She looked slightly happier. 'Pray do not worry, my lord. *I* will sleep on the floor.'

Rob stared. 'I beg your pardon?'

Jemima had put the nightgown away in her bag and was now folding her cloak and laying it down on the floorboards beside the fireplace.

'I will sleep on the floor. I have done so many times before.'

'Have you taken leave of your senses?'

Jemima stopped abruptly at his tone and looked at him, her blue eyes widening. 'Not at all. I merely thought that you could take the bed and I will lie on the floor. I used to sleep on the floor a lot when I was a child.'

'You may well have done so. However, the Countess of Selborne does not sleep on the floor.'

Rob knew he sounded pompous and Jemima's look of amused disgust underlined the fact.

'Good gracious, Robert, you sound so stuffy!'

'Nevertheless...' Rob took a deep breath. '*I* will sleep on the floor. I have done so a great deal on campaign.'

'I dare say,' Jemima said calmly. 'Then we may both sleep on the floor and leave the bed free for some other worthy traveller.'

They looked at each other, then burst out laughing.

'I am going down to the parlour,' Rob said. 'I will be gone a while and when I return—please, Jemima— I would like to find you asleep. In the bed.'

'Very well, Robert,' Jemima said.

Down in the parlour, Rob found the landlord newly washed and humming about his cleaning whilst a small fire glowed in the grate. Mr Hinton pushed a glass of brandy in his direction.

'Take that on the house, my lord, with thanks to your lady wife for her ideas on chimney sweeping.' He paused. 'Had no idea you were married, my lord. From hereabouts, is she, your lady?'

'No,' Rob said. 'Jemima is from London.'

The landlord frowned. 'Reminds me of someone…
It'll come back to me. Family in these parts, has she?'

'Not as far as I know,' Rob said. He wondered how
long he should leave it before he went back up to the
chamber. The parlour was warm and the brandy was
making him sleepy. On the other hand, the sight of Jemima in the four-poster bed was likely to awaken all the
parts that the brandy had not yet reached. He would do
better to drink himself into oblivion, or at least inca-
pability.

Two further brandies and an hour and a half later,
Rob was tolerably certain that Jemima would be asleep.
He crept up the stairs and opened the door of the chamber, letting out a sigh that was three-parts relief and one-
part disappointment as he saw the sleeping figure in the
bed. In fact, it looked as though there were already two
people in the bed, for Jemima had put the monstrously
fat bolster down the middle, leaving a space of approx-
imately six inches for him to lie upon.

She had also left one candle burning. By its light,
Rob could see that his wife was almost entirely buried
under the counterpane, leaving no part of her body visible. A good thing too. He averted his gaze from Jemima's face and the sight of her lustrous hair spread
across the pillow, a deep blue-black in the golden light.
He quickly divested himself of his clothes, blew out the
candle and slid into the tiny space allowed to him.

After a minute he realised that he was holding his
breath for no apparent reason. Beside him, or rather on
the other side of the mountainous bolster, Jemima
breathed with easy regularity. Rob felt vaguely affronted that she should have found it so easy to go to
sleep. The bolster, whilst separating their bodies, did
not divide the pillows and as Rob rolled over in a vain

attempt to become more comfortable, he noticed that a strand of Jemima's hair was resting on his pillow and tickling his nose. He touched it gently. It felt soft and smelled of the same jasmine scent that he had noticed earlier. He resisted the urge to push the bolster aside, pull Jemima into his arms and run his hands through the whole shimmering coal-black mass of her hair. He could see her face in the faint moonlight, pale and serene as a church effigy. Her lashes were dark against the alabaster smoothness of her cheek and her lips curved upwards in a slight smile. She looked eminently kissable. Rob's body started to ache with frustrated passion.

He lay on his side and stared at her face in the moonlight. She looked very young, with her tip-tilted nose and flyaway dark brows. She *was* very young, it was simply that her experience was so very different from that of most young ladies of her age... Yet despite that difference in upbringing he would be the veriest cad to wake her now and make love to her. He should treat her with *more* respect because of her background, not less. And besides, he could not make love to her and inherit the forty thousand pounds.

Rob rolled over on to his back, eyes wide open, sleep receding even as he lay there. What was it that he had said to Jemima the previous day? That he only needed to know that he could not have something to want it very badly? Human nature, perhaps, and just at the moment he was damning his nature to hell. What he wanted was lying right beside him and he definitely could not have her.

He started to count sheep in a vain effort to go to sleep, but when he reached four thousand nine hundred and seventy-three he gave up. Would it be so terrible to break the terms of the will? He could always lie to Churchward—tell him that the marriage was unconsummated. Except Jemima might become pregnant and that would be rather difficult to explain away... Angry with himself for even contemplating such a deceit, Rob rolled on to his stomach and buried his face in his pillow. It smelled of Jemima. Soft, sweet, cool, tempting...

At the end of his tether, Rob flung himself over and tugged violently at the bolster.

It did not budge. Rob pulled it again. There was a ripping sound. Jemima's regular breathing paused and she sighed and turned away from him. Rob paused too. He wondered if she was really asleep.

'Jemima,' he whispered.

There was no reply.

'Jemima!' he said, rather more loudly.

Jemima made a tiny, inarticulate noise of deep sleep.

'Jemima!' Rob shouted.

Someone banged on the wall of the adjoining chamber and some of the plaster crumbled off the wall in response. Jemima did not stir.

Rob flung himself back down on the mattress and within a minute he had fallen asleep.

He awoke as the dawn was streaking the sky and the pale summer light spilled into the bedchamber. He knew almost immediately that he was alone in the bed. He struggled on to one elbow and looked about him. Sure enough, Jemima's side of the bed was empty. The bolster lay in virginal innocence down the middle of the bed, but the other side was bare.

Rob sat up.

Jemima was lying curled up like a small cat on her cloak by the fireplace. She looked tiny and fine-boned, the light glimmering on the fine lawn of her nightdress. Rob smiled. So she had ended sleeping up on the floor after all. Old habits died hard. He eased himself out of bed and scooped her up in his arms. Her head rested gently against his shoulder, her hair spilling softly against his bare chest. She felt very light in his arms. She also felt cold. Rob carried her over to the bed and laid her down. He was about to ease her back under the covers when he froze.

In the pale morning light Jemima's bare feet were clearly visible, small and delicate as the rest of her. Rob took one foot in his hand and ran his fingers over her skin. It was not soft to the touch. There were old scars, weals and the dark smudges of burns. Rob traced the line of one puckered welt along the side of her instep.

For a long moment he stared at it, head bent. He had seen burns before, just as he had seen the evidence of beatings. And now he had seen both on Jemima's body.

Rob took a deep breath. He had known Jemima was a chimney sweep's daughter. He had even known that she had climbed chimneys when she was child, but that had seemed a very long time ago, almost as though it had happened to a different person. Now it was brought home to him just how naïve he had been. A tiny, small-boned child of whatever sex was ideal for sending up a chimney-stack and a man like Alfred Jewell, poor as he had been at the beginning, would not scruple to use his own children to further his business. Jemima had been sent up chimneys and had burned her feet on smouldering soot and breathed in the thick, choking gas. She had struggled to survive in the claustrophobic smokestacks and had climbed for her life. His Jemima.

Rob was overtaken by a wave of fury so immense that he wanted to smash something, anything, to smithereens. Preferably Alfred Jewell, but failing that anything would do. His anger was so intense that he felt physically sick and after it had gone he was left with nothing but pity and a vague surprise that he could feel so strongly for a girl he had known so short a time. A girl. A woman. Jemima. She was his responsibility now and he would guard that with his life.

He wrenched the bolster from the centre of the bed, ignoring the tearing noise as it came away, climbed in beside his wife and drew her into his arms. She burrowed against him with the sleepy guilelessness of a child. Rob held her as delicately as if she was made of china and lay still as the dawn light strengthened in the room and Jemima slept on oblivious.

When Jemima awoke the room was full of sunshine and she was alone. She was also back in the bed and she knew that it must have been Rob who had put her there. She had woken in the night and had found it impossible to go back to sleep, so she had slipped out of the bed and gone over to the window. The town of Burford lay silent away to the east and beyond it the vast estate of Merlinschase, home of the Duke of Merlin. Somewhere out there, so close and yet so far away, was her niece.

Jemima had been fifteen and away at school when Tilly was born. She had known that Jack was sweet on Beth Rosser, the scullery maid at the Duke of Merlin's town house in Bedford Square, whom he had met when he had gone there to sweep the chimneys. Beth was small and thin and exhausted-looking from being at the beck and call of everyone in the house, but she had the kindest face and the sweetest manner that anyone could imagine. Beth had been Jemima's friend as well as

Jack's lover. Jack would take her little presents and would hang about the door, hoping to catch a glimpse of her about her work. He never spoke of her, but Jemima remembered the dreamy look on Jack's face sometimes; he had never looked like that since.

When Beth had fallen pregnant, there the trouble had started. She had not dared to tell anyone until she was more than six months gone and when she did, Jack had immediately wanted to marry her. Jemima had been on holiday from school at the time and she had hidden behind closed doors as Jack and his father argued the matter out. Alfred Jewell forbade his only son to throw himself away on a girl he disparagingly called a kitchen wench. He threw doubt on Jack's paternity of the child and laughed in Jack's face when he demanded to be allowed to marry Beth. When the two of them crept away to try and arrange a clandestine match, Jewell had contemptuously brought them back, thrown Beth out into the street and given Jack a thrashing. Jack had disappeared for more than two weeks and only turned up again in Newgate, locked up for drunk and disorderly behaviour. He would probably have been transported if Alfred Jewell had not stepped in and paid a hefty fine.

Meanwhile Beth had vanished. Turned off from her post, she was found by the landlady of the Saracen's Head, who sent word that Beth had gone into labour prematurely. Though the baby had survived, Beth had died through exhaustion and loss of blood. It was the only time that Jemima had seen Jack cry.

It was Alfred Jewell who had gone to the Duke of Merlin and arranged for the child to be found a place on his estate. Jewell had been keen to see the back of the little girl and forget that the whole episode had ever happened. Jemima had been sent back to school, shaken to the core by what she had seen. And Jack... She thought that he had never been quite the same again.

Now she was so near to Tilly, Jemima felt torn. The urge to see her niece had been strong, for throughout the previous six years she had nurtured ideas of the little girl's development and wondered what she looked like. Dark like Jack, with winsome curls and black eyes? Or fair like her mother, with Beth's pale skin and sweetness of expression?

On the other hand, it made sense to avoid both Tilly and the Duke of Merlin, for chance had an uncanny habit of throwing people together and it could prove very awkward. Jack had been right when he had said it was best to let sleeping dogs lie.

Jemima sat down on the floor and curled up by the fireplace, resting her head against the panelled wall. She sighed. Jack did not want her to interfere and she had to respect his point of view. The past was dead and gone with Beth Rosser.

Jemima slid down on to her velvet cloak and rubbed her cheek against the soft pile. Rob had said that she should not sleep on the floor and she did not really want to. She felt lonely—she wanted to creep back into the bed and cuddle up next to Rob for reassurance. Yet in a strange way he felt part of her loneliness. He might give her comfort, but he was still barely more than a stranger. She could not trust him. Not yet.

She curled up against the cloak. It reminded her of when she was a child and she and Jack had slept in fireplaces, in the ashes and the soot. In some ways she had come a long way and in others she felt as though she had barely changed at all.

Chapter Ten

Jemima sat on the edge of her seat as the carriage turned through the gateposts and made its way up the North Avenue towards Delaval Hall. There was a strange, hollow feeling in her stomach. For all that she had been 'my ladied' from London to Oxfordshire, this was the moment when being Countess of Selborne suddenly hit home. Now, as the thick woodland unfurled on either side of the drive and the white stone house in the distance became progressively larger, she started to realise what it meant to be mistress of Delaval. She trembled at the enormity of it all.

Rob had elected to ride for the final part of their journey that morning. It was a fresh, clear day with the wind blowing down from the hills and a scattering of tiny white clouds breaking the blue of the sky like small fluffy sheep. It was the most perfect day for a homecoming. In between watching the view, Jemima studied her husband as he had his first glimpse of his home for five years. Rob's face was set and hard as he took in the obvious neglect: the waist-high grass in the meadows, the fallen walls and the overgrown rides. Yet beneath his cool demeanour Jemima sensed a repressed excitement and a powerful tension. It made her realise how little she knew or understood of this man who was now her husband.

The coach jolted to a stop on the carriage sweep and a liveried footman came out to open the door. Rob had mentioned that Churchward had arranged for the house to be fully staffed and now Jemima saw that all the servants were lined up on the steps to greet them. An unfamiliar fear clutched at her heart. She had not been born to be a gracious lady. She would just have to make it up as she went along.

Rob was standing by the carriage steps, waiting to hand her down himself. It was a nice touch and Jemima smiled her thanks at him, but although he smiled back she sensed that his mind was elsewhere. Presumably he was concentrating on the Hall, which looked to Jemima like an overgrown doll's house, three storeys of top-heavy design adorned with long windows and lots of ornate stone carving. Jemima raised her brows slightly. Basically, Delaval was an ugly house. She wondered if Rob could see it too.

The butler stepped forward to introduce them to the other servants. It was a process that took some time. Jemima smiled and nodded until her face ached and knew that in her nervousness she would never remember all the names. There were a few moments that stood out: Mrs Cole, the housekeeper, seemed like a lifeline. The estate manager had a small daughter who came forward clutching a posy of cornflowers to present, and lisped out a welcome. Jemima hugged the child, almost crushing the flowers, and nearly cried all over her. Everyone seemed to approve of this.

Then Rob was leading her to the door and, unexpectedly, swept her up in his arms and over the threshold, to deposit her back on her feet on the sparkling tiled floor of the hall.

'Welcome to my home,' he said.

Glancing up into his face, Jemima saw his pride and pleasure. She could hear it in his voice as well. She realised that she had discovered her husband's one true love and she was disconcerted to feel a little jealous.

After three weeks at Delaval, Jemima was forced to admit to herself that matters were not turning out quite as she had envisaged them. Now there was no talk of grand pianos or village schools. She needed nothing but her old clothes and she worked morning, noon and night, scrubbing the floors, polishing the windows, washing the linen, overseeing the transformation of Delaval from neglected country house to gracious home again. She worked alongside the servants, and after three weeks she felt that she knew them as well as she knew her husband little, for in that time Rob had been in her company so rarely that she was afraid she might forget what he looked like.

In a way it was not surprising. Just as she had her work in the house, so Rob had his out and about on the estate, visiting the farms, discussing improvements with his estate manager, going to the markets to buy livestock and machinery now that Mr Churchward had freed up that part of his father's bequest that had come to him on his marriage. Yet Jemima found herself resenting Rob's distant manner. She was beginning to feel like one of the servants herself, and at least they got paid. She remembered his declaration on the day that they had married and how she had been apprehensive but excited at the prospect of his courtship. Such a thought brought a wry smile to her face now that Rob all but ignored her in favour of his long-lost love, his home.

At first the servants had looked askance at Jemima working alongside them, but after a while they had gradually come to appreciate her efforts. Nevertheless, Mrs Cole, the motherly housekeeper, insisted that she take a rest each day in the conservatory and that she should have some time off to go out. As Jemima had no acquaintance in the district and Rob had not shown any interest in introducing her to the neighbouring families, she had taken to walking through the gardens and the surrounding fields whenever it was fine.

It was mid-September now and the first hint of autumn was in the air. Jemima, exploring thoroughly, had decided that the Delaval estate was very beautiful even if the house was not. There was a long, wooded driveway coming in from the north that swept up to the front of the house. To the rear, the formal gardens had disappeared under a year's neglect and roses ran rampant, tangling with blackberry, honeysuckle, foxglove and thyme. Poppies had invaded from the surrounding fields, as had nettles and cow parsley. The peacocks pecked disconsolately at the weed-strewn drive and nested in the broken-down greenhouses.

On one of her walks Jemima had seen Rob at a distance, chatting with his estate manager over the repairs needed to the wall that enclosed the grazing meadow. She had almost gone over to join them, but then Rob had ridden away and the opportunity was lost. Since Jemima did not ride she had been unable to join him on these outings and he had not invited her to do so, though the stables now contained a very pretty, docile mare as well as his own hunter and various carriage horses.

Instead she walked the grassy woodland rides, breathing the scents of warm grass and dry bracken, pushing her way through waist-high nettles, learning about the butterflies and the birds and the animals. She had never lived in the country before. The gentrified surroundings of Strawberry Hill were as close as she had come to rural life and the rest of the time she had lived amidst the bustle of the city. Delaval was very different. The rhythms of the country seemed alien and confusing; at night it was so dark that the stars were diamond-sharp pinpoints of light. The silence seemed alive. Once, when Jemima had heard the bark of a deer from the woodland close by, she had almost jumped out of her skin.

Yet in its own way it was very beautiful and she was fast falling in love with it. She loved the dew-laden spiders' webs on the grass, and the tap of the wood-pecker in the forest and the brush of the wind through the trees. On one early morning walk she had seen a fox standing at the end of the ride, its nose raised to catch her scent. It had looked at her with unfathomable golden eyes before it turned and sauntered away. Jemima had wanted to share all this with Rob, to learn from him and ask questions, but it seemed he had no time for her. He was racing to beat the coming of winter, to secure Delaval before the seasons turned, so that they could start afresh with more hope in the spring.

Jemima's hopes were different. More than once during that first month she thought longingly of a comfortable villa in Twickenham and even dwelt nostalgically on life in the house in Great Portland Street. Jack could not write to her, of course, but her mother had penned a few difficult lines, wishing her well in her new life. As Jack had predicted, Alfred Jewell had washed his hands of his recalcitrant daughter. Mrs Jewell assured Jemima that she had not disclosed her daughter's address or, more importantly, her title, for fear that Alfred would wish to take advantage of his sudden connection with the aristocracy. The letter, laboured and full of things left unsaid, had caused Jemima some tears.

She was cross with herself when she gave way to the blue devils. Just because matters were not turning out quite as she had expected, it was no cause for self-pity. So Rob was obsessed with Delaval and not with her. Jemima reminded herself that he had only married her to secure his inheritance, and if she did not like her new place in the world then it was just too bad. She was a Countess, with an ugly manor house and a loyal staff at her service, and in time she would adjust to all the changes about her. Nevertheless, she was not the only one to notice that all was not well between Rob and herself.

'It's a crying shame,' she overheard Mrs Cole saying to the first housemaid one morning when Jemima had gone to fetch some fresh water for washing the windows and the servants thought that they were alone together.

'There's his lordship out working all the hours God sends and her little ladyship in here doing the same, and never the two of them meet, let alone exchange two words!'

'Too exhausted to exchange more than words anyway, I expect,' the housemaid said. 'Tilbury says the connecting door is always locked.'

Mrs Cole tutted. 'I heard it was a marriage of convenience. That's what they're saying in the village. I heard Lady Marguerite is back from London as well. Wonder what she will make of the whole business?'

'Probably tell them to get down to it and produce an

heir,' the housemaid giggled. 'Beats me, Mrs Cole—him such a handsome man and her ladyship such a pretty little thing! Still, there's no accounting for the quality!'

Mrs Cole put her hands on her hips and straightened up with a groan. 'You tell me, though, Daisy, what's the point in scrubbing up Delaval for the arrival of an heir if Lord and Lady Selborne can't get around to providing one—'

'I expect we shall get down to it at some point,' Jemima said, bustling in with the ewer of water and plonking it down on the window seat. 'It is at number two hundred on my list of things that require attention, Mrs Cole, after beating the guest-room curtains!'

The housekeeper gaped and the housemaid turned bright red. 'Beg pardon, ma'am, didn't see you there.'

'Well, never mind,' Jemima said. 'It would still be true whether you said it or not. Pray forgive me, for I know that I am supposed to ignore such comments, but I come from a very outspoken family and I could not let it pass.'

'Yes, ma'am,' the housekeeper said, looking fascinated and embarrassed in equal measure. 'I'll just get on with polishing the ballroom candlesticks, shall I, ma'am?'

'Pray do,' Jemima said politely. She waited until the door had closed behind the servants before she burst out laughing.

Nevertheless the comment had rankled. It did not surprise her that the servants gossiped; that was simply the way of things. Nor could it be expected that they would not have noticed the locked door between her bedroom and Rob's own. They had probably detected it on the very first night. Jemima knew that a lady would not be concerned about such things. But she was not a lady.

The news that Rob's grandmother had returned home also put her in a fluster. It could only be a matter of time before Lady Marguerite appeared to find out how their precipitate marriage was progressing—and to make pungent comment upon it.

Accordingly, she planned to speak to Rob after dinner that night, but he sent his apologies that he would not be joining her but would be heading straight to bed. Jemima sat in the newly cleaned drawing room, flicking through the pages of an eighteen-month-old copy of the *Ladies Magazine* and quietly seething inside. When she went up to bed she tried the door of Rob's bedchamber, rattling the handle quite loudly, but there was no noise from within.

The following day was very hot, with a strong sun for early autumn. Jemima had spent the day airing the guest rooms in the unlikely event that anyone would ever be invited to come and visit them at Delaval. The furnishings were old-fashioned but of good quality and there was plenty of wear left in them. She knew that decorating and refurbishing the house was the least of Rob's priorities. All of his father's money would go on rebuilding the estate and the farms so that Delaval could become self-supporting once again. His grandmother's money, should he inherit it, would go the same way. Jemima hung the blankets out on a makeshift line between the apple trees in the orchard and reflected once again that at this rate there would be no difficulty in Rob fulfilling the terms of his grandmother's will. The difficulty would come when the one hundred days were up and they could not remember each other's names.

So much for Rob talking about wooing his own wife. If this was his wooing, then men were even less adept in matters of the heart than she had been led to believe.

She was still fulminating about this some five hours later when Rob finally came in from a hard, hot day spent in the lower meadow. Jemima gave him ten minutes, then marched up to the bedroom door and knocked very loudly. She wanted to talk to him and this time she was determined that she should succeed.

After a minute or so the door was opened by Tilbury, Rob's manservant. Jemima could see Rob standing by the chest of drawers, soaping his hands and arms in the big white basin of water. His face was damp and there were droplets of water still in his hair. Jemima felt her stomach clench at the sight of him. His face and forearms were tanned from spending so much time working outdoors but she could see the line of paler skin at his neck where his shirt had shaded him from the sun. The skin there looked vulnerable and soft. Jemima found she wanted to touch it. She folded her arms defensively and stepped into the bedroom. Despite her nervousness she was not going to go away now.

'May I speak with you please, Robert?'

Tilbury was sorting out Rob's evening clothes, moving about the room with the unobtrusive precision that characterised the very best servants. It was the first time that Jemima had seen inside Rob's bedchamber and she looked about her with interest. The room was a mirror image of her own, worn but neat, but with a few personal touches that her own room did not afford. There were portraits of Rob's parents above the mantelpiece and on a side table a fine grouping of china dishes that Jemima thought Rob must have brought back when he was serving in India. The realisation that she knew nothing of his tastes and interests made her feel even more hollow and lonely.

Rob saw Jemima in the doorway, raised his eyebrows slightly and reached for the towel.

'Thank you, Tilbury. Please leave us.'

'My lord,' the valet said expressionlessly. He slipped out, closing the door behind him. Jemima suddenly found herself confronting Rob in his bedroom with no very clear idea of what she was about say.

'Good evening, Jemima,' Rob said, drying his hands and rolling his sleeves down. 'What is it that you wished to say to me?'

Jemima took a breath. It was still there, that hateful distance between them. He sounded as though he was asking his estate manager for a summary of the milk yield. She tilted her chin up towards him. 'I wished to speak to you without the servants present and this was the only way since I never see you alone.'

Rob threw the towel over the end of the bed. He looked tired and worn, exhausted no doubt from working outdoors all day. Jemima felt guilty to be troubling him and immediately repressed the feeling. Her concerns were as valid as anyone else's.

'What is it?' Rob said quietly.

Jemima looked at him. She made a slight gesture. 'Oh, Rob—it is simply that I am concerned for you. You look so tired all the time! Can you not take matters more steadily? You are working yourself into the ground!'

Rob shot her an irritated look. 'You do not understand the ways of the countryside, Jemima. This is the time when the hardest work has to be put in. We cannot sit back and simply wait for winter with the sheep byres tumbling down and the hay rotting in the fields.'

Jemima frowned. The jibe about not understanding had stung when she had spent the best part of the last month trying to learn and Rob had made no effort to teach her.

'Perhaps you are right that I do not know a great deal about life in the country,' she said, as calmly as she could, 'since you have not devoted any great time to explaining it to me. When you spoke of us restoring Delaval, I thought that you meant we would be working on the estate together. Yet we might as well be living in different places for all the time we spend together.'

She saw Rob frown and run a hand over his still-damp hair.

'Jemima, I am very tired—'

'You always are!' Jemima burst out. 'When we meet for dinner you are so exhausted you can barely summon the energy to eat, let alone speak to me! And then we retire to our separate chambers with the door locked between us. The servants have noticed it and they pity me!'

Rob gave a sharp sigh. 'Is that what is troubling you? You must learn not to regard servants' gossip.'

Jemima put her hands on her hips. 'I suppose that Lady Selborne of Delaval is above such things.'

'Of course.'

'But she is not above scrubbing the floors and washing the curtains! You cannot have it every way, Robert. I begin to feel like one of those very servants you so disregard!'

There was a stubborn, withdrawn look on Rob's face. 'I am too tired to discuss such matters now, Jemima. I wish to wash properly and dress for dinner and I cannot do that whilst you are here.'

Jemima felt hot and frustrated. 'Then when can we talk? You have time for everything except me. Over four weeks we have been married and I know as little of you now as I did then!'

Rob pulled his shirt over his head in one fluid movement and tossed it aside. Jemima looked quickly away from the sight of his broad, muscular chest.

'I thought,' Rob said, 'that in London you expressed the wish that we should preserve some distance between the two of us. Have you then changed your mind? Is that was this is all about?'

The colour flamed to Jemima's cheeks. 'Of course not! How arrogant you are! I am not forcing myself on your notice.'

'I am sorry,' Rob said, still in the same odiously polite and distant tone. 'I thought that was precisely what you were doing.'

There was a long silence. Jemima could feel her irritation buzzing in her blood like a fever. What was it about men that enabled them to be so attentive, so charming, when it suited their purpose and then to behave utterly differently thereafter? She had heard said that men were April when they wooed and December when they wed but she had not expected to have it confirmed so quickly. Rob had sweet-talked her into accepting his suit and now he had everything that he wanted and she was dismissed while more important matters such as his dairy herd and his flock of sheep took precedence.

'This floor could do with a clean,' she said suddenly. 'Since that is what you think that I do best—' She grabbed the side of the washing bowl and, without another word, tossed the water all over her husband. Fortunately the bowl was not full or she might have ruined the plaster ceiling of the dining room beneath and undone all her hard work of the previous week. As it was, Rob emerged spluttering and shaking himself.

'The devil! You little vixen!'

'I may be sorry for myself, but you are a pompous, infuriating *idiot*!' Jemima said furiously. 'A pity I did not know that before I married you!'

Rob grabbed her arms. His hands were wet and his torso dripping with soapy water. Jemima's cotton dress immediately soaked through. She struggled for release and found herself clasped more firmly against Rob's chest. She could feel the heat of his body against hers as the dress became as flimsy and transparent as a piece of damp blotting paper.

'Let me go!'

'In a minute,' Rob said pleasantly. 'Who would have thought that you had such a temper?'

'It serves you right for marrying a tradesman's daughter!' Jemima flashed. 'If you wanted a bloodless aristocrat, you should have married your cousin!'

'I am delighted with the arrangement I have made,' Rob said. He held her a little away from him and looked down into her angry little face. Jemima saw the beginnings of a smile in his eyes and felt her legs tremble in response. This was no good at all. She could not remain angry with him when her traitorous body was so susceptible to his touch.

'Let me go,' she said again, but this time it came out as a whisper. Rob was holding her so lightly now that she could have moved away at any moment and yet she did no such thing. She saw his eyes darken, saw him bend his head as he leaned down to kiss her, and slapped his arm away.

'Oh, no, you don't! Not before you talk to me!'

Rob laughed and let her go. There was devilment in his eyes. 'Very well. We talk—and then we kiss.'

'We'll see,' Jemima said.

Rob patted the bed. 'Would you like to sit here, Jemima?'

'No, thank you,' Jemima said. She went across and sat on the window seat. Rob flung himself down on the bedcover. He looked relaxed. He also looked muscular and tanned and rather too dangerously masculine. All the physical labour of the previous weeks had developed in him a physique that the habitués of Gentleman Jackson's saloon would have envied.

Jemima removed her gaze from his chest to meet the quizzical look in his eyes.

'So you wanted to talk to me. I am at your disposal. This is not just about the servants' gossip, I infer.'

'Of course not.' Jemima fidgeted. 'I hear that your grandmother has returned from London.'

Rob looked startled. 'Has she? Damnation. I had hoped she would stay away as long as possible.'

'Well, apparently she is back at Swan Park and no doubt she will be calling here shortly.' Jemima looked at him. 'And I do not doubt that she also hears the gossip, servants' tales or not.'

Rob was frowning. He swung himself off the bed. 'And you think that she will become suspicious about our marriage?'

'She already is,' Jemima pointed out. 'Everything that she hears will only confirm her suspicions.'

Rob walked across to the doorway, then turned back.

'I suppose that we should share a room, for appearances' sake at least.'

'No, thank you,' Jemima said clearly. 'I do not wish to share a bedroom with a man who spends all his waking hours out of my company. Maybe I am insufficiently unfeeling and aristocratic in my way of thinking, but that would make me feel more like a mistress than a wife.'

Rob's eyes glinted. 'There is more to being a mistress than sharing a bedroom, Jemima. Perhaps I should demonstrate—'

'No, thank you,' Jemima said again. She felt nervous, but she kept her gaze steady. 'You have effrontery, Robert Selborne. You ignore me every day for the last three and a half weeks and then you expect—' She stopped as Rob came to a halt in front of her. The wicked light was still in his eyes.

'I expect…what?'

'Well, you don't expect me to sleep with you,' Jemima snapped, 'since you still have sixty-five days to go!'

'Sixty-four days,' Rob said. 'Must you add on additional time?'

The light died from his eyes. He came to sit beside her on the window cushions and took her hands in his. 'Jemima, do you have any idea why I have kept apart from you for so long?'

Jemima's eyes flashed. 'Of course I do not know, since you did not see fit to tell me. How am I to know anything if you do not speak to me? I *assumed* it was because you are obsessed with this ugly house and your estates, Robert.'

Rob looked hurt. 'Delaval is not ugly!' He sounded as though Jemima had insulted his favourite pet. 'How can you say that?'

Jemima laughed. 'It *is* an ugly house, Robert. You are either blind or in love with it if you cannot see that. Which is not to say that it does not have its own charm, for it does. Even I can see that.'

'I suppose that must be true since you have been working so hard to make it spick and span,' Rob said.

Jemima felt slightly mollified. 'I have been working hard. Thank you for noticing.'

Rob's fingers tightened on hers. 'I notice all sorts of things about you, Jemima.' He raised his hand to touch her cheek lightly. 'The way your hair curls when it is damp; the tiny line between your brows when you frown...' His hand moved to trace the line on her face. '...and the way your eyes darken just before I kiss you.' Rob leaned closer. 'They go a cloudy blue, and your lashes tremble—'

'Oh, no,' Jemima said sharply, placing one hand against his bare shoulder to push him away. His skin was warm to the touch and she found herself absent-mindedly rubbing her fingers over the curve of his shoulder. She stopped abruptly and saw that Rob was laughing at her.

'Admit that I almost caught you out there,' he said. His eyes were bright with amusement—and desire.

Jemima moved as far away as she could get from him within the window aperture. She felt shaky but she was not going to succumb—not before she had said her piece.

'It is Delaval that has had all your attention recently, Robert, not I. Your estate is a hard taskmaster.' She put her head on one side to study him. 'Or a very demanding mistress.'

Rob smiled faintly. 'I admit that I have been a little preoccupied with the estate over the past month—'

'A little?'

Rob gave her a shamefaced smile. 'A great deal?'

'To the exclusion of all else,' Jemima said.

'I have been trying to make up for lost time,' Rob said.

'I understand that. But you have missed dinner on six occasions and on five others you have been so late to bed that I have not heard you come up and sometimes you are gone so early in the mornings that I do not see you all day.'

The look Rob gave her made her break off in confusion. 'How wifely of you to notice, my love. Does that mean that you care for me a little?'

'I…' Jemima bit her lip. She was deeply suspicious that he would use her answer to trap her into some other personal admission. And she *did* care for him; that was undeniable. The fact that she resented the hold Delaval had on him would have been absurd if it had not made her realise just how much she did care.

'I do not like to see you wear yourself out,' she temporised. 'It cannot be good for you…'

'Sweet concern.' Rob bent forward and kissed her cheek. 'Would it disturb you to know the other reason for my long hours of work, Jemima?'

Jemima's heartbeat quickened at his nearness. His unshaven cheek brushed the softness of hers and she jumped back.

'I am deliberately trying to avoid you, Jemima,' Rob said softly. 'There is little but you in my mind, whether I am building a wall or milking a cow or discussing the purchase of seed propagators with Jephson…'

Jemima felt her anger start to melt. She smiled a little. 'This is vastly romantic, Robert. Pray continue.'

Rob ran a hand through his hair. 'You may laugh,

Jemima, but you have no notion of your danger. I thought that if I spent each and every day outside, working myself into the ground, I might be so exhausted that I had no time for more…amorous thoughts.' He got up abruptly. 'However, I found that the reverse was true. Physical work seems to make me feel all the more—'

'Ardent?'

'Lustful, licentious, libidinous.' Rob glared at her.

'Impassioned, improvident and imprudent,' Jemima said sweetly. She could not help smiling. 'Oh, Robert—'

'It is *not* funny,' Rob said huffily.

'No, of course not.' Jemima slid off the window seat and went up to him. She put her hands against his chest. 'You could have told me, though.'

'No, I could not. Talking about it makes it worse. It makes me think about you too much and then I want to kiss you. More than just kiss you, to tell the truth. As I said, you have no notion of the danger you are in.'

'But because you did not tell me how you felt, I thought you were avoiding me because you did not like me,' Jemima said. 'I could see that Delaval meant everything to you and so I assumed it would have your best attention.'

Rob grinned. 'I would far rather give you my best attention…'

Jemima backed hastily away. 'You know that you cannot do that.'

'Would you object if I did? I know that a little while ago you were reluctant, my sweet. I have not forgotten that you think that love is a trap.'

'I do not know,' Jemima said, blushing. 'It is true that I have had thoughts of you, Robert.'

Rob looked entranced. 'Sweetheart!'

'But,' Jemima said doggedly, 'I am aware that there are still sixty-four days to go.'

Rob put out a hand and drew her into his arms. He did not kiss her, but held her close against his chest. It was sweet and comforting, but it disturbed her too. He smelled of sandalwood and cool skin and water, and Jemima wanted to turn her cheek and taste him; taste the salt and the faint traces of sweat and the coolness.

She hid her blushing face against him. 'Is it very vulgar to wish to spend time with one's own husband, Robert?'

'Very unfashionable,' Rob said. She could hear the smile in his voice. He loosened his grip a little. 'As it is to wish quite desperately to kiss one's own wife. I fear that we are both quite as bad as each other.'

Jemima put her fingers against his lips. 'Wait! You cannot kiss me.'

Rob groaned. 'Oh, Jemima, please.'

'No, indeed. We are in your bedroom—'

'Yes,' Rob said, an edge to his voice, 'I had observed that.'

'So it would be very dangerous.'

Rob grasped the bedpost in one hand, trapping Jemima between him and the foot of the bed.

'One kiss does not break a vow of celibacy,' he said.

'That depends on—'

'The kiss?'

'On what constitutes celibacy,' Jemima said quickly. 'What do you think, Rob?'

Rob shook his head. 'Oh, no. I will not be drawn into a philosophical discussion at a time like this. Tomorrow maybe, when we go out riding together.'

'Are we going out riding tomorrow?'

'I thought that it would be nice. As we do not spend enough time together...'

'But I cannot ride.'

'Then I will teach you.' Rob laughed. 'That should be enough to kill all passion between us. We shall be brangling within a few minutes. So let us make the most of it now...' He made to draw her closer again.

Jemima slipped under his arm and made for the door. 'When you have taught me to ride, then you may consider whether kissing is permissible or not under the terms of the will.'

'Jemima,' Rob said. 'Hell and the devil!'

But his wife had whisked through the door to her bedroom. He heard the key turn firmly in the lock.

Rob slowly picked up his shirt and tried to ignore the persistent message his body was sending him of how very attractive he found his wife, and how very provoking the whole situation was becoming.

'I hope you are a quick learner,' he muttered to the panels of the closed door, 'or I shall probably expire with frustration.'

Chapter Eleven

The riding lessons were a disaster. Jemima was not afraid of horses—she had been quite accustomed to the dray horses in the streets of London—but she quickly realised that she had no talent for riding. Rob was very patient with her, but Jemima knew that she could never match the powerful precision with which he controlled his black stallion, Arrow. Rob had told her that he had been riding since he was a child, and it showed. When he was in the saddle there was a fluid grace about the movement of man and horse together that quite took her breath away.

Alas, there was no fluid grace about Jemima's own efforts, only a lumpen lurching that left her breathless and the mare bad-tempered. After Jemima had fallen off twice and Poppy had galloped off across the meadow with her bouncing in the saddle like a bag of coal, she had given up altogether and retreated to the gig, which was pulled by a placid pony of some twenty years and never went faster than a slow trot. In this way they progressed about the estate, Rob riding slowly alongside the gig so that he could point things out to her and they could talk. And just occasionally Arrow would become skittish and Rob would gallop off to give him some proper exercise whilst Jemima sat and watched them disappearing over the fields and into the distance.

'Why did you wish to leave Delaval and join the army, Rob?' Jemima asked as one afternoon at the end of September, as they walked together along the northern avenue. She could see the house in the distance like a child's dolls' house, growing larger as they walked towards it.

'When you had all this and it is evident that you love it so, it seems strange that you chose to leave it behind.'

Rob drove his hands into the pockets of his worn shooting jacket.

'It was a great deal to do with this business of being told I could not do something,' he said, with a crooked smile, 'and a little to do with believing that some things are worth fighting for.'

Jemima was watching his face. 'What do you mean by saying that it sprung from a dislike of being told that you could not do something?'

Rob's face lightened into a smile. 'My parents forbade me to go to fight, so of course…' he shrugged '…I was immediately desperate to do it. I was always a most contrary child and my grandparents spoiled me and made me worse. I had good principles to follow, but not the self-discipline to behave well.'

'You do not give that impression now,' Jemima observed, surprised. 'Indeed, you seem very disciplined. Did the army instil that in you?'

'It did. I soon grew up when I was confronted with genuine conflict and I had people relying on me.' Rob expelled a long breath. 'The India campaign had felt like a boy's adventure, but when I went to the Peninsula, that was different. By then I was a hardened soldier and I had seen the sorts of sights I had never dreamed of. In fact, I realised what a spoiled brat I had been in the past.'

They turned down one of the grassy rides that led from the main avenue. The turf was springy beneath their feet and from the grass the late wild flowers peeped; white clover and ox eye daisies. The sunlight cut through the branches in slanting green lines.

'You have not spoken much about your childhood here,' Jemima said. 'Were you happy?'

'I was very happy to live here.' Rob looked about him. 'How could I not love Delaval? I have cared for it with a passion since I was a small boy.'

Jemima smiled at the thought of the serious little child with his intense love of his home. 'And what were your parents like?'

Rob frowned slightly. 'I was a late child. By the time my sister was born Mama was already forty and it was another two years before I put in an appearance. I always felt that there was a huge gulf between my parents and Camilla and me—not just in age. Papa was a very distant parent. For the first sixteen years of my life, until my grandfather died in a shooting accident, Papa was Viscount Selborne, the Earl in waiting. I sometimes wonder whether that frustrated him. He always seemed most irascible.'

'I suppose that it must be strange waiting to step into another man's shoes,' Jemima said. 'Your grandfather must have been very hale.'

'Oh, he was. Had it not been for the accident I believe he might have lived to a hundred.'

'What happened?'

'It was all very unpleasant.' Rob gestured towards

the far side of the wood. 'We had gone out in a party, shooting pheasant, and my grandfather had taken Ferdie with him—my cousin Ferdie Selborne, whom you met at the wedding?' When Jemima nodded, he continued, 'There was a dreadful accident and my grandfather tripped over his own shotgun. He killed himself. Ferdie was utterly distraught. He was only fifteen and he and the beater had been alone with Grandfather when it happened. There was nothing they could do. He had practically blown his head off.'

Jemima shuddered. 'How dreadful for Ferdie.'

'Yes, indeed. To my knowledge he has never been shooting since.'

'And the beater?'

'Fellow called Naylor. He was a groom on the estate. He went off to the wars and we never saw him again.'

'So your father inherited at last, although not under the circumstances that anyone might have wished?' Jemima wondered whether the hot-tempered Earl had felt in some way cheated by his manner of accession. His father's death had not been a natural end and it was not what anyone would have wanted.

'He did. He inherited the earldom and he did not become any less irascible. We all lived here together until I went off to India—my grandmother, my parents, Camilla and I.'

'I should have liked to meet your grandmother,' Jemima said, smiling a little. 'Any lady with the eccentricity to attach such a condition to her will would have been well worth the meeting, I think.'

'She would have liked you,' Rob said. 'She always told me I should marry a girl with something about her, not a milk-and-water miss. I am glad that I would have pleased her in my marriage.'

Jemima felt warmed by the compliment. 'I do not suppose that your father would have approved of me, though. How could he have wished for a tradesman's daughter in the family?'

'Ah, well, my father was different. He valued accomplishments rather than character,' Rob said. 'He was not particularly interested in Camilla and myself as children, for example. Apparently he was pleased and a little surprised when we were born, but after that his interest waned until Camilla could make a good match and I could take on all those responsibilities that the heir to the estate was supposed to fulfil.'

'Was that when you went against his wishes?' Jemima asked. 'He must have been quite shocked.'

She felt a little tentative to be probing family history, but on the other hand it helped her understand more about the reasons Rob had left Delaval—and the devils that now drove him to restore his home to its former glory.

'He was both shocked and angry.' Rob shrugged awkwardly. 'I disappointed him dreadfully, I think. The difficulty was that I felt smothered by his expectations. I was twenty-one and he was expecting me to settle down and produce an heir for Delaval and take up the reins of the estate. I had had that expectation on me for as long as I can remember.' He shifted his shoulders again uncomfortably. 'Camilla had made matters worse in a way, although I do not blame her. She did not marry well, you see, at least by Papa's standards. She fell in love with a sea captain who was visiting his brother in the neighbourhood and she was determined to make the match. He was of good family, but it was not an outstanding alliance. Papa was disappointed but he let it go as Camilla was already three and twenty and had not had a great many suitors. Most of his energies were focussed on me, and on making me fit into his plans.'

Jemima was intrigued. 'What happened when you told him you wanted to join the army?'

Rob stopped walking. Jemima could feel the tension in him, though he spoke dispassionately.

'There was an almighty argument, as you might imagine. It was all fairly predictable. He threatened to disinherit me.'

'Yet still you went away.'

Rob gave her the ghost of a smile. 'The estate is entailed, so I knew he could not deny me Delaval. But, yes—I left him blustering and my mother crying, and I went to India with Sir Arthur Wellesley and then to the Peninsula. I wanted to do something, anything, to prove that I could follow my own course. And I thought that Delaval would always be there waiting for me.' His expression hardened. 'And, of course, it was, but not in the way I had imagined it. Decimated, broken down, deserted. And my parents dead. I cannot forget that the last words we spoke to each other were in anger.'

Jemima went to him and took his hands in hers. She wanted nothing other than to make him feel better and try to assuage some of the guilt that held him fast.

'You could not have known that this would happen, Robert.'

'No.' Rob's grip tightened on her for a moment. 'But I would have liked to make my peace with my father in this world rather than the next.'

Jemima stood on tiptoe and kissed his cheek. 'Perhaps he already knows,' she whispered. 'You are here now and you have already worked so hard…'

There was a second of tension whilst they looked at

one another, then Rob's arms were about her and his cheek was pressed against her hair.

'As have you. I swear, Jemima, that you are so sweet I do not know what I have done to deserve you.'

They stood very still and very quiet for a long moment.

'Did you marry me because you like to go against convention, Rob?' Jemima said, muffled.

Rob tilted her face up to his and smiled down at her. 'No. I married you because I like you. I wanted you with me almost from the first, Jemima, even when we were saying our vows. I knew that our original agreement was not enough, not what I wanted.' He sighed, releasing her. There was a rueful look in his eyes. 'I never thought that keeping the terms of the will would be like this. I did not expect it to be so difficult. A part of me wants to hold you at arm's length to make things easier for us, but another part...' his eyes held hers '...another part of me wants quite the reverse...'

Jemima could not pull her gaze away from his. She felt shivery cold, though the day was warm. There was a question in Rob's face, and when she took one step closer to him, he bent his head. His lips touched hers and lingered for a moment, lightly, almost experimentally. There was a second when Jemima tried not to succumb, tried not to close her eyes and tumble into the sensual spiral that was waiting for her. This went against every sensible tenet that she had learned in her life, and yet it was impossible to resist because she did not want to. And after a moment she gave herself up to Rob, and to the kiss, leaning in to his body, kissing him back mindlessly as the world spun around her and she felt as though she was falling into such a hot, dark and exciting place that she never wanted to escape ever again. They pressed together as the leaves stirred over-head and the shadows danced.

'*I married you because I like you.*'

Liking and loving...Jemima was suddenly unsure where one ended and the other began. She drew away, dazzled by emotions that she was only just beginning to understand.

'Rob...' She smoothed her bodice down with fingers that shook. 'We must not.'

Rob's look was quizzical. 'Why not, sweetheart?'

'Because we are like to forget ourselves.'

Rob took her hand. 'And you were afraid of that, as I recall.'

Jemima evaded his gaze. 'I do not want—'

She stopped. She was shocked to find that what she really wanted to say was: '*I do not want to fall in love with you...*' and hard on the heels of the realisation was the thought that perhaps it was already too late. She *was* starting to fall in love with her own husband. Per-haps it was already too late to withdraw. She thought of Jack and Beth, and the misery and utter cruelty of love. That was not what she wanted. But this could be different. She had to take a risk. She had to try and trust.

'I do not want us to do anything we might regret later,' she said.

Rob leaned one hand against an oak sapling. 'What-ever happens, I should not regret it, Jemima.' He looked at her. 'Would you?'

'I cannot answer that,' Jemima said, in a rush. 'It is not that I do not care for you, Rob, and I want to trust you, but—' She broke off. She did not want to hurt him with her words and she knew that as yet she did not trust him completely. If she did, she would not feel so vulnerable.

'We have as long as we need,' Rob said, pulling her close again. 'We can go very slowly, Jemima...'

Despite that, there was urgency in his hands, in the lips that claimed hers in their next, irresistible kiss. Jemima's lips parted beneath his without question and the kiss became deeper and demanding and utterly overwhelming. It swept her away and she trembled under the onslaught. The silken warmth of his mouth, the ravishing exploration of his tongue, were unfamiliar yet completely seductive. All her defences were tumbling. It was only the small voice of self-preservation in her head that stopped her abandoning herself to him completely. She put one hand against his chest and eased away from him.

'I do believe,' she said, a little breathlessly, 'that you would be the most hardened seducer, Robert Selborne, if only you were free of this stipulation of the will. You sweep all my qualms aside.'

Rob laughed. 'Acquit me of being a rake. If I were, I should never have let you escape from my bedroom that night, will or no will.'

'You will notice that I have not been in your bedroom since.'

'And very wise too. I may not be a rake, but I not a monk either.'

'I have always thought it must be very difficult for monks,' Jemima said, slipping her hand through his arm.

'I have no wish to consider their plight,' Rob said feelingly, 'being so taken up with my own.'

'But you must confess that matters have been very much easier since we have been spending so much time together,' Jemima said. 'We have managed to behave with complete decorum—' She stopped, arrested by the expression in his eyes. It was hot and dark and very dangerous. Her breath caught in her throat.

'Complete decorum?' Rob enquired. He slid his arms about her. 'Is this what you call complete decorum? When I cannot even look at you without wishing to take you to bed—'

'Robert!'

'I beg your pardon, Jemima. I was simply being truthful. Would you prefer me to dissemble?'

'No.' Jemima broke free. 'I would prefer you to remember that there are still fifty-one days to go.' She gave him a wry look. 'Once you have won me over and are free to make love to me, you may not want me any more…'

'Fifty days,' Rob said, 'not fifty-one. And I do believe, madam wife, that there is not the slightest chance that you will escape me.'

Jemima was caught at a disadvantage when the first visitors called at Delaval Hall the following morning. She was standing in the grate in the library fireplace, staring up the chimney and trying to discover the blockage that was making the chimney smoke. They had started checking all the fires the previous day, for it was traditional to have them all swept by Michaelmas day in preparation for winter. Jemima, having spotted several birds' nests and other obstructions, had decreed that a sweep needed to be called out from Cheltenham to give all the flues a good clean before the onset of the cold weather. This was the fireplace that concerned her the most. There was something sticking out of the flue obstruction about halfway up. She could see it herself, but it was out of reach.

'Gracious, child, whatever can you be doing?'

Lady Marguerite Exton's voice seemed to echo around the chimney causing Jemima almost to bump her head. She extracted herself very carefully, climbed out of the grate and stood up, wiping her hands on her apron. She was not very dirty since the soot was stuck on to the side of the chimney rather than on to her, but she suspected that she had a smear on her cheek and that her bonnet was probably a little dusty. She cursed her grandmother-in-law's inconvenient arrival.

'Good morning, ma'am. Pray excuse me—I have been checking on the chimneys in preparation for the arrival of the sweep.'

'Extraordinary,' Lady Marguerite opined. She was looking patrician and elegant in a dress of striped brown silk with matching bonnet and parasol. Her immaculate appearance made Jemima feel very grubby.

Letty rushed forward to kiss Jemima's cheek. She held her at arm's length and giggled. 'Dear me, Jemima, Rob must be a terrible slave driver! To have his wife of barely a month working so hard! We have heard the most shocking tales, you know!'

'Letty…' Lady Marguerite rebuked. She turned to Jemima. 'We have given you and Robert quite long enough on your own, Jemima. Indeed, it is quite surprising to me that you have not grown bored with the sight of each other. A month of unadulterated solitude is surely enough to make even the most doting husband and wife quite desperate for other company.' She looked around. 'Whereabouts is my grandson?'

'Robert and I have not seen a great deal of each other since we came to Delaval, ma'am,' Jemima said, ring-

ing the bell for refreshments. 'He has been busy about
the estate and I have been supervising the improvements
to the house. I believe that he is currently building a
wall in the lower meadow. I will send a servant to ask
him to join us.'

'Very proper,' Lady Marguerite nodded. 'I mean it is
proper that you should not spend too much time together. It is not proper that Robert should be working
on the estate like a labourer. That is quite unsuitable. If
you do not have sufficient servants to do the work, I
shall send some across from Swan Park.'

Jemima caught Letty's eye and tried not to laugh.
Rob's cousin was pulling a face that suggested she was
accustomed to Lady Marguerite's snobbery. It encour-
aged Jemima to stick to her guns.

'I do believe that Robert enjoys the work, ma'am,'
she said mildly. 'He has commented on more than one
occasion how stimulating he finds physical work.'

Which he had, she thought, but not perhaps in the
way that Lady Marguerite might think.

'Enjoys it!' Lady Marguerite looked disgusted. 'I
have no notion what is wrong with the youth of today.'

'I do believe that Robert once helped build the ram-
parts at one of the Peninsular forts,' Letty said, eyes
twinkling. 'No doubt he got his taste for hard work from
there, Grandmama.'

Lady Marguerite wrinkled up her nose as though it
had a bad smell underneath it. 'I always said that the
army was bad for a man. It spreads moral turpitude.'

She took a piece of cake from the plate that the footman was proffering. 'This is very good. Please com-
mend your housekeeper.'

'I shall indeed, ma'am,' Jemima said, pleased that her
mother's plum cake recipe had been appreciated. She

had no intention of laying claim to the praise. No doubt Lady Marguerite would think that cake making was decidedly beneath the Countess of Selborne.

'We came to make sure that you would be able to join us for my ball the week after next,' Letty said, stirring her tea. 'You have had the card? I was hoping that you and Robert would attend, and it would be a pleasant way for you to meet some of our acquaintance.'

Jemima paused. She had no wish to disappoint Letty, whose friendship already warmed her heart, but it was decidedly awkward. She did not wish to bump into anyone who thought that she looked familiar, either through resemblance to Tilly or because they were at Anne Selborne's wedding. On the other hand, she could not skulk in the shadows and become the reclusive countess. People would think she was mad. She really ought to speak to Rob, both about her niece and also about breaking the news of her antecedents to his family. She took another look at Lady Marguerite's face and decided against doing it just now.

'I am sorry,' she excused. 'I would love to be there, Letty, but I fear I have absolutely nothing to wear and I do not believe there is time to purchase anything in Cheltenham now.'

Letty's face wrinkled with disappointment and Jemima felt mean.

'Oh, Jemima, I was so looking forward to it. The party will not be the same without you!'

'Letty is quite right, child,' Lady Marguerite put in unexpectedly. 'We must have the new Earl and Countess of Selborne at our party or everyone will think that there is something havey-cavey going on!'

Jemima tried not to blush guiltily.

'Perhaps we could go shopping in Burford the day after tomorrow,' Letty said, brightening. 'There is a very elegant modiste's shop there, Madame Belinda. If you required anything for the ball I am sure that she could provide it.'

'Burford?' Jemima said. She remembered how close it had been to Merlinschase. 'Oh, no, I do not think—'

'Splendid idea,' Lady Marguerite said. 'Robert!' She smiled as Rob came into the room. 'We are all to go to Burford on Thursday. You will come with us.'

Rob came across and kissed her cheek. 'Good morning, Grandmama! Will I?'

'Certainly.' Lady Marguerite sniffed delicately, then drew back from him. 'It will do you good to get away from all this labouring.'

'I was telling your grandmother how stimulating you have found your work, Robert,' Jemima said sweetly.

Rob came across to her side and sat down next to her on the sofa. He gave her a look that was slightly apprehensive. 'Have you, sweetheart?'

'Indeed.' Jemima smiled at him. 'Remember that you told me that working in the fields made you feel quite—'

'Jemima—'

'Active, assiduous and agricultural,' Jemima finished.

Rob narrowed his eyes. 'Retribution, revenge and reprisal,' he whispered in her ear.

'There is only one drawback in going to Burford,' Letty said. 'I fear that Augusta and Ferdie Selborne and Bertie Pershore must be invited to accompany us, for they are arriving tomorrow and are staying for the ball. Not that there is anything wrong with the boys, but Augusta is another matter. She has no sense of humour—'

'That is the least of her problems,' Rob said.

'How unchivalrous you are!' Letty's eyes sparkled. 'I would never choose to inflict her upon you, Jemima, but as she is Robert's cousin I fear you cannot escape!'

Escape was precisely what Jemima wished to do. She had no wish to meet Miss Selborne again for she had thought Rob's cousin a sharp-tongued creature at the last meeting. Then there was Ferdie Selborne, who was privy to the wedding, and Bertie Pershore, who was the Duke of Merlin's nephew. It was all so intolerably complicated and Jemima felt as though she was walking on eggshells and just waiting for the whole sorry mess to disintegrate under her feet.

'Girl's a dreadful bore,' Lady Marguerite concurred. 'Wish someone would marry her for her money, but almost everyone has realised that if they run through her fortune they are still left with Augusta.'

Letty giggled. 'Oh, dear, you are harsh, Grandmama, but I fear it is true. And she will insist on joining us on the trip and will probably try to cosy up to you, dearest Jemima, so that she may boast of her friend the Countess of Selborne...' Letty slapped a hand over her mouth. 'Oh, how cattish of me! But I am afraid that it is true.'

The thought of the dreadful Augusta cosying up to her was almost too much for Jemima when she remembered the girl's spiteful comments the last time they had met.

She had been afraid that Miss Selborne would remember her and unmask her as a counterfeit Countess, but if what Letty said was correct, Augusta would be too busy ingratiating herself to remember their brief encounter at the wedding. The thought appealed to Jemima's sense of humour.

'I am sure that it will be quite entertaining to invite Miss Selborne to accompany us,' she said.

'I do not suppose,' Letty said hesitantly, 'that your brother, Mr Jewell, would be able to attend my ball? It would be a splendid thing if he were!'

There was a sudden chill in the atmosphere. Lady Marguerite was looking particularly cold.

'I am sorry,' Jemima said. 'I doubt that Jack will be visiting Delaval in the near future.'

Letty drooped and not even a second slice of the plum cake could revive her. Jemima was surprised that a chance encounter had had such an effect on her. Miss Exton was a gregarious girl who must have plenty of admirers. It was malign fate that had made her choice rest on Jack Jewell.

After the ladies had departed to visit their acquaintance in the neighbourhood and Rob had gone back to his work, Jemima returned to the chimney-piece. She could still see the obstruction sticking out into the flue some ten or eleven feet up. By standing on tiptoe in the grate and stretching upwards she was within a few feet of the impediment, whatever it was, but she still could not touch it. She needed to climb up a little.

Jemima hesitated. It was the work of but a few minutes to climb up the flue and investigate, but she knew she should not do it. The Countess of Selborne did not climb chimneys…

With a quick look over her shoulder, Jemima eased off her shoes. The stockings could stay although it was not ideal to climb other than in bare feet. She moved back to the chimney, then paused. Her skirts would hamper her and even though she was only in her old clothes, she should not really climb in her gown. She did not have enough spare dresses to waste this one. Quickly she slipped out of the gown and let it crumple to the floor. Time was of the essence. She hardly wanted the servants to catch her halfway up a chimney.

The climbing came back to her easily. She had never really forgotten it, for at school she would be the tomboy who scrambled up trees and scaled walls in the place of sooty chimneys. Mrs Montagu had never quite managed to persuade her that only hoydens climbed.

This chimney was easy. It was wide, with protruding bricks inside to aid the climber. Jemima set her feet to the lowest step and pulled herself upwards, feeling for hand holds, the skirts of her petticoats brushing the soot from the chimney so that it fell in a soft pile in the grate. She felt her stockings tear on the sharp edges of the bricks, felt her elbow rub uncomfortably against the wall, breathed in the thick smell of soot and felt the familiar press of the chimney stack about her. It was dark and narrow and she was much bigger than she had been when sweeping was her work. Jemima felt slightly panicky.

She put a hand out and touched something metallic, cold and hard. Whatever the blockage in the chimney, it was made of metal. Her searching fingers brushed the edge. It felt like a tin box. She eased it into her hand.

She was about to start her descent into the library when she heard the door open and the sound of voices. Jemima froze, one hand above her head grasping the tin, the other clamped tightly to the wall of the chimney.

'She must have slipped out for a moment.' She heard Rob's voice first. 'I do apologise. I will tell her that you called, Lady Vause.'

There was a murmur of voices, then the sound of the door opening and closing again. Jemima relaxed. She pulled the tin out of its niche and edged down the chimney towards the square of light at the bottom. Suddenly the light was blocked out.

'Jemima!' Rob's voice seemed very loud in the enclosed space. 'Come down that chimney at once!'

Jemima lost her footing and scrabbled desperately to hold on. The tin box fell with a clatter into the grate and Jemima made a grab for another of the brick handholds. She was swinging in the chimney just above Rob's head and she was desperately afraid she would fall off and flatten him.

'Robert!' she said sharply. 'Pray get out of the way! You are putting me off.'

Peering down, she saw that Rob was looking up at her. Or more precisely, he was looking straight up her petticoats. She saw his face break into a grin.

'By God, perhaps there is something in this chimney climbing after all!'

'Please move out of the way!' Jemima shrieked. She swung her legs wildly to try and gain a foothold and she heard Rob give an appreciative whistle. A second later his hands closed very firmly about her waist and he had pulled her out of the chimney and was depositing her on to the library floor in a little pile of soot.

'I could have managed perfectly well on my own,' Jemima flashed, thoroughly ruffled. 'You should have left it to me. I know what I am doing!'

'I beg your pardon,' Rob said, still grinning. 'I was of the opinion that you might fall at any moment and squash me flat. I thought I was helping.'

Jemima smoothed her hair back with a self-conscious hand. There were smudges of soot all down her bare arms and streaks of it dusting her neck and chest above the line of her bodice. Her cap had come off and her hair was tumbling down. It did not help that Rob was looking her up and down in a positively fascinated manner, his dark eyes lingering on the curve of her breasts beneath the soot-smeared bodice, and travelling lower to consider her shredded stockings and bare feet. Jemima brushed her petticoat skirts down, aware that the material was transparent and that Rob could see her legs through it. Not that that mattered—when he had been standing directly beneath her he had seen her legs and more. Jemima felt quite over-heated at the thought.

'I came to tell you that Lady Vause had called,' Rob said, still staring at her with the same strange intensity. 'Jemima, what the devil were you doing up there?'

Jemima gestured to the tin in the grate. It was covered in a thick layer of soot that had solidified into tar.

'There was a blockage up the chimney. I merely went up to investigate.' She tried to make it sound quite an everyday occurrence. 'I think that you will find that the chimney will not smoke now.'

'Well, thank the Lord for that,' Rob said. His lips twitched. His eyes came up to hers and there was an expression in them that made Jemima quake. She had never been particularly self-conscious when climbing before; sweeps quite often climbed in the nude if it meant that they could navigate the chimneys more easily, although Jemima had not favoured this as it gave the body absolutely no protection against scrapes and grazes. Nevertheless, she had never possessed any false modesty about climbing in her underclothes. Until now.

Rob stepped closer. With deliberation he took hold of Jemima's upper arms and bent his head to her collarbone, blowing very gently on the skin. The particles of soot clung to her, but Jemima's skin heated from the contact. She felt the goose pimples run along her skin and her nipples hardened. Rob raised a negligent hand and brushed some of the soot gently from the soft skin of her upper breasts. His touch was light, but the expression in his eyes was anything but impersonal. His hand fell to her bodice, grazed the side of her breast, and a tiny moan escaped Jemima's lips. She felt completely breathless, melting.

'You need dusting down,' her husband said, very softly.

Jemima turned away and hunted about desperately for her pile of clothes. 'N…no I don't. I need to get dressed and to see Lady Vause.'

Rob's hand slid around to the nape of her neck. 'She has gone now.'

'But my clothes—'

'You cannot put them on. They will become dirty.'

Jemima gave a little wail. 'Robert, I cannot stand here in the library in my petticoats.'

'Indeed, you look delightful, my love,' Rob said, his fingers stroking the curve of her neck. 'I had no idea that chimney sweeping could be such an exciting experience.'

He picked her up and placed her gently on the big sofa. Jemima struggled half-heartedly.

'Robert, the servants—'

'Are busy turning away visitors,' Rob said. He touched the curve of her eyebrow. 'You have a smudge of soot here…' He touched the tip of his tongue to the corner of her mouth. 'And here…'

Jemima's lips parted on a gasp and he smothered them with his own. She could not believe that she was in a state of undress and that they were kissing so naughtily on the sofa where Lady Marguerite had recently sat with such perfect propriety. Somehow it made everything seem even worse. More wicked, more exciting.

'I worry about you, Jemima,' Rob said, against her lips. 'You might hurt yourself doing things like that. You really must not climb chimneys any more. Especially not in your underwear.'

'Some sweeps climb naked,' Jemima said not quite innocently, then gasped as her provocation received the response it deserved as Rob's mouth took hers again, roughly this time, plundering, demanding surrender. She slid down further against the cushions.

'Damnation, Jemima,' Rob groaned, when at last he could speak again. 'You said that deliberately! You may climb the chimneys any time!'

He pressed little kisses against her throat and the swell of her breasts until the skin was pink and stung. His hand slid up her leg beneath the shredded petticoats.

The door opened. 'My lord, the chimney sweep is here from Cheltenham—' Giddings, the butler, broke off in shock as his gaze took in the Earl and Countess romping on the sofa. He withdrew and closed the door with studied quietness. Jemima and Rob fell apart. They stared at each other.

'I never thought that I should be grateful for Giddings's intervention at a time like that,' Rob said, trying to master his breathing, 'but if he had not come in then I do not know when I should have stopped.'

'Oh, dear,' Jemima said, rolling away and resuming the search for her gown and shoes, 'we have shocked him, Robert!'

Rob lay back on the sofa and put his hands under his head. He grinned at her as he watched her hunt for her clothing. 'At least that will give the servants something else to talk about,' he said.

Chapter Twelve

'*Dear* Lady Selborne,' Augusta crooned, as she, Jemima and Letty sat in the carriage on the way to Burford two days later, 'it is so utterly splendid to make your acquaintance! You have no idea how I have longed to see Robert married.'

'She means that she longed to see Robert married to her,' Letty whispered in Jemima's ear. 'Pray do not be taken in, Jemima dear!'

Jemima folded her lips on a smile. All the way from Delaval she had been plagued by Augusta's insincerities, just as Letty had predicted. Rob's cousin clearly had no idea that she was buttering up the little sweep's girl whom she had so disparaged at the wedding. It made Jemima feel a little more confident that she could carry off her role as Countess of Selborne with aplomb.

'I am delighted to meet you too, Miss Selborne,' she said politely.

'Oh, call me Gussie,' Miss Selborne murmured. 'All my special friends do!'

Jemima smiled. 'Thank you.'

Augusta inclined her head graciously. The ostrich plumes in her hat bobbed like a débutante at her presentation. To Jemima's eyes she looked far too grand for a country outing, particularly in comparison to Letty, who was looking charming in pale blue muslin.

'I understand that you are from London, Lady Selborne,' Augusta continued. 'Do you not find the country so dreary in comparison? I suppose you shall be persuading Robert to take you to London for the Little Season?'

'I doubt it,' Jemima said dryly. 'Rob's work is here at Delaval for the foreseeable future. We do not have the time nor the inclination to visit Town, Miss Selborne.'

Augusta's lips formed a disapproving moue. 'Oh, but surely... Delaval is so parochial in comparison to the company one meets in London...'

'There is Letty's birthday ball next week,' Jemima pointed out, with a smile for the other girl. 'Surely that will present the perfect opportunity to meet new acquaintance?'

Augusta shrugged. 'I suppose that Merlin will be there. And his son, that rakish Marquis. He might be worth cultivating.'

'The Marquis of Merlin is married now, Augusta,' Letty said, not without satisfaction. 'You could make up to his wife and try to procure an invitation to Merlinschase, I suppose. After all—' she shot Miss Selborne a look of dislike '—a Marchioness is a greater catch as a *special friend* than a mere Countess!'

Jemima could not help laughing, turned it into a cough and buried her nose in her handkerchief. This was an entirely different side to Letty Exton from the sweetness that she had seen before. She inferred that Letty disliked Miss Selborne extremely, though why, she could not guess. There was something more to this than a simple dislike of Miss Selborne's malice.

'I know it is bad of me to bicker with Augusta so,' Letty said later, as she and Jemima walked slowly up Burford High Street that afternoon. The party had gone its separate ways and was to meet at the Lamb Inn later. Fortunately Augusta had elected to accompany Mr Pershore instead of the girls, trying, Letty said, to fix his interest.

'The thing about Augusta is that I know her to be such a troublemaker,' Letty continued. 'She was the same when we were at school. She was always trying to cause trouble for the other girls, especially the ones who were more popular or pretty than she. She is the same with you now! I hate to see that false flattery!'

Jemima patted her hand. 'Pray do not concern yourself, Letty. I met girls like Miss Selborne when I was at school too—I know exactly what they are like! Though I must confess,' she added, 'that until now I have never been in the position where they wished to be my special friend!'

They laughed together. 'Where did you attend school, Jemima?' Letty asked artlessly. 'I went to a seminary in Bath and it was the most tedious bore!'

Jemima felt a pang. Her own education had been so much more than that. Perhaps she had valued it more because she had been so desperate to learn. Or perhaps she had just been fortunate.

'I went to one of Mrs Montagu's schools at Strawberry Hill,' she said. 'It was wonderful.'

'Mrs Montagu!' Letty stared in confusion. 'Lud, then you must be a prodigious bluestocking, Jemima! I had no notion. I am quite in awe of you now!'

Jemima laughed. 'I am scarcely a bluestocking.' She

took Letty's arm. 'And the one thing I am nervous about is choosing a new ball gown! I have not bought a new gown in an age.'

Letty's face cleared. 'Now I may help you there!'

The steep High Street was busy with carriages, horses and carts rumbling down the hill towards the fine old bridge across the Windrush. They walked slowly through the narrow streets, admiring the magnificent church and the neat almshouses on the green next door. The sound of children's games rose over the wall of the school opposite.

Halfway down the main street was Madame Belinda's, a supremely elegant modiste, very superior for a provincial dressmaker. Jemima was not at all sure that she would have had the courage to go in there on her own.

She came out with her ball gown, two other gowns, one for walking and one for evening, a figured silk shawl, two hats and a very pretty bandeau for her hair. There had been plenty of other outfits that Jemima had coveted but, despite Rob's assurances, she felt guilty to have spent as much money as she had. They had little to spare and what there was had to go on restoring the estate. Besides, Jemima could not see why anyone would need a whole wardrobe full of clothes. You could only wear one gown at once, after all.

Jemima was just starting to relax and enjoy the outing properly when the disaster happened. They were walking along Sheep Street, with the intention of meeting the gentlemen at the Lamb for some refreshment before they started the journey back to Delaval. They had left the shops behind and were passing a line of extremely pretty cottages, when the door of the nearest one swung open without warning and two children tumbled out over the threshold. Behind them a woman's voice was raised with a note of alarm, but the girls paid no heed. They were chattering—quarrelling, Jemima realised, over possession of the golden-haired doll that one had clutched in her hand. The girl raised it above her head, out of reach of the other, and pirouetted around. The smaller child was jumping up and laughing, an infectious giggle that was so familiar it tore at Jemima's heart.

A carriage rattled along the road. The woman called again from inside the cottage, then came to the door, a baby in her arms. There was a man standing in the shadows beyond her shoulder but Jemima scarcely noticed him. She was staring at the smaller girl, all tumbled black curls and big black eyes, just like her father. So now she knew. Jack's daughter was the image of him.

There was a shriek as the elder child caught her foot in the cobbles and Jemima jumped, dragging her gaze away from Tilly. She caught the other child almost as a reflex, putting her gently back on her feet. The woman started to thank her and Jemima smiled and said something in return. She was not sure what. She could not concentrate. Jack's daughter was watching her with her solemn dark gaze. She looked well fed and well cared for. She looked healthy and happy. Very happy.

Jemima stood stock still, staring at the little girl. She bore an alarming likeness to Jack—or to Jemima herself. Perhaps there was the merest hint of Beth in the lines of her face and the way her mouth tilted up a little to one side when she smiled. She was smiling at Jemima now, slipping her warm little hand confidingly into Jemima's own and tugging at her. For a moment they stood side by side.

It was the shock on Letty's face that brought Jemima back down to earth. Worse, she could see Augusta Selborne coming towards them from the direction of the High Street. Augusta was leaning on Rob's arm and chattering to him, and they were still some distance away, but Jemima knew that they had seen her. They had seen her and they had seen Tilly, and they were coming closer by the second. Jemima felt a little sick.

She released Tilly gently and smiled down at the little girl.

'You had better go with your mama and your sister, poppet. Perhaps we shall see you again soon.'

The woman was still thanking her as she shepherded the children in front of her into the house. The little dark girl went last, clutching the woman's skirt.

'Come along, Tilly,' the woman said a little impatiently. She turned to the man, who had stepped past her now and out on to the pavement. 'Good day, your Grace. Thank you for your visit.'

The gentleman raised his hat and the door closed quietly behind the woman and her children. Jemima struggled to move. Her knees were suddenly rather shaky. To have stumbled across Tilly here seemed the worst possible coincidence, but to do it in company was even more unfortunate. And in addition to the little girl, she had also stumbled upon Tilly's guardian, the fearsome Duke of Merlin. Even now he was putting a hand under her elbow to steady her and any moment he would recognise her and then she would be even more deeply in the suds.

'Are you quite well, ma'am?' the Duke asked.

Jemima looked up into his face and registered the shrewd, dark eyes, and hard, hawklike features. It was a long time since they had met, but she had not forgotten his face and it seemed he had not forgotten hers. How could he, with Tilly to remind him? She saw the recognition come into his eyes and with it a mixture of shock and deep disapproval.

'How do you do, Miss Jewell?' the Duke of Merlin said frostily, releasing her arm abruptly. 'It is a great surprise to see you here.'

There could be no explanations on the pavements of Burford. The Duke bowed coldly and Jemima thought that probably he would have moved on there and then had it not been that she was in company with Letty Exton. This was another disaster. Jemima saw the Duke hesitate as he recognised Letty, and then he looked back at her with the suspicion and dislike deepening in his face. Jemima knew exactly what he must be thinking— that she had come to cause trouble, or to ask for money, or to presume on a connection that was tenuous at best. He would imagine that she had already ingratiated herself with Letty and her family and that maybe she had presented herself under false pretences. Jemima struggled to think of a way that she could explain herself, but no easy solution presented itself. She felt as though she had lost all her normal composure.

'Uncle Merlin!' Letty said. 'What a surprise! How do you do, sir?'

'How do you do, my dear.' The Duke was smiling at Letty but it faded quickly enough when Letty said, 'I believe that you must already know my companion, sir, but she is no longer Miss Jewell, rather Lady Selborne.'

The Duke absorbed this latest piece of information with no more than a flicker of a disapproving eyebrow, but Jemima felt the force of his anger. His tone was arctic. 'Indeed? My congratulations, Lady Selborne.'

There was a curious silence. Jemima's mind was totally blank. She did not know how to start to explain. It was complicated enough trying to think what to say about Tilly, let alone explain her marriage to Rob, the Duke's godson.

And Letty, looking from one to the other, suddenly seemed to recall the strange circumstances of the encounter, and the child who looked just like Jemima, for she blushed bright red and stammered, 'I…I beg your pardon, sir… Did you wish to speak with Lady Selborne alone?'

The Duke's lips quirked mirthlessly. 'I imagine that I should, but not here. We seem to be attracting quite a crowd…'

It was true. Not only had Rob and Augusta and Bertie Pershore come upon them now, but a number of curious passers-by were lingering in the street. People were starting to stare. Jemima wanted to sink with despair.

'Your Grace!' Augusta Selborne was pushing forward. 'What a pleasant surprise.'

Her sharp gaze turned to Jemima. 'And Lady Selborne, what a dark horse you are! I had no notion that you had family here in Burford!'

Jemima felt angry and vulnerable. It seemed imperative to prevent Augusta from saying anything else stupid, but she could not think what to say. She could summon up no easy excuse that would not seem like an obvious lie. Her desperate gaze sought Rob. He was standing a little back from the others and he had not yet greeted his godfather. His jaw was set hard and there was an angry light in his dark eyes. As Jemima looked

at him he turned, and his cold gaze settled on her. Her
heart froze at what she saw there.

'Robert—' she said.

'Robert.' The Duke greeted his godson with an ironic
inclination of the head. 'How pleasant to see you again!
It seems that we have urgent matters on which we need
to catch up. I deeply regret that I am engaged for the
rest of the afternoon or I would most certainly discuss
them now. Does tomorrow suit?'

Rob nodded. 'Thank you, sir.' His tone was clipped.

'I will ride over to Delaval in the morning,' the Duke
continued. He nodded to the group. 'Until then, Robert.'
His gaze fell on Jemima and hardened. 'Lady Selborne…'

There was a moment of silence after he had gone,
then Letty caught Augusta's arm and hustled her along
the pavement.

'Come along, Augusta! Grandmama will be waiting
at the inn.'

Augusta's pansy brown eyes mocked Jemima's face.
'And won't she be pleased to hear our news!'

For a moment Jemima thought that Rob was going
to turn on his cousin, but after a second he took a very
deep breath and instead offered Jemima his arm. Jemima felt a sick lurch in her stomach. She wished that she
had trusted Rob and chosen to explain everything to him
before now. She wished she had told him about Tilly.
She wished she had disclosed her connection with the
Duke of Merlin. But it was too late for that now.

She looked at him. Rob's eyes were very dark and
expressionless. He looked towards the window of the
cottage where both little girls, one dark, one fair, were
clambering up on the seat to stare and wave at them.

Jemima opened her mouth to speak, then saw Augusta and Letty watching her and closed it again.

They fell into step behind Letty, Augusta and Bertie. Augusta showed every sign of falling back and trying to eavesdrop, but Letty marched her along the pavement like a sergeant major. Rob slowed his steps to put a little distance between them and the rest of the party.

'What an extraordinary resemblance that child bore to you,' he said pleasantly, quite as though he was discussing the weather. 'I believe that she is Merlin's ward although I have never seen her before. But evidently you knew that already.'

Jemima felt his impenetrable gaze on her like a physical touch. She shivered under it.

'I…yes…I did know.' Jemima groped for words. 'The Duke of Merlin—' she began.

'Yes? I collect that you already know my godfather,' Rob said ironically.

Jemima cast him a quick look. 'We met some time ago.'

'I see.'

'I had not seen him since. We—'

'And the child?' Rob interrupted her.

It was so unlike him to interrupt that Jemima's gaze flew to his face. She stammered a little.

'I am sorry that I did not tell you about her.'

'So am I,' Rob said, a little grimly. 'I am sorry that you saw fit not to tell me anything at all.'

Jemima could sense his tension for it was implicit in every line of his body. He had his hand on her arm, steering her along the pavement, and she was grateful to him. The town seemed crowded, but she could not seem to focus properly on the people who passed by.

'She is a connection of yours, I infer?' Rob continued.

They had almost reached the door of the inn. Jemima could see Letty practically dragging Augusta over the doorstep whilst Augusta craned her neck to try and see what Rob and Jemima were discussing behind them.

Jemima stopped. Rob was watching her very closely and suddenly she could read the expression in his eyes and all her emotions came alive, for under the huge self-control that she could see he was exerting was an anger burning bright and hot. In that second she realised exactly what he was thinking—that Tilly Jewell was her own child and that, intolerably, the Duke of Merlin could well be the child's father...

Jemima withdrew her hand quickly from his, feeling the colour come into her face, a colour that she knew would make her look even more guilty.

'Oh!' she said. She pressed her hand to her mouth. 'Oh, Rob. You think that Tilly is my daughter—'

There was a step beside them and Ferdie's jovial voice cut the atmosphere like a knife through muslin.

'There you are, Robert! Wondered where you'd got to! The others are all ready to go. The fellow with the piano is positive that it is going to rain and he suggests that he sends it over to Delaval on the cart when the weather is dry.' Ferdie grinned, apparently oblivious to what he had interrupted. 'Has Rob been telling you about the purchase he's made for you, Jemima? A grand piano for a wedding gift!' He clapped Rob on the shoulder. 'Told him he must be besotted to go to the trouble of transporting it all the way to Delaval on these roads!'

Jemima pulled herself together. Rob was looking impassive again, but she could see the muscle that twitched in his cheek. She wanted to cry.

'A wedding gift,' she said slowly. 'How...very generous of you, my dear. Thank you for remembering that I was interested in music.'

She saw Rob make an equal effort to match her composure. 'You are very welcome, my love,' he said.

Lady Marguerite and the rest of the party were emerging from the inn and the carriages were being brought around. Everyone was acting as though there was nothing wrong, and yet it felt to Jemima as though they were all caught in some horrible pretence. Lady Marguerite's expression was wooden, Letty looked frightened, Augusta had a high, angry colour and Bertie Pershore simply looked embarrassed. With a flash of insight, Jemima realised that Augusta must have made some loaded remark about the encounter with the Duke of Merlin and that Lady Marguerite must have put her in her place.

Jemima closed her eyes briefly, then opened them again. She did not for one moment delude herself that Lady Marguerite had any sympathy for her. It was simply *bad ton* to make a scene in public.

She swallowed hard and squared her shoulders. She knew that Rob would protect her in front of his family, but she had no notion what would happen once they were private together. She remembered the flash of fury she had seen in his eyes. Even if she explained to him that Tilly was not hers, would he still be furious with her? She had knowingly kept her previous connection with the Duke of Merlin a secret from him. She wished fervently now that she had not kept any secrets, for suddenly she was left feeling very alone.

It was starting to rain as they left Burford, big drops falling from fat grey clouds, but Rob did not notice.

The gentlemen were all on horseback whilst Jemima had the Delaval carriage to herself and Lady Marguerite, Letty and Augusta shared the carriage behind. Letty had tried to insist that she should accompany Jemima, but Rob had overruled her. He thought that his wife probably needed some time to collect her thoughts. Seeing the child had evidently been a shock to her. Or perhaps, Rob thought, clamping down on his violent fury, seeing the Duke of Merlin had been the greater surprise.

He tried to be rational and go over the facts as he knew them. Jemima and his godfather were evidently acquainted. What was not clear was the extent of that acquaintance. If it had been straightforward, Merlin would surely have cleared up the situation there and then. The fact that he had not suggested that the circumstances were delicate. Rob tried not to jump to conclusions and found himself positively leaping ahead, despite his best intentions. Jemima had been Merlin's mistress and the child was the outcome of their liaison.

He stopped his runaway thoughts very deliberately, allowed his anger to abate and tried not to pull on the reins too much in case he damaged Arrow in the process. The others were giving him a wide berth and he did not blame them. He knew he must look grim. What was intolerable was the thought that all the party knew as much as he and must be speculating along much the same lines. He had been cuckolded before marriage; his wife had had an illegitimate child; he would be a laughing-stock…

This last hurt less than the thought that Jemima had not trusted him. It threw a great many of his assumptions into confusion. Despite the fact that they had known each other but a short time, he had thought that he understood her. He had thought her honest. It seemed that he had been mistaken.

His anger and his disappointment were stark and painful. He had wanted his virginal bride to be precisely that. He had thought that this wooing of her, which had been progressing so agreeably in the last few weeks, would have a particularly sweet end.

He had been taken in by her innocent protestations. When he had kissed her she had withdrawn with a modesty that had seemed entirely genuine. Over the past week or so he had been leading her step by step towards exploiting the natural sensuality that he sensed within her. Except she might already have explored that all too well...

Rob frowned. Beneath his anger some shame stirred. He knew nothing of Jemima's life in the Jewell household or the circumstances that might have led her to throw herself on the mercies of a rich protector. He was also making assumptions about his own godfather, a man he admired and whose integrity he had never questioned until now. He was condemning Jemima unheard simply because the facts looked bad. And because he was jealous. Damnably jealous.

'Oh, Rob. You think that Tilly is my daughter—'

Rob frowned. He had seen the precise second that Jemima had woken from her shocked trance, had seen the guilty colour that had come into her cheeks and the horror in her eyes. It had seemed quite clear. And yet...

The child had looked exactly like her. The same heart-shaped face, the same silky black hair, the same... No. Different eyes. Eyes as black as soot rather than the colour of lavender. It was a small thing, but it made him wonder.

Rob became aware that the rain was pelting down

now, running in rivulets down his face. Ferdie brought his horse alongside.

'I say, old fellow, would you mind awfully if we all put up at Delaval, just until the storm eases? It's closer than Swan Park…'

It was about the last thing that Rob wanted, but he did not have much choice. With a gruff word of acquiescence he urged his horse forward so that he could give instructions to the coachman.

His mind returned with inevitability to the puzzle in hand. If the child in Burford was not Jemima's daughter, then who was she? He needed to talk to his wife. Very urgently. And now he would have to fight his way through a crowd to do it.

Rob had no opportunity for a private word with Jemima before dinner, and as the rainstorm had not abated by dusk, it was agreed that their guests should stay the night.

It seemed the worse possible time for them to be hosting their first visitors. Not only was the house still in a state of upheaval and the servants flustered by the arrival of unexpected guests, but as time wore on he could feel the chasm between himself and Jemima widening whilst his sense of impatience almost got the better of him. He wanted to pick her up and carry her out of the dining room under the noses of their guests. He wanted to shut the two of them away and ignore their visitors until the secret that lay between them was explained. Neither option was possible.

Rob watched his wife all through dinner, whilst he answered what felt to be an interminable series of questions from his grandmother about the restoration of Delaval and chafed at the need for propriety and good manners. He felt very uncomfortable. All the family were behaving as though nothing was amiss and yet they all knew that there was something very wrong. He felt as though he was acting a part in a very bad play.

Jemima was also putting on a sterling performance, but occasionally her shoulders would slump and she would look tired. Rob thought that she looked small and vulnerable and he could not help feeling a pang for her.

Jemima looked up and caught his eye. She did not look away. Rather her gaze seemed to convey an urgent need to talk to him. Rob felt slightly better. At least she still wanted to speak to him. She was not trying to avoid him. That had to be a good sign.

Chapter Thirteen

It was late before Rob had the chance to speak to his wife alone. Ferdie and Bertie had escaped to the local hostelry as soon as they decently could and the ladies had retired, full of tea and gossip. Rob and Jemima had fulfilled their role as hosts admirably, but Rob was profoundly relieved to see his visitors safely to their rooms. He spent a long time over his own toilet, waiting to be sure that all his guests had retired and that Jemima would be alone, then he went along the corridor to her chamber, knocked at the bedroom door and went in. The room was empty, but from the dressing room came the murmur of voices. After a second's hesitation, Rob went in there as well.

Jemima was sitting on a tapestry stool at her dressing table and Ella, her maid, was brushing her hair. She was dressed in her nightrail and in the candlelight the fine lawn material looked thin and insubstantial. The maid looked up, saw Rob in the mirror, and the hand holding the brush stilled. Jemima was saying something to her, but now she looked up too, an arrested expression coming into her eyes. Ella took one look at Rob's face, dropped a curtsy and slipped past him, closing the door behind her.

Rob leaned back against the door, feeling the cool smoothness of the panels against his hands. Now that the moment of truth had arrived he felt strangely apprehensive. Perhaps there were things that he did not wish to know at all. But it was too late for that now.

'May we speak?' he asked.

'Of course.'

Jemima sounded very composed, but he saw the anxious way in which she pressed her hand to her throat. She got up and came across to him. The light shone through the transparent cotton of the nightrail. Rob picked up the nearest thing to hand—a silky dressing robe with an oriental design—and passed it to her.

'You had better wear this,' he said shortly.

She secured the dressing gown about herself and tied it. Her hands were not quite steady. Then she turned to face him. There was a silence.

'I do not know where to start,' she said, and he could hear the raw nervousness in her voice. His heart started to pound, though he kept his tone level.

'Wherever you prefer. With either the Duke of Merlin—or the child that looks exactly like you.'

'The child, then,' Jemima said. 'For she came first.' She gave him a faint smile and he realised that his feelings had showed all too clearly on his face.

'I know that you thought me Merlin's mistress,' she said, 'but I swear it is not so.'

Rob felt his breath coming a little easier. 'Never?'

'Never.' Jemima hesitated. 'I have been no man's mistress.'

'Then the child—' Rob said.

'Is my niece.' Jemima looked up and met his eyes

very straight. 'Tilly is not my daughter. She is my niece.'

'Your niece?' Rob stared blankly. He had not thought of this. Something that felt like a crushing weight was lifting from his chest. He felt a little stupid. 'You have a niece?'

'I do. Tilly is Jack's daughter.'

Rob strode over to the window and stood inhaling the cool, rain swept air. He felt inexpressibly relieved. 'You had best tell me the whole. How old is she?'

'She is six. Jack was seventeen when she was born.'

'And her mother?'

'Beth is dead. She was my friend.'

'I see,' Rob said. His mind was spinning.

'She looks very like you,' he said.

Jemima smiled a little. 'I know. It was a shock for me too.'

Rob sat down beside her on the bed. 'Tell me all about it,' he said.

He listened whilst Jemima talked; of the climbing days and life in Nutner Street and the camaraderie of the sweeps and Beth, who had been Jack's girl and Jemima's friend. She told him what had happened when Beth had died and the Duke of Merlin had offered Tilly a home. The candle burned down, casting their shadows against the wall.

'I thought that you seemed a little shocked when I mentioned Merlin to you,' Rob said ruefully. 'I assumed it was because you were overawed at the thought of the Duke being my godfather whereas, in fact, you were surprised for an entirely different reason...' He shook his head. 'Oh, Jemima, why did you not tell me?'

He saw Jemima knit her fingers together. She was shaking a little and he wanted to cover her fingers with his and reassure her. But a part of him was still angry with her and could not quite let it go. He sat still and watched her.

'I should have done,' she said, head bent. 'I should have trusted you.' She looked up, her expression twisted. 'When I agreed to marry you, Rob, I knew nothing of your connection with the Duke of Merlin. I did not even know that Merlinschase was close to Delaval. And until today I did not know where Tilly was. So you see...' she shrugged dispiritedly '...I had no reason to speak.'

Rob's eyes narrowed. 'But as soon as you heard of my connection with Merlin you must have known there would be a danger.'

Jemima stared past him into the heart of the fire. 'I knew there was a danger that Merlin might remember me, but I thought it slight. We had only met twice. The other thing that I did not know was that Tilly looks just like me.' She gave a bitter smile. 'Or that I look like her.'

Rob took her hand. 'So you did not deliberately seek her out...'

Jemima looked up and met his eyes. In the candlelit dark she looked very young. 'No. I swear it. Oh, a part of me has always wanted to see Tilly, to make sure that she was well and happy...' She shrugged, her shoulders looking thin under the nightrail. 'But another part knew it might be upsetting and dangerous, and that it was best to leave it be. Jack always said that. Father would taunt Jack with little pieces of information about Tilly.' She looked at Rob. 'You know—"I hear that your daughter is already better at her letters than you have ever been" or "It is fortunate I took that baby away from you for her to have any chance of success in life''—that sort of thing.'

Rob's mouth tightened into a thin line. His opinion of Alfred Jewell, never of the highest, was going downhill more rapidly than a snowball in winter.

'In the event, Jack was wise,' Jemima said wryly. 'I now know that Tilly is happy and healthy, but I wish that I had never seen her. Merlin thinks that I am here to make trouble, I know he does, yet it was never my intention!'

'We may sort that out tomorrow,' Rob said, stroking her hand. The release of tension, the relief where the anger had been, was very powerful.

'I suppose so.' Jemima's shoulders still drooped. 'I am sorry, Rob.'

'For what?'

'For being so foolish. And most of all for not telling you before.'

Rob edged a little closer. 'Why did you not?'

Jemima's face puckered. 'I do not know really. I *wanted* to tell you, but secrecy has been a bit of a habit for me and I told myself that I did not know you well enough.' Jemima's lavender-blue eyes were dull. 'Now you are angry with me, and your grandmother thinks I am a fallen woman and that hatchet-faced Augusta will spread dreadful rumours, and if she remembers where she saw me before it will make matters much worse...'

'And which of those is the most important?'

Jemima looked at him. 'That you are angry with me,' she whispered.

Rob put his arms about her and drew her head down to his shoulder. 'I am not angry with you.'

'Well, you should be.' Jemima sat up and pushed him away almost angrily. 'You are too *nice*, Robert Selborne! I thought that the very first time I met you. I thought then that some unscrupulous person would take advantage of you.'

'It is fortunate then that you caught me first. You may take advantage of me with my blessing.'

Jemima gave him a watery smile. 'Oh, Rob. But now that everyone has seen me and Tilly as well… I cannot believe I have been so stupid!'

Rob gave her a hug. 'I shall speak to Grandmama after I have spoken to Merlin. We shall sort matters out.' He looked at her. 'Do I have your permission to tell Grandmama the truth? It is the only way, I fear.'

He saw Jemima bite her lip before she acquiesced. 'I suppose so.' She sighed. 'It is difficult to imagine how I could sink any further in Lady Marguerite's estimation. It might have helped me to redeem myself had I been *enceinte* but I will have to disappoint her, I fear.'

'For now, perhaps.'

He saw Jemima blush slightly. 'Rob…' she did not meet his eyes '…would you have been so very angry with me if Tilly *had* been my daughter?'

There was a silence. Rob struggled with himself. He wanted to be honest with her. 'I would have been shocked—and disappointed. I *was* shocked, when I thought that Tilly was yours.'

'Of course. I know that men wish their brides to be innocent…' Jemima looked up. Her eyes were shy. 'You have no cause to worry, you know. I told you that before.'

Rob pulled her back into his arms, holding her tightly. 'I cannot pretend that I am not glad, Jemima. But if Tilly had been yours then I would not have put you aside. You have become too important to me.'

Their gazes locked. Rob lowered his head very gently and kissed her lips. Then he put her firmly from him.

'Get into bed.'

Jemima's eyes were huge. 'Rob—'

'Don't worry. I am going to stay with you, but only because I do not wish Augusta to see me creeping from bedroom to bedroom like an actor in a bad play. It would be just like her to be spying in the corridors.'

Jemima was frowning. 'If she remembers me—'

'Then we shall tell the truth. You look very tired. Pray do not worry about this now.'

Jemima plucked his sleeve. 'But your relatives… Your grandmother will not acknowledge me again once she knows my background.'

'She will have to if she wishes to speak to *me* again.' Rob urged her towards the bed, pulling the covers back for her. Jemima sat down on the edge of the bed and obediently swung her legs under the pile of blankets. And then she stopped, her gaze narrowing on his face.

'What is it?'

Rob wrenched his gaze up to meet hers. 'Your feet. I saw them before, when we stayed the night at the inn and I put you to bed. But I had forgot…'

Jemima wiggled defensively under the covers and pulled the sheet up to her chin. 'They do not hurt. All the burns healed long ago.'

She sounded matter-of-fact. Rob sat down on the edge of the bed next to her. 'Do you have any scars elsewhere?'

'The elbows and heels are the worst,' Jemima said. 'You use them to wedge yourself into a chimney so they tend to take the greatest punishment.'

She eased one arm out modestly from under the bedclothes and held it up so that the fine material of the sleeve fell back.

'I fear that I may never wear elegant summer dresses with the shorter sleeve…'

Rob could see what she meant. The skin of her elbow was puckered and hard, and there were scars along her arm. They were old injuries, but the scars were still purple and angry. He ran his fingers gently over the skin there.

'Are these the worst scars that you have?'

Jemima had recovered herself. Her blue eyes sparkled at him. 'Is this some kind of perverse competition, Robert? Do you have war injuries that are worse than my climbing scars?'

Rob started to laugh. His hands went to the sash tying his dressing robe. 'I could show you.'

Jemima's eyes widened in alarm. 'No, thank you! I gained the distinct impression that you were naked beneath your robe.'

The silence in the room held a different quality now. 'I am,' Rob said. 'I always sleep naked.'

He saw Jemima swallow hard. All he could see of her was her face and neck above the scalloped neckline of the nightrail, but it was enough. Her eyes held a slumberous quality now, warm and blue. Her hair was tumbled over the pillows and smelled faintly of jasmine. The nightrail was modest, but he could see the swell of her breasts beneath the lace at the top and the sight filled him with instant lust. There was a pulse beating in the hollow of her throat as she watched his face.

'Robert—'

Rob leaned over and stopped her words with his lips. She responded instantly, her mouth soft and full beneath his own, parting for him, letting him in. He took what she offered, pressing her back against the pillows, angling his head so that he might deepen the kiss. Her body shifted beneath the covers, accommodating itself to his. Her hand came up to touch his face in the gentlest caress, then tangle in the lapels of his dressing robe, drawing him closer.

Rob drew back a little so that he could trail soft kisses down the satin skin of her neck, pausing to press his lips to the hollow where the pulse still beat its frantic rhythm. The candle had burned down low now and the light was very soft. Jemima's eyes were closed, the lashes dark on her cheek, her head slightly turned away against the whiteness of the pillow. Her lips were already stung pink with his kisses and her body was soft and open to him. Rob's throat closed with a mixture of desire and tenderness. He wanted to possess her and claim what was already his own.

His mouth returned to hers with an urgency that drove all other thoughts aside. He felt her small hands sliding over his robe, then under it, drifting across his bare chest. He threw back the covers, let the dressing robe fall to the floor and slid into the bed.

Jemima turned onto her side so that they faced one another. She did not speak. They lay there studying each other for a long minute, then Jemima put a hand out and touched his cheek again, and he turned his lips against the palm.

'Rough,' she said, rubbing experimentally with her fingers.

Rob felt his body react. He was wound up as tightly as a spring. He put his hand out and brushed the hair away from Jemima's face. It curled softly about his fingers and he rubbed a strand across his lips.

His fingers continued their exploration down to the

edge of the lawn nightrail. The skin was soft beneath his touch. Jemima's breasts rose and fell quickly as the tempo of her breathing increased. She could not help herself. She was feeling the exquisite relief of a secret that had finally been told. Like Rob, she felt the sweet taste of reconciliation.

Rob's palm skimmed the tip of her breast as his hand came to rest on the thin material just below its curve. Jemima squirmed.

'Rob…' Her voice was very soft.

'Mmm?' Rob did not raise his head. His fingers went to the buttons that ran down the front of the nightdress. He opened one. Then another.

Jemima's hand came up to still his. 'You know that we should not be doing this.'

'That is a matter of opinion.'

'My opinion is that we are breaking the vow of celibacy. Or that we are in grave danger of doing so.'

Now Rob did look up, and the heated, dangerous darkness of his eyes made her catch her breath. He laughed and his fingers resumed their slow movement downwards.

'Are we then to discuss celibacy tonight?'

Jemima struggled between practicality and desire. 'I think we should.'

Rob leaned over and kissed her very lightly, taking her bottom lip gently between his teeth. His hand slid into the bodice of the nightgown and cupped Jemima's breast. The jolt to her senses made her gasp and Rob took advantage with a ruthless kiss, sliding his tongue into her mouth, tasting, teasing, driving her to the edge of wildness. Jemima dug her fingers into his shoulders and revelled in the gasp that she wrung from him in turn.

'Define celibacy.' Rob's lips hovered over hers. His hand was stroking up the curve of her breast from beneath, raising tiny shivers through her whole body. Never had Jemima felt less like indulging in word games, but she had a mission to accomplish and if Rob was determined to throw away forty thousand pounds it was down to her to save him.

'Celibacy is…' She tried to focus.

'Yes?'

'I…I do not have the dictionary to hand…'

Rob bent his head and took the tip of her breast in his mouth. Jemima's back arched and she let out a despairing groan.

'If you cannot come up with a definition,' Rob said, and she could hear the laughter in his voice, 'then what can I do but continue until you do?'

He circled her breast slowly, deliberately, with his tongue before flicking the tip.

'Celibacy is chastity,' Jemima managed to whisper. She cleared her throat. 'Celibacy is chastity and this, Robert, is not chaste at all.'

There was a pause. Jemima opened her eyes to see Rob poised above her. The dark hair was tumbled across his brow and the lean planes of his face were taut with desire. Her fascinated gaze moved lower, to where the bodice of her nightrail fell open. Rob's hand was resting on the curve of her breast, dark against the pale skin, and the sight shot her through with such fierce desire that she was left weak and trembling.

'I think that you should leave,' she said.

Rob's gaze held hers. 'Do you want me to leave?'

'No,' Jemima said. 'I do not want you to, but I still think that you should.'

Rob sighed. She felt the bed shift under his weight

as he sat up and reached for his dressing robe. The candle was burning very low now, but in the pale light she caught sight of his nakedness before he flung the robe about himself. She stared.

'Don't,' Rob said, and there was a wrench in his voice. 'Do not look at me like that, Jemima, or I swear that will be an end to all celibacy.'

Jemima's face flamed. So firm and hard and sculpted... She was aching to feel those hard lines against her. She screwed up her face in an agony of frustrated wanting.

'I am sorry,' she said.

'I'm not.' Rob bent and dropped a lingering kiss on her parted lips. 'You are a stronger person than I am, Jemima Selborne.'

'If you go through the two dressing rooms then you may reach your own bedroom without stepping on to the landing,' Jemima said.

'Thank you.' Rob ran a hand through his hair. 'I should hate Augusta to see me in such a state of frustration.'

'And how many more days is it?' Jemima asked.

She saw Rob smile as he bent to kiss her again. 'Forty-seven. I fear that our troubles may only be beginning, Jemima.' His lips brushed hers again. 'Now that we have started, I am not at all certain that we can stop.'

Chapter Fourteen

Robert and his godfather met at an early hour the next day. Ferdie and Bertie had not even stirred after a heavy night at the local hostelry and Rob was hoping that the other guests would be similarly tardy in rising, at least until he and Merlin had concocted a story that would be acceptable for general consumption. He offered the Duke a cup of strong coffee, took one himself and went to sit down opposite his godfather.

'I am grateful that you did not greet me with pistols at dawn, Robert,' the Duke said wryly, pulling an appreciative face as he tasted the coffee. 'Hmm. This is very good. A vast improvement on the mud served up in your father's day.'

Rob laughed. 'It is Jemima's doing. She has wrought wonders with everything from the poultry to the pantry.'

Merlin nodded slowly. 'And with you, I think.' He fixed his godson with a shrewd eye. 'She has told you everything?'

Rob nodded. 'Last night. I confess it would have been helpful to know before rather than after the event, but...' he shrugged '...I know now.'

He saw his godfather relax infinitesimally. 'I imagine

that you might have been thinking all kinds of nefarious things about me?'

Rob looked a little shamefaced. 'Forgive me, sir. Whatever suspicions I harboured about both you and my wife did not withstand the test of my affections. I knew that neither of you could be false.'

Merlin nodded. There was a twinkle in his eye. 'Nicely put, Robert.' He laughed. 'I am glad that you esteem me as much as you seem to admire Lady Selborne.' His laughter faded. 'You know, of course, that she is a chimney sweep's daughter?'

Rob put his coffee cup down a little sharply. He stifled the pang of irritation the Duke's words raised in him. 'I do know that.'

He saw his godfather's lips twitch. 'No need to take offence, dear boy! It was a statement of fact rather than a judgement. I esteem Lady Selborne very highly. Do you know that she and I discussed philosophy when we first met? She is a credit to Mrs Montagu's schooling.' He smiled. 'I must apologise to her for my somewhat abrupt behaviour yesterday. I should have known that she was not in Burford to cause trouble. A most unfortunate coincidence, I suppose.'

'Mrs Montagu's schooling may have been sound, sir,' Rob said, 'but it was not so efficient on geography. When Jemima married me she had no notion that Delaval was close to Merlinschase.'

The Duke sighed. 'Nor that you were my godson?'

'Indeed, sir.' Rob shifted. 'That being the case, I wonder if we might devise some sort explanation that will suit? Not for the immediate family—I thought to tell them the truth, but for curious acquaintance…'

Merlin inclined his head. 'Did you have anything in mind?'

Rob hesitated. 'I thought that Jemima's niece might well be a connection of the family? Some sort of irregular alliance a few generations back could account for it.'

Merlin laughed. 'Why not? My grandfather was considered a terrible rake. I am sure that one more illegitimate connection would not malign him more than he deserves! And that would be entirely consistent with my acting as guardian to little Miss Tilly.'

'Excellent, sir.' Rob grinned. 'We might go a step further and suggest that that was how Jemima and I came to be acquainted? She was visiting her niece and I met her and was instantly smitten.'

'Part of that is true at least,' the Duke said drily. 'But you feel that you need to tell your grandmother the truth?'

There was a peremptory knock on the study door.

'I should think so too, Robert!' Lady Marguerite said, sweeping into the room and giving her hand to Merlin with a gracious inclination of her head. 'I refuse to be left outside the door like the veriest housemaid! How am I to help dear Jemima if I do not know what is going on?'

She sat down and reached for the coffee pot, ignoring her grandson's look of amazement.

'Well?' she said impatiently. 'You may speak now, Robert. I am quite agog.'

'I am most dreadfully sorry about yesterday,' Letty Exton said, in a rush. She had cornered Jemima after breakfast and asked if the two of them might walk a little together, the day being fine after the thunderstorm the night before. 'I mean, I am sorry about Augusta's behaviour, and I am sorry that we went to Burford and—' her blue eyes were quite stricken '—I am most desperately sorry if I have caused trouble for you, dearest Jemima.'

Jemima was touched. Letty had no reason to think well of her and yet, unlike Augusta, she had assumed that the encounter with Tilly had an innocent explanation rather than a scandalous one. Since Rob had explained the entire matter to Lady Marguerite, Jemima felt comfortable in speaking to Letty. Miss Exton was her only friend in her new life, and Jemima was anxious not to lose that friendship. She shook her head.

'Dear Letty—please stop! What happened yesterday was in no way your fault. Indeed, it was mine, for I should have avoided Burford and the potential embarrassment of seeing Tilly, at least until I had had the opportunity to discuss it with Rob and decide what to do.'

Letty peeked at her from under her bonnet. 'Tilly—is that her name? She is a prodigiously pretty child, Jemima, and so very like you.' She clapped her hand to her mouth. 'Oh, I did not mean to imply—'

'Tilly is my niece, Letty,' Jemima said, deciding to cut straight to the truth in order to spare Letty further embarrassment. 'She was born out of wedlock, but had the good fortune to become the Duke of Merlin's ward. When I married Rob and came to Delaval I had no notion that I would be in such proximity to her, nor indeed that Rob had any connection with the Duke.' She sighed. 'You can imagine my mortification when I saw the child and realised that not only did she bear a startling resemblance to me, but that everyone else had seen it too!'

'Yes, indeed,' Letty said. 'A speaking likeness.' She

cast Jemima a look. 'And then there was the Duke himself...'

'Oh, yes.' Jemima smiled ruefully. 'I can imagine what everyone was thinking there! And meanwhile the *Duke* was thinking that I was only here to cause trouble! It was a devilishly difficult situation!'

They were walking slowly along the gravel path towards what had once been the lake. All that was visible now was a large pond covered in water lilies, which were curling up at the edges with the approach of autumn. Damselflies hovered above the reeds. Jemima tilted her parasol against the October sun.

'You had not previously mentioned the matter to Robert?' Letty ventured.

Jemima shook her head. 'I had not.' She gave Letty a little smile. 'You may imagine how he felt—in common with everyone else, he suspected that Tilly was my daughter. I did not have the opportunity to explain to him until last night.'

Letty shivered. 'Oh, Jemima! And you looked so composed at dinner, whilst in reality I suppose you were not feeling at all the thing!'

'It was one of the worst evenings of my life,' Jemima said with feeling.

'I hope that all is sorted out with Uncle Merlin now,' Letty said. 'I know he is rather frightening at times, but he has a kind heart underneath.'

Jemima thought of the scene that had enacted itself in the library that morning. If the previous evening had been tense and difficult, then the morning had promised to be just as hard in a different way. Fortunately Rob had already smoothed matters over with the Duke and Lady Marguerite, and Merlin at least had been charm personified. Lady Marguerite's reaction to having a chimney sweep as a granddaughter-in-law was rather more difficult to gauge.

'All is agreed,' she said. 'There is to be an irregular connection between our two families—it is necessarily irregular, I am afraid, to explain the fact that it has never been mentioned before. Tilly is now a distant cousin of mine, and in fact I met Robert through the connection, since he is the Duke's godson and Tilly is the Duke's ward.' She smiled at Letty. 'It is rather neat, if fictitious.'

'I suppose that most people will believe it,' Letty said with a smile. 'But I do thank you for telling me the truth, dearest Jemima.'

Jemima gestured to the tumbledown summer-house that sat on a little rise above the bank. 'Shall we sit awhile, Letty? I would like to talk and it is not often one gets the chance.' She gave a rueful smile. 'I have a dreadful suspicion that now your grandmother knows the whole, I do not believe we shall have the chance to meet again at all!'

Letty bent on her a look of lively amazement. 'Oh, surely it cannot be so bad? Although the matter is unfortunate, Grandmama will see that no blame can attach to you.'

Jemima took a deep breath. 'If that were all, then I might hope for her indulgence,' she said. 'Unfortunately, Rob has also told her that I am a chimney sweep's daughter and that he and I married in order to meet the terms of his father's will. There!' She gave a long sigh. 'I have said it all!'

There was a clatter as Letty dropped her parasol on the wooden floor of the summer-house. She bent down to retrieve it, her eyes still fixed on Jemima's face. 'A sweep's daughter? You?'

She sounded so incredulous that Jemima smiled. 'I fear so.'

'Well…but…' Letty turned pink. 'That is not so bad. I mean, a wife takes her husband's place in society, after all, and plenty of gentlemen marry ladies who are not…I mean…they marry the daughters of cits and tradesmen—'

She broke off. 'Oh, dear, I did not mean it to sound like that! Besides, you went to Mrs Montagu's school, did you not? And no one would guess…' She put her hands up to her scarlet cheeks. 'Drat! I was so determined not to sound snobbish like Augusta and I have just made the most utter mull of it!'

Jemima laughed. 'You are not a snob, Letty. I expect I took you by surprise. I do apologise for shocking you.'

'I am not shocked,' Letty said stalwartly. Jemima could tell she was lying and that she was in fact shocked to the core. 'Only…you said that you married Rob to fulfil the terms of his father's will?'

Jemima nodded. 'I fear so. He was required to marry a lady who attended Anne Selborne's wedding. He asked me.'

She was surprised to see Letty's eyes light up like stars. 'But that is capital, Jemima! I thought that you meant you had made an arranged marriage, but now I see that Rob chose you!'

'The field was not large,' Jemima pointed out drily.

'No, but he preferred you to Augusta,' Letty said incontrovertibly.

'That,' Jemima said, 'is not flattering, Letty!'

They laughed together. 'Anyway,' Letty said shyly, 'however the marriage started, it is clear to see that Rob adores you, Jemima.' She gave a little sigh. 'He *is* lovely, isn't he? I had the most shocking crush on him when I was younger. I used to follow him everywhere and make a frightful fool of myself.'

'Well,' Jemima said, 'Rob is very fond of you so I do not suppose it did any harm. Have you never wished to marry, Letty?'

Letty's pretty little face dropped slightly. 'I suppose not. That is, I have never met a man who engaged my interest sufficiently to make me wish to marry him. And no one asked me, so…'

'No one asked you?' Jemima raised her brows. She found that very difficult to believe. Miss Exton, she was sure, should have been beating the suitors off with sticks.

'Did you have a season?' she asked.

'Oh, yes,' Letty rubbed her fingers over the smooth handle of her parasol. 'Uncle Simon, Rob's father, paid for me to have my come out, but Augusta—' Her face crumpled. 'I should not tell tales out of school.'

Jemima frowned. 'Has Augusta done something particular to upset you, Letty?'

Letty grasped Jemima's hand gratefully. 'Not precisely, but…' Letty wrinkled up her nose '…Augusta ruined my season, you see. At the time I did not realise what she was doing, but now I see…'

'What happened?' Jemima asked.

'I was only seventeen and fresh from the country,' Letty said. 'Whenever I seemed to attract a beau, there would be Augusta, sparkling and distracting their attention… She had plenty of Town bronze, you see, and she made me feel very green.'

Jemima was beginning to think that something needed to be done to fix Augusta.

'She must have been jealous of you, Letty. You are far prettier than she is.'

'Blondes were not in fashion,' Letty said sadly. 'I was considered Unfortunate.'

'Oh, dear. How silly. So your season was not a success.'

'No, and then there was no more money to go up to London, so I stayed in the country with Grandmama. And though I met some gentlemen in Town on this visit, Augusta said that they would only be tempted to take me off the shelf now that I am coming into some money. That rather spoilt it for me, I confess.'

'I am not surprised,' Jemima said briskly, hating Augusta's malicious little digs. 'It seems a great pity that you were obliged to invite Miss Selborne to your birthday ball.'

'Yes, I thought so.' Letty sighed. 'Bertie Pershore is very sweet and Ferdie is quite charming, but Augusta is enough to ruin any house party.'

Jemima laughed and patted her hand. 'Just remember that you have the looks and the fortune, Letty!'

Letty twinkled. 'I confess it will be prodigiously nice to be a little bit rich. We have always been quite dreadfully poor, you see. Although one should not refine too much upon material things, it will be nice to have beef for dinner occasionally!'

'Your fortune is in trust?' Jemima enquired.

'Yes. Papa left me a competence, not a fortune, but it will seem like riches to me.' Letty gave a shy smile. 'The Extons have never been rich, you see. My parents died when I was very young, Jemima, and Grandmama has always brought me up.'

Jemima thought about the frosty Lady Marguerite and wondered what on earth it had been like to be a small girl in such a household.

'Did you like that?'

'Oh, yes,' Letty beamed. 'Grandmama is exceedingly kind under her crusty exterior!'

'Is she?' Jemima could not help the incredulity sounding in her voice and Letty gave a peal of laughter.

'Yes, she is! Once she decides to like you, you will see for yourself.'

'I hardly think that that is likely to happen now,' Jemima said, a little sadly. 'She cannot but disapprove of me.'

Letty shook her head. 'Grandmama wishes above all things to see Rob happy and settled at Delaval, Jemima. That is the only thing that will concern her.'

Jemima wished that she had Letty's confidence. She could imagine Lady Marguerite sweeping from the house in high dudgeon, never to return.

Jemima watched as Letty pleated her skirt material with tiny, jerky movements. Clearly there was still something troubling her new friend.

A second later, Letty said, 'You said that Tilly was your niece, Jemima…'

'Yes?'

'Then she must be your brother's child? Or perhaps…' Letty brightened '…you have other siblings, Jemima?'

Jemima felt a huge pang of sympathy for her. Letty looked so hopeful, yet it was impossible. Even without Tilly it was impossible.

'Tilly is Jack's daughter,' she said gently. 'I am sorry, Letty.'

Letty bit her lip. 'It does not matter. I thought she must be. She has his eyes.'

There was a silence. Jemima could tell that Letty wanted to ask more questions, but was too well bred to persist. Besides, what could she tell her friend?

'My brother is a chimney sweep; he is barely literate; he has fathered an illegitimate child and it is foolish to think that there could ever be anything between the two of you when you are the sheltered child of a gentleman and he is so very far beneath you…'

Letty had said it herself when she had observed that a wife took on her husband's position in society. The reverse was never true. Jemima sighed. She could also have said that Jack was loyal, brave, kind and had his own code of honour, but it would make no odds. He and Letty could never be together.

'I suppose I shall end up marrying Ferdie Selborne or Mr Pershore,' Letty said with a sigh.

Jemima smiled. 'I should not be too hasty to do that,' she said. 'Not unless you care for either of them, of course.'

Letty giggled. 'Oh, I like them both prodigiously, but love…? Ferdie looks like a heron and is a dreadful libertine. Grandmama would have apoplexy if I said I wished to marry Ferdie!'

'And Mr Pershore? He is no rake.'

Letty giggled even more. 'Bertie? No, indeed he is not. But you must have observed, Jemima, that Bertie, whilst being the sweetest creature in Christendom, is not the world's finest mind!'

'Oh, Letty,' Jemima said, laughing, 'that is a little unkind.'

'And he drinks. Did you see him at breakfast?'

'I thought he was drinking water?'

'By the bucketful. Apparently he got so foxed at the Speckled Hen last night that Ferdie had to carry him home! He was completely insensible. He only got up for breakfast because he is afraid of Grandmama.' She smiled. 'Oh, look! Here he comes now.' She raised her voice. 'Would you care to sit down, Mr Pershore? You are looking very peaky.'

Bertie Pershore was indeed looking very sickly indeed. He tottered towards them and lowered himself on to the bench gingerly, wincing as the sunlight caught his eyes.

'Servant, Lady Selborne, servant, Miss Exton,' he muttered. 'Must apologise… Always was sensitive to turtle soup!'

'Of course,' Jemima said sympathetically. 'Did you have a pleasant evening yesterday, Mr Pershore?'

'Don't remember any of yesterday night, ma'am,' Bertie said, wincing again. 'Turtle soup is the devil for playing havoc with my memory.'

Letty giggled. 'Come, come, Bertie, we know that you were down at the Speckled Hen with Ferdie! Where is Ferdie now?'

'Going over the stables with Rob,' Bertie groaned.

'And did you not wish to join them?' Jemima asked.

Bertie turned an even more ashen grey. 'No, thank you, ma'am. Smell of the stables, you know. Turns the stomach.'

'You should go and lie down until you recover from the soup,' Letty said, giggling. 'Quickly, Mr Pershore! Grandmama is coming.'

Between them they hoisted a groaning Mr Pershore to his feet, took an arm each, and steered him down the path towards the house.

'Mr Pershore!' Lady Marguerite was bearing down on them at full speed. Bertie groaned again.

'Don't leave me!'

'Mr Pershore.' Lady Marguerite's cool blue eyes surveyed the hapless gentleman. 'Do not stand around in the full sun if you are feeling delicate. I have a restor-

ative that will do the trick. Go inside and one of the
footmen will bring it to you.'

'Very good of you, ma'am, but I am not sure there
is a restorative for turtle soup—' Bertie began.

'Soup, fiddlesticks! You are foxed, man, good and
proper. Stop pretending.'

'Don't know what they put in the ale at that inn,'
Bertie muttered, going scarlet. 'I swear to you, ma'am,
that I can hold my liquor better than this.'

Lady Marguerite shooed him towards the house. 'Run
along, Bertie. And perhaps, if you are very good from
now on, Merlin need not hear about this.'

'You probably know that the Duke of Merlin is Bertie's uncle,' Letty whispered in Jemima's ear. 'He is a
terrible tartar with poor Bertie!'

Jemima was feeling a little sick. She was sure that
any moment now Lady Marguerite would probably turn
around and rip her to shreds…

'Now then, girls—' Lady Marguerite turned back to
them '—we are to go calling this morning.' She turned
to Jemima. 'There are various ladies in the neighbourhood who are anxious to meet you, my dear, and I
would like to introduce you to some of the guests who
are to be at Letty's ball. That way you will already have
an acquaintance when you go to the ball, and need not
feel so new.'

'That is very kind of you, ma'am,' Jemima said, reel-
ing from being called 'my dear' and trying not to sound
too astonished. Had Rob not spoken to his grandmother
after all?

'Robert should have thought of it already, of course,'
Lady Marguerite said, 'but gentlemen are very slow
about these things and I hear that he has been keeping
you very much to himself.' She caught Jemima's blush

and smiled. 'No need to look embarrassed, child. That is as it should be. I am glad to see him so happy.' She looked around. 'Lud, Augusta is coming this way. Come along, girls, before she catches up with us.'

'She has decided to like you,' Letty whispered to Jemima, as they hurried to keep up. 'I told you she would!'

'Stop whispering, Letty dear,' Lady Marguerite said sharply, from in front. 'It is most vulgar.'

'Your grandmother reminds me of Mrs Montagu,' Jemima said in an undertone, when she was sure that Lady Marguerite was far enough ahead of them not to overhear. 'She could always tell if we were talking in class even when her back was turned.'

'Splendid woman, Mrs Montagu,' Lady Marguerite called over her shoulder. 'I was delighted to hear that you were one of her pupils, Jemima dear.'

Letty and Jemima exchanged a look and giggled. 'Why do you think your grandmother has decided to like me?' she whispered to Letty.

'Because Rob loves you,' Letty said artlessly. 'We have all observed it, dearest Jemima. He is utterly sweet on you.'

And she scampered to catch up with Lady Marguerite, leaving Jemima to follow behind more slowly.

'Rob loves you… He is utterly sweet on you.'

There was no reason for Letty to be correct, of course. Jemima knew that Rob had shown her tenderness and understanding and kindness beyond anything that she had experienced before. But love? There she was a novice, with no means of judging. He had spoken to her of desire and passion, but he had said no words of love. Yet still a small part of her hoped that it was true.

* * *

The carriage rattled down the green country lanes as they travelled the neighbourhood making their calls. Everyone was most anxious to meet the new Lady Selborne, and though Jemima met with much veiled curiosity about the suddenness of her marriage, most people were friendly and Letty and Lady Marguerite were staunch in their support of her.

'I am glad that Sir Henry and Lady Vause will be attending the ball,' Letty said, as the carriage pulled away from Verne Manor, the last call of the morning. 'I like Chlorinda and I have often thought that she would make the perfect wife for Bertie Pershore.'

'Henwit,' Lady Marguerite said succinctly, though she was not referring to Letty. 'One henwit in the family is enough. Bertie needs to marry a clever woman.'

Letty shivered. 'Was that not a dreadful story that Lady Vause was telling us? A man murdered at the Speckled Hen last night, and Ferdie and Bertie both there the very same evening!'

'That's what you get for drinking in a common tavern,' Lady Marguerite said sharply. 'Ferdie always was a ramshackle fellow.'

'Oh, Ferdie is all right, Grandmama,' Letty said smiling. 'He is quite harmless really.'

They were driving through the Wychwood Forest on their way back to Delaval. The place made Jemima shiver a little. This was no pleasant woodland like the one that encircled Delaval. Here the trees pressed together closely, rank on rank like soldiers lined up for battle. It was thick and dark along the track and made her nervous. She was still not completely at ease in the country.

Letty peered out of the window. 'This is where Tom,

Dick and Harry were hanged on the gibbet, Jemima. You have heard the tale of the highwaymen? It always seems to me a haunted place.'

'Young girls, too much imagination,' Lady Marguerite said.

'I did not think that there were many highwaymen these days,' Jemima said. 'Highway robbery seems quite out of fashion.'

'Of course it is,' Lady Marguerite said crossly. 'Very bad *ton*.'

The words had barely left her mouth when a shot rang out. The coach rocked as the horses plunged between the shafts. There was an explosion of noise. The coachman was shouting and the groom was running to the horses' heads as he tried to prevent them from toppling the coach into the ditch.

'Stand and deliver!'

'Botheration!' Lady Marguerite grumbled.

'No highwaymen in Wychwood?' Letty murmured, as the door of the carriage was wrenched open. 'There are now.'

Chapter Fifteen

At first glance the man standing in the doorway of the coach was the archetypal highwayman. He had scuffed black leather boots, black trousers, a shabby black tricorne pulled down low over his eyes and a neckcloth over the lower part of his face. His eyes above the mask were black as coal and a lock of equally dark hair escaped from beneath the hat. About his shoulders was a black cloak, but on closer inspection Jemima realised that it was in fact a large soot sack, split in half and draped around him. She looked at the man's face again. She opened her mouth to speak. One of the pistols moved in her direction.

'Out!'

Jemima closed her mouth again.

'I most certainly will *not* get out of my carriage on the whim of some scoundrel!' Lady Marguerite looked down her nose. 'Be off with you, man!'

'Grandmama,' Letty said in an agonised whisper. 'Pray do as he says.'

'Certainly not,' Lady Marguerite said, sitting back against the cushions as though the matter was quite decided. 'I dislike to be inconvenienced like this.'

The highwayman looked amused and not in the least discomposed. The lines about his eyes crinkled as he smiled. 'Very well, ma'am.' He gave a little half-bow. The pistol moved again as he turned towards Jemima and Letty. 'Ladies, if you please…'

Jemima jumped down to the ground whilst Letty, every inch the lady, gave her hand to the highwayman and descended the carriage steps very prettily.

'Would you like my jewellery?' she asked. 'I have a very elegant pair of earrings and a matching necklace.'

'Letty,' Jemima said, 'you are not supposed to *offer*…'

Letty was slipping the earrings off and handing them over. She put her hands up to unfasten the necklace, fumbling a little with the catch. 'Oh, I cannot quite manage it.'

The highwayman stepped forward gallantly. 'Allow me, ma'am.'

'Oh, for pity's sake, I would offer to help myself if I thought you wanted it!' Jemima snapped, as the highwayman stowed one pistol in his belt and lifted Letty's hair to unfasten the necklace. Letty was blushing now. The edge of the highwayman's cloak brushed her breast and his gloved fingers tangled in her hair.

'Do apologise, ma'am,' the highwayman said to Letty, stowing the jewellery in his pocket and stepping back. 'No wish to importune a lady.'

'That is quite all right,' Letty breathed.

Jemima rolled her eyes in exasperation.

The highwayman took Letty's arm and guided her back to the coach. 'Shan't keep you a moment, ma'am,' he said. 'Need a word with Lady Selborne.'

Jemima drew away from the coach and into the thick shadow at the edge of the wood. She watched him settle

Letty back in the carriage and turn towards her. As he reached her side he pulled down his neckcloth. Jemima gave a sigh that was sharp with irritation.

'Jack,' she hissed, 'what the *devil* do you think you are about?'

Jack's hand closed about her wrist as he pulled her deeper into the shade. 'Quiet! I don't have much time.'

Jemima freed herself. 'What are you doing here? And what are you playing at, stopping the coach? Don't you know that highway robbery is a crime?'

'It was all I could think of,' Jack said. There was a white line about his mouth and his eyes were tired. 'I'm in trouble, Jem. I could hardly stroll up to the house or send you a note, could I? I need your help.'

Jemima flashed a quick look back at the carriage. Letty was watching them and talking animatedly to Lady Marguerite at the same time. She looked pink and excited. Jemima sighed.

'Tell me what's going on. Quickly. Tell me in the cant, so no one can overhear.'

As cover, she started to unfasten her necklace and fiddled about with it a little more, keeping her eyes riveted on Jack's face.

Jack rested his broad shoulders against the nearest tree. He lapsed into the sweep's cant, the language they had talked in since they were children.

'The out and out last night—'

'At the Speckled Hen?'

'That's the one. They're trying to pin it on me.'

Jemima's eyes widened in amazement. 'They are trying to frame you for murder?'

'Quiet!' Jack said. 'What's the point of me speaking in cant if you blurt it out like that?'

'Sorry,' Jemima said, recovering herself. 'What were you doing there in the first place?'

'Can't go into that now.' Jack slid her necklace absentmindedly into his pocket. 'There was something rum going on and I landed in the middle of it. Took a topper and the next thing I knew they were trying to fit me up. They locked me in the clink, but I got out and ran.'

'How did you escape?' Jemima asked. She knew the gaol in Burford was close by the church and it was no mean feat to break out.

'I climbed,' Jack said succinctly. 'It's the one thing I can do.'

'And the pops?' Jemima gestured towards the pistols.

Jack grinned. 'Bought them from a real scamp who was picked up on Otmoor Heath and was in the jail with me.'

Jemima nodded towards Jack's horse, which was helping itself to a blackberry bush. 'And the nag?'

'Mangy fellow. Bought him in Aylesbury. He walked all the way here. Won't go at more than a trot. Luckily he was still at the inn when I went back.'

Jemima stared. 'You went *back*?'

'Had to. I needed to find out how to get hold of you.'

Jemima rubbed her forehead. 'Jack, this is not amusing.'

'I don't need you to tell me that.' Jack looked her over. 'Don't you have any more jewellery, Jem? Can only make so much fuss over one necklace.'

'If I had known you were coming, I would have worn the contents of my entire jewellery case,' his sister said drily. She could see Letty's anxious little face still peering at them through the coach window.

'I have to go. There's a place on the estate you can

stay and I'll come to you tonight.' Jemima raised her voice. 'You're fit for nothing but the pigsty, you scoundrel. We have the very place for you on the Home Farm. Now, get you gone!'

She pushed her purse into his hands.

Jack squeezed her hand as he took it. 'Thank you,' he whispered. 'Bring some food with you.'

'Give yourself up!' Jemima said, whirling away and hurrying toward the carriage. 'You'll only get caught, you villain!'

The highwayman raised his hand in a salute. 'Thank you, ma'am.' He sketched a bow in Letty's direction and vaulted on to the horse, which looked affronted at being expected to carry so much weight. Jemima was afraid it would keel right over under the strain.

As soon as she was safely in the carriage the coachman let off a volley of shot from his blunderbuss, which only served to raise the crows from the trees and frighten the horses. Lady Marguerite called him sharply to order.

'Drive on! We have wasted enough time on this incompetent thief!'

'Why incompetent, Grandmama?' Letty questioned. 'He seemed quite accomplished to me.'

'In the art of seduction, perhaps.' Lady Marguerite sniffed. 'Can't abide these handsome fellows!'

'It was a shame that he did not try to steal a kiss.' Letty sighed.

'Yes, it was,' Jemima concurred, 'for then you might have glimpsed his face and been able to describe him to the constable.'

'Quite right,' Lady Marguerite approved. 'The man should be caught and damned well hung!'

Letty sighed. 'I thought that he looked as though he was—'

'Letty!'

'I was only going to say that he looked as though he was down on his luck, Grandmama,' Letty said. 'Poor man, I do believe that was a sack he was wearing. It must be dreadful to be a criminal.'

Jemima turned away and looked fixedly out of the window. What Jack was doing at Delaval was one question that required an answer, and a second was how he had managed to get himself tied up in the murder at the inn. Jemima frowned out at the passing countryside. This was a devilish pickle Jack was in, for if he was already a wanted man the constable would be scouring the neighbourhood for him. News of the highway robbery would only add to his tally of crimes.

Jemima sighed. She suddenly felt very tired. No more secrets, she had said to Rob. But this… This might be too much for even Rob's generosity to take. It could be one secret too far.

The constable, when he arrived, was reassuringly inept and the witnesses soon improved upon the confusion with their descriptions of the highwayman of Wychwood Forest.

'He was a big man, very fat,' Lady Marguerite said. 'And he had a North Country accent.'

'He was tall, dark and handsome,' Letty said breathlessly. 'No, I didn't see his face or his hair. How do I know he was dark?' She screwed up her face. 'I suppose I don't really… Except that I just *know*…'

'He was about five foot seven inches tall,' Jemima said, knocking at least six inches off Jack's height, 'and

he was fair. Yes, I did see a bit of his hair, which is
how I know. He was riding a brown horse.'

'No, it was piebald,' Letty objected.

'Skewbald,' Lady Marguerite said.

They were sitting in the drawing room at Delaval,
with Rob and Ferdie present to give them support in
the unlikely event that any of them should be overcome
at relating their experiences. The constable, Mr Scholes,
was looking flustered and was perspiring heavily as he
tried to make sense of the conflicting evidence. He
sucked his pencil and flicked the pages of his notebook.

'Lady Marguerite,' he appealed, 'you say that the fellow let you remain in the carriage and did not take any
of your money or jewellery?'

'Certainly he did not,' Lady Marguerite said. 'I was
not going to hand it over to any old riff-raff.'

'Whereas he took your necklace and earrings, Miss
Exton?'

'Oh, yes, but I gave them to him,' Letty said help-
fully. 'He did not really steal them...'

The constable frowned. 'Lady Selborne?'

'He took my pearl necklace and my purse,' Jemima
said composedly. 'I was not wearing any other jewellery.'

She was very aware that Rob was watching her. He
had not moved or spoken through the entire interview
and curiously his silence was more difficult to bear than
any number of questions. When they had returned
home, Letty's excited descriptions had released Jemima
from the need to speak at all, and whilst she had reassured Rob that she was unhurt, she had not told him
any more of the encounter than that. She had not confided in him, and every second that went past seemed
to make it more difficult.

Rob was scrutinising her with a very perceptive regard. Jemima reflected that either she had a guilty conscience or Rob already suspected that she knew more than she was telling.

'So…' the constable said heavily, reviewing his notes. 'He was tall, fat, shortish, fair, dark, spoke like a northerner and rode a brown piebald horse—'

'Skewbald,' Lady Marguerite corrected. 'I know about horses, my good man. M'father bred them.'

The constable sighed and put his notebook away.

'He sounds a desperate fellow,' Ferdie drawled. 'Do you think him the chap you are seeking from last night, Scholes? The one who escaped the gaol after the murder?'

'Very probably, sir,' the constable said.

'A murderer!' Letty said, whitening. 'Oh, no!'

'No cause to worry yourself, ma'am,' the constable said with heavy-handed gallantry. 'Doubt he'll be on the loose for long.' He turned to Ferdie. 'You were in the Speckled Hen yourself last night, weren't you, sir?'

'Bertie Pershore and I took some ale there,' Ferdie admitted, shifting a little under Lady Marguerite's disapproving glare. 'Don't know anything about a murder, mind. Knifed, was he?'

'No,' the constable said, seeming disappointed. 'Hit his head. No doubt about foul play, though.' He turned to Rob. 'You might remember him, my lord. Henry Naylor. Groom here in your grandfather's day, he was. Went to the wars and had just come back again.' He shook his head. 'A sorry end.'

Jemima was puzzling over the name Naylor. She knew that she had heard it somewhere before but she could not quite recall where. She saw Ferdie and Rob exchange a look and it puzzled her even more. Ferdie was looking ill at ease now and quite unlike his usual urbane self.

'I do not believe that the highwayman could have been a northerner,' Letty said suddenly. She blushed as everyone stopped talking and looked at her. 'He was speaking London cant,' she said in a rush. She looked at Jemima appealingly. 'When he was talking to you, Jemima...I heard him.'

Jemima felt a little sick. 'Was that what it was?' she said lightly. 'I did not understand him, I am afraid.'

'I should think not,' Lady Marguerite said. 'London cant! Whatever next, Letty? You're as likely to know cant as I am to know Chinese!'

Letty flushed bright red but looked stubborn. 'I heard it.' She looked at Jemima again.

Jemima shook her head very slightly and Letty fell suddenly silent, her eyes widening. Looking up, Jemima saw that Rob's gaze was riveted on her with quizzical interest.

The constable got up to leave. Ferdie showed him to the door whilst Rob went across to the sideboard to pour a glass of Constantia for his grandmother. Jemima got up and moved across to the long windows. She knew that Rob would follow her; she could feel him watching her and felt her skin prickle under his scrutiny. A second later she repressed a shiver as he spoke in her ear.

'London cant,' he said. 'How very interesting.'

Jemima looked up and met his eyes. He was leaning very close to her and his gaze was challenging. Jemima's heart skipped a beat.

'You know, don't you?' she whispered.

'That I have a highwayman as a brother-in-law?' Rob's brows lifted. 'What the devil are you up to, Jemima?'

'I don't know yet.' Jemima cast a quick look round the room. They were barely out of earshot of the others. She put a hand on Rob's lapel and drew him closer still. He came, but his face was hard.

'Jack is in some sort of trouble,' she said. 'He has been framed for the murder last night.' Jemima gripped Rob's jacket. 'He is in hiding. I have said that I will go and see him tonight.'

'I do not want my wife running around the country-side at night,' Rob said. 'It is not safe.' His eyes were cold.

'Please, Rob,' Jemima pleaded with him. 'I will be quite safe. I need to find out what has happened.'

Rob's jaw set. 'Why did you not tell me sooner?' he asked. 'Why did you say nothing when you came back?'

Jemima felt a little sick. 'I could not. We have visitors. And then the constable arrived! There was no chance.'

Rob's cold expression did not alter. 'There was plenty of time if you had wanted to do it.'

'What are you two whispering about?' Lady Marguerite demanded, from across the room. 'You know that a husband and wife should never whisper intimately together!'

Jemima caught Rob's sleeve as he turned away.

'Robert—'

'No,' her husband said. His face was set hard. 'We may talk of this later, Jemima.'

Jemima watched him go. She knew that he was right. She had hesitated over whether to tell Rob about Jack, and what to tell him. And then the secret had caught up with her, as secrets had a habit of doing. She could not blame Letty, whose innocent remarks about the cant had

never been intended to cause trouble. She thought that
Rob had suspected even before then. She was not prac-
tised at deception, particularly when her loyalties were
torn.

She doubted that Rob would see it that way, though.
To him it could only appear that she had failed to trust
him a second time. First Tilly, now Jack. He had forgiven her Tilly and she had promised that there would
be no more secrets. She had kept her word for all of
two days.

And to make matters worse, she was going to go
against Rob's express wishes. Jemima squared her
shoulders. She could not leave Jack alone and friend-
less. No matter what Rob had said, she would have to
seek Jack out.

The disused pigsty made a cosy enough shelter for
an autumn night. Jack Jewell hooked the reins of the
exhausted horse over the broken end of a wooden beam,
and went back out into the forest to hunt for some wood
to make a small fire. The wood was dry and burned
well, its resinous scent mingling with the pine fragrance
of the trees that surrounded the pig man's hut. It was a
risk, but Jack reckoned that no one but Jemima would
be wandering in the woods that night to see or smell
the smoke. He hoped she would hurry up. He was starv-
ing hungry.

The fire made him feel a little better. He sat down
on his makeshift cloak and stared at the flames. Fire
had been his life and almost the death of him on more
than one occasion. It was as familiar as an old friend,
which was good because just at the moment he needed
all the friends he could get. Jack was still not sure how
he had stumbled into such a mess, and he had even less

idea how he would get out of it again. He wondered if Jemima would tell that swell of a husband what was going on. He absentmindedly chewed a piece of dry straw. He was not sure about Robert Selborne. The man seemed straight enough and he had seemed to like Jemima a lot. Jack had seen the look on Rob's face when he had been standing at the altar and there was more to it than a gentleman taking a fancy to a pretty little piece. But even so, he was not sure that he would trust him.

The horse made a deep sighing sound, an indication of its disgust that there was not a scrap to eat. Jack felt much the same. He gave it an encouraging pat. He was beginning to feel quite affectionately towards the old nag, his companion in criminality. Jack had not been in gaol since the long-ago incident after Beth's death, but he had no illusions what would happen to him if the constable caught him. Never mind Newgate—he would be on his way to meet his maker before he could draw breath. Murder and highway robbery were capital offences, after all.

The shadows shifted as the fire flickered. The door of the pig man's hut squeaked a little in the draught. A twig cracked. Jack cocked his head. Was that a step outside? No doubt it was Jemima with a fat marketing basket stuffed full of food. His mouth watered but he reached for one of the pistols at the same time. It would not do to be too careless.

The door opened an inch. Someone was definitely outside, and probably not Jemima, who would not be so timid. Jack eased himself to his feet and tiptoed across to the door. It opened slowly. Jack raised the pistol and the firelight glinted along the barrel. He had never shot anyone in his life but he thought that at close range he would probably manage not to miss…

'You!' he said. 'Not the visitor I was expecting.'

Letty Exton stepped into the room and closed the door behind her very precisely.

'Would you mind putting the pistol away, Mr Jewell?' she said. 'You are making me nervous.'

Jack lowered the pistol again and stuck it in his belt. He watched her as she came forward into the firelight. She was dressed in a rich velvet cloak with a hood and it made her look as though she was on her way to a *ton* ball. When she put the hood back, the firelight burnished her curls to a copper halo. She had a small stoop of hay in her hand and she fed it to the horse, which guzzled it greedily.

'Piebald,' she said, with satisfaction, stroking its nose. 'I knew it was.'

'For pity's sake,' Jack said, 'this isn't a game, you know.'

Letty's blue gaze fixed on his face. Jack felt his throat close. He swallowed hard.

'I know,' she said.

She put the basket down on the earthen floor.

'I brought you some food.'

Jack looked at the basket and then back at her face. 'Thank you.'

Letty gave a little sigh of exasperation and sank to her knees on the floor, unpacking the contents on to Jack's cloak as though it were a picnic.

'Cheese, game pie, apple tart—no cream, I'm afraid—ham and two sweet pears from the hot houses. Oh, and a pint of ale. I hope that's all right?'

She looked so anxious that Jack felt his stomach clench. 'Perfect,' he said.

He sat down and started to eat. Letty bit into one of the pears. The juice ran down her chin. She licked it up, saw Jack watching her and stopped, making a business of packing the food wrappings back in her basket. There was a long silence whilst Jack ate.

At the end he said, 'It'll never work, you know.'

Letty looked up. 'We'll see,' she said tranquilly. She tidied up the leftovers, wiped her hands and got to her feet.

'I think I had better go now.'

'Yes,' Jack said. 'I think you had.'

Chapter Sixteen

'Pork pie, apples, cheese, a side of beef and a pint of ale,' Jemima said. 'Don't just stare at it, Jack! I thought you would be famished!'

She watched in exasperation as her brother slowly reached for an apple and sank his teeth into it. He did not seem particularly hungry, but that might be attributable to his nerves on finding himself in such a situation. She started to eat some of the cheese herself. It was strong and delicious.

'Talk,' Jemima said, with her mouthful. 'I don't have long. Rob doesn't know I am here. Worse, he will have to tell our guests that I'm sick.' She sighed. 'Now they'll be even more convinced I'm pregnant.'

Jack gave her a quick look. 'Are you?'

'No.'

Jack raised his brows. 'So you haven't told your husband about it being me who stopped the coach?'

Jemima tried not to look as shifty as she felt. 'He knows. I haven't had time to talk to him properly. I told you—we have visitors.'

She felt Jack's gaze resting on her. 'I thought there

were supposed to be no secrets in marriage, Jem. Is everything all right between the two of you?'

'Of course it is.' Jemima took a swig of ale and avoided his eyes. 'You'll need to move on tomorrow in case they're searching for you. There's an old charcoal burner's hut on the other side of the estate. It shouldn't be for long. Just until we can sort this out.'

'Don't change the subject,' Jack said. 'We were talking of you and the swell.'

'No we weren't. Everything's fine.'

'Do you like him?'

Jemima sighed. 'Yes. Yes, I do.'

Jack turned to look at her. 'Do you love him?'

Jemima pulled a face and looked away. 'I don't know.'

'No shame in it if you do. Except you don't trust him, do you?' Jack shifted a little. 'You'd have told him what you were up to if you did.'

'Never mind that.' Jemima did not want to talk about it. It made her feel worse. She started to eat the pork pie while Jack tossed the apple core to the horse. 'Tell me what's going on, Jack.'

Jack sighed. 'I wouldn't be here if I knew the answer to that.'

'No? Well, tell me what you do know, then. Why did you come to Delaval in the first place?'

Jack settled down. 'I came to see you. And to warn you.'

Jemima paused in her chewing. 'Warn me about what?'

'Someone's been asking questions about you. You know, sniffing around. I thought it might be your fancy in-laws wanting to discredit you, so I came as quick as I could to let you know.' Jack sighed. 'Truth to tell, it's no fun at home without you, sis. Father's simmered down now about you leaving. Seems almost pleased to have you off his hands. Mother's really proud.' He gave her a mocking look. 'A real live Countess as a daughter!'

Jemima looked horrified. 'And Father?'

'He doesn't know. It's our little secret, Mother and me. Makes her happy. As for Father, I'm hoping he'll get stuck up a chimney one of these days.'

'Jack!'

Jack shrugged. 'So who do you think it is, snitching around for information about you?'

'I don't know.' Jemima took a mouthful of ale and handed the bottle over. 'Rob has a cousin who's a nasty piece of work. It could be her. She met me at the wedding and she might have recognised me, but she could be waiting to denounce me at some point in the future.' Jemima shivered. 'Horrible girl! She was vile to Letty as well.'

She saw Jack's head come up sharply. 'Letty?'

'Letty Exton. The girl who was in the coach with me this afternoon. Surely you remember her from London—pretty with golden curls. She's lovely.'

'I remember. What about her?'

'Augusta spoiled her come out.'

'Shrew,' Jack said. He let his head sink down on his knees. 'So it could be her. At least you're forewarned, Jem.'

'Yes. Thank you.' Jemima frowned. 'So how did you get into this mess, Jack?'

Jack lay back and closed his eyes. 'I fell in with a man called Harry Naylor the other side of Oxford. We travelled together. He was coming back to Delaval after the wars. Wounded at Corunna, he said.'

'Naylor. Oh, yes. He was a groom here a few years ago, apparently.'

'Weaselly fellow. Didn't care for him, but as he knew the way and I couldn't read the road signs…' Jack yawned. 'We got to the Speckled Hen last night and had a bit of a barney over who should buy the drinks. He'd been touching me for cash since Oxford and I was a bit pi—a bit annoyed. So we had words and he went off to talk to a friend and I took my drink into a corner.'

'Did anyone see you quarrelling?' Jemima asked.

'Yes. Unfortunately.'

'Oh, dear.' Jemima pushed the remains of the pork pie towards him. 'Are you sure you're not hungry?'

Jack looked shifty. 'No, thanks. I'll have a drink though, before you finish that ale.'

He tilted the bottle, wiped his lips on his sleeve and continued, 'Later on some flash coves came in. One was the swell at your wedding.'

'Ferdie Selborne.'

'That's right. With some other chinless wonder. They played a few games of cards and then I saw Harry edge on up to them.'

Jemima put down the piece of beef she was eating. 'Harry Naylor spoke to Ferdie?'

'That's right. Saw it with my own eyes. They were arguing fit to bust.'

'About what?'

'No idea, Jem.' Jack looked annoyed. 'If I knew that I'd know everything, wouldn't I? Next thing I knew, I was in the corridor, having come back from taking a—'

'Yes, all right,' Jemima said hastily. 'Spare me the details.'

'It's important. The jakes were outside, you see. I never got back to the bar. Suppose I'd taken too much

ale and the next I knew I woke up in my room upstairs
with the landlord pounding on the door and shouting to
me to come out and saying that Harry Naylor was murdered and the constable on the way. They carted me off
to Burford gaol before you could say knife.'

'So you scaled the wall and ran away, thereby con-
firming everyone's view that you were the murderer.'

Jack looked defensive. 'I didn't want to be a sitting
duck, did I? They wouldn't have asked too many questions. A convenient stranger to pin a murder on…I'd
have been hanged before you could say—'

'Highwayman,' Jemima finished.

'Yes,' Jack said. He sighed. 'That was stupid, but like
I said, I couldn't just come to the door. Or write you a
note, for that matter. I'll give all the jewellery back.'

'That horse doesn't look up to a life of crime,' Jemima said, lobbing the piebald another apple.

'It isn't. Neither am I. That's why I need you and
your Earl to sort this out for me.'

Jemima got up and brushed the crumbs from her
skirts. 'I'll talk to Rob about it. But…Ferdie Selborne…
He's Rob's cousin, you know, and one of his best
friends. I don't think he'll believe it.'

Jack shrugged dispiritedly. 'Then you know what I'm
up against, don't you?'

'I'll leave you the food,' Jemima said, blinking a little
owlishly and suddenly realising how much of the ale
she had drunk. 'And don't forget to move to the charcoal burner's hut tomorrow. We'll come some time in
the afternoon.'

Jack stood up. 'You're a great girl, Jem.'

Jemima gave him a hug. 'And you're an idiot.' She
stood back and looked at him.

'Jack…'

'Yes?'

'There's something I should tell you. I saw Tilly a few days ago.'

Jack's dark face was suddenly still.

'I'm sorry,' Jemima said in a rush. 'You were right and I was wrong. I should have left well alone.'

'But you didn't?'

'I didn't speak to her, if that's what you mean.' Jemima put a hand on his arm. 'She's well, Jack. And happy. I thought I should leave it at that.'

Jack covered her fingers with his own. 'Did it cause trouble with the lord?'

'Rob. His name's Rob, for goodness sake. And, yes, it did, I suppose. Just for a bit.'

Jack laughed. 'Now who's stupid? I suppose he thought she was yours.'

'Something like that. I told him the truth. I hope you don't mind.'

Jack shook his head. 'Seems you may trust your Lord Selborne after all, Jem. You should make your mind up, you know.'

'His name is Rob,' Jemima said for a third time. 'And now I'm going back to him. Good night, Jack.'

'I knew you would go,' Rob said. He was standing in Jemima's bedroom, waiting for her, and he was white with anger.

Jemima threw her cloak over the back of the chair and turned to face him. 'Why did you not stop me then, Robert?'

Rob looked contemptuous. 'Because I wanted to see what would happen. I wanted to see if you respected my wishes sufficiently to do as I asked.'

Jemima winced. She felt guilty and knew she

sounded defensive. 'I could not simply leave my brother hiding out there.'

'There was no need for that.' Rob strode over to the window. 'I would gladly have gone with you to find Jack tomorrow and try to sort the entire matter out. You needed only to trust me.'

Jemima felt her irritation catch. 'You did not say so! If I had known—'

Rob gave her a look that silenced her. 'I told you that we would talk about it. But you did not wait for that.'

They stared at each other for a long, angry moment, then Jemima's shoulders slumped. 'I am sorry. After Tilly, I thought…'

'Yes?'

'That you would not forgive me another indiscretion.'

'Strange,' Rob said, with biting sarcasm, 'when what I find hard to forgive is another secret.'

Jemima thought of what Jack had said only an hour ago about love and loyalty.

'I did not intend to hold secrets,' she said slowly. 'I only did it…'

'Because your loyalty is to Jack,' Rob said. His face was in shadow. 'I understand. He is your brother, after all.'

'No,' Jemima said. That felt wrong. She narrowed her gaze as she tried to work it out.

'My first loyalty is to you,' she said.

Rob looked up. There was a fierce light in his dark eyes. 'I do not think so, Jemima. If you believe that, you delude yourself.'

Jemima frowned. It was something new to see this inflexibility in Rob, to hear the hardness in his voice. And yet had she not seen warnings of it before, in the anger he had shown over her father's violence, in the

stubbornness with which he had pursued his career in
the army and the equal determination he had shown in
restoring Delaval? She had always known that there was
a core of steel beneath Rob's tenderness.

'I have trusted Jack all my life,' she said, a little catch
in her voice, 'and I have known you but a short time.'

'I understand,' Rob said again. He sounded tired now,
his anger gone.

They looked at one another. Jemima had the strangest
feeling that she was on the verge of losing something
precious before she had really had it. All this time Rob
had been courting her, leading her to trust him by slow
steps. He had shown her nothing but generosity and
she... Jemima swallowed hard. She had repaid that
kindness as best she could, but perhaps her best had not
been good enough.

'What is it that you want?' she said, watching his
face. 'Rob, I do not understand—'

'I want your trust,' Rob said.

Jemima shook her head slightly. 'But you already
have it!'

Rob's gaze did not falter. 'You always hold something back.'

'I...' Jemima's first instinct was to deny it, but she
stopped, for there was more than an element of truth in
what Rob had said. He knew it and she knew it too.

Rob took her hand. 'I do not like compromises, Jemima. I want everything.'

Jemima scanned his face. 'You have it.'

'All your trust. All your loyalty. All your love.' Rob
released her. 'Think about it, Jemima. All or nothing.'

Jemima stared at him. 'Nothing?'

'It is still not too late to have the marriage annulled

and give you that house in Twickenham,' Rob said, with a lopsided smile. 'If that is what you prefer.'

'No!' Jemima could not smother the instinctive cry that rose to her lips. 'That is absurd!'

'Why?' Rob raised an ironic brow. 'That was what we originally intended.'

Jemima frowned. They had come so far from that original position that sometimes it was difficult to remember just where they had started. But one thing she did know in her heart of hearts. Her life and Rob's had become so entwined in the tapestry of Delaval that to tear herself away would be a wrench she was not sure she could survive.

'No,' she said again, and her voice was thick with tears this time. She stared at Rob through the blur. 'I do not understand. All this because of tonight?'

'No,' Rob said. He sighed. 'All this because I cannot settle for second best, Jemima.' He strode over to the fireplace. 'I promised that I would give you as much time as you needed, did I not? I promised that we could go as slowly as you wished.' He brought his hand down flat on the mantelpiece and the china jumped. 'I lied. I cannot do that any more. I have tried to be patient and twice you have kept secrets from me, so now I am not prepared to compromise any longer. Either you trust me or you do not. And if you do not, you are free to go. Make up your mind.'

Jemima bit her lip hard, struggling against the urge to cry. This felt all wrong, and yet she could not blame Rob, for he spoke nothing but the truth. She had risked everything by holding things back from him and it was only now, when she realised how close she was to losing him, that she could see how much more important he was than anything else in the world.

Rob glanced at the ormolu clock. 'It is very late. I should leave you now. Tomorrow, if you wish it, you may tell me about Jack and I shall see what I can do to help him.'

He was already halfway to the door. Jemima put out a hand. 'Wait!'

Rob stopped. The expression on his face was that of a polite stranger. 'Yes?'

'I am sorry,' Jemima said, in a rush. 'I do not know what else to say, Rob. You have a right to be angry with me. I cannot deny it. But I do not want to leave Delaval. I love it here.' Her voice broke. 'Oh, Rob…'

Rob's expression was still hard. 'Perhaps we should talk about this tomorrow, Jemima.'

'If you wish,' Jemima said. She set her jaw. 'There is something I want to tell you now, though. I know I have made mistakes, Rob, but I do not intend to make the mistake of leaving you, or agreeing to an annulment. They are not easy to obtain, you know.'

She saw a spark of humour in Rob's eyes and her heart leapt at the thought that perhaps all was not lost after all. 'Really?' her husband drawled. 'Is that so, my dear?'

'Yes.' Jemima's heart was beating very fast. Instinct told her that she had his full attention now. 'Especially if a couple has lived together as we have done. You would not find it easy to claim, for instance, that you were impotent.'

Rob smothered a laugh. 'I confess that I would be in two minds whether to take that course or not.'

'Understandably,' Jemima said. 'And,' she added, greatly daring, 'once I had told the courts of your undeniable prowess, those particular grounds for annulment would be entirely closed to you.'

Rob's lips twitched. He took several steps closer to her. 'Perhaps I could think of something else.'

Jemima faced him out. 'Perhaps I could counter your claims. Or perhaps…' she took two steps that brought her to within a foot of him '…I could persuade you to change your mind.'

There was a second of stillness and then Rob grabbed her. His fingers dug into her upper arms and he pulled her tight against him.

'Devil take it,' he said, 'you would not have to try very hard.'

His mouth came down hard on hers and Jemima responded shamelessly, entangling her hands in his hair, pressing herself against him. Her head began to spin as the kiss deepened and she parted her lips under his, tasting, exploring, her need for him as great as his for her.

They drew apart slowly. Rob's breathing was ragged and his eyes were dark with desire. Jemima felt her legs tremble. She held her breath. 'Does this mean that you forgive me?'

Rob kissed her again, a brief, hard kiss. 'I suppose I do.'

Jemima rested her head against his shoulder. 'It will be the last time, Rob. I swear it.'

'Just prove it,' Rob said. 'Please.' He stepped back. 'I should go.'

'You will have to help me undress,' Jemima said, avoiding his eyes. 'Everyone thinks that I am sick and I cannot call my maid or I will give the game away.'

Rob groaned and she added hastily, 'You need only unfasten the buttons for me. I cannot reach them myself, but I can manage the rest.'

'Turn around, then,' Rob said.

Jemima looked at him. She raised her chin. 'I am not trying to seduce you, you know,' she said. 'I have not forgotten your grandmother's will.'

Rob groaned again. He ran a hand through his hair. 'I can assure you that I am within an ace of forgetting it.'

Jemima's face warmed. He turned her around. His fingers were busy on the buttons that fastened the back of her gown. Jemima's heart was beating very hard now and all she seemed aware of was the heat and the beat in her blood. She felt the bodice of the gown loosen and slip away as the dress fell to puddle about her feet.

'No stays,' Rob murmured. 'That's a blessing.' He bent to kiss the side of her neck, then trailed little kisses across her bare back above the neckline of her chemise, leaving Jemima's spine tingling. She turned around, crossing her arms firmly over her breasts.

'I can manage for myself now, thank you,' she said.

Rob did not reply. He calmly leaned across and blew out the candle, then scooped her up and placed her on the bed. Jemima could not see him, but every one of her senses was heightened, devastatingly aware of him. She could feel him beside her in the dark; feel his warmth and the brush of his body against hers. His voice came very softly out of the darkness.

'How much do you trust me, Jemima?'

Jemima cleared her throat. 'Ah…um…totally, Robert.'

'You have had your doubts before.'

Jemima took a deep breath and let go of her fears. 'I know that you would never hurt me.'

'And do you still think that love is a trap?'

Jemima squeezed her eyes tight shut. 'Not precisely... I think that physical love is...can be...rather pleasant...'

She heard him laugh. 'That's my Jemima. Still holding something back...' He shifted beside her. 'Will you entrust yourself to me tonight?'

Jemima's breath caught. Her heart bumped painfully against her ribs. 'Rob, the terms of the will—'

'I know. But there are other ways...'

She felt him draw the chemise away from her. There was nothing but her stockings left now and Rob had discovered that too, running his hand up her leg to the soft skin above her garter. His fingers stroked and cajoled, tempting her beyond endurance. His mouth covered hers, hard and urgent.

Jemima was slow burning for him now as his hands and mouth moved over her body with a leisurely thoroughness that awakened and learned and teased and tormented by turns. She was also achingly aware of his own self-control and the fact that he was still fully dressed whilst she was almost naked. In some ways it added to the excitement and in others it was desperately frustrating as her hands met with layers of material when she wanted nothing between them. She struggled and groaned with disappointment until he trapped her marauding hands between their bodies and returned to her mouth to kiss her fiercely, stealing her last remaining breath. And when she freed her hands again in a ruthless attempt to part him from his clothes, Rob simply laughed and lowered his mouth to her breasts, kissing and caressing until Jemima lay exhausted and supine with longing.

'Do you still trust me?' he asked.

Jemima turned her head on the pillow. 'Oh, yes... I

can see that trusting you is a very…pleasurable experience…'

Rob kissed her again, long and slow, sliding his hand up her thigh, parting her legs to caress and tease until she squirmed. He smothered her cries with his mouth on hers.

'Since I cannot make love to you fully tonight,' he whispered, 'there are other things that I would like to do instead. May I?'

There was a long, hot silence. Jemima's whole body was clenched so tightly she was afraid that she might burst. Rob's fingers had already resumed their slow torment and she felt her body move instinctively at his command. Her dazed mind was not even sure that it understood what he had truly meant, but when she breathed her assent she soon found out. Rob slid down the bed and she felt the soft caress of his hair as it brushed her bare stomach. She had already tensed in anticipation of some undreamed-of pleasure when his tongue took the place of his fingers, and Jemima felt as though her body had fragmented into a million tiny, blissful pieces.

In the end the rapture was so exquisite that she had to bite the pillow to prevent herself from crying out and rousing the whole house, and when she discovered that Rob was not intending to let it rest with that first dazzling explosion of pleasure, she abandoned herself to pure sensation for the rest of the night.

Chapter Seventeen

'Jemima? Wake up, sweetheart...'

The morning sunlight was patterning squares of light across the floor and Jemima blinked and stretched. She felt warm and heavy and utterly blissful. She was lying in Rob's arms and he was...naked, she realised. As she stirred, he moved a little away from her and she immediately felt bereft.

Rob's breath tickled her ear. 'I have to leave you now, before the servants arrive. How are you, sweetheart?'

'Happy,' Jemima murmured.

She opened her eyes properly and turned within his arms.

At some point within that heated night she had imagined that she would never be able to face Rob again in the daylight. He had taken her body for his own and evoked the most exquisite response from her and had her trembling with a shameless desire. Yet now he was smiling at her with such tenderness that she felt her embarrassment melt away.

Then she frowned. 'Rob... It was lovely for me, but you—'

Rob grinned. 'I have never enjoyed a night more, Jemima.'

Jemima blushed. 'No, but…'

'Pray do not worry, sweetheart. I am sure that we may redress the balance soon.'

'I needed to talk to you,' Jemima murmured, 'but somehow it did not happen.'

Rob eased himself out of bed and started to dress in slightly haphazard fashion. 'You know that I am to go out shooting with Ferdie and Bertie this morning? I shall be back as soon as I can and then we must talk. I promise to go with you to see your brother this afternoon if you wish me to.'

'Thank you,' Jemima murmured. All her fears seemed so far from this sunlit room and yet they were out there, waiting to pounce. Rob still had no notion that Jack thought Ferdie had been involved in Naylor's death. When she told him… She turned aside from the thought, not wanting it to spoil the sunlit morning.

She caught Rob's sleeve as he bent to kiss her. 'Rob…I meant what I said. Last night was wonderful but it was…' she wrinkled her brow '…unfinished, somehow, and I am not sure that I can stand much more of this.'

'Neither can I,' Rob said. He sighed, and then his brow cleared. 'I did enjoy you, though.'

'Rob!' Jemima squeaked, as his hands delved beneath the sheets. She stilled. 'You have forgiven me, then,' she said.

'You trusted me,' Rob said. He kissed her lingeringly. 'I will see you later, sweet.'

'Be careful,' Jemima called, suddenly anxious, and saw Rob grin in response.

After Rob had gone out she lay still. The dreaminess

induced by the previous night was on her still and she did not feel like getting up. She lay and looked at the sunlight stippling the ceiling. Was this love, then, this happy languor? Or had she fallen into precisely the trap that she had seen capture so many before her: the confusing of intense physical attraction with love?

She could hear Rob's voice next door as he chatted to his valet and just the sound of it made her smile. So perhaps…

There was a knock at the door and Ella came in with the hot chocolate. Her gaze went from Jemima's clothes, scattered across the floor, to her mistress's bare shoulders as she sat curled up dreamily in the bed. Ella giggled.

'I see that you were feeling better last night, my lady.'

Jemima smiled too. 'I was, thank you, Ella.'

The maid started to tidy the room.

There was a knock at the door. Jemima hastily reached for her dressing-robe to cover her nakedness.

'May I come in?' Letty was in the doorway. She had a box in her hand and she put it down on a side table. 'I do apologise for bursting in like this, Jemima, but Grandmama is talking about returning to Swan Park this afternoon and I wanted to make sure that you were quite well. After our ordeal yesterday and your sickness last night, I mean…'

'Of course.' Jemima gestured to her to come into the room. 'Ella, would you come back in a little, please? I think I shall take my morning chocolate with Miss Exton.'

'Thank you for sending her away,' Letty said artlessly, when the maid had closed the door behind her.

'I wanted to talk to you, dearest Jemima, and I was afraid that someone would overhear…'

'Of course,' Jemima said, smiling a little. 'What did you wish to discuss, Letty?'

'Well…' Letty blushed. 'It was about what I said to the constable yesterday. You see, I never thought… And then you gave me *such* a look, and I realised that you did not wish me to mention it, and I wondered…' She spread her hands helplessly. 'Just what is going on, Jemima? I know that the highwayman is your brother—'

'You do?'

'Yes. No! That is, I am sure that Mr Jewell is not a highwayman, but I wondered if it was a disguise?'

Jemima made a quick decision. Letty was a sad rattle, but she was sure that she could trust her.

'Letty, you must not breathe a word.'

Letty's eyes had grown huge and blue. 'Oh, no, indeed I won't!'

'And you mustn't do anything about it.'

Letty looked guilty. 'Oh, no, of course not.'

'Jack is in some trouble,' Jemima continued, improvising lightly, 'but I am sure that it will be resolved soon. I have told Rob and he will help put all to rights.'

'You have told Rob about it?' Letty looked nervous. 'Was that wise? I mean, he might be stuffy about it and I observed that he did not like Jack—Mr Jewell—a great deal…'

'When did you observe that?' Jemima said curiously.

'Oh, when we met you that time in Mr Churchward's office, of course! Rob was all formal and Mr Jewell was all stiff and it was clear that they did not know what to make of each other.'

Jemima raised her brows, wondering just how much more Letty had noticed.

'You must not develop a *tendre* for Jack, Letty,' she warned. 'I know that he is most handsome, but you are a lady, my love, and I am sorry to say that Jack is no gentleman in the accepted sense. Our family is in trade and as such he is beneath you.'

'Rob chose to marry *you*,' Letty said mulishly.

'I know.' Jemima sighed. 'And you know that that is different, Letty. A wife takes her husband's place in the world, and besides, Rob married me as a matter of convenience.'

Letty gave a giggle. 'Fiddlesticks! Convenience, indeed. He is head over ears for you, Jemima, and you for him too. You should see your reflection this morning if you do not believe me! There!' Her eyes sparkled. 'I am not such a lady, I suppose, to make reference to such things!'

'Oh, dear,' Jemima said. She looked about the room. Half her clothes were still dropped carelessly on the floor as Ella had not had time to tidy them all away. The bedclothes were tangled and there was a dent in the pillow where Rob's head had been. She caught sight of her reflection in the pier glass. Her hair was tousled about her shoulders and there was an indefinable something about her expression that morning, sated and happy and ever so slightly wicked. The signs were all there to read. She bit her lip.

'Oh, dear,' she said again.

Letty patted her hand.

'You should not worry about caring for Rob. Augusta and spiteful people may say that to feel or show affection is lower class, but that is only because no one could possibly love her! Why, Grandmama is *aux anges* to see such a love match, and when you provide an heir for Delaval—' She broke off. 'Oh, dear, I have gone a little too far this time, haven't I?'

'I am not *enceinte*,' Jemima said hastily, 'although I know that Lady Marguerite thinks me so.'

'I expect you soon will be at this rate,' Letty said. She pressed her hand to her mouth. 'Oh, I am so tactless. I always say exactly what comes in to my head. Grandmama is always thinking me indelicate!'

'Well,' Jemima said, trying not to laugh, 'I confess that you do take my breath away sometimes, Letty. Perhaps we should change the subject now.'

'Yes,' Letty said. She gestured to the tin box on the table. 'I found this in the library yesterday, but with all the excitement I forgot to give it to you. I looked inside, I am afraid. My deplorable curiosity! It seems to be a diary, but I swear I have not read it.' She jumped up. 'I must go and get ready to leave for Swan Park, I suppose. I will see you later, Jemima?'

'Of course.' Jemima smiled at her. She put out a hand and drew the tin box towards her. Since finding it up the chimney a few days ago she had completely forgotten about it. The lid came open easily enough, for Letty's curious fingers had loosened the tar that had held it closed. Inside was a pile of paper, close written and crossed. With a tiny frown, Jemima lay back on her pillows and started to read.

'This has to stop.' Jack Jewell leaned his head back against the sun-warmed wood of the charcoal burner's hut. The sun beat down on his face and he closed his eyes.

'It will.' Beside him, Letty Exton tilted the brim of her straw hat to enable her to rest her head next to his. Her stripy parasol shaded her face. The edge of its shadow just caught Jack and he smiled a little. It felt as though she was touching him. Even though his eyes were closed he could sense how close she was. He could smell her. Her scent was a mixture of roses and honeysuckle and it played havoc with his self-control. He shifted a little away.

'We are to return to Swan Park today.' Letty spoke softly. 'It is my birthday ball in two days.'

Jack opened his eyes and squinted against the sun. 'Am I invited?'

Letty smiled. 'If you would like to attend, Mr Jewell, then you are most welcome.'

She sounded like a Duchess. Jack wanted to kiss her. He turned his head slightly and saw that she was watching him with those glorious sky blue eyes.

'I saw your daughter,' she said. 'I thought that I should tell you.'

There was a silence. Jack held her gaze, black on blue. His heart was beating fast. He cleared his throat.

'Does it make a difference?' he asked.

Letty did not answer immediately. Her face was grave in repose.

'No,' she said after a moment. 'Except that I wished that she was mine.'

Jack closed his eyes. It was the closest thing that he had had to a declaration of love in six years. His heart ached.

He opened his eyes again. Letty was still watching him, his pocket princess who seemed so sure that they should be together. Her certainty shook him. He wished that he had half her strength of character.

'It should make a difference.' He spoke roughly. 'I'm not for the likes of you.' He searched desperately for the most convincing reason, the biggest issue that could ever divide them. 'I cannot even read or write.'

'Do you want to?' Letty asked.

Jack almost laughed. His shoulders slumped against the wall. 'Sometimes I do. I never cared when I was a child. Now I think it might be useful.'

Letty wriggled closer. He felt her soft breath against his cheek and forced himself not to turn his head. It took every ounce of willpower that he had.

'I have a bargain for you, Mr Jewell,' she said. 'I will teach you to read...'

'Yes?'

'If you teach me sweep's cant,' Letty finished. She held out her hand. 'Is it a deal?'

Jack grinned. He put his hand into hers. 'Done,' he said.

'I admit that it looks bad.' Rob said later that evening, when everyone had departed for Swan Park and he and Jemima were alone. He put the sheets of paper down on his desk and turned to face Jemima. She was sitting on the window seat, her feet curled up beneath her, her expression serious. The tin box lay on the desk between them. 'It is written in Ferdie's handwriting and...' Rob hesitated '...it does state that he was responsible for my grandfather's death—'

'It says that he shot him,' Jemima said baldly. 'Your grandfather did not accidentally shoot himself. It was Ferdie's fault.' She uncurled herself and slid off the seat.

Rob tapped the diary. 'I suppose it is a confession of sorts. He sounds deeply affected by the whole experience. A most terrible accident.'

'I know,' Jemima said. She too had been moved by

the sad desperation of the writing and she had no doubts that it had been a dreadful accident, just as Rob had said. She frowned a little. 'Why do you think that he wrote it down, Robert?'

Rob shook his head. 'Perhaps he could not bear to keep it bottled up. Sometimes it helps a little to write things down.'

'And why hide it up the chimney?' Jemima frowned. 'It makes no sense.'

Rob shook his head. 'Only Ferdie could answer that, and I am not at all sure that we should raise this with him.'

Jemima looked up sharply. 'But it is a motive for murder,' she said.

Rob looked at her. 'You mean Naylor?'

'Of course. He was with Ferdie when your grandfather died. Both of them kept it a secret.' Jemima made a gesture. 'Naylor went away. And then he came back and Jack saw him arguing with Ferdie... And now he is dead.'

'I cannot believe it,' Rob said. His face was very pale and set in the candlelight. 'Not Ferdie. He can be feckless and he is a libertine, but...' He turned to look at Jemima and his expression softened slightly. 'I am sorry, Jemima. It is not that I think Jack is lying.' He grimaced. 'I simply believe that there has to be some other explanation.'

'What explanation can possibly cover the case?' Jemima ran a hand through her hair. 'Goodness knows, I like Ferdie, but I cannot see how to explain this!'

Rob got up and drove his hands into his pockets. 'Bertie was with Ferdie at the inn! If anything had happened, surely Bertie would have known? Ferdie could not simply stroll out, murder Harry Naylor and come back to the card table as though nothing had happened!'

Jemima made a gesture. 'I agree it sounds far-fetched. But the confession...'

Rob looked stubborn. 'That does not mean that Ferdie killed Naylor. Jemima, you are talking about my cousin.'

Jemima put her hands on her hips. She understood that Rob had a loyalty to his cousin, but she also had a loyalty to Jack, and he was in hiding for his life.

'Just because he is your cousin it does not mean that he could not have done it,' she said.

'No, of course not.' Rob ran his hand over his hair. He swung round. 'But I know Ferdie, Jemima! He would never hurt anyone deliberately, let alone murder them! He cannot have killed Naylor.'

Jemima rubbed her forehead. She knew what he meant. Ferdie seemed quite harmless. There was something gentle about him.

'But will you speak to him, Rob?' She pleaded.

'Very well. I will,' Rob said. His face was drawn. 'But I will not do it until after Letty's birthday.'

Jemima's head jerked up. 'Must you wait?'

'Yes,' Rob said. He spread his hands. 'There would not be a great deal for Letty to celebrate were I to accuse Ferdie of murder the day before her party.'

Jemima sighed. She knew he was right. And a part of her did not want him to accuse Ferdie at all. She could not believe that it was true.

Rob picked up the sheets of paper again. 'Thank you for bringing this to me,' he said, 'and not going direct to the constable.' He shot her a look. 'Did you not wish to do so, to save Jack's skin?'

Jemima looked at him. There was no sound in the

room but for the spit of the fire. She gave a little smile. 'I confess that I should prefer it if we could clear Jack's name straight away. It is awkward for him to be in hiding. I think he may even decide to turn himself in if matters go on too long.'

'It should not be for much longer,' Rob said.

'No, I know. It is difficult for me, but...' Jemima shrugged lightly '...you are my husband and my first loyalty is to you.'

Rob put out a hand and pulled her into the crook of his arm.

'I am sorry,' he said.

'Sorry?' Jemima turned her head against his shoulder and looked at him.

'About what I said last night. I was jealous.' Rob rubbed his jaw. 'Damnably jealous, to tell the truth.'

Jemima eased away from him slightly. 'Jealous of Jack?'

'I envied how close you were to him.' Rob looked at her sideways. 'I always have done. Right from the start, when he escorted you to the church for our wedding and I knew he did not like me.' He smoothed the hair away from her face. 'It was not just Jack, I am afraid. When Ferdie was so charming to you that day I wanted to run him through.'

'Rob!' Jemima was entranced.

'I had no idea I was so possessive,' Rob finished ruefully. 'I did not like myself very much for it, but I could not help it.'

'I do not believe you should reproach yourself,' Jemima said, pressing a soft kiss to his cheek. 'I should be the same.'

Rob pressed his cheek against her hair. 'Truly?'

'Truly. Look what a fuss I made about all the time

you spent on the estate when secretly I thought that you should be with me.'

Rob dropped a kiss on her lips.

They sat very quietly for a little.

'We have the place to ourselves this evening,' Jemima said dreamily. 'It is pleasant, is it not?' She started to rub her fingers absentmindedly over Rob's cuff. 'You could read your newspaper and I could sew, like an old married couple. Or perhaps we could do something else. Robert...'

Rob made an enquiring noise.

'You know that you said we could find a way to redress the balance after last night...' Jemima said.

She felt Rob go very still. 'Yes?'

'I thought, perhaps,' Jemima said, blushing a little, 'that you might show me how that would work.' She looked up and met Rob's gaze. There was nothing sleepy in it now. 'If you do not mind,' she added politely.

She saw the corner of Rob's mouth lift in a smile.

'I admire your spirit of fair play,' he said, as he drew her to her feet.

Chapter Eighteen

Jack Jewell paused, one hand on the stone banister that led up the wide steps to the terrace at Swan Park. The doors to the ballroom were open and the silver drapes swayed in the autumn breeze, affording a brief glimpse into the lighted world beyond. A thousand silver candles glittered in the sconces. Fabulous silver flowers and decorations adorned the ballroom. Jack stood in the shadows and watched as Miss Lettice Exton celebrated her coming of age.

He had never intended to be there. He knew the whole thing was preposterous. He knew that he should go away and never see her again. He knew that there was no future for them. He stood in the darkness, straining for a single glimpse of his one true love.

The drapes shifted and a figure stepped out of the ballroom, a wraith in silver gauze. Jack caught his breath. He watched as Letty came forward to the balustrade, leaned one elbow on the stone and rested her chin on her hand. She looked sad. And it was her birthday.

Jack kept perfectly still. Behind Letty he could see a couple swirling past the long windows, dancing the quadrille. Jack heard the applause when the dance came to an end, followed by snatches of conversation. He heard the tinkle of the music and the clatter as the servants hurried to keep the buffet tables laden with food. He smiled to see Jemima, stunning in green velvet, dancing with a most patrician-looking gentleman. His little sister, the Countess of Selborne. Some fairy tales did work out, and others did not.

On the terrace Letty stood like a drooping flower. The orchestra struck up for a polonaise. Jack took the steps two at a time.

'Would you care to dance, Miss Exton?'

Letty put her hand into his. In the moonlight her eyes were a bright silver blue, like the stars.

'You came to my party,' she said, and gave Jack the biggest smile that he had ever seen. He bowed.

'You invited me.'

Letty held him at arm's length. 'Jack, your clothes!'

'Do you like them?'

Letty's eyes sparkled. 'You look very fine. You did not steal them, did you?'

Jack laughed. 'On my honour, no.'

'And are you still a wanted man?'

Jack shook his head. 'No. Had you not heard the news? I thought it was all over the county. Mr Beaumaris, the parson, told the constable that he had seen Naylor on the night of the accident. Apparently he was dead drunk. Hit his head on the lych gate, so Beaumaris said, but he staggered off into the dark before the parson could help.'

'Why did he not say so sooner?' Letty said indignantly.

Jack smiled at the protective anger in her tone. 'Beaumaris has been away for a few days. He only got back today.'

Letty sighed, mollified. 'Then I suppose I must forgive him.' She paused. 'Does Jemima know?'

'Not yet. I am only just returned from Burford.'

A little frown puckered Letty's forehead. 'But the highway robbery, Jack? What about that?'

Jack grinned. 'There was no reliable description of the highwayman,' he said. 'Only you or Jemima or your grandmother could give me away.'

'Jemima and I never would,' Letty said with a confidence that shook Jack's heart, 'but I cannot be sure of Grandmama.'

'She doesn't like me,' Jack said roughly, 'and I understand why.'

Letty was shaking her head. 'Grandmama is not like that, Jack. Yes, she is protective of me, but there is no snobbery in her. Look at the way she has taken to Jemima! She loves Jemima because Rob loves her...'

Jack felt a mixture of happiness and desperation. 'That is different,' he said, and they both knew he spoke the truth.

The music struck up and they started to dance. Jack had never danced a polonaise and had absolutely no idea how to go on, so Letty had to give him intensive instruction whilst trying not to laugh.

'No, circle to the left... And now to the right... Give me your right hand...'

She gave up, and collapsed against his side, laughing silently, one hand pressed to her ribs in a vain attempt to keep the laughter inside.

'Oh, Jack, you are utterly hopeless...'

'I know,' Jack said gravely.

Letty's laughter died. For a second they looked at one another.

'I came to say goodbye,' Jack said.

Letty bit her lip. Her eyes were very wide. 'Are we not to see each other again, then?'

'I thought not, no.'

'It will not be easy, with your sister married to my cousin.'

'No.'

Letty withdrew from him a little way. 'I could go inside and tell them that we are betrothed,' she said.

Jack's heart jumped. He knew she would do it too, his dauntless girl. No dictates of society or class or even common sense could stop her.

He kept his tone neutral, betraying none of the longing and the hopelessness inside. 'I do beg you not to do that,' he said.

'You would not wish it?' Her brows were arched with sudden displeasure, her tone even more clear-cut than before. 'You would not wish to marry me?'

Jack shook his head slightly, more in denial of the situation than to confirm her words. 'Letty—'

'Answer my question, if you please, Mr Jewell. It is not every day that I make a proposal to a gentleman and I need to be perfectly clear of the outcome.'

Jack stared at her face, etched silver in the moonlight.

'I love you,' he said. 'But I cannot marry you.'

It seemed that, after all, he had said the right thing. He saw Letty's eyes widen and the tears come into them, though she was smiling at the same time. He opened his mouth to say more, but she put her gloved fingers against his lips.

'Hush,' she said. 'It is not every day that I kiss a gentleman.'

And she stood up on tiptoe to press her lips to his.

* * *

Jemima had been dancing with the Duke of Merlin
an experience that had been enjoyable in one sense
since the Duke was an exceptionally good dancer, and
quite nerve-racking in another, since she was still rather
in awe of him. They had spoken of music, with Jemima
admitting cautiously to her plans for a music room at
Delaval and music lessons at the school in the village
Merlin had seemed genuinely interested and had asked
some searching questions. At the end of the dance he
handed her over to Bertie Pershore, who had put his
name down for the polonaise, and who approached his
uncle with some trepidation.

'Take Lady Selborne away and dance with her, Ber
tie,' Merlin said affably. He raised his voice. 'You
dance divinely, ma'am. May I have the cotillion before
supper?'

Having ensured Jemima's social success, Merlin then
withdrew to the end of the ballroom and was seen in
conversation with Lady Marguerite.

'Two terrifying tartars together,' Bertie observed, as
he and Jemima took their place in the set. 'Must con
gratulate you, Lady Selborne. Took me years to win
Merlin over and I think he still regards me as an over
grown schoolboy.' Bertie's face fell. 'Probably because
I am an overgrown schoolboy. Anyway, don't know
how you did it!'

'You're lovely, Bertie,' Jemima said warmly. 'Don'
worry, the Duke knows your true worth.'

Bertie smiled. 'I say, Jemima, you're quite a girl
yourself. Wish I could find one like you. Don't have
any sisters, do you?'

'I'm afraid not,' Jemima said. 'You do not wish to marry Miss Vause?'

'Girl's wetter than a weekend in Scotland,' Bertie said. 'I think I need a managing female.'

'Miss Selborne?'

Bertie shuddered. 'No, thank you. Miss Selborne is always so cross.'

Looking at Augusta, Jemima could see what Bertie meant. Miss Selborne was standing in a small group that included several eligible gentlemen, but she was scowling across the ballroom at Chlorinda Vause, who was chatting to Rob. Jemima wondered if it was true that she really had wanted to marry Rob herself, or whether she was simply envious of any young lady who was prettier than she was. Remembering Letty's comments about her come out, she thought that it must be so. It was a shame, for Miss Selborne spoiled any good looks she might have by scowling so hard.

The ball had been a raging success. They were now well past the supper interval and all the guests appeared to have been enjoying themselves prodigiously. Jemima had danced with Rob four times already, to the apparent disapproval of Lady Marguerite who had berated them for being tiresomely unfashionable. There had been a twinkle in her eye as she had said so.

Bertie excused himself and wandered off to find his next partner, but Jemima stayed where she was, her gaze travelling on to Rob. She realised that tonight was the first time she had ever seen him in such a setting. He looked distinguished, handsome and utterly delicious. Jemima paused. The dancers blurred before her eyes.

'I want everything. All your trust. All your loyalty. All your love.'

She had given him the trust, the loyalty and as much passion as the terms of the will allowed, though she felt that their interpretation of abstinence was becoming ever more flexible with each passing day. But there was more than trust and passion. Rob wanted everything, everything that she could give.

'You always hold something back,' he had said.

Standing there in the ballroom, Jemima felt a huge wash of love and longing that left her shaking. By slow degrees she had abandoned all of her fears: the cynicism that held her back from believing in an honest love, the mistrust that made her deny physical attraction. And now she felt a little foolish that it had taken her so long to realise how much she loved Rob. For she did love him with all her heart.

The drapes stirred beside her and Letty stepped into the ballroom. She looked very pink and pretty, and a little startled.

'Oh, Jemima! Were you outside?'

'No,' Jemima said, shaking herself out of her pre-occupation. 'I was just…standing here…'

'Watching Rob,' Letty said. Her eyes were very bright. 'You love him, do you not?'

'Yes,' Jemima said. 'I feel a little slow. I have only just realised it.'

Letty scanned the ballroom. She frowned. 'Augusta is planning something. I can tell. She has that look on her face.'

Jemima followed her gaze. Augusta Selborne was still holding court to her small, admiring circle, and as she saw Jemima watching, she gave a small, feline smile. Her triumphant tones seared the air.

'Nothing but a chimney sweep's daughter, to be the Countess of Selborne…'

Jemima caught her breath.

'Oh, no,' Letty said, in a whisper. 'The silly fool! It will never work!' She shot Jemima a look, and then took her elbow in a comforting grasp. 'She is trying to discredit you, Jemima, but she has not the least idea of Grandmama's support for you, nor of the Duke of Merlin's involvement. She is about to humiliate herself dreadfully!'

Jemima took a deep steadying breath. She hoped that Letty was right. Within a minute or two either she or Augusta would be severely socially embarrassed.

Augusta's audience was looking shocked, though whether at Augusta's gossip or the news about Jemima was not clear. The scandal spread out from the group like ripples in a pool. Heads started to turn. Across the ballroom, Jemima saw Ferdie grab Rob's sleeve and say something urgent in his ear. She saw Rob start across the floor towards her. Augusta's voice soared.

'She met Robert when she was hired to dance at a wedding... Well, you know what men are... I knew there was something rather *déclassé* about the girl.'

Rob reached Jemima's side and took her hand very firmly in his own. There was a hard, angry light in his eyes, but he found time to smile reassuringly at Jemima before he turned to his cousin.

'You embarrass no one but yourself with your words, Augusta,' he said, with silken politeness. 'I assure you that there is no one who could bring greater honour to the role of Countess of Selborne than Jemima. I am proud that she is my wife.'

Jemima felt the tears prick her eyes. Her fingers clung to Rob's and she smiled mistily at him. Such a public declaration of his love for her...

And now Lady Marguerite Exton had turned from her

conversation with the Duke of Merlin and was looking Augusta up and down in disgust. By the time that she had finished, Augusta seemed to have shrunk slightly. All conversation in the ballroom seemed to die away.

'I must add my own support to my grandson's moving tribute, Miss Selborne,' she said, studying Augusta with a coldness that made the girl draw back. 'Jemima graces the position of Countess of Selborne. Her background is of no importance to me, just as it is not important to me that you are the granddaughter of a soap manufacturer.'

Somebody tittered. Augusta flushed bright red. 'That is different! My grandfather owned five factories!'

'Oh, my dear,' Lady Marguerite said, 'I am sorry that that matters to you. All that matters to me is that I see my grandchildren happy.' She turned to Rob and Jemima and held her hand out. 'And as Rob and Jemima are evidently very happy indeed, then I too am content.'

Bertie Pershore was trying to draw Augusta away, trying to save the situation before it was too late. Augusta, however, was standing rooted to the spot as though she had grown out of the ballroom floor. She pointed a shaking finger at Jemima.

'Maybe you would not be so content, madam, if you knew that you already had a great-grandchild, albeit not one of Lord Selborne's fathering! There is a child living not so far from here who is the image of Lady Selborne. I think that tells us all we need to know of our new Countess.'

This time the silence in the ballroom had a different quality. It was the stunned silence of horror. There was no room left for malicious gossip. This accusation was too damning, too public and too shocking.

Jemima heard Letty catch her breath in outrage. She

felt her legs tremble beneath her and then Rob's arm was about her and she could feel the anger in him, so protectively fierce that it seared her soul.

'Hold your tongue, Augusta!' Rob said. 'You know nothing! Tilly Astley is not Jemima's daughter and your slander reflects badly on no one but yourself.'

The drapes by the open window stirred as someone stepped into the room behind them.

'I'm afraid that Selborne is utterly in the right of it, ma'am,' Jack Jewell said, coming forward. He gave Augusta Selborne a contemptuous look. 'You have completely the wrong end of the stick. Miss Astley is *my* daughter, not m'sister's.' He went up to Rob and offered his hand. 'Since this seems to be the evening for tributes,' he said with a grin, 'perhaps I should add mine. Damned glad to have you as a brother-in-law, Selborne.'

Jemima blinked as Rob took Jack's hand and shook it heartily. 'Glad to see you, Jewell. Very glad,' he added with a grin of his own. 'Have you come to dance at my cousin's ball?'

Jack turned to Letty and gave her an elegant bow. 'Your servant, Miss Exton. I do apologise for my late arrival. May I offer you my congratulations on your birthday?'

Letty dropped a curtsy and gave Jack a dazzling smile. 'I was not expecting to see you again, Mr Jewell, but you are very welcome.'

She gave Jack her hand and he seemed disinclined to release her again. The crowd in the ballroom was transfixed, sensing more drama to come. Rob flashed Jemima a smile, then shepherded Letty and Jack towards Lady Marguerite. Jemima caught her breath.

'Grandmama,' Rob said clearly, 'you will remember Mr Jewell.'

Jack bowed. 'Lady Marguerite…'

'Mr Jewell.' Surely that was a hint of warmth in Lady Marguerite's frosty tones? It was impossible to tell, but Jemima thought she caught a glint of a smile in the lady's cool blue eyes. She looked across at Rob again and saw that he was smiling too.

Letty, taking courage from her cousin, stepped forward to introduce Jack to the Duke of Merlin. 'I hope, your Grace, that I may present Mr Jewell to you?'

Merlin bent and kissed Letty's cheek. 'You may do anything you wish on your birthday, my dear. Mr Jewell…' He held a hand out to Jack. 'I am delighted to make your acquaintance again. As Miss Astley's guardian—' he turned and glared witheringly at Augusta Selborne '—it is always a pleasure to see you.'

A murmur of comment broke the charged silence in the ballroom, but when Letty turned towards Augusta there was a pin-dropping quiet once more.

'This is Miss Augusta Selborne,' Letty said clearly. 'I am afraid that no one likes her very much.' She gestured to one of the footmen to come over and took a glass of red wine from his tray.

'Four years ago Augusta managed to spoil my come-out,' Letty continued conversationally, to the ballroom at large, 'and tonight she has tried to spoil my birthday ball, but I am happy to say that she has not succeeded.' She smiled sweetly at her erstwhile school friend. 'I think that you should go home now, Augusta. Red wine is so staining.' And she emptied the glass over Augusta's elegantly coiffured head.

'Grandmama always said that I had no decorum,' she said.

It was already past dawn and breakfast had been taken when the last of the carriages rolled out of the gates of Swan Park and Rob went in search of his wife. Despite the fact that he had tried to keep her by his side, Jemima had been so much in demand that he had had to relinquish her to a succession of gentlemen, all of whom wished to dance with her. He had last seen her taking breakfast with her brother and the Duke and Duchess of Merlin, but then she had vanished. Rob had searched high and low, and had ended in their turret bedroom.

The window leading out to the balcony was open and the drapes were blowing in the slight breeze. The room was empty. Suppressing a shudder, Rob went out onto the balcony. He had always been afraid of heights and although there was plenty of space, he edged along, feeling his way along the wall and refusing to look over the parapet and down on to the cobbles below. By the time that he had reached the corner where the stone steps ran up to the roof, he was in a cold sweat.

'Jemima?' He could hear the quaver in his voice. The breeze caught the name and whisked it away as it whistled over the battlements. Rob made the mistake of looking down and felt a little sick.

'Rob? I'm up here.'

He might have known that she would be up on the roof. First climbing chimneys and then on the roof. Rob winced. He loved his wife and he would not have changed her for anything, but sometimes her pastimes made him shudder.

He tilted his head up to see if he could see her. It was another mistake. White clouds tinged faintly with the pink of dawn swung drunkenly overhead against the pale blue sky. The cawing of the rooks sounded sinister, as though they were waiting for him to fall. Rob closed his eyes as the whole balcony started to tilt and spin.

'Jemima,' he said again, very deliberately, 'would you please come down?'

'Why don't you come up?' Jemima asked innocently.

Rob could see her now, or at least he could see her feet and ankles, and the hem of her green ball gown. He squinted to see if he had the angle correct to see more, and managed to catch a glimpse of silky stockings. It was almost sufficient to make him forget his vertigo.

'I cannot come up,' he said, groping his way to the bottom of the stone stair and hanging on for dear life. 'Please come down.'

'But there is such a lovely view up here!' Rob saw Jemima settle on the edge of the battlements in a froth of white petticoats. She was sitting directly above his head. Rob groaned aloud.

'Jemima, you are making me feel ill. I am afraid of heights.'

There was a pause. Rob opened his eyes again to see Jemima leaning over and her face peering down at him. He had a perfect view into the bodice of the green velvet dress. Her breasts seemed to be straining at the neckline, trying to break free. Rob took a deep breath.

'Wait a moment. I am coming up.'

'Rob, no! Wait!' Jemima sounded genuinely distraught. 'If you are afraid of heights then you must not attempt to come up here. You could become disorientated and fall off.'

'Thank you so much,' Rob said grimly, setting his teeth. He started up the stone steps, clinging to the handrail and keeping his eyes averted from the sheer wall of the house. How many steps to the roof parapet?

Ten? Twelve? It felt like hundreds. Then he felt Jemima's hand close strongly about his wrist, pulling him up, and he was standing on the roof and feeling as though he was being tossed on a very stormy sea indeed. He tried to focus, saw the ground far below, taunting him, and wished he had not looked.

'Come and sit here.' Jemima had a solicitous arm about him and drew him to the corner where the chimneystack protruded from the roof. 'It is sheltered and we can sit comfortably. Why did you do that, Rob? You knew that I would have come down.'

Rob sank down onto the sloping roof and settled himself comfortably in the corner. The chimney-stack felt reassuringly solid against his shoulder and from here he could not see the ground.

'Sometimes we cannot let our fears dictate to us,' he said, slumping a little against the solid brick of the chimney.

Jemima scrambled up next to him.

'I suppose I should not do this in such a pretty dress. It was just so fresh and clear up here that I wanted to see the view.'

Rob shuddered again and closed his eyes.

'It was very brave of you, Rob,' Jemima continued softly. 'Do you feel better now that you are up here?'

'No, I feel damnable.' Rob opened his eyes and looked at her. 'Talk to me. It will help me concentrate.'

'It was a lovely ball, wasn't it?' Jemima said, smiling. 'And so eventful!' She giggled. 'When Letty tipped the wine over Augusta I thought that everyone was going to cheer!'

'Letty has been waiting a long time to do that.' Rob grimaced. 'Augusta has made her life a misery ever since they were at school together. With any luck we shall not see much of her in future.'

'I thought that your grandmother was marvellous,' Jemima said. 'So much hauteur! And the Duke of Merlin looking down his nose at Augusta! Priceless!' She sobered. 'I am sorry, Rob. Augusta is your cousin, after all is said and done.'

Rob shrugged. 'I still have Grandmama and Letty, and at this rate I shall have Jack as well…'

'Yes…' Jemima's smile faded. 'Was it not extraordinary when he came in? Such an entrance!'

'Your brother has great style,' Rob agreed, with a wry smile.

Jemima rested her head briefly against his shoulder. 'I have so much to thank you for,' she said softly. 'The way that you greeted Jack like a friend and introduced him to your grandmother in front of everyone…'

'It was the least that I could do,' Rob said feelingly, 'after he had gone so far to help me.'

Jemima moved slightly and her hair brushed his cheek. It felt soft and sweet.

'When Jack told everyone about Tilly, I realised that he had already spoken of it to Letty,' she said. 'I was quite amazed. They cannot have met above half a dozen times and yet all that is important already seems settled between them.'

'Sometimes it only takes one meeting to settle matters,' Rob said softly. He smiled. 'Letty will have to be prepared to fight for him, though. Half the ladies in the room were desperate to dance with him! How does he do it?'

'Jack is a rogue,' Jemima said. 'The ladies love that spice of danger.'

'And yet I feel that Letty would be quite safe with him.'

'I think that you are right. But...' Jemima wrinkled her brow. 'I believe Jack loves Letty and I am certain she loves him, but surely it cannot happen, Rob? Jack has a trade. He is not a rich man, and he is far beneath her. I cannot see your grandmother ever agreeing to it.'

'We shall see,' Rob said. He put his arm about her and Jemima wriggled closer to him. 'Grandmama seemed quite cordial to him this evening. And she did not give him away, did she?'

Jemima looked at him. 'You mean she did not identify him as the highwayman? Perhaps she did not know.'

'She knew,' Rob said with a grin. 'She told me Jack was the highwayman several nights ago. She also confessed to me that she had made enquiries about you. When I told her about how we met, she already knew. She knew everything about you.'

Jemima pursed her lips. 'So it was Lady Marguerite. I wondered.'

'What was?'

'Jack came here originally to warn me that someone was asking questions about me. I wondered who it was...' Jemima sighed. 'So she knew everything and never said a word.'

'I believe that what she said tonight was true,' Rob said. 'She asked me that day if I loved you and when I said that I did, she told me that that was all that mattered.'

Rob leaned his cheek against Jemima's. It was cool from the fresh air. Sitting here, his arm about her, their bodies pressed close, he felt a contentment that nothing could touch.

'You heard that Harry Naylor was not murdered after all?' Jemima said softly. 'Jack told me last night.'

'I heard.' Rob pressed a kiss against her hair. 'I am so glad. For many reasons.'

'Jack has the devil's own luck,' Jemima said. 'To go and turn himself in, only to find there is no crime to answer.' She sighed. 'What do you mean to do about Ferdie, Rob?'

Rob frowned. It was the only thing that was left to decide. 'I do not know. I will have to think about it, but not now.' He smiled at her. 'Mornings are for fresh beginnings.'

Jemima spoke softly. 'Speaking of which, there is something that I have been remiss in telling you, Robert.' Rob stiffened and Jemima leaned a little closer so that the soft curve of her body pressed against his.

'It is nothing bad,' she said. 'I said just now that I had a great deal to thank you for.' She hesitated. 'When you sprang to my defence so eloquently this evening, I…' She broke off, biting her lip. 'I wanted to cry,' she said. 'I had only just realised that I loved you, you see, and there you were, proving in front of all those people just how much you loved me…'

Rob felt the pleasure kick through his body, followed by a rush of protective love so strong he almost squeezed the breath out of her. He let her go and turned his face against her hair.

'So you love me? Oh, Jemima, I have so wanted to hear you say that.'

She turned a smiling look on him. 'I am sorry that I took so long. You have been very patient with me.'

Rob did not feel patient at all. In fact, he knew that if he had to be patient for very much longer he would probably expire with frustrated love and passion. He kissed her with love and desire and gentleness, revelling in their new-found joy, and then he let her go.

'There is something that you could do for me, sweetheart,' he said.

Jemima's eyes were huge. 'Yes?'

'You can help me down the stairs,' Rob said.

Chapter Nineteen

By the time that they regained their bedroom, Rob was a trembling wreck and Jemima was almost as pale with fear as he was himself.

'You should never have come up on to the roof,' she scolded as she helped him to lie down on the bed and took one of his shaking hands in her own. 'I had no notion that your terror of heights was so extreme. You should have told me...'

Rob lay still and waited for the room to stop spinning and his breathing to settle. 'I shall be very well again soon. Please do not distress yourself.' He opened his eyes and smiled at her. Jemima's piquant little face looked stricken as she gazed down at him. She was clutching his hand tightly in one of her own and stroking his cheek with her other hand. It was very nice. Rob gave a small sigh.

'Jemima, dearest...'

'Yes, love?'

'It would probably help me to breathe if you were to take off my jacket.'

Rob struggled into a sitting position and Jemima obligingly helped to slide the jacket from his shoulders.

Excellent. He lay down again with another small sigh and Jemima pressed a soft kiss on his brow. She smelled sweetly of rose water and honey. The round neck of the green dress afforded him a wondrous view of her breasts as she leaned over him to stroke his fevered brow. Rob gave a sigh of genuine emotion. He was starting to feel rather hot and the rest of his clothing felt rather too tight.

'Is there anything else I can do to make you feel better?' Jemima asked.

Rob could think of several things. He gave her a feeble smile.

'I confess that I do find my neckcloth rather constricting. And the waistcoat...'

The waistcoat was easily dealt with, but the neckcloth caused Jemima rather more of a problem since it was so intricately tied that she only seemed able to tie it into more of a knot. Rob lay still, almost fidgeting with frustration beneath her ministering fingers as she pulled and twitched it and finally gave a sigh of exasperation.

'I believe I shall have to call Tilbury—'

'No.' Rob put out a hand and caught her wrist. 'The poor fellow will be sleeping. You will find you get a better purchase if you move up here.' He patted the bed beside him.

Dark eyes met lavender blue for a long moment and Rob knew that she had divined his true motives. He repressed a grin and tried to look innocent.

'I have a better idea,' Jemima said briskly. Before Rob could draw breath she had swung herself up on to the bed, climbed over and knelt above him, the froth of her velvet skirts spilling over them both and on to the coverlet.

'Good God, Jemima!' Rob tried to sit up and was

forced firmly back by one of Jemima's hands on his shirtfront.

'Robert, dearest, you really must rest and not give way to violent impulses. You have sustained a horrid shock you know.'

'Yes, but…' Rob struggled and felt her thighs clasp tightly about him to keep him still. His whole body responded to the embrace of hers, tightening intolerably. His breeches had become at least two sizes too small for him.

'Jemima, what the devil are you doing?' he ground out.

'It seemed to me that I would have more purchase for unfastening your neckcloth if I was on top of you,' Jemima said, a little breathlessly. 'Pray do hold still, Robert, or I shall never be able to do it.'

'I had no idea that your legs were so strong,' Rob said faintly. His mind was teeming with erotic images.

'It is the benefit of years of climbing,' Jemima said briskly. 'I have almost finished…'

She leaned over him calmly and started to untangle the cravat at his throat. The glorious green velvet dress rustled and the neck dipped as she worked. The swell of her breasts strained at the rounded edge of the gown. After five seconds of mental torture Rob gave an infuriated shout, ripped the neckcloth apart and threw it on the floor, grabbed his wife around the waist and tumbled her over on to the bed beside him.

'You minx, you did that on purpose!'

Jemima giggled. 'I am sorry. I thought you deserved it for pretending to be in pain.'

'I am in pain now,' Rob said feelingly. He pulled her to him and his mouth swooped down to claim hers. It was hot and fierce and it silenced her completely. Their lips parted and Jemima gasped, 'Do not forget the will, Robert—'

Rob shook his head. There was a heat and a tenderness inside him and he held her a little way away from him, scanning her face.

'No,' he said. 'I do not forget it. It no longer matters to me.'

Jemima's eyes widened as she took in his meaning. Her lips curved instinctively and he bent to kiss her again, unable to resist. She pulled back.

'No, wait! It is only six more weeks, Robert! We have waited this long for your fortune—'

'Yes,' Rob said, 'and I am not prepared to wait any longer for you.'

Jemima gave a little wail as his busy fingers pulled one of the diamond-headed pins from her hair, then another, then another. He stowed them on the nightstand whilst the mass of her hair came tumbling down.

'No, Rob, you mustn't! It isn't worth losing the money.'

'That, my love, is where you are most profoundly mistaken,' Rob said. He ran his hands through her hair, slipping his fingers through the shining strands, then entangling his hand in it and pulling it to one side to allow him to kiss her exposed throat. Desire swept through him in an irresistible tide. She was sweet and warm and soft. She was *his* and she loved him. That was all that mattered.

His lips brushed the hollow at the base of her throat where her pulse hammered, his teeth nipped the lobe of her ear, and Jemima gave another wail, though this one was already half-hearted.

'Robert—'

Rob started to loosen the row of tiny buttons on the

front of the bodice of the velvet ball gown. 'What sort of a man would I be if I said that I was in love with my wife, I wanted to make love to her, but I wanted the money more?'

'A practical one,' Jemima sniffed, trying to capture his marauding hands. 'You have done so much for Delaval already—do not risk it all for this.'

Rob seized her and gave her a vigorous kiss. 'Jemima, sweetheart, I can forgive your lack of enthusiasm now—just—if you make up for it later…' He drew the bodice of the dress apart to reveal the crisp chemise and petticoats beneath and bent his head to kiss the top of her breasts.

'As for Delaval,' he murmured, 'I was in a fair way to becoming obsessed with it until you pointed out the error of my ways. So now I am putting you first, as is right and just.'

He drew the chemise down slightly and touched the tip of his tongue to the cleft between her breasts, brushing his fingertips over the sensitive pinpoints of her nipples, where they hardened through the cotton shift.

'Robert,' Jemima gasped, 'pray reconsider.'

'Too late. I am decided.' Rob took a deep breath. 'How the devil do I get you out of this dress?'

It was a tussle, but the amusement and the struggles soon gave way to genuine passion as the green dress crumpled to the floor to be swiftly followed by Jemima's stays. She took a deep breath as she was released from their restraining hold and spread her arms wide, whereupon Rob took full advantage to peel the chemise down to her waist and take one hard nipple in his mouth. Jemima arched against Rob's gentle, questing lips and tongue as he drove her mad with longing. His hands were on her bare waist and he held her still for his mouth to take its pleasure—and to pleasure her as well. It was intense and exquisite, and the touch of his mouth on her breasts and the caress of his hands on her stomach made her squirm with desperate need. She needed to touch him back; she needed to feel the smooth skin and taut muscle of his body pressed against hers. No concerns of modesty or reticence could stop her now. She tugged fiercely at his shirt and sent it flying across the room, and reached out to pull him against her with all the pent-up desire of abstinence.

A little shudder went through both of them as their bodies finally made contact, skin on skin, warm and smooth, hard and soft, rough and gentle... Jemima's blood fizzed with sensual arousal as she turned her face up to Rob's again and they kissed, their tongues tangling in intimate fusion.

And then Rob had sent his boots crashing to join the pile of clothes littering the floor, and he had tugged Jemima's chemise down over her bottom and tossed it aside, and he was unfastening his breeches and Jemima thought that she would melt with love and longing and wild desire. He looked down at her and she caught her breath at the heat and hunger in his eyes.

She lay back and held her arms out to him.

'You still have time to leave me and take the forty thousand pounds instead.'

Rob did not even hesitate. He took her in his arms and rolled her beneath him, his hands caressing her stomach and sliding over her hips until she opened to him, urgent and ardent as he.

He bent over and brushed the tumbled hair from about her face with a gentle hand, bending his lips to the damp hollow of her collarbone, tracing the pulse there as Jemima's body jumped beneath his touch.

'Not for a million pounds,' he whispered, and then she reached out to him and he took her and Jemima's mind splintered into a blinding pleasure and her body tumbled into boundless, blissful delight.

'Robert, I have been thinking,' Jemima said, as they walked slowly up the oak staircase at Delaval that evening. 'It is about the forty thousand pounds.'

Rob raised his brows. 'I see. Would you care to go somewhere more private to discuss this?'

'No, I do not think so,' Jemima said. She fiddled nervously with the fringe of her shawl. 'That would be a very bad idea. You see, I think that we should avoid any opportunity for intimacy for the few next weeks, and that way the situation may be retrieved...'

Rob gave her a look that brought the colour into her face. 'I do not think so,' he said drily. 'Not unless your recollection of the events of this morning and my own vary fundamentally.'

Jemima blushed. 'Yes... No—what I mean is that if we keep to the letter of the agreement from now on, we might be forgiven one small aberration.'

Rob started to laugh. 'One small aberration? Is that what you call it? Jemima, we made love three times—'

'Hush!' Jemima besought. She looked over her shoulder. 'Come into the bedroom where no one can hear you!'

'Besides,' Rob continued after the door had shut behind them, 'who is to forgive us? Churchward? The poor man would die of embarrassment if I vouchsafed to him the events of this morning.'

'I thought, perhaps, that as it was left to your own conscience...' Jemima dropped her shawl onto the chair and went across to the dressing table. She started to unpin her hair, watching Rob's face in the mirror.

'I mean, no one knows except you and I, and Churchward will accept whatever you tell him.'

Rob was watching her too. He lay back on the bed and put his hands behind his head. 'What would you do in my position, Jemima?'

Jemima paused. 'I suppose that I would tell the truth,' she said, after a moment.

'Yet you think that I should lie?' Rob sounded almost hurt.

Jemima swung round on the stool. 'No, of course not. It is merely that I know how much you care for Delaval and how important the money is for the restoration.' She sighed, her shoulders slumping. 'Of course, I see it was a silly idea. You shall just have to tell Churchward that you were unable to fulfil the terms of the will.'

Rob held out a hand to her and she came to sit beside him on the bed. He entwined his fingers with hers.

'There is another reason why it would be a bad idea,' Rob said softly. Looking up, Jemima caught his eye and blushed hotly.

'I rather enjoyed this morning,' Rob said, 'and now that I have already broken the terms of the will I intend to continue doing so at every available opportunity.'

'Robert!' Jemima said, trying to sound shocked. She smiled a little and rubbed her fingers over the back of his hand.

Rob sat up slightly and started to unfasten the silver filigree clasp that held up her gown.

'Go and lock the door,' he said softly.

'Robert!' This time Jemima was a little shocked, but she was intrigued as well. She went across and turned the key in the lock. When she turned back, Rob was still lying there, watching her with bright, speculative eyes.

'Robert, it is only early evening—' she began.

Rob smiled. 'And we have plenty of days to make up for,' he said. 'I intend to keep you up for the whole night.'

Jemima's eyes widened. A delicious languor was warming her veins. 'The whole night? Surely not *actually* all of the night?'

'The whole of the night,' Rob repeated, as he started to undo his cuffs.

Chapter Twenty

'I am very sorry to have deceived you,' Letty said, as together she and Jemima strolled through the shrubbery at Delaval a few days later. The crisp autumn leaves crunched beneath the soles of their boots. 'It was very wrong of me.'

Jemima smiled. 'I knew that you liked Jack, I simply did not realise how serious it was. I thought—forgive me, Letty—that you were just taken with his handsome face...'

'Oh, I was,' Letty, said, dimpling, 'but more besides.'

'And Jack loves you too,' Jemima said. 'He says that he did from the start. I have never seen anything quite so instantaneous.'

'Maybe you have,' Letty said slyly. 'How did you feel when you first saw Rob?'

Jemima raised her brows. 'Dizzy, shaken, light-headed...'

'There you are, then,' Letty said, satisfied. 'And now?'

Jemima's smile grew. 'Dizzy, shaken and light-headed... I was slow to realise that I loved Rob, I do admit that.'

Letty laughed.

'Do you think that Lady Marguerite will agree to the match?' Jemima asked cautiously.

Letty looked pensive. 'I think so. She was very cordial to Jack the night of the ball and she has permitted him to call since. She told me that she always admired a man who could make an entrance.'

Jemima's lips twitched. Jack had certainly done that. 'And then she did not turn him over for the highway robbery,' she pointed out.

'No, and she said the other day that he would make a very good gentleman farmer. I think,' Letty said, 'that it will be all right.'

Jemima nodded. Certainly it would not be easy for an illiterate sweep to become a gentleman farmer, but Letty had such an air of quiet determination about her that Jemima was almost convinced that matters would work out.

'Ferdie will be going back to Town today,' Letty said. 'Now that Augusta is gone and Bertie has gone to Merlinschase for a while, I do believe that Ferdie is quite bored!'

Jemima was thinking about Ferdie's confession. She and Rob had discussed the letter and Rob had felt very strongly that he did not wish to raise the matter with Ferdie now that the business of Naylor was sorted out. He had argued that sleeping dogs should be left to lie, and Jemima had agreed with him. What virtue was there is stirring up an old incident that had clearly caused Ferdie so much grief at the time?

She thought of this when Ferdie came to see them later to say his farewells.

'I came to say goodbye,' Ferdie said. He sat down,

smiling at them. 'I say, you two look very cheerful this morning! Glad to see that country living agrees with some people. Can't wait to get back to Town myself.'

'Would you care to join us for luncheon?' Rob asked. 'You are very welcome if you wish.'

Ferdie shook his head. 'Truth is, old fellow, there is something that I have to tell you and I'd prefer to get it over with. I've been working up to this since before Letty's ball.' He put a hand out as Jemima started to get to her feet. 'No, please stay, Lady Selborne. I would like you to hear it too. I need a witness.'

Jemima and Rob exchanged a look. 'Then pray tell us, Ferdie,' Rob said.

Ferdie shifted in his seat. All the lines were drawn tight on his face and he was gripping his hands together so tightly that they were a pale blue. Jemima almost expected to hear them crack.

'Fact is,' Ferdie said conversationally, 'it's to do with Naylor and old Lord Selborne and myself. Y'see, when old Lord Selborne died, it was I who pulled the trigger and Naylor and I were the only two who knew of it to this day.'

His moustache drooped like a mournful dog's ears. 'It was an accident, naturally, but the fact remains that it was my fault. We said that my grandfather had tripped and his gun gone off and killed him, but I was the one who tripped—and who shot him. Shot my own grandfather.' He shook his head. 'Cannot quite believe it myself.'

'Who is "we", Ferdie?' Rob asked.

'Harry Naylor and myself,' Ferdie said. 'Here's the thing. Naylor was my beater that day and he was the only other man present when I shot Grandfather. I was all to pieces. Couldn't believe what I'd done, trying to raise the old man, only it was too late. Half his head blown off.' He saw Jemima wince. 'Not pretty. So next thing I knew, everyone was coming running and Naylor was telling everyone that it was an accident and the old man had fallen on his own gun. I didn't say a word. Everyone thought that I was too shocked to speak, and the truth is I was—at the enormity of what I'd done. Anyway, Naylor kept up the pretence and I kept silent and it went on and gradually I began to believe the story myself.' He stopped. 'Dash it, you don't seem very surprised, Rob. Thought I would set the house by the ears!'

Rob shook his head slowly. 'I confess I suspected something of the sort. I remember overhearing Papa say at the time that the angle of the bullet seemed all wrong for Grandfather to have done it himself. The rumours were soon suppressed but I did not forget them. Then Jemima found the diary.'

Jemima got up and went across to the bureau. She turned the key in the lock and opened the draw, extracting the old tin with its pitiful, charred pages. Ferdie had turned very pale as he saw the manuscript. He held out his hands and they were shaking. 'My diary! I thought Naylor had it! He told me he'd hidden it.'

'He did,' Jemima said. 'Up the chimney. Maybe he never had the chance to retrieve it.'

Ferdie turned the flimsy pages over between his fingers. One tear plopped on to the paper, then another.

'Devil take it,' he said shakily, 'I'm as weak and unmanned as a kitten! Beg pardon, Lady Selborne.'

'Dearest Ferdie,' Jemima said, abandoning etiquette and going over to give him a big hug, 'pray do not regard it. My brother Jack always says there is no shame in a grown man crying.'

'Jack Jewell crying?' The image so struck Ferdie that

his shoulders stopped heaving. 'Can't see it myself. Man's built like a house.'

'Well, you would be surprised,' Jemima said.

'Why did you never say anything before, Ferdie?' Rob asked quietly. 'Why carry that burden all these years?'

'Thought it had all gone away,' Ferdie said miserably. 'Least said, soonest mended, what? Naylor had gone to the wars, y'father had inherited... Thought it was all right and tight. Couldn't quite forget it, though.'

Rob shook his head. 'And then Naylor came back. And touched you for money, unless I miss my guess. Had he been blackmailing you for many years, Ferdie?'

Jemima remembered Jack saying that Ferdie had seemed unconscionably shocked to see Harry Naylor and that they had quarrelled at some point in the evening.

'Naylor was never supposed to come back,' Ferdie said. He sounded aggrieved. 'I paid him to stay away. Paid more that I could afford. Fellow didn't even have the decency to get himself killed in the Peninsula. And then to come back and touch me for money again! Damned disgrace.'

'But you didn't kill him,' Rob said. 'Beaumaris said it was an accident.'

'I didn't kill him,' Ferdie agreed, 'but I was dashed grateful to the man who did! And now it turns out it was all an accident. Pity, really.' Ferdie's shoulders slumped. 'Couldn't stand it any more, old fellow. Had to tell you. Should have told you all years ago. Finally got around to it now.'

Jemima squeezed his hand. 'You have punished yourself so much over the years, Ferdie, have you not? But it was only an accident.'

Ferdie squeezed hers back gratefully. 'Thank you, Jemima. I confess I feel much better having spoken of it.' He looked across at Rob.

'Will you… I suppose that you will have to tell someone? Report it, I mean…'

Jemima met Rob's eyes. She did not say anything.

'I cannot see what purpose that would serve,' Rob said slowly. 'Both our grandparents are dead now and nothing can alter that. And you have lived with it for a long time, Ferdie. Best to let it go, now.'

Ferdie stood up. There was an odd, blind look in his eyes. 'Thank you, Robert. Think I'll go away now, if it's all right with you. Your servant, Jemima.' He gave Jemima a neat bow. 'I hope to see you soon in Town.'

'I hope Ferdie isn't driving his curricle,' Jemima said, after he had gone out. 'He is like to end up in the ditch if he is.'

'I think he was riding,' Rob said, with a grin. 'And his horse knows its own way.' He looked at her. 'Did I do the right thing?'

Jemima put her hands into his. 'I do not know, Rob. But you did what I would have done.'

She freed herself and went across to the sofa where Ferdie had discarded the sheets of the diary. Picking them up, she handed them to her husband. 'What do you want to do with these?'

Rob paused for a minute, then looked towards the fireplace.

'It's a good fire, isn't it?'

'The best.' Jemima smiled. 'I built it myself.'

'And it draws well.'

'Of course. That chimney is clean as a new pin.'

Rob tossed the diary sheets into the flames and drew his wife into the crook of his arm. 'That's that, then,' he said.

It was the fifth of November when Mr Churchward arrived at Delaval after a long and arduous journey from London. The nights were drawing in now and a spell of poor weather had turned the road into a rutted mire. Mr Churchward was tired, hungry and extremely apprehensive.

As he drew close to the house he saw that there was a huge bonfire in the long meadow. The orange light lit up the murky sky and the sparks were flying, caught on a stiff autumn breeze. Mr Churchward raised his eyebrows. Perhaps Lord and Lady Selborne had tired of trying to instil some order into their estate and were burning it down instead. The he realised that it was Guy Fawkes' Night and his heart sank. He felt like the perfect candidate to be on top of the bonfire. But he could not let his courage fail him now. He had come all the way from London to break the news and that was what he would do. He ordered the carriage into the stable yard.

In the barn at the end of the stables, Lord and Lady Selborne were personally investigating the quality of the hay that had been stored for the winter. At least that was how the expedition had started. Tipsy with sweeps' scrumpy, they had walked arm in arm to the stables, where Rob had proudly displayed the huge piles of hay, the product of much of his hard work in the past few months. He had picked Jemima up and thrown her into the haystack to demonstrate just how sweet and soft it was, and then he had thrown himself down beside her. Much of what had happened next was inevitable.

It was the unexpected sound of carriage wheels on the cobbles and the sound of raised voices that had finally caught Jemima's attention and she had rolled out of her husband's arms, sat up and peered around the corner of the barn door.

'It is Mr Churchward!' she hissed. 'Whatever can he want? And whatever is he doing arriving at this time of night?'

'Catching us *in flagrante*,' Rob said, with a grin. He got to his feet, helped her up and tried to brush the hay off his clothes. Then, giving up, he sauntered out into the stable yard to greet his guest, a wide smile on his face.

'Churchward! What an unexpected pleasure. You have found us in the middle of our Guy Fawkes's celebrations.'

Mr Churchward's face looked strained in the flaring torchlight. 'Good evening, my lord. Lady Selborne.' He bowed awkwardly. 'Pray forgive my unheralded arrival. I have some very grave news to impart to you, my lord, pertaining to your late grandmother's will…'

Jemima could see Rob frowning and thought that he had probably partaken of too much wine to be able to make much sense of this. She took the lawyer's arm.

'Pray come inside, Mr Churchward, and take some food and drink. You must be exhausted after your long journey…'

Churchward, however, seemed incapable of consuming any refreshments until he had said his piece. He followed them into the study, refused the seat that Rob offered, and stood looking a little forlorn as his curious hosts waited expectantly for him to begin.

'I do apologise, my lord,' Churchward said. He took a document out of his case and stood holding it out, looking a little at a loss. 'I came as quickly as I could to give you this. I...' He paused. 'I did think about destroying it, my lord, and pretending that it had never been received in my office, but alas...' he shook his head '...when the moment came I found myself quite unable to falsify the record.'

Rob and Jemima exchanged a look at this terrible admission. It was almost impossible to imagine the upright lawyer doing anything so shocking.

Rob took the paper and unfolded it, then looked up sharply. 'But this is my grandmother's will, Churchward. We are already aware of the terms—'

'The second page, my lord!' the lawyer said, in anguish.

Rob raised his brows. He turned to the second sheet of paper and read out, *'Should my grandson marry, then his marriage vows must of course take precedence over this other vow of celibacy. I should not wish the terms of my will to come between Robert and his bride, and I applaud him on his good sense in choosing to marry when young people today so often show a distressing tendency towards waywardness...'*

Rob stopped. His eyes met Jemima's.

'Oh, Rob,' Jemima said, ' a second page to the will!'

'I am most dreadfully sorry,' Churchward said, polishing his glasses on the sleeve of his jacket. 'The sheet had fallen down behind my cabinet—indeed, I did not find it again until this very morning—and as the first page of the will concluded on such a final note, signed appropriately and so forth...' He cleared his throat unhappily. 'I am sorry that I never suspected there was anything missing. So careless of me!' He polished his glasses again. 'I cannot conceive how I could be so inefficient...'

He stopped. Neither the Earl nor the Countess of Selborne were paying him any attention at all. They were staring at each other with a mixture of shock and starry-eyed affection that made Mr Churchward feel quite *de trop*.

'One hundred days,' Rob said, wincing.

'Oh, dear,' Mr Churchward said.

'You mean seventy-five days,' Jemima pointed out with a slight smile.

'Eighty.'

'I have told you before, Robert, that that depends on your definition of celibacy—'

'Ah…' Mr Churchward said. He looked from one to the other and turned slightly pink. 'Ah…excellent. Well, I see no need to dwell any further on the terms of the will. I shall arrange for the capital to be released…'

'Thank you, Churchward,' Rob said, without taking his eyes off his wife. Very slowly he entangled Jemima's fingers in his and drew her towards him.

'Very well, then,' Churchward said, a little helplessly. He stuffed the late Dowager Countess's will back into his case and fastened the buckles, his fingers shaking a little in his haste to escape. 'Thank you Lord Selborne, Lady Selborne.'

'I will ring the bell and ask the servants to take you to your room, Mr Churchward,' Jemima said, making no move to free herself from Rob's embrace.

'I will find my own way,' Mr Churchward said hastily.

Neither his lordship nor his ladyship answered him and as Churchward closed the door behind him he saw that Rob was already drawing Jemima closer into his arms. Churchward hurried out into the hall. There were two torches flaring in the walls, mirroring the firelight that still danced and glowed down in the meadow. In the drawing room doorway, Churchward could see the figures of Letty Exton and Jack Jewell locked in an ardent embrace.

Mr Churchward blinked and hurried towards the door. Perhaps it would be wiser to stay at the Speckled Hen. He did not feel quite comfortable remaining at Delaval tonight.

Down by the bonfire the dancing seemed to becoming even wilder. Shadowy black figures jumped and spun like a scene from a primitive painting. He could see Lady Marguerite Exton, her skirts held up in one hand, dancing with what looked like a Master Sweep.

'Good gracious!' Mr Churchward said, pushing his glasses back up his nose with a nervous gesture. 'Good gracious! Delaval is becoming a paradigm of passion! Amorous, abandoned and…' he smiled a little '…rather amusing.'

Back in the study, Rob had let Jemima go sufficiently to draw breath.

'Which vow do you prefer, Rob,' she asked, smoothing the material of his shirt with gentle fingers, 'the one you took to win your grandmother's fortune, or the one you made to me, to love and to cherish?'

Rob tilted her chin up so that lips were very close to his. 'To cherish and to adore,' he said. 'That is the vow that I intend to keep, Jemima. Forever.'

*   *   *   *   *

Regency romance…and revenge by bestselling author Nicola Cornick

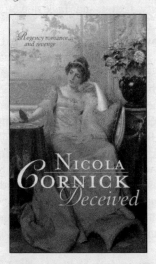

Princess Isabella never imagined it could come to this. Bad enough she faces imprisonment for debts not her own. Even worse that she must make a hasty marriage of convenience with Marcus, the Earl of Stockhaven.

As the London gossips eagerly gather to watch the fun, Isabella struggles to maintain a polite distance in her marriage. But the more Isabella challenges Marcus's iron determination to have a marriage in more than name only, the hotter their passion burns. This time, will it consume them both – or fuel a love greater than they dare dream?

Available at WHSmith, Tesco, ASDA and all good bookshops

www.millsandboon.co.uk

M&B

0406/10/QUEENS 07 V2

Queens of Romance

An outstanding collection by international bestselling authors

16th March 2007

20th April 2007

18th May 2007

15th June 2007

Collect all 4 superb books!

www.millsandboon.co.uk

BL/41/QOR x4

Queens of Romance

An outstanding collection by international bestselling authors.

Collect all 4 superb books!

*Available at WH Smith, Tesco, ASDA, Borders, Eason, Sainsbury's
and all good paperback bookshops*

www.millsandboon.co.uk

Medieval
LORDS & LADIES
COLLECTION

When courageous knights risked all to win the hand of their lady!

Volume 1: Conquest Brides – July 2007
Gentle Conqueror by Julia Byrne
Madselin's Choice by Elizabeth Henshall

Volume 2: Blackmail & Betrayal – August 2007
A Knight in Waiting by Juliet Landon
Betrayed Hearts by Elizabeth Henshall

Volume 3: War of the Roses – September 2007
Loyal Hearts by Sarah Westleigh
The Traitor's Daughter by Joanna Makepeace

6 volumes in all to collect!

M&B

0707/11/MB096 V2

Who can resist a dashing highwayman?

Ally Grayson never wanted to be a heroine –
she dreamed of writing great stories, not living in a
fairy tale. But when she's abducted by a charming
highwayman right out of a novel, Ally finds herself
thoroughly enchanted.

But when Mark, her burdensome fiancé, is revealed
to be none other than the rogue of her dreams,
Ally must make a choice: plunge into a world of
murder and deceit without a protector, or place her
trust in the man who has lied to her...

Available 15th June 2007

www.millsandboon.co.uk

M&B

Victorian London is brought to vibrant life in this mesmeric new novel!

London, 1876

All her life, Olivia Moreland has denied her clairvoyant abilities, working instead to disprove the mediums that flock to London. But when Stephen, Lord St Leger, requests her help in investigating an alleged psychic, she can't ignore the ominous presence she feels within the walls of his ancient estate. Nor can she ignore the intimate connection she feels to Stephen, as if she has somehow known him before…

Available 20th April 2007

www.millsandboon.co.uk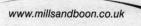

MILLS & BOON®
Historical

Rich, vivid and passionate

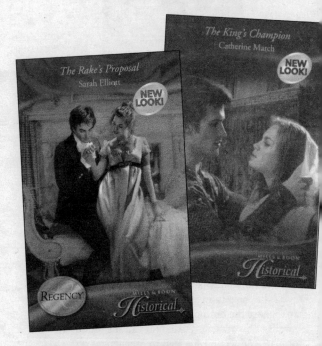

4 brand-new titles each month

Available on the first Friday of every month
from WHSmith, ASDA, Tesco
and all good bookshops
www.millsandboon.co.uk

GEN/04/RTL10V2